ENDGAME
IN BERLIN

ENDGAME IN BERLIN

by
William
Harrington

DONALD I. FINE, INC.
New York

c.1

c.1

Copyright © 1991 by William Harrington

All rights reserved, including the right of reproduction in whole or in part in
any form. Published in the United States of America by Donald I. Fine, Inc.
and in Canada by General Publishing Company Lmited.

Library of Congress Cataloging-in-Publication Data
Harrington, William, 1931–
Endgame in Berlin / by William Harrington.
p.   cm.
ISBN 1-55611-313-7
I. Title.
PS3558.A63E48   1991
813′.54—dc20   91-55186
CIP

Manufactured in the United States of America

10 9 8 7 6 5 4 3 2 1

Designed by Irving Perkins Associates

To Myra and Stuart and Catherine and Dick

GLOSSARY OF NAMES AND
━━━ ABBREVIATIONS ━━━

BND (*Bundesnachtrichtendienst*): Federal Intelligence Service. The security service of the Federal Republic of Germany (West Germany), subsequently of the united Germany.

BD (*Bundesrepublik Deutschland*): Federal Republic of Germany, or West Germany.

Bundeswehr: Federal Army. The army of the Federal Republic of Germany (West Germany).

CIA: Central Intelligence Agency, U.S. Sometimes called The Office.

COS: Chief of Station, the head of a CIA station.

DCI: Director of Central Intelligence, the head of the CIA.

DDO: Deputy Director for Operations. Head of the CIA's Directorate for Operations (DO). The spymaster of the CIA, as distinct from its administrative and other operations.

DDR (*Deutsche Demokratische Republik*): German Democratic Republic, or East Germany.

DGSE (*Direction Générale de la Sécurité Extérieure*): French foreign intelligence agency.

Élysée Cell: Very small secret French security group given the special duty of preventing the assassination of the president of France. Not supposed to exist. Suspected of terminating individuals identified as likely involved in plots to assassinate the president.

GIGN (*Groupe d'Intervention de la Gendarmerie Nationale*):

French elite police force charged with combating terrorism. It is known for the use of torture and assassination—whatever may be judged necessary to defend the French nation against terrorism.

HVA (*Hauptverwaltung Aufklärung*): Chief Administration, Intelligence. An elite group within *Stasi,* commanded by General Markus Wolf, HVA was a highly successful East German espionage agency that scored major successes against the West German government. Abolished with reunification.

KGB (*Komitet Gosudarstvennoi Bezopastnosti*): Committee for State Security. Intelligence insiders often call it The Committee. The pervasive security agency of the Soviet Union. In past decades it has gone under various names—the Cheka, GPU, OGPU, NKVD, MGB, and MVD. In the past it acquired a bloody reputation for brutal suppression of every form of dissent within the Soviet Union. Its foreign-intelligence operations were conducted by First Directorate, an elite group. Today it professes to have dropped most of its internal-security functions and to concentrate only on foreign intelligence.

MI5: Military Intelligence, Department 5. The British military intelligence office that deals with internal spying and subversion. Like the CIA, it has no powers of arrest and must rely on Special Branch, Scotland Yard when it wants to arrest someone and present evidence in court.

MI6: Military Intelligence, Department 6. Also known as SIS, which stands for Secret Intelligence Service. The British military intelligence office that conducts overseas espionage.

Mossad: The Central Institute for Intelligence and Special Assignments. Israeli intelligence. Often called The Institute.

Mukhabarat el-Alam: General Intelligence Agency of Egypt.

NIO: National Intelligence Officer. A senior intelligence analyst within the CIA. Ordinarily, an NIO is responsible for a region.

NSA: National Security Agency. U.S. agency responsible for intercepting and decoding other nations' signals, whether

by radio, telephone line, cable, or whatever. Also charged
with preventing other nations' doing the same to the U.S.
SIS: Secret Intelligence Service. Another name for MI6.
Stasi (*Ministerium für Staats-Sicherheit*): Ministry for State
Security. The KGB of the German Democratic Republic
(East Germany), abolished just before reunification.
UB: Polish Intelligence.

> With the end of the Cold War, two for-
> mer opponents face off once again as
> the United States and Russia embark on
> a new form of conflict – industrial
> espionage.

Дйккенс...

Dickens. How many years had passed since he had last thought of that name? The Englishman who had so vividly limned the cruel contrast between the capitalist exploiters and the exploited working class in England. There was much to learn from Dickens, the teachers had emphasized thirty years ago. Correct English and—half-conscious, only it was true—a correct characterization of the tragedy of capitalism.

Yes. So . . . A hell of a lot of difference any of that made now.

Kedrov had walked away from the conference table for a few minutes and stood at a window, smoking a cigarette and looking down on the iced-over river and on new snow accumulating on top of the old. That was what had made him think of Dickens. On a snowy night like this, in London, the old capitalist had left his counting house with a warm greatcoat around his body, on his way to an ample dinner in a fine restaurant. His wretched clerk had ventured out into the same cold with nothing but a shawl around his shoulders, on his way home to a poor supper. You must never forget that scene, his teachers had said: and Colonel Nikolai Pavlovich Kedrov, KGB, had not.

And, the teacher had said, how could a system that not only tolerated such injustice but actually sponsored and protected it expect to survive against the honest rage of the toilers?

Colonel Kedrov glanced back toward the conference table, where a dozen men from the system founded on the honest rage

of the toilers sat around a table covered with green cloth, facing
bottles of mineral water and vodka, scribbling idly on pads while
the presiding officer spoke.

The Conference on the Applications of Higher Technology
had droned on for five days. Some of the more flippant conferees
had dubbed it the Frustration Conference. In plenary sessions,
Kedrov had heard some twenty-five reports from ministers,
deputy ministers, factory directors, scientists, technicians, and
a few angry citizens.

Now in executive sessions, the meaning of those reports was
being made painfully clear. Speaking was presiding officer Pyotr
Georgievich Semyonov, Minister for Economics, once Minister
for State Planning, a Marxist title no longer fashionable. He
settled and spread in his chair until he filled it, like bread dough
that spreads and fills a pan. Balding, with a fringe of white hair,
he kept his lips and fingers doubly busy rotating a fat cigar that
had gone out—doubly busy because he was also talking and
gesticulating in his characteristic way: with practiced gestures
and careful variations of voice, like the actor he was.

Kedrov watched Semyonov with some amusement. They had
something in common, the two of them: Semyonov had come to
prominence under Khrushchev, Kedrov under Brezhnev; not
many men with that kind of background were still sitting in the
executive sessions of important government conferences.

Semyonov was ten years older than Kedrov, old enough to
have shaken the hand of Stalin, old enough to hold personal
memories of the dreaded Lavrenti Beria, old enough to have
had his first significant promotion from Georgi Malenkov. He
had become, in the 1970s, a deputy member of the Politburo
and was then known as an ideologue, a keeper of the Marxist
faith. His retreat from orthodoxy had been gradual and su-
premely skilled. Although he had never made a clean break,
when dogmatic Marxist-Leninist theory became abhorrent, lo,
critics could cite speeches and papers by Pyotr Georgievich
Semyonov analyzing the failures of Stalin, Khrushchev, and
Brezhnev. In time he even spoke critically of Lenin himself;
when a motion was made in the Supreme Soviet to remove the

body of Lenin from its mausoleum on Red Square and give it "decent burial," Semyonov spoke in favor.

Kedrov was envious of Semyonov's deft reversal. His own had been awkward and contemptuously noted.

Semyonov was trying now to sum up some of the more important findings. One old Bolshevik habit clung to him. He never said in ten words what he could say in a hundred.

"Our mandate directs us to avoid such questions as ownership and control of the means of production. Those questions will be discussed and decided elsewhere. Our mandate is to search for ways to remedy the chronic shortfalls in our production goals, whoever owns the farms and factories. Our mandate is to find short-term solutions to the problem of supplying our people's needs—and beyond that to find ways to make our products competitive in world markets. Our technocrats—" Semyonov paused and nodded at some of the junior ministers who sat uncomfortably at the table "—have emphasized most dramatically what they have called the primitive state of our higher technology."

Only two men in this executive session were not directly involved in problems of the economy and production, Kedrov and the man who now interrupted with a question.

"Is our technology really so deficient, Pyotr Georgievich?" asked Marshal Mikhail Josefovich Malinovski. "I have observed something rather different."

"Indeed you have, Marshal," said Semyonov dryly. "For decades the best technology we had was directed to the armed forces."

"We had to defend the country against the fascists and imperialists," said Malinovski.

"Of course," said Semyonov with a nod toward the marshal that was almost a bow. "But now we are threatened by something very different. Anarchy. If we cannot supply our population with the basic needs of life—"

"And higher technology is the cure-all?"

"A very important element of the cure," said Semyonov.

Marshal Malinovski frowned and shook his head. He cast his

eyes toward the ceiling, where nine of the twenty bulbs in a dusty crystal chandelier were burned out—which was why dim, yellowish incandescent light lent an air of shabbiness to the whole room.

"Allow me to give you an example, Marshal," said Dimitri Vasilievich Pavlov, Deputy Minister for Manufacturing.

The marshal nodded at Pavlov. He was accustomed to giving people permission to speak.

"The Japanese," said Pavlov, "can design and produce a new automobile in months. They simulate their designs and even their production processes on Cray Y-MP supercomputers. They know before they build the first prototype exactly how the car will perform and how it can be most efficiently manufactured. Ford and General Motors do the same. In our automobile factories we stumble through a trial-and-error process at every stage. Our automobiles are obsolete before they are made, are too expensive to produce, and cannot compete in any market. We cannot sell them abroad. We could not *give them away* abroad. Our own people are scornful of them."

Kedrov had smiled to himself when he heard that. Only seven years ago Dimitri Vasilievich Pavlov, then a factory director, had argued smoothly in another economic conference that the Volga sedan his factory produced was a fine, solidly built automobile, superior in every way to the "frivolous" cars being built in the West and in Japan. Semyonov himself had said at the time that the Zhiguli and Volga were representative of the excellence of socialist industry.

"Miracle machines, these supercomputers," said Marshal Malinovski to himself, not without a suggestion of scorn.

"Another example, Marshal," said Pavlov. "The American chemical manufacturer DuPont used Cray computers to simulate the process for manufacturing a new polyamaride fiber they call Kevlar. They needed to know if certain monomers they planned to use would break down under the heat and other strains of the manufacturing process. And through computer simulation, they found out, before they so much as built one machine. In our plants we would have had to build the machinery and try it to get the answers to such questions."

"I must admit the Americans predict the weather far more accurately than we do," said the marshal. "I suppose this has implications for agriculture as well as for military operations."

Semyonov spoke again. He held up his left hand and used his right to tap fingers and count his points. "In the Western countries and Japan, sophisticated robots perform many delicate manufacturing processes. We don't have computers that can control such robots. Supercomputers perform constant quality checks on the production lines. Supercomputers analyze every aspect of production and move materials, machines, and labor to the right places at the right time. Our factories sit idle for hours, often for days, waiting for the arrival of some essential."

"Grain rots in the fields," said Kedrov from his place at the window, "because the trucks to haul it are somewhere else hauling something that would not rot, something that could wait."

"Even this problem your computers could solve?" asked Marshal Malinovski with amused cynicism.

"Even that problem," said Semyonov. "Rational allocation of resources."

Pavlov smiled sarcastically. "You cannot rationally allocate what you do not have," he said. "Computers cannot do everything."

"They cannot bring rain," said the marshal.

"Nevertheless," said Semyonov, "we must have computers. Supercomputers. What they call multiprocessor supercomputers. Also, we must have the sophisticated software it takes to make them function. A recommendation that we make whatever sacrifice may be necessary to get these things will be a principal part of the report of this conference."

It was well that those who had surrendered the faith only reluctantly or not at all could still meet apart, as in the old days, and make decisions that would one way or another be imposed on the new system. (New system! What system was that? There was no new system, only confusion.)

Malinovski, Semyonov, and Kedrov sat over a supper of ground lamb sausages and sauerkraut dumplings, heavy food to be washed down with vodka and glasses of scalding tea.

They had steamed themselves in a Turkish bath and were taking this supper in a private dining room adjacent to the bathhouse. Here they could be assured of absolute privacy as they sat, still sweating profusely, in towel robes and eat and drink as men of their rank had done in the old days, without fear of reproof.

Both of the others greatly outranked Kedrov, which made him wonder just why they had invited him to join them for this supper. He had wondered in fact why he had been appointed KGB delegate to the Conference on the Applications of Higher Technology. His official title was Third Deputy Commandant of the First Chief Directorate—the number-four man in the KGB directorate for foreign operations. The First Chief Directorate was by far the most important directorate in the KGB; still, Kedrov, with a practiced sense of hierarchy, knew the Chairman had reached well down into the organization to select the KGB representative to the Conference.

Maybe the Chairman had done it to spare the KGB too close identification with the Frustration Conference. Whatever the reason, Kedrov had not regarded the appointment as any kind of honor or anything likely to win him reward or promotion.

Marshal Malinovski drained the last of the vodka from his glass and reached for the bottle. "So, Comrade Colonel," he said. "Does the KGB agree with the gloomy comparison of our technology with that of the imperialists?"

"Our best information, Comrade Marshal, is that the situation is as bad as the most pessimistic report we heard . . . and probably worse."

In private conversation these unrepentant Communists returned to the jargon they had grown up with. It was out of style now to call anyone "comrade." You could draw a frown, even a reproof. A society that had failed to establish a new superintendence had mindlessly rushed to jettison even the superficial trappings of the old. Plus much that was not superficial.

Banners. Pictures. Slogans. Flags. Uniforms. Medals. Courtesies. Rank. Preference.

Ten thousand statues of Stalin had been torn down, most of

them smashed. There had been no such thing as the Battle of Stalingrad. It was the Battle of Volgograd now. Those changes had happened a long time ago, and for good reason, in many people's minds. But who would have thought the nation would ever actually tear down statues and pictures of Lenin? Who would have believed Leningrad would legislate a return to its old name, St. Petersburg? Who could believe a political party, tiny though it was, would loudly advocate the return of the House of Romanov . . . and would be *allowed* to advocate it?

In the conference room, Mikhail Josefovich Malinovski had still worn his uniform as Marshal of the Soviet Union, with his decorations. It would have been difficult to imagine him except as an officer in uniform. A Georgian, he had the thick-set body and the bull neck of his fellow Georgian, Stalin, with the heavy black brows of Brezhnev. He wore little round steel-rimmed eyeglasses and had worn them even in the steam room, since he could see nothing without them. He had driven a tank into Berlin in 1945—until a German civilian woman hit that tank with a *panzerfaust* rocket. The marshal carried the burn scars from that day on his back and legs. His only other combat experience had been in Afghanistan, where as a general commanding an army division, he had nearly been killed when another missile fired from a hand-held launcher landed among his staff and annihilated eight men. If Malinovski had not just then stepped a few meters away to urinate, he would have been killed, too. As it was, the explosion threw him five or six meters. The damage to his head had made him all but blind. Twice in combat, twice wounded. In the army his nickname was *Karandash*, The Pencil. He had spent all but a few months of his career as a desk officer—at least there, it was said, he had never been wounded.

He loved food, as did Semyonov—perhaps, Kedrov speculated, because they had lived through years when people starved. A man who had experienced that would be sure to keep his belly full.

As for himself, Kedrov had never known hunger. He had suffered it, but he had not known it. He was born in 1943 and did not remember the bad years of the Great Patriotic War. All he knew of the great war was what he heard people say, and for the first ten years of his life it had seemed that his elders spoke of little else. Two uncles of his, and an aunt, had been killed, all three with the First Byelorussian Front under the command of Marshal Zhukov. His father had been wounded while serving with the Eighth Guards Army under Colonel General Chuikov.

Photos of the two uncles and the aunt had hung in the family flat in Moscow. As Nikolai Pavlovich grew up, he had found fascination in the picture of his aunt Lidya Nikolayevna Kedrov. She was a military policewoman and had been twenty-two years old when she was shot by a fascist.

The photo had been taken not long before. She had been pretty, so far as he had been able to tell from a somewhat blurred picture. Her face was young, of course, but even through the blur of the photography he could see that her features had been regular and unscarred. She had worn her blonde hair long, and she was wearing a beret cocked far over on one side of her head. Her military blouse was loose but belted tightly at the waist in the traditional Russian style. Her boots came to her knees, but her skirt was quite short, leaving maybe twenty-five centimeters of bare legs showing. It was her exposed legs that had intrigued the young Nikolai Pavlovich. A hundred nights he had masturbated over her picture, aroused by those twenty-five centimeters of bare legs. In his fantasies, she was his bride.

His mother had told him when he was seventeen that Lidya Nikolayevna was said to have given her body to four hundred men during the years of the Great Patriotic War. He was not to mention this to his father. The stories had come back with returning soldiers.

No matter. That was yet another reason for the young man's fascination with his aunt. Another was that he imagined he looked like her, more than like his stocky father and uncles.

Colonel Kedrov was not yet fifty years old. He was blond, like his aunt, and his hair was still thick and healthy. The face he'd had in his twenties—long, strong, with a cleft chin, a heavy lower lip, big blue eyes with a penetrating gaze—had not yet disappeared behind deepening lines and recent looseness of flesh, nor had it been submerged in weariness and cynicism, though these qualities distinctly marked it. His food and vodka did not settle immediately into flesh and more flesh, and he remained straight and erect and was able to maintain a suppleness of movement that had long since been lost to his two companions. If he didn't look like his young aunt, so long dead, then maybe he looked like Edward Fox in the role of General Brian Horrocks in the motion picture *A Bridge Too Far.* He'd seen the *Bridge* movie in London some years ago and had been amused by a woman companion's insistence that he looked a lot like the actor. He'd been amused but . . . the actor was obviously far more handsome.

Kedrov loved the sauerkraut dumplings, which were called *varenky z kvashenoiu kapustoiu.* The sauerkraut was finely chopped, fried until dry, then immersed in a sauce of sautéed onions, with plenty of butter and coarse pepper, and finally some sour cream. The mix was folded into thin dumplings, which were then boiled. It would have been impossible to eat them without vodka.

"So, what is the answer?" asked Marshal Malinovski, directing his question at both his supper companions. "The Motherland has proved its ability to overcome technological disadvantages. We required four years to catch up with the West's fission-bomb technology—but only months to catch up with them on the thermonuclear bomb. We put satellites in space *before* they did. Why can't we do it again?"

"Comrade Marshal," said Semyonov. "We *can* do it again . . . given time. And that is the problem. Given four years, or five, our scientists and technicians can build a multiprocessor supercomputer. But by then the West will have built . . . god knows what."

"With every day we fall further behind," said Kedrov. "Only the damned supercomputers can design supercomputers! Only they can control the extremely sophisticated and delicate processes required to manufacture the chips that are their brains. They program themselves, writing in a few days programs our people would take months to write. They detect their own errors and reprogram themselves to avoid those errors in the future!"

"A vicious circle," the marshal commented glumly. "Can we not make a jump ahead? We did just that in missile design."

"Thirty years ago," said Kedrov. "But missiles don't design missiles. And missiles don't manage the processes that manufacture missiles. What is more—"

Marshal Malinovski banged his fist on the table. "What are we talking about?" he asked. "Survival, is it not? So what is the goddamned answer?"

"There are three possibilities," said Semyonov. "The first is to develop our own supercomputers—"

"Which possibility we have already eliminated," said the marshal.

Semyonov nodded agreement. "The second possibility would be to buy computers and programs from the United States or Japan. And that might be possible, since the United States has removed its export ban on higher technology. This possibility has two problems. First, it is doubtful the Americans or Japanese would actually sell us any significant number of these big machines. Their companies already have many orders for their newest and best supercomputers. What we would need is their entire output for a year or more."

"And how would we pay for these machines?" Kedrov asked. "Surely they are—"

"That is the other problem that eliminates this possibility," said Semyonov. "To buy what we need, even if we could buy it, would cost billions in hard currency—which we don't have. Sixty percent of our hard currency comes from the export of oil, and I need hardly tell you that oil production has fallen sharply over the past three years. Most of those hard-currency credits are spent to buy grain. If we did not buy grain we would have the money to buy computers, but we can't let our people go hungry while we spend billions to import technology."

"Turn then to your third possibility," said Marshal Malinovski. "I think I know what it is."

Semyonov smiled and turned toward Colonel Kedrov. "The assignment has already been made," he said. "Your attendance at this conference has been your initial briefing, Nikolai Pavlovich. The problem has become the responsibility of the Committee for State Security."

Committee for State Security was the full and official title of the KGB—*Komitet Gosudarstvennoi Bezopastnosti*. Often it was called, simply, The Committee.

So *that* was why he had been assigned to attend the sessions of the Conference on the Applications of Higher Technology. Both his supper companions had known it all along. They had been acting out a little drama for him, another element of his briefing.

"Chairman Vyshevskii has told us that you of all men have the special abilities to achieve our purposes," said Semyonov. "You have in fact been honored, Nikolai Pavlovich. You will command a special mission. You will be given every resource you could possibly need."

"You may call on the resources of the armed forces, Comrade Colonel," said Marshal Malinovski.

"And what precisely am I to do?" Kedrov asked. "Exactly what is it that is expected?"

"Tomorrow," said the marshal. "Tomorrow you will be given an additional technical briefing. And then you will visit the special training school at Zagorsk, where you will choose the members of your team."

An honor. Kedrov knew he had been right when he guessed his appointment to the Frustration Conference was nothing likely to win him honor, reward, or promotion.

"I hope I am worthy of the assignment," he said quietly as he lifted his glass of vodka.

"You speak English and German fluently," said the marshal. "You have lived in the West. You know how to work there. You have served most effectively in the West. You know something about computer science and can readily learn more, far more quickly than someone who had to learn everything from the beginning." The marshal picked up a sauerkraut dumpling with his fingers, contemplated it for a moment as though he thought he saw a speck on it, then popped it in his mouth. "I can think of no one I would rather have assigned to this critical venture."

Not before three in the morning did Colonel Kedrov pull his car into the parking lot beside his apartment building on Gorki Street. The police guard was asleep in his box, but Kedrov did not care and did not think of reporting him. He walked through the crunching snow to the front of the building and looked up. He could see lights still burning in his flat on the eleventh floor.

The building offered no service at this hour. He let himself in with his key and crossed the dark lobby. The old woman *dezhurnaya* was not sitting in her chair and had probably long since gone to bed. The elevator had of course been out of service since ten o'clock. Walking up eleven flights more evenings than not had maybe been what kept him from going to fat. It did something for his heart and lungs, surely.

Kedrov took no notice that the walls of the stairwells were cracked and peeling and hardly any notice of the stench of urine. The walls of the lobby and halls were in the same condition, and if people didn't piss in the halls, they certainly did open their doors and toss out trash, which usually stayed there for weeks before it was collected. He did take notice of missing light bulbs, which left the stairwells dangerously dark. He would speak to the building director about that.

With some people, a word from a colonel of the KGB was still enough to get things done.

A woman climbing these stairs had been attacked by a drunk last month. He had stolen the groceries she was carrying. Nothing of the kind had ever before happened in this building, from the day it was opened in 1954. It had always been the residence of people of some status, officers of the government and Party, and no one had ever dared commit a crime here before. Another evidence of the disintegration of society.

He unlocked his door and walked into his flat. The lights were on. Mriya was asleep under a blanket on the sofa. Kedrov smiled. She might have gone on to bed but had stayed up and kept the lights on for him. Likely there was something to eat, too.

He woke her gently, even before he took off his hat and greatcoat.

Mriya Aronovna Meyerhold had been his lover for eleven years. Mriya was nine years younger than he, but she didn't look that much younger. Her fifty-cigarettes-a-day smoking habit had coarsened her skin. In fact, as she woke now and stretched and smiled a welcome at him, she reached for a packet of cigarettes and for her American cigarette lighter. She was a big woman, tall, not overweight but solid: a formidable woman, many said. She had her hair bleached to make her a blonde and had it cut short so she would not have to spend much time caring for it. Right now, as she held her cigarette between her lips and worked the lighter with her right hand, she ran her left hand over her head, which was all the attention she would give her sleep-tousled hair. Her brows were thick and dark above brown eyes in deep retreat and with a slant some called oriental. The shape and color of her eyes seemed to make it impossible for Mriya to give anything a casual glance; her eyes always communicated intensity and meaning, whether she meant to or not.

She was wearing a heavy gray sweater with the sleeves pulled back to her elbows, a black wool skirt, and knee-length black wool socks. The flat was cold as always.

She stretched. "I have some *baklazhannaia ikra*," she said. "I'd like to say I made it, but in fact I bought it. Are you hungry?"

He was not, of course, but he supposed she had stood in line for an hour to buy half a kilo of what they called poor man's caviar, a spread made of eggplant, tomatoes, onions, green pepper, and garlic. It was eaten on pumpernickel, and he had always considered it far tastier than caviar. He nodded and said he had hoped she would have something good waiting.

While Kedrov hung his coat and hat in the one closet in the flat, Mriya carried the bread and *baklazhan* to the living room. She put it out with a bottle of vodka and two glasses.

"Something extremely important?" she asked, referring obviously to the hour.

"Life or death," he said.

"You mean...?"

"For the nation, maybe. For us, probably."

Mriya smiled cautiously. "You've used those words to describe assignments before."

Kedrov shrugged and spread his hands toward the walls. It was a gesture he had shown her often, meaning that they could never be sure what they said was not overheard. The living quarters of any citizen might have listening devices planted in the walls. The living quarters of an officer of the KGB were much more likely to be wired.

He smiled weakly at her. "I have been given an important assignment. It is vital to the survival of the Motherland, against economic chaos. Naturally, it is vital to me. To us. I must... devote myself to it wholeheartedly."

Mriya nodded. She used a knife to cover a hunk of pumpernickel with the dark spread. "Will I be involved?" she asked.

Mriya worked for the KGB, for the First Chief Directorate, often under the supervision of Colonel Kedrov. Their superiors emphatically did not like the relationship, but they had tolerated it. She too was a linguist, fluent in English, German, and French. She had spent much time in the West and functioned there with easy confidence. They had worked together on crucial assignments, with significant success. Like any of the world's very few effective hierarchies, the First Chief Directorate was result-oriented. Unlike the typical hierarchy, it would tolerate a good deal of eccentricity from people who succeeded.

"I am to assemble a team," said Kedrov. "Until I know the exact nature of the assignment and the talents existing in the personnel pool from which I can draw, I am not sure whether or not I can make you a member of the team. I will be going to Western Europe, maybe even to the United States, and you know I will have you with me if I possibly can."

I am to assemble a team. Until I know the exact nature of the assignment and the talents existing in the personnel pool from which I can draw, I am not sure whether or not I can make you a member of the team. I will be going to Western Europe, maybe even to the United States, and you know I will have you with me if I possibly can.

Major Yuryev switched off the recorder. "After that," he said, "they changed the subject and said nothing more significant." He smiled coldly. "Unless the Chairman wishes to listen to their endearments."

"That will not be necessary," said Chairman Vyshevskii.

First Deputy Chairman Andronikov crushed a cigarette in the big bronze ashtray on the Chairman's desk. "We can solve the problem very simply by just denying him the right to assign her to his mission," he said.

"Too crude, too simple," said the Chairman. "No. Let him take her with him if he wants to." He turned to Yuryev. "It will be your job, Ivan Stepanovich, to stalk them—without their knowing it of course—as Javert stalked Valjean."

Yuryev frowned. He had no idea who Javert and Valjean might have been. But he would find out. And he would play Javert to Kedrov's Valjean. Kedrov would not take a breath outside his notice. "I will carry out the assignment exactly as you say. You can depend on me."

Chairman Vyshevskii glanced at Andronikov, then nodded at Yuryev. "We *will* depend on you, Ivan Stepanovich," he said. "And let this be clearly understood: Colonel Kedrov is the man best qualified to carry out this mission. That is why we are sending him, in spite of our problems with him. Your mission is to watch him, report constantly, and to do whatever must be done to prevent his—well, to prevent his failing, for whatever reason. He must not be *allowed* to fail. Is that clear enough?"

"It is clear, Comrade Chairman."

———————— 2 ————————

OLGA ALEXANDROVNA CHERNOV had been bold enough to ask Colonel Kedrov not to smoke in her office, and he was uncomfortable—though not nearly so uncomfortable as Mriya would have been if she had been asked not to smoke. It was another manifestation of the breakdown of society, that a woman no more than thirty or thirty-five years old should demand that a man of his age and rank amend his conduct to suit her. A bold and rude innovation, this, asking people not to smoke—American in origin.

Except for this, it was pleasant to sit here with Olga Alexandrovna, for she was an affable and extraordinarily capable young woman who had immediately invited him to address her by her first name and patronymic and had poured him a glass of steaming tea. She was attractive, too, though intense and sober.

Olga Alexandrovna called to Kedrov's mind the word *solid*. It was the word that characterized her personality as he had seen it so far. It was the word that characterized her person: the dour expression on her face and the way she held her body— rigid, as if she were ready to spring. It characterized her womanly figure, too: defiant in its generosity. And her personality: totally self-confident.

Probably she could not have talked at all without her blackboard and chalk. She was up and down from her chair constantly, erasing an idea and sketching out a new one, filling the board

16

with lines and words that would have been meaningless to anyone not listening to her and following her conversation. He had before observed this nervous obsession with diagrams; it was an idiosyncrasy of computer-oriented scientists. They could not think, apparently, except in interconnected blocks.

Her office was decorated, if it could be said to be decorated at all, with computer junk—that is, with green and silver circuit boards, presumably obsolete or defective, and even a disk drive with its cover removed to expose the rust-colored disks and the read-write heads on the ends of their hinged arms.

She was far more specific than anyone who had spoken to him so far. "Our national problem, Nikolai Pavlovich—besides misplaced priorities for too many years—is that we are at least half a decade behind in the field of semiconductors. I assume you know what I refer to."

"Yes. Chips."

They had adopted the English word. Chip. чип.

Olga Alexandrovna nodded. "We have the technology to manufacture the rest of a supercomputer." She smiled scornfully. "I mean, we can make the steel cabinets. Wire. Little electric motors to run the drives and cooling fans. Even fat awkward Russian fingers can insert pins in holes. What we do not have is the technology to make the semiconductors, the chips. Oh, you understand, of course, that we can make the simpler chips that control earlier generations of computers. What we cannot do is make the chips that control machines like the Cray Y-MP or similar super-supercomputers being introduced by companies like Hitachi and NEC."

"I understand," he said.

She shrugged. "We can do it in time. The problem is, we don't have time. The 1990s are the decade of the supercomputer. Without them, our industry cannot compete in any field. What is more, as you have probably heard, we need supercomputers to make supercomputers."

"So I've heard," said Kedrov.

"Something else that may be of interest to you, Nikolai Pavlovich," she said as she stood and picked up her chalk. On the blackboard she wrote the word *codes*. "There is not a code one of these machines cannot crack. What is more, they can create codes that nothing we have can decipher. They can read everything of ours that they intercept. We will be able to read nothing of theirs."

She drew a box around *codes* and sat down again.

"You understand my mission, Olga Alexandrovna," he said.

"I understand you can tell me where to start."

"First, you should read a body of documents," she said. "I cannot allow them to be taken from the Institute, so you will have to read them here. I should think it will take you about two days. For the moment, I will tell you enough to make the documents more nearly comprehensible to one who is not, after all, a computer scientist."

"I must be at Zagorsk this afternoon," he said.

"Of course. Then return."

"I will."

She stood and picked up her chalk. She began to diagram. "The human brain," she said, "can assimilate information at speeds that remain far beyond the capacity of any computer." She reached for her glass of tea. "For my brain to inspect this object in my hand, its appearance, the feel of it, and so on, and to recognize it as a glass of tea, requires my brain to perform— as we estimate—one hundred billion logical floating-point operations per second. A computer being developed at Cambridge, Massachusetts, in the United States, may exceed this capacity within the year. Still, it will not match the human brain in cognitive abilities, for a variety of reasons we cannot go into now."

"I am glad to hear it," said Kedrov dryly.

"The typical supercomputer can do about 2.5 billion operations per second. Our own are still operating in the hundreds-of-millions range. I will oversimplify, Nikolai Pavlovich. One of the reasons why the supercomputers work so fast is that the electrical impulses within them have far shorter distances to travel—because their chips, besides being more sophisticated, are also more compact. Electrical impulses travel through the computer at the speed of light, but when you are talking about billions of operations per second, an infinitesimally small distance makes a significant difference. We can make the chips that do all the operations. But because our chips must be immensely larger, our computers take ten or fifteen seconds to do what the Western supercomputers do in one one-hundredth of a second."

"Which means," said Kedrov, "that conditions change faster than our computers can analyze them."

"Precisely."

"In specific terms, Olga Alexandrovna—"

She began to diagram again. "Making chips means etching a complex pattern of components and circuits on a thin silicon wafer," she said. "In the past—oversimplifying once again—designers drew patterns, the patterns were photographed, and the patterns were photographically reduced as small as possible. The tiny patterns were then projected onto the surface of the silicon wafer and etched there. But... the distances now involved are shorter than the wavelengths of light! This technology, of which we are masters, is *obsolete!*"

"The supercomputers—"

"Still rely, most of them, on optical etching. But the new generation, the super-supercomputers, must be controlled by chips manufactured by a new technology."

"Which is?"

"There are two possibilities," she said. "One is X-ray technology, because X-rays have a shorter wavelength than light. The other—the more promising technology—is called e-beam lithography. The full name is direct electron-beam lithography. The possibilities—"

"Olga Alexandrovna... put this in terms an old man can understand."

She grinned. *"Old man!* Nikolai Pavlovich, my *husband,* at forty years, should be as young as you. But—think of this. The human hair is seventy-five microns wide. An e-beam lithography machine can etch a circuit that is one-*quarter* of a micron wide." Her smile disappeared. "Think of a television tube. A beam of electrons scans lines to make the picture. Think of an electron beam scanning lines a billion times finer, etching a tiny circuit. That is what we don't have, Nikolai Pavlovich. It is what we *must* have!"

"And where do we get it?" he asked bluntly.

She began scratching on her blackboard again. He had to admit, her diagrams made the conversation easier to manage.

"This technology," she said, drawing blocks and writing in them, "has two elements. One is making the machines. We can do that. Not immediately. It will be exceedingly difficult. But we can do it." She drew a big X over the block where she had printed *make*. "The second element is—" She printed a second word on the blackboard, *how*. She tapped her finger on the word, smearing it but leaving it legible. "Western corporations have spent hundreds of millions—of however you want to put it, rubles, British pounds, American dollars—developing this technology. It is unbelievably complex. They have experimented with it over the past twenty years. What we need, Nikolai Pavlovich—"

"Is the benefit of their trials and errors," he said.

Olga Alexandrovna sat down and put her hand down firmly on his. "If I knew what they have learned in the past twenty years, what mistakes they have made and where correction of those mistakes has led them, I could—my colleagues and I could bring our country into competition with them in ten months!"

Kedrov nodded. "Then my job is simple," he said. "All I have to do is steal what they have learned."

She squeezed his hand as though they were lovers—though he fully understood it was from commitment and enthusiasm. "Direct electron-beam lithography!" she whispered hoarsely. "Not a panacea, Nikolai Pavlovich. Not the solution to all problems. But if you could bring back from the West the secret of e-beam lithography, you will truly be a hero of the Soviet Union!"

It was well after noon when he and Olga Alexandrovna Chernov finished their meeting, and she invited him to take lunch with her in the Institute dining room. Knowing that scientists at the Institute ate well, Kedrov accepted.

They sat at a table apart. Her colleagues understood that Olga Alexandrovna was meeting with a colonel from the KGB, and they stayed away from her for two reasons. First, they supposed that whatever she was discussing with him was private; and, second, they dared an impertinence they would not have dared five years ago: ostentatiously to avoid the company of an officer of an agency they scorned.

Kedrov did not even notice. He assumed they stayed away from him out of grudging respect, out of uncertainty, even fear. He had been accustomed to that for twenty years and had not yet become accustomed to the idea that in the new Soviet Union some people might be ready to snub him.

He was not accustomed, either, to the experience of a young woman whose acquaintance he had made only this morning being so bold as to ask him personal questions.

"How did it happen, Nikolai Pavlovich, that you chose The Committee for a career? You will forgive my asking, I hope. I ask everyone questions like this."

They sat over a lunch of white fish in a cream sauce, with a bottle of vodka between them. His mother had asked this question. No one else had ever asked it. He wasn't sure how to answer.

"When I applied for affiliation with the Committee for State Security, it offered a young man a splendid career," he said. "In fact, it still does."

"A splendid career..." the young woman said thoughtfully.

"Yes," he said simply. He did not choose to explain further.

Only those who thoroughly understood the structure of the agency understood that an officer of the First Chief Directorate had nothing to do with internal security, nothing to do with political control or dissent, nothing to do with the apparatus of terror. Olga Alexandrovna did not understand that the First Chief Directorate did indeed offer a splendid career. The KGB offered all its full-time employees better pay than almost any other career. Immediate access to the special apartments, the special stores, the special restaurants, the separate medical services, the separate entertainments and holidays that were available only to the gentry of the government and the Party. A special status within the protection of the organization. First

Chief Directorate offered even more. Agents of the First Chief Directorate comprised an elite.

He wore suits tailored in London. He was immediately recognizable on the streets as a man with special status, because he dressed as very few Russians could dress, no matter what they paid. He wore shoes made in Italy. He wore American slingshot underpants. He owned a Japanese camera and a Japanese tape recorder and player, and in his flat in the building on Gorki Street he played tapes of English and American musical plays—*Les Miserables, Phantom of the Opera, La Cage aux Folles*, and so on. He had eaten in the finest restaurants of Paris and London, stayed in the great hotels.

Olga Alexandrovna tipped her head a little to one side and looked at him as if she had not really seen him before. If he judged correctly, she had just revised her appraisal of him in some significant way: revised and then immediately dismissed the thought.

"I have served abroad almost all my years in the KGB," he said. He meant for her to understand he was not a policeman. "In Germany most of the time. In England sometimes."

"Yes, of course," she said. "You are a spy. That is why we are together today."

"During the years when our country was constantly threatened by the imperialists, I contributed what I could to our survival. That threat has diminished somewhat. A new one has arisen: as ominous as the old one but far more subtle."

Olga Alexandrovna grinned. "Nikolai Pavlovich," she said. "Drama is out of style. We face a very practical difficulty. If you read the foreign press, you read that our one-time enemies now wish us well. They actually want us to succeed."

"You believe that?" he asked.

"We are no longer called an evil empire," she said.

"Will they then give us the technology we need?" he asked.

"No. You will have to steal it."

Kedrov shrugged. "Is this so very different?" he asked.

For a moment she sat looking down at her plate, using her fork to assemble a bite of fish. "Is it not different, Nikolai Pavlovich?" she asked.

"No. Nothing has changed. Remember the words of the famous German, Karl von Clausewitz: 'War is a continuation of policy by other means.' The war is not over, Olga Alexandrovna. The imperialists still threaten our existence, and we fight on by other means."

Nikolai Pavlovich Kedrov could not imagine living where winter did not mean deep snow and penetrating cold, where men and women did not enshroud themselves in wool and fur and warm themselves with hot drinks and occasional steam baths and shut themselves up in small rooms redolent with cooking smells and the honest rankness of their own bodies. No matter how attractive the Mediterranean or Caribbean might be, for a few weeks, a few months, their enticements paled beside the communal coziness Russians made for themselves on long winter nights in retreat from the remorseless cold. Driving in his Zhiguli out of Moscow toward Zagorsk, he fought patches of ice and snow on the inadequately cleared pavement. The heater in the car was weak—not adequate even for a London winter—and he wore his greatcoat and gloves and fur hat as he drove.

Zagorsk. The training school there was secret. It was new. It was charged with training selected agents for the new task.

Only those who thoroughly understood the history of the KGB since 1989 understood that Chairman Vyshevskii had quietly advised the President and the Council of Ministers that whether authorized or not, the agency intended to de-emphasize its internal security role and in the future focus its attention and resources on foreign operations. The Chairman had not said so, but he and his deputies had taken careful note of the fate of internal security policemen in Romania, Czechoslovakia, and Germany. They were firmly decided not to risk such a fate for themselves. Suddenly Second Chief Directorate had been de-emphasized. So had Fifth Directorate, whose role had been to suppress dissent. Suddenly First Chief Directorate had, in effect, *become* the KGB.

Many of the bully-boy policemen of Second Chief Directorate had been cashiered. A few of them, together with a few from

Fifth Directorate, were being retrained. At Zagorsk.

More important were the agents being assimilated into the KGB from the security agencies of the former fraternal republics. The best of them, the ones best able to function effectively in the West, were German. Kedrov himself had seen to it that the most talented people from the now-abolished German agencies were not lost but summoned to Moscow and then to Zagorsk for retraining and reassignment.

Now abolished was the *Ministerium für Staats-Sicherheit*, once called *Stasi*—the Ministry for State Security, the KGB of the former German Democratic Republic. Within *Stasi*, an elite group had operated under the title *Hauptverwaltung Aufklärung*, HVA—Chief Adminisration, Intelligence. The spymaster of HVA, General Markus Wolf, had anticipated by more than ten years the new assignment First Chief Directorate of the KGB had now undertaken: industrial espionage, leapfrogging Western research and development by stealing the results and so speeding industrial development. Almost all of the best agents of HVA were now at Zagorsk, most of them as instructors.

Colonel Kedrov had authority to recruit anyone he wanted at Zagorsk. With maybe an exception or two, he already knew who he wanted. He had worked with these men and women before and had already judged them.

The new training school at Zagorsk had once been a mental hospital—that is, ostensibly a mental hospital, actually a prison where noisy nonconformists had been silenced. Its sixty rooms had been refurnished to make a dormitory for the trainees. Its four wards had been converted to classrooms. The rest of its facilities, kitchen, cafeteria, laundry, and so on were useful to the school. The formidable security fence that surrounded the place caused no special notice in the neighborhood. It had always been there. Not one person in ten in the area had ever guessed what was inside that fence, and no one at all understood that the institution was now something very different.

In Moscow, number-four officer in First Chief Directorate was not impressive rank. At Zagorsk it inspired deference. The director of the school welcomed Colonel Kedrov, then vacated his office and told the colonel to consider it his own. In mid-afternoon Kedrov sat down behind the director's desk and focused his attention on a stack of files.

He had eleven files. Six were ones he had asked for. Five were files suggested by the director.

Kurt Horst Steiner. There was a man he wanted. He reviewed the file. Born in 1961 in Oranienburg. Father, a machinist. Mother, a hotel maid. Excelled in *das Polytechnikum*, completed the twelve-year course, not just the ten-year course, and earned a full state scholarship to attend the University of Leipzig. Competed for a place on the Olympic team of the German Democratic Republic as a pole vaulter, but did not qualify for the 1980 Olympics. Politically active. A member of the Communist Party. Graduated from Leipzig in 1983 with a diploma in applied sciences, mathematics, and Marxism-Leninism. Fluent in Russian, English, and Latin.

Applied to the *Ministerium für Staats-Sicherheit* immediately on graduation. Was accepted and assigned to *Hauptver-waltung Aufklärung*. Trained in Berlin and Moscow.

His first assignment was a test: a not-unusual one for a new HVA agent. He was sent to Cairo, carrying an Irish passport—forged, of course—in the guise of a representative of an Irish brewery that wanted to export its ale to Egypt for consumption in Cairo hotels and on Nile cruisers. He was in Egypt just three days. He found the man he had come to find, a defector from the KGB, and killed him with a knife. He did that the first day. The second day he went out to see the pyramids. The third day, he spent four hours in the Egyptian Museum before returning to the airport for a flight to Paris.

After that, Kedrov did not need to read the file to recall the details of the career of Kurt Horst Steiner. The young man's next assignment had brought him under the direct command of Colonel Kedrov.

He opened the second of the files he had asked for.

Kristin Kuniczak. Born in Cracow in 1964. Father, a professor at Jagiellonian University. Mother, a professor at Cracow Technical University. Educated in anticipation that she too would become a university professor, possibly of Polish and Russian literature, in which studies she concentrated. Became fluent in German and Russian. Married 1981 to Pawel Kuniczak, ostensibly actor, actually paid informer for UB, Polish Intelligence. Gave birth to a son four months later while still only seventeen years old. Arrested and imprisoned on suspicion of smothering the infant, released when an autopsy proved the child had not died so. Did not return to university. Toured Poland with theatrical troupe, playing bit parts under Kuniczak. Recruited by Janusz Prus, senior UB agent, to act as *agent provocateur* among actors and expose anti-Soviet group in theatrical troupe. Succeeded in so doing, resulting in several prosecutions. In 1982 became mistress to Prus and moved into his flat in Warsaw.

Where she met Colonel Nikolai Pavlovich Kedrov, and from that point forward he did not need to read the file to follow the career of Kristin Kuniczak.

She was an exceptionally attractive young woman. Even a man who did not know her history—pregnant at seventeen, married, *agent provocateur*, mistress of a senior security police agent while still technically married to a minor informer—could not have failed to be intrigued by her, just from her looks and personality.

Kedrov had been intrigued. He had suggested to Prus that he should sacrifice his mistress to the cause of Marxism-Leninism. Kedrov could not have guessed how pleased Prus was with that suggestion. Prus's wife had learned about the pretty, dark-haired, dark-eyed mistress. That was one problem. That the eighteen-year-old Kristin was limitlessly ambitious was another. Prus had been happy to ship her off to KGB training school in Moscow.

Kristin Kuniczak was the only other woman Kedrov had slept with since he had established his relationship with Mriya Aronovna.

She was waiting to see him, so he interviewed her first, before Steiner.

"Nikolai Pavlovich," she greeted him with that guileless and yet devilish smile that had so beguiled him when he first met her. "It is good to see you again."

"Would you like to work with me again, Kristin?"

"I can think of no higher privilege," she said in flawless, unaccented Russian. It was difficult—no, impossible—to measure the proportions in which sincerity and mockery were mixed in her voice and words. "Anyway, I am bored with Zagorsk."

Kedrov doubted that. Kristin was never long bored, wherever she went. Her pixyish nature and earthy physical allure took care of that. She was not a dazzling beauty. She was, in the first place, quite petite, no more than 1.6 meters tall, no more than fifty kilograms. Her belly and backside were flat, her breasts small, as he well remembered. Her hair was dark brown, so very dark it was almost black, and she wore it long, yet fluffed out so her head was surrounded by it as if by a fur cap. Her features were simple: a wide mouth with thin lips, dark eyes under dark brows, altogether a face well shaped, nothing wrong with it, still nothing stunning. Somehow her buoyant, iconoclastic personality projected from her dancing eyes and evocative smile, as if there were a light burning inside her that threw out a vivid image.

Another element of Kristin Kuniczak was that her past was littered with the wreckage of people who had underestimated her: first her husband, and others since. That she was so easily underestimated helped to make her an effective agent.

And she *was* an effective agent. That was why she was here at Zagorsk, selected for the special training that prepared the best for the new mission.

"Bored or not," he said to her, "I hope you are learning what they're teaching here. The world has changed. *We* must change."

"Or die," she said simply.

"I am not quite ready to brief you on your new assignment," he said. "I promise you it will be interesting. And important. I have ordered the director of the school to expedite the remainder of your training. In a few days I'll return to brief you and the others chosen." He paused and smiled. "I trust you have not lost your taste for Rhine wines."

Kristin grinned, "So, To the Rhine. With all due respect to the Soviet Union, Nikolai Pavlovich, what is most boring about

Zagorsk is the table they set. I dream of German restaurants."

"As do I," he said.

Kedrov vividly remembered the day in a fine Berlin restaurant—in fact the dining room of the Hotel Bristol-Kempinski—
when his dinner companion, a British agent, had stared for a
moment at a beautiful young woman who was speaking French
and had said—

"Ah . . . the French! How would you like to have *her* for your
best friend?"

And Kedrov had looked across the room at an erect, hard-
faced, close-cropped German, a forbidding fellow he did not
think he would want to know, and had said—

"In a fight, I'd rather have the German over there."

That German had not been Kurt Horst Steiner. But he might
have been. Forty-four years as citizens of a fraternal republic
had not changed them. Germans of the former Democratic Republic were hardly distinguishable from Germans of the Third
Reich.

Actually, Steiner was not the typical German Kedrov thought
he was. A little more than thirty years old, Steiner retained a
naive charm that did not, in Kedrov's frame of reference, serve
a man well.

Yet it had served Steiner well. People who should have been
more perspicacious did not see past the handsome, youthful face
to the cruel man inside. In many ways Kurt Horst Steiner was
just what he looked like: young, innocent, happily handsome,
shallow. In some ways he was exactly that. In others he was
the product of his background.

How described? So handsome his handsomeness verged on
feminine delicacy. Sturdy and muscular—still the young man
who had hoped to vault at the 1980 Olympics. Blond. Ready
with a disarming smile. In one sense, forgettable. In another,
probably in the way women saw him, disturbingly unforgetta-
ble.

"It is an honor to see you again, Comrade Colonel," said Kurt
stiffly before he sat down.

There was no point in asking Kurt Horst Steiner if he was ready to accept a new assignment under the command of Colonel Kedrov, KGB. Of course he was. Willing? No, eager.

"I am sure you understand, Comrade Colonel," he said, sadly but still with some stiffness remaining in his voice, "that I am a man without a country."

"But not without a cause," said Kedrov. He would judge Steiner by his reaction to this meaningless response. "Still a man with much to achieve."

Steiner nodded solemnly. "I agree, Comrade Colonel."

"Your new training, Kurt?"

"It is excellent, Comrade Colonel."

Kedrov nodded. "It was meant to be. It must be. I am taking you with me on a new assignment, by far the most important either one of us has ever known."

"I will do my best."

"I have no doubt. Be sure you meet Kristin Kuniczak, if you haven't already. She will be working with us."

Steiner was unable to conceal his surprise, his dismay. "Comrade Kuniczak?" he asked.

"Learn not to call people comrade anymore, Steiner," said Kedrov. "Even in Moscow."

"*Jawohl!*"

Kedrov smiled. "Your training, Steiner. Your new training, here at Zagorsk. Aren't they teaching you to talk like the impudent youths of the West? Take it seriously, my young friend. Remember the *gammler?*"

"What the West called ... "

"Beatniks," said Kedrov. "Pseudo-intellectuals—"

"Scum!" Steiner spat.

"Remember them, Kurt. Don't mimic them, but remember that what they represented comes even closer to the social climate of *our* countries today than does the tidy disciplined societies we sustained. They represent the new world in which you and I have to function and survive."

"Surely, Comrade Colonel—"

"I exaggerate," said Kedrov. "But learn from your training here at Zagorsk. I expect you let your hair to grow much longer,

Kurt. You are going to serve our cause in a different world."

"I have served in that different world, Nikolai Pavlolich," said Steiner, using Kedrov's first name and patronymic for the first time.

"You have served in it," said Kedrov. "Now you are going to be *of* it."

"What more can I do for you, Nikolai Pavlovich?" asked Olga Alexandrovna Chernov.

Kedrov shook his head. "You have served our country extremely well," he said, conscious that she might not very much care if she had served the Motherland very well or not.

He had, as she had suggested he should, spent two days at the Institute, poring over files she had selected for him. He now knew more about the manufacture of semiconductors than he had ever expected to know, had ever dreamed he would want to know.

"I can remember, Olga Alexandrovna, the first time I ever saw an electric typewriter, the first time I saw a Xerox machine, the first time I saw a computer. I can remember the first time I ever saw a television set! Semiconductors . . . " He shook his head.

"The target company, Nikolai Pavlovich," she said grimly.

"Yes. I have chosen agents who will be able to approach the technicians of a target company. Young. Knowledgeable. Adaptable."

"From your reading of the files, have you chosen a target?"

"I want your opinion."

"Tell me first what company you choose."

"Laser Solutions, Incorporated," he said.

Olga Alexandrovna reached across her desk and put her hand down firmly on his. "An excellent choice, Nikolai Pavlovich," she said. "It is the one I would have chosen myself. Hitachi . . . " She shrugged. "Well, maybe. Intel . . . maybe. LSI, Laser Solutions, Incorporated . . . the first choice. Penetrate LSI and you have penetrated the company on the leading edge of e-beam lithography."

"On the leading edge of something else, Olga Alexandrovna."

"Oh? You see something else in those files?"

"What is your judgment," he asked, "of massively parallel processing?"

"An American specialty," she said. "It may be extremely important. The difficulty is, it's mostly in the minds of the computer scientists who are working on it. To capture that technology, we would have to have access to one of those minds for a considerable period of time. A far more difficult task for you, I should think."

"But worth the effort it we could do it."

"Well worth whatever it might require."

She stood at the window and watched him drive out of the parking lot. After a long moment's hesitation she picked up the telephone and dialed a number.

"Ivan Stepanovich? Olga Alexandrovna here. The colonel will move against Laser Solutions, Incorporated."

"Good," said the KGB major.

"Maybe not so good," she said. "LSI is a multinational corporation. It has research and manufacturing facilities in the United States, Britain, Germany, and Japan."

"Did he make a wise choice of companies to penetrate?" asked Major Yuryev.

"He read the files and understood what he read—as not many of you would, if you don't mind my saying so. LSI is heavily committed to direct-write electron-beam lithography, also to fiber-optic technology for the transfer of signals inside the computer. Colonel Kedrov also identified massively parallel processing as a technology we should have. LSI is working on that, too."

"What is massively parallel processing?"

"I won't try to explain on the telephone. You should read the documents. Let me say this: that in the short run it can be even more important to us than e-beam lithography."

"Then the colonel has chosen well," said Yuryev.

"Yes, but we must remember, Ivan Stepanovich, that LSI has many government contracts and is surrounded by heavy security. The task Colonel Kedrov has undertaken will be anything but easy."

"We will not allow him to fail, Olga Alexandrovna."

3

RUSSELL TOBIN SETTLED comfortably into his window seat in the first-class section of Air France Flight 203, Paris to New York. He had brought a book with him, Anne Rice's *Queen of the Damned,* and he meant to read and snooze.

Tomorrow was going to be a challenging day, but there was nothing he could do to prepare for it and no reason why he should not relax all the way across the Atlantic. He slipped out of his shoes, a pair of black Gucci loafers, loosened his necktie, and pulled the menu card from the seat pocket before him to see what was going to be served for dinner.

"Roos-ell . . . It is *good* to see you."

This could not be a coincidence. Very little that involved André Guyard was ever a coincidence. If he was aboard this flight and seated beside Russell Tobin, he had arranged it. The Frenchman sat down in the aisle seat and shrugged and twisted as he fastened the belt.

"Five years?" Tobin asked.

"And three months," said Guyard. "But I have kept track of you. When they knocked holes in the Berlin Wall, I stared hard at my television, expecting to see you out there pounding away with a big hammer."

"Actually," said Tobin, "I was at home in my flat, working on my résumé. I suddenly felt very obsolete and had begun to wonder if I wouldn't have to look for a new kind of job."

"Ah-hah!" Guyard laughed. "Our kind will never become obsolete Roos-ell. Never."

"Well, I wondered for a while if we hadn't suddenly run out of enemies," said Tobin.

Guyard raised a hand, and a cabin attendant came immediately to his side. *"Deux Courvoisiers, s'il vous plaît,"* he said to her. *"Et une minérale gaseuse avec deux verres."*

Tobin tucked his book into the pocket ahead of him. Obviously, he was not going to do much reading after all.

André Guyard lit a cigarette. They sat in no-smoking seats, and the Defense de Fumer signs were lighted, but neither of those facts deterred him. Nothing would deter him, Tobin remembered. The man did not just smoke, he drew blue smoke from strong French cigarettes into his lungs as if taking nourishment from it.

The cabin staff said nothing. Tobin guessed they had some idea who he was. Likely the company had told them that one of their passengers was a high-ranking officer of DGSE, *Direction Générale de la Sécurité Extérieure.* It wasn't true, exactly, but likely that was what they had been told. It was enough to engender awed deference from the cabin staff.

"The conference?" asked Guyard.

Tobin nodded. "Yes. The conference."

That was not the whole truth either. It was true that he was on his way to Washington to attend the same international conference Guyard was undoubtedly going to attend. He expected, however, that another conference he would be attending would be more important. Tomorrow's meeting was with the DCI. He would make the session of the international conference only when his meeting at Langley was over.

"I hope we find the answer to the question," said Guyard mock-ingenuously.

"We know the answer to the question, André."

"Zagorsk."

"Right. The best of them. Of the others, some are dead. Some are hiding. Some have retired."

"Very few came to us," said Guyard. "Did many come to you?"

"Not many. And the ones who came didn't have much to sell.

An unhappy lot of men and women. Obsolete. Two years ago, one of the Germans said to me, 'I have learned the details of how and how much your National Security Agency plans to reduce its European activities. I have current and accurate information, but nobody wants it. I have no one to report to. Why did I bother?'"

Guyard sucked hard on his cigarette and raised his chin high as he drew the smoke into his lungs. "Reduction indeed," he said ironically. "Your National Security Agency has *increased* its European activities."

"I wouldn't know," said Tobin.

"No, no, of course not," said Guyard. "So insignificant an NIO would not be trusted with such sensitive information."

Tobin shrugged. It was a comment to which he would not respond—indeed, Guyard did not expect him to.

"I understand, just the same," said the Frenchman, "that the NSA has accepted its new definition with enthusiasm, and, though it fumbled its way a little at first, is now functioning effectively in the new role."

Again, Tobin only listened. What Guyard was talking about was the major shift in emphasis at NSA.

For decades the National Security Agency had monitored other nations' communications, intercepting, recording, and when necessary decoding radio signals, telephone conversations, and telemetry. It intercepted not only broadcast communications but also tapped cables and installed eavesdropping devices. NSA afforded the United States an astonishingly rich source of intelligence information.

For example, in the late 1970s NSA installed a sophisticated electronic tap on a Soviet underwater communications cable in the Sea of Okhotsk, just off the east coast of the Soviet Union. For several years NSA intercepted secret Soviet military communications, including detailed information about missile tests.

On October 10, 1985, NSA listened to a dozen telephone conversations between the president of Egypt and his foreign minister. President Mubarak had told the government of the United States that the PLO terrorists who had hijacked the *Achille Lauro* and murdered Leon Klinghoffer in his wheelchair were

not in Egypt. To his foreign minister, Mubarak was saying the
United States was crazy to think an Arab nation would hand
over Arab brothers. No, the four PLO terrorists would fly to
PLO headquarters, then in Algeria, aboard an Egyptair 727.
Mubarak told his foreign minister the flight number, time of
departure, and flight plan. Four F–14 fighters from the carrier
Saratoga intercepted the Egyptair plane over the Mediterranean and forced it to land on a NATO base in Sicily, where the
hijackers were taken off.

The principal mission of NSA had always been to learn everything it could about Soviet military strength and movements in
Eastern Europe. It maintained major listening posts all along
the western side of the Iron Curtain. Other listening posts were
aboard ships at sea, on high-flying aircraft, and even in orbiting
satellites. Although NSA could not always decode what it intercepted, very little communications traffic moved within or to
and from the Soviet Union that NSA did not intercept and
analyze.

What Guyard was suggesting now was that the end of the
dangerous military confrontation between the United States and
the Soviet Union had not meant the dismantling of the NSA
apparatus in Europe. To the contrary, the United States was
intercepting more information than ever before—information of
a different kind, because NSA had been assigned a new role.

He was correct, as Tobin well knew. NSA continued to intercept all the information it could from inside the Soviet Union.
Unstable and weakened, the Soviet Union was still a nuclear
superpower.

NSA's new responsibilities included monitoring communications that might afford leads about imminent terrorist activity
and that might help law enforcement agencies to interdict drug
shipments anywhere in the world. The new emphasis, though,
was economic information.

For a very long time the intercepts had included industrial
secrets. It was all but unavoidable that a system that monitored
every form of communication should from time to time gather
information relating not strictly to defense, but to economic
conditions within friendly countries as well as unfriendly ones.

The White House had used the information sometimes when it suggested an economic crisis in one or more of those nations. Decisions about trade policy and economic and military assistance had been based on intercepted business information. Use of these intercepts had been clearly in the economic self-interest of the United States.

What did law and ethics dictate about disclosure of such information to American corporations, particularly when most of this kind of information came from friendly countries, even firm allies?

What ethics required was muddied by the fact that NSA intercepts also proved that other nations were eavesdropping on American business communications to the extent they could. What the law required was muddied by the fact that changing the law would require an open debate in Congress. A complicated dialogue had been going on for more than a year within the American intelligence community, with the White House and the Congressional Oversight Committee also involved. Ten thousand questions remained unanswered. Among the most thorny of them: Which American corporations would be given what information? That question alone was well nigh impossible to answer.

As the Air France 747 taxied out toward a runway the cabin attendants brought Guyard and Tobin their brandy and mineral water, together with a little tray of hors d'oeuvres: caviar on crackers. To serve during takeoff was another violation of rules, but the cabin staff were plainly ready to break any rule to serve and impress their distinguished passenger.

A high-ranking officer of DGE—*Direction Générale de la Sécurité Extérieure.* If that was what someone had told them he was, they had been told something less than the truth. If they had been told who he really was, they might not have understood it. The agency he worked for was not well known. But if they had been told the truth and understood it, they would have been still more deferential. André Guyard was number-two man in GIGN—*Groupe d'Intervention de la Gendarmerie Nationale.*

GIGN was a specialized elite police unit established in 1983 (and succeeding the infamous *Action,* which President Mitter-

rand had insisted on abolishing) to combat terrorism. André
Guyard had in reality a license supposed to have been held by
the fictional James Bond but not in fact held by any British
officer. Officers of GIGN had a license to kill. Having once assured himself to his complete but personal satisfaction that a
subject was genuinely a threat to the security of France, likely
to commit some major offense against the nation, André Guyard
had a license to kill that subject. He had that license and he
used it. Tobin had seen him use it.

Somehow the French managed philosophically to reconcile
their vaunted commitment to the rights of man with a readiness
to use outright brutality in the service of their country.

It was difficult to believe that this squat, solid, somber man,
this hacking chain-smoker who appeared in danger of setting
fire to his mustache, was one of France's most trusted security
officers. Tobin had seen him put a 7.65mm bullet through the
back of a man's head and knew he was no innocent. More than
that, he had seen Guyard in the exercise of a finely tuned Ma-
chiavellian sagacity. He was not just a killer. Not at all. The
willingness to kill was just a part of his professional armory.

Takeoffs from Charles de Gaulle Airport were often mysterious to passengers who could not understand why a 747 sometimes cruised at two thousand feet or less over the French
countryside for ten or fifteen minutes, leaving people in the
cabins to wonder if something was wrong with the airplane and
they were going to return to the airport. Then the pilots would
tip the nose up finally, and the airplane would begin a steep
climb.

This takeoff was like that, and when the plane went into its
climb, Tobin and Guyard had to grab at their glasses and the
bottle of mineral water.

"Do you remember Klaus Ostreicher?" Guyard asked Tobin.
Tobin nodded. "Did he survive?"

"Yes. He has a new name and a new appearance, and he is
very much alive. Not obsolete."

"Where is he?" Tobin asked.

Guyard could not contain his satisfaction in knowing something Tobin did not know. *"Bundesnachtrichtendienst,"* he said.

Formerly the Federal Intelligence Service of West Germany, BND was now the intelligence service of the reunited Germany. Almost none of the chief agents of *Hauptverwaltung Aufklärung* came over. It had been natural to suppose many of them would, but very few did.

"They are committed to economic espionage," said Guyard.

"You are not surprised."

Guyard shrugged, that vividly expressive Gallic shrug that only Frenchmen used. "For the Germans the Cold War is not over. They have now the opportunity to fight the old fight again, in a different way but on their own terms and by techniques in which they are very effective."

"Remember what von Clausewitz said," Tobin suggested. "'War is a continuation of policy by other means.' Well, the Cold War was a continuation of policy by other means. Industrial espionage is a continuation of war by still other means. The policy von Clausewitz referred to was to gain an advantage over your neighbors, even to dominate your part of the world, or all the world. The policy hasn't changed. Only the means."

Guyard smiled. "Our profession produces relatively few philosophers, Roos-ell. Clearly you are one."

A cabin attendant came by with the bottle and poured more brandy. The airplane climbed through a layer of cloud, and soon the more observant and thoughtful of the passengers in the dimly lighted belly of the 747 were aware of their isolation in a vast dark world. Tobin pulled his novel from the seat pocket and hoped Guyard would understand that he wanted to read.

"I think often," said the Frenchman, "of the days when we worked together. Days of greater certainties, Roos-ell."

Greater certainties. Tobin understood what he meant.

When Russ Tobin graduated with a degree in European history from Stanford University in June of 1963, the CIA recruiter had not been embarrassed to suggest that service with the intelligence agency was akin to service in the Peace Corps. Neither Tobin nor the recruiter had dreamed that a few years later students would riot when they learned a CIA recruiter was on campus. Tobin saw the CIA as the recruiter suggested: a government agency where a bright young man might do valuable service to his country.

President Kennedy had repeatedly called the nation's young people to the service of their country.

No one doubted the country needed service. Just before Russ Tobin began his junior year at the university, East Germany closed the border between East and West Berlin and began construction of the Berlin Wall. That same month Cuba demanded the United States surrender its naval base at Guantánamo. Shortly after that the Soviet Union resumed atmospheric nuclear testing. A few months later the United States resumed. Eight months before Russ Tobin graduated, reconnaissance flights over Cuba discovered bases under construction that would have put the entire western hemisphere within easy range of Soviet nuclear attack. For a week the United States and the Soviet Union stood on the brink—a word of the time—of nuclear war. In 1963 the Cold War was as cold as it ever got.

And that year, too, Russell Tobin was as idealistic as he ever got.

He asked the CIA recruiter if it would not be well for him to spend a couple of years in military service before he came to the Agency. The answer was no, anybody could serve in the army but only a select few qualified for the Central Intelligence Agency. In a time of Cold War you could do a lot more for your country with the Agency than you could do in any of the armed services.

So Russ Tobin agreed to try to qualify. The security check was embarrassingly thorough. An FBI agent called on Tobin's high school football coach and interrogated him for half an hour about the young man's family, friends, ideas, and attitudes— without suggesting the reason for the questions. Another agent aggressively questioned a girl Tobin had dated during his junior year in college, mostly about her, not his, affiliation with the American Civil Liberties Union. Agents visited family neighbors.

Tobin himself was asked why he subscribed to *The American Scholar* (because a free one-year subscription came with membership in Phi Beta Kappa), why he had gone to Mexico during spring break in his senior year (to see the fleshpots of Tijuana), and if his close friendship with a fraternity brother and roommate had any sexual overtones (it did not).

The visit to Tijuana . . . an odd couple of nights spent witnessing indescribable squalor and all that went with it. In a college boy it had generated mixed emotions: first, the sympathy a liberal conscience was supposed to engender, yet a powerfully stimulated curiosity about the opportunities for experience a young man might find in desperately deprived (and deliciously depraved?) poor girls and women. The miserable poverty he saw pressed strongly in on him with a strangely stirred compound of erotic stimulation and a heady sense of menace. Life and death were closer here than they were in Bakersfield, California—closer both ways: to each other and to him, Russell Tobin.

He was with three friends. The first night they saw lewd shows and fended off every proposition—three husky young Americans, ingenuously handsome and conspicuously naive. Back in San Diego the next day they argued about whether or not they had acted like boy tourists. Two of them promised they would accept a proposition tonight. One said he wouldn't. Russ said he would wait and see.

"C'mon, football asshole," Nick had jeered. "What are you saving it for?"

"If you're a virgin, you've got a problem, you son of a bitch. I'm not, and I can get it without paying for it."

"Yeah, maybe, but think of the *simplicity* of it. You'll never see her again. If you walk off with a dose, you can't find her to blame her. If you leave something in her that she doesn't want, she can't find you."

"Hell of a philosophy," Brady had said. He was the one who was insisting he wouldn't.

"A better deal than you get from some saintly little bitch in a tartan skirt and dark blue cardigan," Nick had said. "Wham bam, thank you, ma'am. If you got tears, cry 'em someplace where I don't have to see them."

"You son of a bitch..."

Brady chose not to go with them the second night. The remaining three cruised. They shopped. They said no to four propositions, then returned and let the second pair of girls try again.

Sure, they had a friend. She'd come to the motel.

She did. Nick and Stan clung to the arms of two chubby little girls who looked like they were sixteen or seventeen. The third one would be Russ's, and when she showed up she looked more like thirty-five: a hard woman with hair dyed a garish red, wearing a thick smear of lipstick, dressed in a tight short skirt and an overflowing halter.

They had rented just one room. Stan said he and his girl would stand on the balcony outside and smoke cigarettes until Nick and his girl were finished with the bed. The girls laughed. They didn't have all night, they said. Everybody together. More fun that way, anyway. Two couples in the bed! A lot more fun!

"You 'n me in the bathroom, buddy," the tawdry pro had said to Russ. "You get the best deal. You sit on the potty, an' I'll suck you. You get the *best* deal."

They went in the bathroom. She closed the door but didn't lock it, then undressed. She lit a cigarette.

"Look, I... how much, anyway?"

"Twenty American dollars, lover boy. In advance."

Russ fished the money out of his pocket. "But... just sit down on the edge of the tub and talk. I don't really want anything."

She took the money. "Figure I carry a bug?" she had asked, half-hostile.

"I don't know," he had said, half-ashamed. "I just don't feel like it."

"You can have one of the others afterward," she had said. "Not for *this* money, but—"

"It's all right," he had said.

She sat on the edge of the bathtub as he had suggested, naked, and smoked her cigarette. Her nakedness did not arouse him. If it had, the waterbugs wandering around inside the old-fashioned tub would have subdued him. He thought about asking her about her life, why she was a hooker, what kind of living did she make . . . all that. He was surprised to find he was too shy to ask. She represented something he didn't know much about, he decided. Life.

Before the night was over he learned something about it. When they got back to their car—it was Nick's—they found it had been broken into. Nothing was gone but a gasoline credit card—because there had been nothing else in the car.

Nick drove toward the edge of town, toward the highway to the border, out of the lighted and busy part of town along a dark street. He hadn't gone a block on that street before they saw flashing red lights behind. A police car.

The car pulled up beside them. Two khaki-clad Tijuana policemen got out. You have a taillight out, one of them told Nick in reasonably good English. Nick was courteous, said he'd get it fixed; said he'd get it fixed right there in Tijuana, before they drove to the border. No, said the Tijuana cop. We go to the station. You and your friends go to jail tonight. Tomorrow—

It would be some years before Russ again felt such terror. He had heard, they all had heard, lurid tales of what happened to *norte americanos* held overnight in the Tijuana jail. It was an element of California folklore.

"Hey, uh, can't we work this out some way?" Nick had said. He had in mind a bribe. "I mean, like on a friendly basis?"

The Tijuana cop shook his head scornfully. "You two in police car," he had said, pointing at Russ and Brad. "Emilio comes with you."

Terror. Or panic. Or maybe simply scorn for the goddam spic. Whatever. They would talk about it later. Endlessly. Three strong university athletes, three lithe and muscular young men. Two fat greasers. Two fat Mexican cops.

From whatever motive—though they would later agree it had been from unalloyed fear—Nick swung hard and jammed a nose-crushing fist into the face of the Tijuana policeman.

Everything happened and was over in an instant, it seemed. Realistically, it was over in a quarter of a minute. The second officer, the one called Emilio, had grabbed for his pistol. Russ struck him on the back of his neck, not with a karate chop, just with his fist but with the force of a university jock still in superb shape. It staggered Emilio. Then Russ grabbed the man by his black, greasy hair and beat his face against the fender of the police car until the Mexican went slack and dropped to the ground. At the same time Nick was pounding the face and chest of the first policeman with both fists.

Stan raised his foot and slammed a heel down on the ear of the man Russ had felled. Then he joined Nick in pounding the other one.

Both policemen were unconscious, maybe dead. Certainly both were injured. Both lay silent and bloody.

"*Jesus!*" Stan had gasped.

"Across the fuckin' border!"

They drove to the border without incident and returned to their motel in San Diego, where Brady was sitting in the room, watching television and drinking beer.

"You don't look to me like guys who got satisfactorily laid," Brady had said.

The incident in Tijuana did not rate so much as a mention in southern California newspapers. The boys never knew how badly they had hurt the two Tijuana policemen, even if they had killed them.

The three boys—not the fourth—talked the episode through endlessly, until they graduated and no longer saw each other. They agreed they felt guilty. None of them felt so guilty as to be interested in confessing. Stan wondered if racism had moved them. Nick and Russ agreed it had not.

Nick and Stan suffered exceptionally virulent strains of gonorrhea, which required months to cure.

Russ elected not to mention the subject at all to the CIA recruiters.

During a protracted interview, a half-comical, semi-mysterious representative of the CIA, solemnly asked a series of hypothetical questions, such as—

—If he married and later learned that his wife's father had been a member of a subversive organization twenty years ago, would he consider himself obligated to report the matter? (Yes, if he were a CIA agent, otherwise no.)

—If the United States lost a nuclear war and a substantial part of its urban population had died, would he favor trying to adapt to the new order the Soviet Union would impose or would he favor retreating into the mountains to help organize a guerrilla resistance unit? (The latter.)

—If he woke some morning after a heavy binge and discovered that a friend had taken advantage of his drunkenness to perform a homosexual act on him during the night, what would he do? (He couldn't imagine the circumstance ever arising, because he never drank that much.)

—If the people of the United States elected a socialist president who tried to dismantle the CIA, would he accept the dismantling or look for a way to keep the agency clandestinely alive. (He would obey the law.)

The final question was not hypothetical. The man had fixed narrowed eyes on Tobin and asked him if he accepted Jesus Christ as his personal savior. Tobin told him if the answer to that question made any difference to the CIA, then he didn't want the job.

Two weeks after that interview he received formal notification that the CIA had accepted him for training.

During ten months of training, much of which consisted of indoctrination, Tobin decided there was an element of Mickey Mouse in the whole business. He continued, just the same, to see the agency as offering him an opportunity to serve his country. He retained a degree of skepticism, but he judged the positives to outweigh the negatives.

His final examination, as it was called, was a farce. The agency had secured the cooperation of a pharmacist and his wife in the town of Lancaster, Ohio: an enthusiast for the Junior Chamber of Commerce and his Junior League wife. They agreed she would use indelible ink and write two initials inside the cups of all her brassieres. Tobin was to travel to the town and learn

what those two initials were—without, of course, being identified or discovered by people who were expecting him. He had
one week to complete the mission.

He flew to Columbus, rented a car, and drove south to Lancaster. It was a town of some thirty thousand, where an unex-
plained stranger would be noticed before long. He used the
telephone book to learn the business and home addresses of the
pharmacist. He stopped into the pharmacy and bought a can of
shaving cream to get a look at the pharmacist. He noticed the
photographs of two children on the wall behind the pharmacist's
counter. He drove by the home and saw a small brick ranch
house in a subdivision cul-de-sac where even an unfamiliar car
on the street would be noticed. He did not see the wife, but he
noted the red Chevrolet Corvair in the driveway. Parked that
afternoon in the parking lot at the nearby elementary school,
he saw the red Corvair again. She had come to pick up her
children, and he got a look at her—a handsome blonde whose
spare figure impressed him as one who might not need a brassiere.

He returned the rented car to Avis, then went to Hertz and
rented another one. In Columbus, he found a thrift shop and
bought some baggy and well-worn khaki pants, a khaki shirt,
and a Cincinnati Reds baseball cap. In another store he bought
two ballpoint pens he stuck in the pocket of the shirt. He drove
the rented car out on a country road near a lake or reservoir
and amused himself for a quarter of an hour by throwing hand-
fuls of wet mud at the car. He smeared some mud on the Cincinnati Reds baseball cap.

The next morning he did not shave. He dressed in the used
khakis and the cap and drove the muddy car to Lancaster. He
spent most of the day sitting at the bars in half a dozen beer
joints, feigning a little fuzziness as he nursed a single beer in
each and drawing drinkers who were really fuzzy into conversation. Sooner or later he turned the talk toward the pharmacist's wife—

"Went ta high school with this chick called Millie . . . She's
married to that guy that's got the drugstore. Wha's his name?

Fletcher? She's got high and mighty. Won' even say hello."

The first eight people he tried this on did not respond. The ninth said, "Aw, she ain't got stuck up. Not really. Maybe you just come on her at the wrong time."

Encouraging the conversation to continue, Tobin learned that Millie Fletcher had two children, played bridge, and loved to swim. She swam competitively and trained for it. ("I mean, she's got medals! You oughta see her shoulders. You talk about *muscles* on a woman!") In winter she swam three or four times a week in an indoor pool, the man said. He was the janitor and saw her at the swimming club, and he swore she always said hello to him. Whenever the weather was warm, she swam in the country club pool—even when the water was too cold for most people. She swam two miles every morning.

A habit. A pattern of conduct that made Tobin's assignment easier.

Back to Columbus. The third day he bought mustard yellow slacks and a white golf shirt, also a putter. Stopping by the Scioto Country Club—which he had learned was the most exclusive and expensive club in central Ohio—he walked around swinging his putter and smiling and had no difficulty swiping a rain hat with the club's logo. At Lancaster Country Club he strolled in wearing his Scioto hat and carrying the putter. He walked into the men's locker room and found what he had hoped would be the case: that the men did not lock their clothes in steel lockers but hung them in open wooden cubbies—just as they did in Bakersfield, California. Lancaster was a town where people did not have to lock up their belongings while they played or swam.

Later that afternoon, in the thrift shop on Fifth Avenue in Columbus, he bought a set of green work clothes. He bought a used tool box. At a hardware store he bought a one-gallon gasoline can. At a nearby station he bought two quarts of motor oil and poured it in the gas can.

On his fourth day he wadded up the khaki work clothes in the tool box, soaked them in motor oil and added about a quart of gasoline. He closed the tool box and put it in the trunk of the

Hertz car. He poured some more gasoline on a pair of under-pants and used them as a rag to wipe his fingerprints off the tool box.

By ten in the morning he was at the Lancaster Country Club, dressed in green work clothes and carrying a tool box, rag wrapped around handle. The red Corvair was in the parking lot. He'd been prepared to come back the next morning and the next, but he wouldn't have to; Millie Fletcher was there.

He walked around the clubhouse, pretending to be a workman come to repair something. He checked the pool. There she was, grimly swimming laps, alone except for a man sitting on the edge of the pool. He may have been her coach.

He went to the door of the women's locker room. There he put down his tool box, opened it, and lit the khaki clothes. When the fire was burning fiercely, filling the central hallway of the clubhouse with black smoke, he pulled the lever on the fire alarm.

People scattered. They ran outside. He walked into the wom-en's locker room and began to examine the clothes hanging in the cubbies. Only four cubbies had clothes in them—three women on the golf course, one in the pool. Brassieres. He found the inked initials in the second one he looked at. GW, whatever those meant. GW. He touched the sweaty bra gingerly, then hurried out of the locker room.

Half an hour later he ran the Hertz car through a wash. An hour later he checked out of his Columbus motel. Three hours later he was on a plane to Washington.

At Langley, they laughed. "Crude but effective, Tobin. And the initials, incidentally, stood for 'Good Work.'"

During the detailed critique they had made it plain they did not think it such good work. The pharmacist had telephoned his contact, laughing, and said he guessed the CIA trainee had been there, since someone had set a smoky fire outside the locker room where his wife's clothes were hanging. Tobin's work had been effective, but it was hardly inconspicuous.

Anyway, he had passed.

In the summer of 1964 Russell Tobin was sworn in as an employee—which was all the word they used: *employee*—of the

Central Intelligence Agency. He was assigned a desk in a shared office at Langley and for six months worked as a junior intelligence analyst, trying to make sense out of contradictory reports coming in from all over the world. He pored over tens of thousands of documents, trying to relate one to another. When a glimmer of consistency seemed to appear, the next document extinguished that faint glimmer and left the whole collection of data completely senseless.

He wrote memorandum after memorandum, pointing out dim and ambiguous patterns he barely saw himself, wondering if anyone up the line took his notes seriously.

Then suddenly in February of 1965 he was transferred. Sent as a civilian to the army language school at Ford Ord, California, he spent the next year in immersion courses in German and Russian. When he finished he could converse fluently in either language, on almost any subject. More ominously, he had learned what to ask for in a Moscow store if he wanted, say, a tube of toothpaste—where in fact to go to buy a tube of toothpaste, how to react if a tube of toothpaste was not to be had . . . and so on. He learned, especially, what Russians didn't know about the world outside the Soviet Union.

He learned that although a visitor in the Soviet Union would see many drunks on the streets, in the underground stations, and so on, the Soviet citizen would know nothing about alcoholism. It was Soviet doctrine that, although a few people did get drunk from time to time, alcoholism was a disease suffered only by the desperate wretches of the capitalist world, not the socialist states, so there was really no such problem in the Soviet Union. It would be highly suspicious to talk about alcoholism in Moscow. How would anyone get the idea that such a phenomenon existed there?

He was not dropped into the Soviet Union as a clandestine spy. He went to Moscow as a second secretary in the economics section of the United States Embassy, a position that put him instantly under KGB surveillance. If he had not been a CIA agent, his predecessors in such positions had been; and, more significant, almost all second secretaries in Soviet embassies were KGB agents.

They played games. Men and women came to him, offering to trade sensitive information for refuge in the United States. A charming young woman he met at an embassy cocktail party confessed she was in love with him. A taxi driver claimed he was a cashiered major of the Red Army and offered, out of his bitterness, to disclose information about Soviet antitank missiles. Tobin found microphones in his flat—and left them in place. He allowed the young woman to come there and sleep with him; and when she asked him if he could get her out of the Soviet Union, he very simply said he didn't know how.

After a few months, these crude gambits ceased. He had earlier passed his tests with the CIA, and now he had passed with the KGB. In a significant sense he had earned acceptance as a member of the intelligence community: clever and competent and not to be nullified with easy tricks. The CIA took note. The KGB took note. He had successfully completed a *rite de passage*.

Guyard had begun to study the dinner menu from the seat pocket, and he spoke without looking up. "Roos-ell . . . Your former wife was in Paris a month ago."

"Which one?"

"Ah, yes. There were two. The one who visited Paris was Helen Willsberger. She went on from Paris to Berlin."

"I saw her in Berlin. I had dinner with her."

"A charming lady," said Guyard. "She must have inherited a great deal of money from Willsberger."

"You had her under surveillance?"

Guyard nodded. "Even though only the ex-wife. Even the ex-wife of an American NIO has a degree of protection while visiting Paris. We had noted that it was her first visit to France since Willsberger died eleven years ago, and we thought that a suggestive circumstance. You will be glad to know that no one approached her, that nothing unusual happened."

Tobin grinned and shook his head. "You never cease to amaze me. I mean, the French system has never ceased to amaze me."

Guyard was studying the menu from the seat pocket. "Vigilance," he said. "It is how smaller countries survive."

"Superpowers, too," said Tobin.

"Yes. Coupled now and then with vigorous prosecution of the national self-interest. The entrecôte appears unfortunately to be the only promising item on this menu. I suppose you will be spending the night in New York and flying to Washington in the morning?"

"Actually," said Tobin, "I'm flying to Washington immediately after we land."

"Ah. I have booked a room near the LaGuardia Airport so I can take an early shuttle flight. I didn't know there was a good flight on to Washington after landing at Kennedy after eight o'clock and making the transfer to LaGuardia."

"I'm flying down on a government Lear jet. You're welcome to come with me."

"I am grateful," said Guyard.

4

THE OFFICE OF the Director of Central Intelligence was a sumptuous corner suite in the Old Executive Office Building, immediately adjacent to the White House. The current DCI, Admiral Hawthorne E. Pemberton, treated the great old Victorian rooms as if he did not mean to stay there long—which probably he wouldn't. DCIs came and went. This DCI had made no noticeable changes; the office was furnished just as it had been under his last two predecessors, with a huge antique desk faced by armchairs upholstered in peach silk.

Like several DCIs before him, he kept his most important files in two bulging black leather briefcases, which were carried in for him when he came in the morning and carried out when he left. So far as Tobin could see, Admiral Pemberton had nothing personal on his desk, not even a family photo, not even the obligatory autographed picture of the president.

Director Pemberton was a man unsubtly conscious that he was extraordinarily handsome. He was six feet two. His hair was white. His face was strong and regular, with a pronounced cleft in his chin. This morning he was wearing a gray suit, and he looked like one of the models who had posed for the whiskey ads that used to appear on the back covers of magazines. He was conspicuously comfortable in his self-confidence. That was one of the qualities the president prized in him: that he dazzled the congressional committees before which he was often called to testify.

He had good reason for this self-esteem. He was an intelligent man with a phenomenally retentive memory. His detractors suggested he was more clever than astute, and some insinuated that his successive promotions in the navy had been as much a matter of his wealth and background as his ability. He had in fact learned to sail off Newport, and his family were major contributors to the Republican Party, nationally and in Pennsylvania. Tobin had no way of evaluating the insinuations. He did have information and experience on which to judge Admiral Pemberton's competence as DCI; and he judged HEP, as the admiral has signed his notes, as one of the two or three most able DCIs under whom he had served.

The third man in the room was William R. Roper, Deputy Director for Operations: a compact, rotund man, no more than five feet nine, bald, with liver spots on his shiny pate, and beady, shifty, dark little eyes. Like most DDOs in the past, Roper was a career man in the CIA. He had been with the Agency for thirty years, twenty of those years in the Operations Directorate. He was a graduate of Yale and affected the postures he identified with an Ivy Leaguer. He worked at appearing calm, a little aloof, always on top of whatever situation he faced. He was noted for an odd habit of sometimes speaking crude slang and ungrammatical sentences—whether by accident or as an affectation, nobody knew. He was Tobin's immediate superior, though Tobin had direct access to the DCI; and in Tobin's judgment it was Roper, not Pemberton, who was more clever than astute.

After a perfunctory exchange of greetings and inquiries after each other's health and families, Director Pemberton sat down behind his desk, and Tobin and Roper took the chairs facing him.

"We've got a bunch of disparate facts, Russ," said the DCI. "We've been matching them this way and that. We're going to brief you on all of this and see what you think. Why don't you start, Bill?"

Roper put his coffee cup in his saucer on the DCI's desk. "Let's start with Japan," he said. "Ever been in Kyoto?"

"I've never been to Japan," said Tobin.

"Ever hear of a company called Kazo, Limited?"

"Electronics," said Tobin. "Computers."

"Kazo maintains its chief research lab near Kyoto: the old imperial city, the one with all the palaces and temples. The lab is out in the woods, on a lake. A picturesque spot, I'm told. Why they have it there, I don't know. Maybe to get their scientific types away from the distractions of Tokyo. Anyway, that's where she is, and that's where they're working on the 256–megabit chip. That's a memory chip, not a microprocessor. It's two or three generations ahead of what's being used now."

"They'll be able to do some damned interesting things with it," said the DCI. "Think of a symphony recorded, not on a tape or any kind of disk, but on a chip the size of your fingernail, and the music is transmitted into the amplifier without any mechanical motion. Think of carrying in your breast pocket a tiny computer that has the entire text of, say, the Washington telephone directory in it, so you can type a name on its little keypad and get the number instantly. Or type the number and get the name."

"The 256–megabit chip," said the DDO, "has all kinds of implications: economic, political, and military. If Kazo makes the breakthrough—"

"Aren't other companies working on it, too?" Tobin asked.

"Yeah, several. Hitachi, which is fiercely competitive," said the DDO. "Nippon Electric Company—NEC. In the States, Intel is of course working on it. So is IBM. Then, too, and an aggressive goddamned competitor, is LSI, Laser Solutions, Incorporated. LSI is an international joint venture: American, British, German, and Japanese. Given a guess, I'd 've figured Hitachi and LSI were on top. But—"

"The Japanese have concentrated on the dense memory chip," said the DCI. "Packing more and more onto one chip. American companies have concentrated more on new microprocessors and on massively parallel processing—that is, supersupercomputers. Billions of dollars are being spent on research and development. I mean *billions*."

"So what happened in Kyoto?"

"This gets highly confidential, Russ," said the DCI.

"What doesn't?" asked Tobin dryly.

Russ Tobin was an NIO, a National Intelligence Officer—a senior intelligence analyst who reported directly to the DCI, though he was technically still within Operations Directorate. No one in the Agency, with only two exceptions, the DCI and the DDO, had higher clearance and more complete access. Officially, his jurisdiction was Germany. Unofficially, it was Western Europe.

The DCI smiled, acknowledging he'd had no reason to remind a man like Tobin that information was confidential. "It involves NSA intercepts," he said. That explained the disquiet. "Inside a friendly country."

Tobin grinned. "They're *all* friendly now," he said. "Isn't that the official line?"

"No defense orientation," said the DDO grimly.

"*Everything* has a defense orientation," said Tobin. "One way or another."

Admiral Pemberton frowned thoughtfully at Tobin. "Okay," he conceded. "With your own proviso: one way or another."

"Specifically," said the DDO. "Specifically, the Kazo laboratories in Kyoto communicate with Kazo corporate headquarters in Tokyo by microwave. *Coded* microwave. Gobbling up the microwave transmissions ain't no big deal for NSA. If you needed to know where we intercept the transmissions, I'd tell you. But you don't. Cracking the code was something else. We figured it'd be worth it and used our priority to get time on a Cray C–90. We're sitting on information worth tens of billions. You know what the problem is."

"Who gets a look at it," said Tobin.

"Right. But that's not your problem or mine. Our problem has to do with the leak out of Kazo. Kazo in Tokyo has been absolutely hysterical about it. Information has got loose. Or so they figure. They're *hysterical*. They've got the store bet on this chip, and if somebody has stole it . . . "

Tobin lifted his coffee cup. "How good is the stolen information?" he asked. "How valuable?"

The DCI and the DDO exchanged glances. The DCI spoke. "Russ . . . to evaluate that, we had to take the specifics of what we'd found out to . . . well—"

"To American competitors," said Tobin.

"How else could we evaluate? Congress says no. We swore our contacts to secrecy. We swore them not to use what they learned. What the hell could we do? We have to know how good the info was."

"How good is it?" Tobin persisted.

Roper answered. "Not so damned good," he said. "Put it another way, though. Whoever got it won't make the same mistakes Kazo has made. Won't ride up a box canyon. I mean, whoever got the info knows what false leads Kazo followed, so they won't follow those leads. That makes the info pretty valuable, right?"

"Who lifted it?" Tobin asked.

"Who you figure?" asked the DDO.

"Zagorsk."

The DDO nodded. "Not for sure. But very damn likely."

The DCI spoke. "You remember Lida Zdravchev? The Bulgarian? What in the world would she have been doing in Kyoto?"

"Zagorsk?" asked Tobin.

"Russ," said the DCI solemnly. "We have a resource in Zagorsk. Lida Zdravchev spent six months there. Four months later she was in Kyoto. She spoke fluent Japanese. Ostensibly she was a commercial aide to the Bulgarian consulate in Tokyo, touring Japan and looking for consumer technology like VCRs the Japanese might license for manufacture in Bulgaria. We cannot positively identify her with the leak from Kazo. But . . . who else? The Zagorsk connection is all but totally persuasive."

"I can see that," said Tobin. "How did the leak happen?"

"A young engineer disappeared over a long weekend. He stumbled into a Tokyo drying-out station—y' know? One of those street stations the Jap cops keep on the streets, so drunks can come in and get sobered up a little before they try to go home. Anyway, this kid shows up at this station at two A.M. on a Tuesday morning, staggering drunk and sobbing. When the hangover set in, the police had to forcibly restrain him from committing suicide. Company security men had meanwhile discovered he'd been doing a lot of copying on one of the office copy machines. He denies he took any copies outside the office, says every copy he made can be found in his files. It's tough to prove he's lying."

"What's the connection with Lida Zdravchev?" Tobin asked.

"The Japanese don't make that connection," said the DDO. "We do. She flew back to Europe the day before the young engineer showed up in Tokyo."

"The NSA intercepts," said the DCI, "are a lot of hysterical babble between Tokyo and Kyoto. This young man was working on the 256–megabit chip, and they're afraid he—"

"A reasonable assumption," Russ interrupted.

"Ain't all we got to worry about," said the DDO. "I guess you know a town by the name of Dahlem?"

"Berlin," said Tobin. "It's a district in Berlin. A suburb, we'd call it. Known for the great Dahlem Museum. Pretty place. I had a flat there once."

"Can you think of any reason why Colonel Kedrov would be in Dahlem?"

"Laser Solutions, Incorporated," said Tobin. "They've established a research lab there."

"Why Dahlem?" asked Roper.

"Why not? It's always been a fashionable place. Some important Nazis lived there in the thirties and forties. On the edge of the Grunewald, the huge, wooded park southwest of the center of Berlin. Easy distance from the Kurfürstendamm, the Fifth Avenue of Berlin. Close to the Wannsee, for swimming, boating. A short cab ride to Tempelhof Airport. Besides, I've heard that Laser Solutions thought establishing an important facility there made a political statement that Berlin was once again the center of Germany. Anyway, it's there: one of the world's most sophisticated research and development laboratories. But why is Kedrov there? Doing what?"

"Taking a weekend off, from the look of it," said the DDO. "He popped in from Moscow, rented a little car at Tempelhof, and drove out to Dahlem, where he checked into a little inn on the edge of the Grunewald. Der Löwe, it's called—The Lion."

"I know it well," said Tobin. "The place has a nine-hole golf course and is favored by business types who like to knock the ball."

"Well, he wasn't there playing golf. Not at this time of year. He spent the weekend. We don't know why. We didn't have him watched."

"You didn't notify me," said Tobin.

"You were in London. Then you went to Paris and flew here. We're notifying you now."

"Was he alone?"

"He had a woman with him. A big woman, a chain-smoker."

"Mriya Meyerhold," said Tobin.

"Came into town Friday afternoon, left Monday morning," said the DDO. "Can you think of any other reason why he'd be there? Any reason other than Laser Solutions?"

Tobin shook his head.

"LSI is a joint venture," said the Director of Central Intelligence. "Kazo is a participating company. In a sense, it all comes together in LSI. The 256–megabit chip. Electron-beam lithography. Massively parallel processing. A penetration of that company would be a goddamned nightmare."

"Dahlem is on your turf, Russ," said the Deputy Director for Operations. "And I guess that gives us a lot to talk about."

Tobin was the name on her office door.

Audrey S. Tobin, M.D.
Certified, American Board of Psychiatry
Adult and Adolescent Psychiatry—Psychopharmacology

She had kept his name. It was a joke between them. "If you were English and born Tickhill, then married a Tobin, you'd keep the Tobin, too," she had said. His response had been, "Well, it's about all you got out of the marriage. So, welcome." She had concluded the dialogue by saying, "I got something else out of it, of course. A few wonderful months. And American citizenship."

Their two grand mistakes had been equally disastrous. She had married a patient. He had married his psychotherapist.

They still loved each other. Or maybe they did. They said they did.

Audrey lived in an elegant white frame house in Chevy Chase, Maryland. The house had always impressed Russ as much too much for one woman and her elderly mother, but he understood very well how a person who had lived her childhood in half of a narrow, soot-stained brick row house in Camden Town could exult in a plethora of big, airy rooms in a house situated on three acres of lawn and groves.

"Damned stud," she whispered huskily. ("Dawmned stood," she pronounced it. She had carefully cultivated a public-school accent, but in private moments, particularly when a little emotion was involved, Camden Town sounded through now and again.) "Never run out of it, do you?"

They had just coupled on her bed, and she was commenting on how much vigor remained in a fifty-year-old man who had flown the Atlantic the night before; spent half his day in a challenging meeting with the DCI and DDO; whiled away two hours at an international conference on the mysterious dispersal of Eastern European espionage agents; and finally had come to her office in a cab only to discover he had to wait an hour for her before she could get away and drive out to Chevy Chase. They were going out to dinner and would return to this bedroom later, but he had expressed an interest in coming to the bedroom *now* as soon as they could break away from their tea with her mother.

Mrs. Tickhill had sniffed her disapproval when Audrey told her she and Russ were going to relax in her bedroom for an hour before they left for dinner. "Well, I s'pose tay-ee is nowt nearly so interesting as . . . relaxing."

Audrey sat now on a Victorian chair upholstered in black horsehair. She was naked except for a black garter belt, one leg extended as she pulled on a dark, sheer stocking. Her sandy-red hair was pulled back and tied behind her head. She had already repaired her makeup, of which she wore very little: only a little mascara, a bit of powder, and pink lipstick sparingly applied to her full lips. Her greenish-blue eyes flitted back and forth between Russ's face and her hands that were attaching the garter to the stocking.

She was more than six feet tall, nearly as tall as he was. Her legs were extraordinarily long. She had gained a little weight since Russ had last seen her seven months ago. The new flesh was on her hips, behind especially, and maybe in her breasts.

Russ had always liked Audrey's breasts, more than he had ever liked any other woman's. ("'Ere I am, an M.D. from University of London with residency in psychoyatry at St. Stephen's, postgraduate in psychoyatry in Berlin and at Columbia, a board-certified psychoyatrist, and what you appreciate is moy *tits!*") They were white, and the nipples were vivid pink. He had never seen any others exactly like them.

"How have you been?" she asked.

"How are you asking? Doctor-patient?"

"I couldn't be your doctor again if life depended," she said. "But suppose I *were* your doctor."

Russ shrugged. "Problem's still there, but you taught me to live with it."

"Ninety percent of psychiatry," she said as she smoothed the stocking over her leg. Calm, she pronounced *psychiatry* normally.

"So . . . you think I'm not bad for an old fart."

"Forget old, Russ. That you're not. I date a guy who's twenty-eight and is older than you."

Russ was fifty. Passing that birthday two months ago had been emotionally difficult. He had marked it alone, sitting in a favorite small café in Berlin, drinking a bottle of wine and eating sauerbraten. He had wished he'd had a different table, though. His chair had faced a mirror across the room, and he'd sat facing himself, unable not to stare at his own image.

He was six feet two. He weighed a little more than he should but not much more. His black hair had backed off a little on either side of his forehead, leaving a devil's point at the middle of his forehead. His face was looser than it had been a very few years ago; and it was deeply lined around the eyes and a little jowly.

The more he had stared at himself in that mirror, the more he had seen what he didn't want to see: world-weary cynicism, or something that looked like that to him. The once-bright hazel eyes were dull now; they were the eyes of a tired man. Tired ... not so much physically fatigued as disappointed and, far too often, just bored.

"I wouldn't be twenty-eight again for a half million a year," he said.

"You need more sessions," she said.

"Seriously, Audrey," he said. "You made a world of difference. I mean, in the professional sense. I don't know how I'd have hacked it another ten years if—"

"You would have," she said. "That's you. You'd have gone on till you died. And you will."

He shook his head. "I'm entitled to retire."

"Sure. This week Director has called you back to Washington to heap something more on your shoulders. You'll retire after you settle that. Except that you won't, because then he'll have something else for you. You're a patriot when patriotism is out of fashion."

Russ sat up and turned and put his feet on the floor. "I'm not an anachronism, Audrey."

"Hell, no," she said. "You're the best man I've ever known. Bar none."

"I blush."

"No, you don't. You're not capable of it."

He went in the bathroom.

He had met Dr. Audrey Tickhill in London in 1982. It had been arranged by a friend who had believed Russ Tobin should meet the newly licensed young psychiatrist. They had understood it was a professional introduction, not just a social one.

He had needed help. Confidential help. The problem was simple. Tension. Pressure. Endemic in middle-aged males: usually the effect of real or imagined expectations on the part of wife and children, sometimes employer. It would have been easy for Audrey or any other psychoanalyst to cope with, except that in Russ's case the tension arose from nothing imagined but from the stark fact that successive promotions had put him in a job where he had to send other people out to risk their lives, and already two of them had died. Taking risks himself had been far easier emotionally than asking others to take them.

His chief symptom was nothing unusual. He was drinking too much.

At first he hadn't been able to believe that this tall, sandy-haired, busty English girl was a competent psychiatrist. He had confided in her a little and immediately discovered she understood more than he could have imagined. He admitted to her that he needed professional help.

The doctor-patient relationship had to be unconventional. While it was not unusual for a patient to wish to keep it confidential that he had placed himself under the care of a psychotherapist, that confidentiality was difficult to maintain when the patient was a senior intelligence agent. He dared not let the Agency learn that he was seeing a psychiatrist. William J. Casey had been DCI then, and the very thought of an active agent lying on a couch and spilling his memory to a psychiatrist would have sent Casey into a frenzy.

Doctor and patient, then, maintained the fiction that the relationship was purely social. Russ never visited Audrey's office. She saw him in her flat, sometimes in his, and often over dinner, where they sat at a private table in a corner and their solemn conversation looked like talk between lovers, anything but therapy sessions between doctor and patient.

Everything changed one night in July. Early morning, actually. The sun rises very early at that time of year in London, and dawn found Russell Tobin beating on the door of Audrey's flat in Bayswater—drunk, disheveled, and tearful.

She let him in. For a long moment she thought she would not, but he was conspicuously intoxicated on a very public street and was likely to be picked up by the police. She let him in, and he collapsed on her sofa and began to sob.

It was fortunate, they agreed later, that he had not made much sense. He told her far more than he should have told her, even if she was his doctor. He said something about a man named Fritz. Fritz was dead, she gathered. A police organization Russ called UB had arrested Fritz and killed him, almost certainly after protracted torture. Fritz had not wanted to go to Poland. He had considered the risk too great. Russ had paid him extra to encourage him to take that risk. The risk was not too great for the likely result of Fritz's mission. It had not been too great for the CIA, certainly not for the BND. It had been too great for Fritz.

He couldn't do it anymore, Russ had said. He would resign. He would go home and get a job in business.

"I believe the way you say it is that you were 'working' Fritz," she had said. "Isn't that right? So if you hadn't worked Fritz, someone else would have."

"Sure. And if Eichmann hadn't obeyed his orders to murder Jews, someone else would have."

"Murder is what the people who caught your man committed. You didn't. You didn't commit a crime. You didn't send Fritz to commit a crime, except a crime against the so-called laws of a criminal state. And, yes, what you sent Fritz to do had to be done. He didn't succeed, so somebody else has to do it. And if you don't work the next Fritz—you, who care about your people—then he'll be worked by somebody who cares less."

"I can make my own rationalizations," he had said with the dull sullenness of a drunk.

"In psychoanalytic jargon," she had said, "the term *rationalization* means developing self-satisfying but incorrect reasons for behavior. Laymen have picked that up and made rationalization a bad word. Which is stupid. What's wrong with reason and rationality? Break my logic, Russ. If you can."

She let him sleep on her sofa. Later she phoned her office and took the day off. She stayed with Russ and in mid-morning made him breakfast.

After that, they were not just doctor and patient anymore. He did the cliché thing; he fell in love with his therapist. She knew better, but she fell in love with him.

He talked more about resigning from the CIA. Besides the guilt, there was the pressure, he said: the unrelenting pressure.

"Let us suppose," she had said, "you found yourself a job with a big American corporation. Do you think there would be no pressures?"

"But they wouldn't involve life and death."

"*Precisely*. The pressures would be just as great, the tension probably even greater, and the stakes, by comparison, would be petty. You would suffer the same pressures for not very much."

"You're saying I have no alternatives."

"I don't know where you'll find alternatives," she had said. "You pay the price of being intelligent and well educated. Or maybe you don't. The working types in Camden Town think they live under pressure, too."

Even after they married, his therapy continued. He could live with pressure and tension—that was her point. Everyone did, she insisted. Partly it was a matter of self-image, self-confidence.

She had grinned at him one night over a candlelight dinner and laughed. "How in hell did I ever get myself in the position of trying to give *you* more self-confidence?"

He was transferred to Berlin. She left London and went with him, giving up her practice. For a year, during much of which she did not see him, she lived in a West Berlin flat and did postdoctorate work in psychiatry.

She suspected but did not know that twice during the year he crossed the Sector Border, the first time just from West Berlin to East Berlin, but once from West Germany to East Germany, for a month-long stay.

At the end of that month he recrossed between Sonneburg and Neustadt. In a wet and misty woods, a civilian ruffian in the employ of *Stasi* had abruptly materialized out of the dark and challenged him with a pistol. Russ had escaped and completed his crossing only because the *Stasi* man, starting to lead him away, had lost his balance on wet foliage on a steep slope. As the man stumbled, Russ had grabbed a rock and used it to crush his skull.

Back in Berlin, Audrey could not understand the artificial exhilaration she saw in her husband—saw it in his unnaturally glittering eyes—and guessed he had killed someone. She was wrong in her guess that he had taken revenge for Fritz.

She did not know or suspect that during that year Russell

Tobin came very close to resigning from the CIA. Called back to Washington, he had been told that the Reagan Administration placed great emphasis on developments in Central America and would be calling in senior agents for reassignment to that region. Specifically, *he* might be called.

Tobin had shrugged and said he spoke German and Russian, not Spanish, and had spent seventeen years serving in Europe, where he knew what he was doing. Central America, he said, was peanuts.

Two days later he was summoned to a private meeting with William Casey himself, in the corner suite in the Old Executive Office Building.

Casey had been blunt. "You want me to understand you *refuse* to serve in Central America? Tell me yes or no, 'cause if you refuse—"

"Central America is a sideshow," Tobin had said. "What the hell could possibly ever happen there that would make any difference?"

"Russ, you don't know what the fuck you're talkin' about. Anyway, the President is most anxious about what's happening in Nicaragua."

"Nicaragua!" Tobin had snorted. "The future of civilization will be decided on the East-West boundary in the middle of Europe. Us against them. That's where it is. That's what counts. I was trained to serve on that boundary. That's where I *have* served. Over the past ten years I've sent back facts and figures about the strength and disposition of Soviet armored divisions. My people have found out where missiles are sited and what they're aimed at. I'm working resources in the DDR, Poland, Czechoslovakia, and Hungary. I'm working where it's going to happen, if it happens. And, by God, I'm not going down to some two-bit banana republic and worry about the squabbles among a handful of grubby spics."

"What if you're ordered?"

"I won't go."

Casey had stared at him in unbelieving anger, his heavy-lidded, watery blue eyes blinking in disbelief, his loose, fleshy lips audibly flapping.

Tobin had seized on the momentary paralysis of the DCI to lower the intensity of the confrontation. "You're supposed to be damned good about how you use resources. What kind of deployment of human resources would it be to pull experienced agents out of Europe and send them where they don't speak the language and don't know the country?"

"And don't give a damn," Casey had added.

"And don't give a damn," Tobin had agreed bluntly.

Casey had risen from behind his desk, saying he was late for an appointment at the White House, and he had left Tobin without indicating what he intended to do. Tobin heard nothing more about transfer. He never again had direct communication with Casey.

The next year he took extended leave from Europe, as he was entitled to do, and returned to the States for rest and to spend time at Langley learning about new electronic resources.

Audrey came with him, of course. He rented a furnished apartment in Georgetown. He applied to the Agency for special assistance in obtaining naturalization for Audrey. She did not qualify under the law, but occasionally the wife of an agent was naturalized under a private bill enacted by Congress. The Senate Bill extending American citizenship to Audrey Tickhill Tobin was introduced by Senators Moynihan and Goldwater, senior members of the Senate Select Committee on Intelligence. Russ learned later that his request to the Agency went to the senators with an endorsement by Casey.

While her bill was pending, Audrey applied to do postdoctorate work at Columbia University. When Russ was reassigned to Berlin, she told him she wanted to stay in New York until she completed her work. She told him, in fact, that she had already made such an impression at Columbia—and Columbia had made such an impression on her—that she might not ever want to return to London or Berlin.

He understood what she was saying. Their divorce did not become final until two years later.

Audrey had pulled on the second stocking and now fastened a black bra. She got up and went to her walk-in closet for her dress.

"Want to go back to Europe with me?" Russ asked her.

"Why?"

"Because I've never stopped loving you," he said.

"Half-true," she said. "You never stopped what you started. But I'm not sure, my dearest friend, you ever loved me. I'm not sure you're capable of it."

"Try again," he said.

She shook her head. "We had a wonderful time . . . and also the worst goddamned experience I've ever had in my life. You're horny, you come see me. I probably will be, too. But to depend on you, Russ Tobin . . ." She shook her head. "Never again. Never . . . again."

5

COINCIDENCE: THE GERMAN research and development laboratories of Laser Solutions, Incorporated occupied a new three-story building at the northwest corner of a busy street and highway intersection in the Berlin suburb of Dahlem. It was on that very same intersection in the spring of 1945, that a German sniper shot and killed the young and attractive military police-woman Lidya Nikolayevna Kedrov while she was directing Soviet tank and truck traffic.

Colonel Kedrov had no idea this was where it had happened. Nor had he the slightest suspicion of another unlikely coincidence: that the clerk who checked him in and out of the inn called Der Löwe was the man who had killed his aunt. That German, whose name was Hans Günsche, had been a fourteen-year-old military-school cadet, serving in the *Volkssturm*, Hitler's last-stand home guard. The boy had taken immense pride in having killed a Russian. He had been the only one in his company to accomplish such a feat.

Today, Hans Günsche was one of the few people left in Dahlem who remembered 1945. He had long since resolved to put those bad old days out of memory and had extended the usual courtesies to the Russian man and woman as he checked them in for a weekend at Der Löwe and later checked them out. It did not occur to him to be otherwise than courteous, though Russian soldiers in 1945 had raped his mother four times and his sister more than a dozen times.

The Russian occupation hadn't lasted long. Dahlem was in the American Sector, and shortly the stinking, boorish Russians had pulled out, taking with them everything they could carry, leaving hundreds of girls and women pregnant, and leaving scores of civilian men dead. The Americans had come then, swaggering and yet conspicuously uncertain, and they proved incapable of more than a few brutalities.

The war had not marked Dahlem badly. It had not been bombed the way other districts had, and it retained some of the old charm that had made it so attractive a residential district before the war.

Der Löwe, for example, was an eighteenth-century stone building, still retaining a few patches of the yellowish stucco that had once covered it. It had been a hunting lodge for the Prussian aristocracy. A few homes were almost as old. They shared the district with stark, cold modern office buildings. Hans Günsche liked to say that Der Löwe had stood for two hundred years before those buildings were put up and would still be there, receiving guests, when the last of the ugly office blocks had been knocked down.

The LSI building had all the architectural distinction of a grossly oversized soda-cracker box. Like so many other unimaginative office buildings all over the world, its facade was of dark, reflecting glass, with not so much as a single feature to relieve its square lines. Like nearly every small modern industrial building in the world, it was identified by a modest white-letters-on-dull-black signboard that stood on the lawn.

LSI
VERSUCHSRÄUME

The German on the sign was a concession. Inside, little German was spoken, except by the support staff: the secretaries and clerks, the porters and janitors. Many of the technological staff were German, but all of them were bilingual; all of them spoke English at least, and a few of them spoke Japanese as well. English was the official corporate language. No one worked at the technological or managerial level who was not fluent in English.

The director of the Dahlem laboratory was a German, a native Berliner, named Max Wenzel. He was also a vice president of LSI. When Russ Tobin arrived late on Monday morning, three weeks after Kedrov's weekend in Dahlem, a stiffly erect Director Wenzel received him in his office but said immediately that he had booked a table for their lunch, in a club on one of the top floors of the Mercedes-Benz building downtown.

"Let me introduce Jane Mahoney," Tobin said. "She is an associate of mine and will be working with me on the problem I've come to bring to your attention."

Wenzel bowed to the blonde young woman and extended his hand. "A pleasure," he said. "You are of course included in my invitation to lunch."

"I appreciate the invitation, but I'm afraid I have another appointment," she said, gracefully bowing herself out of a luncheon she knew he didn't really want to invite her to.

They sat down at Wenzel's desk and Tobin apprised him of the reason for his visit.

"Yes," said Wenzel. "I have had repeated warnings from the company."

"Before we leave your office and go to lunch, I want to show you a couple of pictures," said Tobin. He handed Wenzel a gray clasp envelope containing two photographs: one of Colonel Kedrov, one of Mriya Meyerhold. "Keep those," he said. "Have you ever seen either of those people?"

Wenzel shook his head. "I am quite sure I haven't."

"One is a high-ranking officer of the KGB. The other is his girlfriend, but she's a KGB agent, too. You know what Zagorsk is?"

"I'm afraid I don't."

"It's a training center where the KGB reprograms agents for industrial espionage. We use the name as a shorthand term for industrial espionage. Kedrov and Meyerhold are principals in Zagorsk."

"Technology," said Wenzel. "Civilian technology."

"The distinction between military and civilian has gotten a

little blurred," said Tobin. *"Enemies. Competitors.* The end result of competition might not be so very different from the end result of war."

The LSI laboratory building, the director's office, and Max Wenzel had something in common, Tobin thought as he glanced at Jane Mahoney for her reaction as they watched Wenzel frown over the two pictures. Offices, building, and Wenzel himself— all were utilitarian. Wenzel's desk was clear. The only paper in sight was in a pair of stacked black plastic boxes. Two pens in a marble-base penholder looked as though he never touched them. On the credenza behind the desk, the latest and most sophisticated IBM desktop computer sat ready for Wenzel's command.

Wenzel himself was tall and gaunt. His long face was thin and pale, though he could never shave his black whiskers so close they wouldn't darken the skin of his cheeks. His lips were thin and startlingly red. He wore his hair clipped short on the sides, in the old Prussian manner—maybe because that was all the gray hair he had. He wore big rimless eyeglasses.

Wenzel's chauffeur drove him and Russ downtown in a long black Mercedes that Tobin recognized as armored. They sat down to a sumptuous lunch that began with whiskies, proceeded through salad, filet of sole in a delicately flavored white sauce, with white wine, then cheese with fruit and coffee and brandy. Tobin wondered if Wenzel meant to return to work that afternoon, but he guessed after a while that the man was one of those fortunate individuals little affected by food and drink.

"Security is a personnel question, of course," Wenzel said. "We can adopt procedures to prevent documents and devices from escaping our laboratories. How do you prevent the escape of what your staff carries in their brains?"

"I suppose you can't," said Tobin.

"Have you read Solzhenitsyn's *The First Circle?*" Wenzel asked. "In it he describes what the Russians used to call by a slang term, *sharaska.* It was a scientific research center in which all the scientists were prisoners, called *zeks.* Secrets could escape even from there."

"You have to depend on your people," said Tobin.

"In industries based on technology we are dependent on people, not just for their abilities, but for their integrity as well. In fact . . . accountants can scribble out all the numbers they want to represent assets: buildings, equipment, all that. A company like LSI has only one asset. Just one. Brains. People and their brains. The rest of it is—"

"*Dreck*," said Tobin. The German word meant shit.

"Yes, exactly. The bean counters cannot understand. But— well. I would be happy to have you review our security arrangements."

"I doubt I could contribute anything," said Tobin. "I wanted you to understand that the visit of Colonel Kedrov and Mriya Meyerhold to Dahlem could be dangerously significant. You are a prime target. It's not likely they came here for nothing. Watch for any unusual activity by your key people. If you want to put anyone under surveillance, call me. I can arrange something discreet. I will be working closely with the *Bundesnachtrichtendienst*. We must keep in touch."

In the months when people came to play golf, an exuberant crowd would elbow up to the little bar at Der Löwe in early evening. They came to drink and exult or lament their shots off the tees, their chips, their putts—mostly their putts. Often, the gray and bald Hans Günsche would leave the desk and come back to join their celebration for a few minutes. In the cold months, when the ground on the course was frozen and footsteps would break the frozen blades of grass, the bar was never quite deserted but never occupied by more than a few men and women. It was quiet then, and people sat at the heavy oak tables, in the subdued light from small incandescent lamps with dark red shades, and talked solemnly.

In winter, Der Löwe was a favorite rendezvous for lovers, particularly those with problems, such as inconvenient marriages. It was also the favorite bar of the oddly varied scientists from the Laser Solutions laboratory, half a kilometer away. Most of them didn't come when a noisy crowd filled the bar. When the golfers were gone for the winter, the computer scientists arrived. They sat over dark beer and sketched mysterious patterns on sheets of paper. Sometimes they pulled calculators from their pockets and appeared to try to solve complex problems of mathematics while they chuckled and sipped beer.

Günsche didn't readily relate to these people. They were not outgoing like the golfers. On the other hand, the work at the front desk was much slower in winter, and he spent more time in the bar and gained some distinct impressions of the scientists from LSI.

One of them was in trouble, he guessed.

He didn't know their names, but the young man was from LSI, and he supposed the young woman was, too. They had begun to see each other only about two weeks ago. They made an odd couple: odd even by the standards of that multinational, multilingual, even multiracial establishment. The young man was an Indian or Pakistani. The young woman was European: Aryan, also, to use the word the stiff old men had long ago taught him to use. Hans Günsche had matured beyond everything he had learned as a loyal member of the Hitler Youth, but it still troubled him—out of some other source but that early training, he insisted to himself—to see a white girl becoming increasingly intimate with a brown boy.

Mahmud Nedim understood what was expected of him. He should receive the blessing bestowed on him by God (the Beneficent, the Merciful) with humble gratitude—always remembering, though, that such a blessing rarely came without a price. The price to him was a challenge he must meet. How he met it would determine what kind of man he was, whether he was worthy of the blessing, whether he deserved the respect of his family and his community. God had sent the blessing, and God had sent temptation as a test.

His father would expect him to receive the blessing and face the challenge with such thoughts, confident in the strength of his faith, worthy of the love of God.

That was what his father would expect. His father had hardly ever set foot outside Rawalpindi, much less outside of Pakistan. He had never ventured into the lands of what he called the unbelievers, and very likely he never would. He was a respected lawyer in Rawalpindi, so learned in the laws of God and man that even the judges deferred to him. He was prosperous from the fees and bribes customarily paid to lawyers who could make arrangements. And he was a believer.

Mahmud had been astonished to learn that among the Western technicians—the Japanese especially—*belief* was a bad word. *Faith* was even worse. One of his English colleagues defined faith as "an obsession with believing what is conspicuously untrue." To believe something meant that you accepted as true something you could not prove. The Americans used a slang expression—"gut feeling"—and to the highly educated rationalists of the computer laboratories that was the same thing as believing. It had been difficult for Mahmud to learn that new meaning. To him, belief implied certainty; but when in staff meetings he had said he believed something, his colleagues had scoffed and asked him how he sustained his belief.

The difficulty was that they were of a different world, a different culture from the one that had shaped his life and thought. They were as scornful of his world of received truths and certainties as his father was of their world without truths and certainties. "They believe in money and gadgets," was how his father put it. "Your father believes in spooks and spirits," his colleagues laughed.

Even before he left home, Mahmud had noticed something. His father prayed for long life, but when he suffered a heart attack he demanded treatment with Western medicine. He scorned the unbelievers, but his life depended on them. His father conducted much business by telephone. His documents were typed on electric typewriters. He took pride in his Xerox copying machine, almost the first in Rawalpindi, and became most impatient when it failed and he had to wait three days for service. They had an electric refrigerator in their home, also two wireless sets and a television set. His father drove a Fiat automobile. Gadgets. His father had all those and demanded

more. Yet, he scorned the unbelievers who invented and manufactured them.

At first, when he arrived in the West, Mahmud had hoped he
could reconcile the two worlds. Not for the worlds, not even for
his father, just for himself. It had proved impossible. He wasn't
sure he could ever go home.

And now—

This beautiful little Western girl. That she could love him was
really impossible. How could she? In the physical sense at least,
she was everything a man could possibly want in a girl. She had
a pretty face and a pretty body. Her personality dazzled him,
partly maybe because it was unlike any he had ever seen in a
girl at home. At the same time it troubled him. She was never
solemn. She laughed at everything. She venerated nothing: not
God, not country, not community, not friendship, not even science—and certainly not the company where she worked or her
superiors there. Obviously, she would not venerate a husband,
either.

Her name was Anne-Lise Hein. She was a linguist, an inter-
preter in Russian and Polish for Deutsche Handelsbank. Her
first job each morning, she had told Mahmud, was to dictate a
German-language summary of the news from six Russian and
three Polish newspapers. After that she spent her hours trans-
lating letters, memoranda, and other documents. Often she sat
in meetings and translated conversation. It was boring, she said
with a husky laugh, but it paid well.

"But Anne-Lise," he had said gravely—"do you feel no obligation of loyalty to Deutsche Handelsbank?"

She had tipped her head and grinned at him. "Until I get
better job somewhere else," she said. "Or rich man offers to
marrying me."

She was the epitome of the modern Western woman, he had
decided. But why—why would she be interested in *him?*

"Why not?" she had said in reply to his earnest question. "I'm
not virgin, Mahmud. Why not experience the kind of man you
are?" She had shrugged. "You look good to me."

This evening she sat beside him on the bench that faced

the table, not in the chair opposite. They'd drunk two beers. Beer was, of course, forbidden by God. It was one of the sins—or . . . rather one of the adjustments he had made to the Western world. Anyway, they had drunk two beers, and he anticipated she would call for more. She had been laughing and chatting, and now her hand was stroking his leg.

"Old sobersides!" she laughed. They spoke English, the language they had in common, though English was her weak language, and she spoke it clumsily. "You want I go away?" She moved her hand up his leg and rubbed his excited male parts. "I don't think so!"

"Anne-Lise!" he gasped. He had never experienced this kind of touch before, had never expected to. "Is this . . . ?"

"What, my boy?" she asked in that husky voice that so stimulated him. "Is this 'proper?' Is this 'polite?' Hmm?" She closed her hand around his penis and scrotum, so tightly he felt pain— but also a rush of excitement. "You want me for take my hand away?"

Mahmud shook his head. "No," he whispered hoarsely.

With her other hand she reached for her stein of frothy German beer. "No. You learn. Slowly, yes. But you learn. I could make a good man of you."

For an instant his thought was: what kind of man, in the sight of God and man? But that thought endured only for the instant, and he returned all his attention to Anne-Lise. He wondered if he dared touch her. He wondered how she would react if he put his hand on her crotch or her breast.

"You will must make up your mind, my dark friend," she said. "I am most curious, but my curiousness endures not long."

Mahmud stared intently at her smile. He'd had to search in his thesaurus for a word. *Lascivious.* Her smile was lascivious. Until he arrived in Berlin he had never known a girl who would have dared smile that way.

"Oh, Christ . . . " Anne-Lise muttered.

A woman approached their table. Debora Benson. An American. A system analyst and designer at LSI. Mahmud had wondered whether Debora had extended him her friendship because she genuinely liked him or because as an American she thought she had to prove she could share friendship with a person of another race.

"Do you mind if I have a beer with you?" Debora asked.

"Please sit down, Debora," said Mahmud.

Some of their colleagues at LSI thought Debora was icy, aloof, that she considered herself superior, that in fact she thought Americans were superior by definition. Others said she was warily defensive for hidden reasons. As she sat down now, she extended only a restrained greeting to Anne-Lise. Until Anne-Lise began to appear, Debora had sat here many nights with Mahmud alone, and they had talked about everything in the world. They had relieved each other's loneliness.

"I hear the 200–beam machine ran great this afternoon," said Debora Benson in the flat voice she characteristically used when she was talking about technology. "Let's hope it doesn't make scrambled eggs tomorrow."

"It might do that," he said.

"No. No, it will make two hundred perfect chips."

Mahmud raised his chin a little. He meant to signal Debora not to discuss the subject in front of Anne-Lise. He realized it was well known that LSI was working on a 200–beam machine, so she wasn't disclosing anything; but he never spoke of any aspect of his work in front of people who were not entitled to know.

She was talking about a machine that projected two hundred electron beams onto a silicon wafer. The powerful beam started as one and was split into two hundred parallel beams during projection. The projector moved through a pattern to etch a single chip. The two hundred beams etched two hundred identical chips simultaneously. This was essential to the manufacture of extremely dense memory chips on an economically feasible basis.

This was Mahmud's field: electron-beam lithography.

Debora was a pallid young woman: pallid of complexion, pallid of personality. Though probably no one had ever called her beautiful, she was pretty. Her eyes were blue. Her hair would have been mousy brown, but she bleached it. She kept it cut so it covered her ears but not her neck. She smiled in a subdued way, as if she were afraid it was undignified to smile broadly; and when she laughed, it was from between barely parted lips. The contrast between Debora and Anne-Lise was that Anne-Lise's exuberant personality sparkled, while Debora's hid in shadow.

Her field was massively parallel processing. She was an exceptionally gifted mathematician, which significantly reinforced her talents as a program designer.

"Is it that your work is going well?" asked Anne-Lise.

Debora nodded. "Reasonably well. In spite of the Japanese commitment to vector processing."

"Vector processing. This is . . . ?"

"Conventional computers," said Debora, "are vector processors. They line up billions of calculations and process them one at a time. The best microprocessors run billions and billions of calculations per second, but there is a limit to the complexity and speed of microprocessors. Besides, they get more and more expensive. Parallel processors break a problem into fragments and assign each fragment to a simpler microprocessor. A massively parallel processor might be thought of as a thousand desktop computers all lined up and working together as a team."

"Why do the Japanese resist this?" asked Anne-Lise.

"They think it may be impossible to write the programs to make all the processors march in line and to assemble the results of all the processors' work into a single result."

"*Is* this impossible?" asked Anne-Lise.

"No. We've done it. It's an American specialty."

Anne-Lise moved her hand under the table to caress Mahmud's penis. Debora could not see and did not guess why her friend started. Anne-Lise spoke, "Mahmud never speaks of his work. I could guess he carries from the building the trash paper."

Debora smiled. "I can assure you Mahmud does not carry out the trash."

"He is an important man?"

"He is a brilliant computer engineer," said Debora.

Anne-Lise smiled lazily and suggestively at Mahmud. "You

see? I have to ask your friend to learn what an important man you are." She glanced at Debora. "Is this called modest?"

"Mahmud is a very modest man," she said, dully serious.

Anne-Lise cocked her head to one side and smiled defiantly at the compact, dark-skinned Pakistani. "Mahmud is to take me downtown this evening, to buy me nice dinner." She gave his private parts a playful squeeze. "Is not so?"

Mriya Aronovna Meyerhold drew smoke into her lungs from the last cigarette in the second pack she had smoked today. She had decided to mistrust the diminutive young woman who sat across the table from her. Her judgment was intuitive. You could not rely always and exclusively on reason. Sometimes you had to act and judge on the basis of feeling.

They spoke Russian. "Nikolai Pavlovich is satisfied well enough with your last report," said Mriya Aronovna. "He is anxious to hear another."

"It is like trying to cozy up to a dead fish," said the younger woman. "He has a troubled conscience, and he is afraid."

"Maybe he is not the right choice," said Mriya Aronovna.

"I didn't make it."

"It was made on the basis that he is unmarried and a naive young man who is not quite sure how to cope with a world he never saw before."

They sat toward the rear of a cellar bar just east of Friederichstrasse. The intensity of their conversation had caused the men in the bar to assume they were lesbian lovers: a contrasting pair, one with a taut boyish figure, wearing a stylish miniskirted black dress, the other a heavier and older woman dressed in the dark blue uniform of an Aeroflot ticket agent. They were the focus of some curious glances, but no one approached them. Earlier this bar had been crowded shoulder to shoulder. Now the four musicians who had shaken the place with raucous dance music had packed their instruments and switched off their amplifiers. They sat at the bar, drinking, and they were the most likely men in the place to approach the two women at the rear table.

"When you last spoke with Nikolai Pavlovich, you mentioned a woman. Debora . . . ?"

"Debora Benson. The genius of massively parallel processing."

"Have you seen her again?"

"I saw her this evening. She sat down with me and Mahmud at Der Löwe. They were soulmates before I came along."

"Soulmates. Just soulmates?"

"She is as timid and distant as he is. Maybe more so. She resents me."

"Nikolai Pavlovich wants you to move faster. He says you will know how."

Kristin Kuniczak smiled lazily. "An inborn talent," she said.

"He wants to hear from you again before the end of the week— at which time he hopes to hear you report progress."

"If I am entirely unsubtle—"

"Nikolai Pavlovich said to tell you he relies on your instincts in these matters."

"How kind of him."

"Yes. Now . . . it would be better if we did not leave together."

"I want to use the toilet. You go first."

Meyerhold counted off marks and put them on the table to pay the bar tab. She smiled woodenly, nodded, and walked out of the bar.

On the street, she glanced around, hoping to see a taxi. If she couldn't find a cab, she'd have to walk to a bus stop and wait—which did not appeal to her at all.

She did not notice the small man who stared at her from a doorway across the street.

Russ Tobin started his white Porsche Targa and rushed forward to be at the curb before a cruising cab could possibly come along. He rolled down the window.

"Mriya Aronovna!"

She jerked her head to turn her eyes away from him, as if she were a woman accosted by a man trying to pick her up. She strode off along the sidewalk.

"*Mriya!*"

She stopped and stared into the car. Her body stiffened, and she drew a deep breath.

"It's been a long time, Mriya," he said in Russian. "Come on. Get in. I'll take you home. Better, I'll drive around a while so we can talk. We can find a taxi later, and you can go home in that."

She hesitated only for a moment, then reached for the door, opened it, and sat down beside him in the car.

The small man stepped out of his doorway across the street, peered intently at the license plate on the Porsche, then took out a notebook and wrote it down.

"You know, it's a burden to follow you. You keep late hours. But I decided to do it personally. I didn't want anyone else to make the contact." He frowned and grinned at her uniform. "Aeroflot. Not a very inventive cover, Mriya. Do you actually sell tickets?"

"I'm a supervisor," she said.

"Not much of a cover."

"It would have been all right for a short time, if I hadn't been seen by you."

Mriya Aronovna Meyerhold had aged. He hoped he could believe she had aged more than he had in the same time. She looked tired. He had misunderstood her before, but he thought she looked discouraged. Not disillusioned. A woman who had never had illusions could not be disillusioned. This one seemed discouraged, as if she had given up.

"The world has changed since we last met."

She shook her head. "Not really."

She fumbled in her purse. He knew she was looking for cigarettes, and he was sorry he hadn't brought any. He drove south to Unter den Linden, west past the Brandenburg Gate, and into the great park, the Tiergarten.

"Nothing has changed, Tobin," she said.

"*They* haven't changed?"

"No. It's the same thing, always. They will never change. They never forget, never forgive."

He turned off the main road through the park and onto a side road, where he could pull the car to the side and stop.

He had hardly stopped when Mriya Aronovna fell across the gearshift and steering wheel and into his arms. "Oh, Tobin! Tobin!" she wept. "For god's sake, why couldn't it be different?"

6

RUSSELL TOBIN HAD spent more of his adult life in Berlin than
in any other city. He had learned how to live there; and that
was important, to know how to live in a city. He'd never learned
to live in Washington, and he couldn't imagine living in New
York. Other men talked about retirement to Florida or the Costa
del Sol. When Tobin thought of retirement, more often than not
he thought of buying a bigger, more expensive, more permanent
flat in Berlin and living out his years there. He'd learned to feel
comfortable in Berlin. He knew where to find what he wanted.

For now, he lived in what had been East Berlin: in half of a
small, soot-blackened brick house behind a two-meter brick wall
with a wrought-iron gate, on Joachimstrasse. He had agreed
with his neighbors that he would share responsibility for the
shrubs and flower beds in the narrow "garden" between the wall
and the stoop. He was gone so much of the time that he could
not do his share, so he made it up to them—he hoped they
thought he made it up—by bringing them bottles of whiskey
from the duty-free shops, or occasionally a box of chocolates or
a bottle of French perfume.

The neighborhood was what the old Berlin had been, the
kaisers' Berlin: determinedly solid, honest, and lace-curtain
modest, the kind of Victorian neighborhood you saw in Ham-
mersmith on the way in from Heathrow Airport. You were more
likely to find that kind of neighborhood in what had been the
Russian Zone than in the western zones. The burgers of West

Berlin had bulldozed their rubble away and built new, and some parts of the western city looked distressingly like Fort Worth. The easterners hadn't had the resources to do that and had rebuilt as much as they could. Ironically, these patched-up houses from the days of Kaiser Wilhelm I had become some of the most sought-after and lovingly restored houses in the reunited city. The former East Berliners had rushed across the ruin of the Wall to find homes in the modern neighborhoods of West Berlin, while many westerners came the other way, looking for tradition and charm.

The morning after his postmidnight rendezvous with Mriya Meyerhold, Russ slept until nine. In his fiftieth year, he had learned to indulge himself by sleeping in after a late night. He made coffee in his little kitchen and carried it into his living room, then went out to pick his morning papers off the stoop. The morning was oppressed by a raucous noise. Even inside the house he had heard it and could hear it. He stood at the window and looked out. Birds. Thousands of black birds—starlings, blackbirds, grackles?—wheeling over the neighborhood and swooping down to peck at the tiny patches of grass behind the walls. Maybe a migrating flock. Maybe a sign of spring.

He had lain awake for sometime last night, trying to analyze Mriya's surprising eruption of emotion. It could have been calculated. She was capable of feigning emotion. On the other hand, she had reason for her tears.

The reason had driven her to him in 1984. A KGB agent already sharing living quarters on and off with Colonel Kedrov, she had approached Tobin in an all-night café in Hamburg. The place was on Budapester Strasse, so close to the St. Pauli-Reeperbahn red-light district that he had taken the somewhat coarse young woman for a St. Pauli girl, stopping in the café for coffee and a pastry on her way home. But she had addressed him by name.

An offer. She would give him information. In return she wanted an option. "If I elect. A place to go, where they will know me and give me refuge instantly, without question. Then ... safety. In the States, probably. And enough money to live comfortably."

He had agreed to her terms. She was not the first agent he had turned, and he didn't trust her any more than he had trusted the others. Her approach itself was so suspicious that he almost marked her for a quiet neutralization. He treated the information she turned over as highly questionable and subjected it to exceptional verification requirements.

Nothing failed. Everything she delivered proved valid. What was more, it was useful. She had been turned. There was no question about it.

Maybe her most valuable service was her contribution to the resolution of the Otto Reuss affair.

Reuss was an agent of HVA, *Hauptverwaltung Aufklärung*. In 1985 he was a major in the *Bundeswehr*, the West German army, and was serving as an aide to the corps commander of the frontier force the West Germans maintained on the Sector Border.

In such a position, Reuss had access to *Bundeswehr* and NATO plans to defend Western Europe against an all-out invasion by the Warsaw Pact. He learned that, in spite of the demands of West German politicians that every square meter of the Federal Republic be defended to the death, the plan was to give up ground gradually, exacting as great cost as possible, until NATO forces could mount a major counterattack. For this reason, the frontier defense force consisted chiefly of *Jagd Kommandos*, fast tank units whose mission was to destroy as many invading tanks as possible. As necessary, the *Jagd Kommandos* would fall back. Behind them lay two lines of dug-in defenses. It was important for the Warsaw Pact planners to know this. The plan was contrary to their expectation that the *Bundeswehr* would lunge forward in the event of attack and try to fight the battles on East German territory.

By the time Mriya Meyerhold betrayed Otto Reuss, he had already done the damage. The point was to prevent his doing more. A group met to see if there was any way to trick him into sending misinformation to HVA.

They never had a chance to find out. Shortly the word came that Major Otto Reuss had disappeared.

For six months he did not surface. Everyone assumed he had

somehow learned he was in danger and had fled home to East Germany. Then General Markus Wolf announced that the "brutal murder" of Otto Reuss meant the end of an informal gentlemen's agreement that captured agents would be imprisoned pending possible exchange. He announced the execution of two agents of the BND, one of the CIA.

Murder? The facts emerged gradually, initially through a Belgian dealer in small arms who had ample motive to talk to the BND. Otto Reuss had lived with a mistress in a villa at Bad Godesberg, a few miles up the Rhine from Bonn. On the night of October 4, 1985, a squad of men in German police uniforms had burst into the villa and "arrested" him. One of those men had been André Guyard. Guyard himself had shot Reuss in the head, only two kilometers from the villa. Later in the night they had dropped the body down an abandoned mine shaft in the Saar.

The French did not always cooperate with their opposite numbers in other countries.

Meyerhold's *bona fides* looked proved. On the other hand, could anyone have been sure that General Wolf had not decided to sacrifice Reuss for the prospect of conveying major disinformation via Meyerhold? Reuss, after all, may have done as much as he could; perhaps he was asking to be recalled.

No one could be sure. Except that she gave no major disinformation. She identified agents, and that was all. And never again an important one like Reuss.

Tobin suspected in time that she'd had a personal motive in exposing Reuss. He wondered, in fact, if she had not grown impatient with him, decided he wasn't moving fast enough on Reuss, and taken her information to Guyard. Of course, there were always at least two other possibilities: first, that Kedrov himself, for whatever motive, had ordered her to expose Reuss, second, that the KGB, just as likely as General Wolf, had been ready to dispense with the services of Otto Reuss and had betrayed him, using Meyerhold as the knife.

Finally, some small disinformation began to come. Either someone was feeding it to her, or she knew what she was doing. Whichever way, she was of no more use. Tobin stopped working her. Or she stopped working Tobin. It could have been either way.

Whatever—last night she had once more proved useful. After ten minutes gently sobbing on his shoulder, she had pulled herself together, and they had talked.

The Bristol-Kempinski Hotel was on the Kurfürstendamm, only a few blocks from the blackened ruin of the Kaiser Wilhelm Memorial Church, where the tower clocks stood stopped at 7:30 since 1943. The English word for the church was *Memorial*. It was a memorial to the horrors of war, a ruin left standing as a reminder. Tobin had always liked the German word better. *Denkmal*. Literally it meant, "Think of this time" or "Think of what happened here." The contrast between the fashionable, expensive shops that lined the Kurfürstendamm and the bomb-ravaged church made the *Denkmal* even more dramatic.

The *Ober*, or headwaiter, at the Kempinski looked up at Tobin with a troubled frown and asked if he had booked a table.

"I'm meeting a friend, Karl."

"Ah. Certainly, Herr Tobin. And he is . . . ?"

"Colonel Kedrov."

The headwaiter's face darkened for an instant. To anyone else he would have said there was no one by that name in the restaurant. To Tobin, he nodded and pointed across the room, where Kedrov sat with Mriya Meyerhold at a table near a window.

She knew he would be coming. That was the service she had performed last night.

"Nikolai Pavlovich!" Tobin said in Russian, affecting surprise.

Kedrov did not *affect* surprise. He *was* surprised, and dismayed, and suspicious that this meeting was not accidental. He stood. "Russell Georgievich! This is unexpected!"

Russ glanced at Mriya. She had told Russ she and Kedrov would be having lunch here today. Obviously, she had not told Kedrov that Tobin would appear. Kedrov did not feign surprise this well.

Kedrov's still-trim frame was covered by a well-tailored gray suit, white shirt, striped tie—even a handkerchief in his breast pocket. He was no typical Russian, in Tobin's judgment, not this straight, calmly self-confident, blond man. Maybe he was representative of what the Russian aristocracy had been. He was unlike the piggish Soviet leaders in the line from Stalin through Malenkov, Krushchev, and Brezhnev. He could hardly have been more unlike the reptilian line: Lenin through Vyshevskii by way of Lavrenti Beria. Tobin could imagine that the pigs and reptiles hated this man. It would be instinctive with them, hardly to be avoided. The ugly suffered their ugliness and hated the handsome.

"Sit down and have a drink with us, Russell," said Mriya. She crushed a cigarette in an ashtray. "We are talking about nothing more significant than the weather."

Russ nodded at her. "I'll sit down and have lunch, if I'm not intruding. I seem to have come in for lunch without having booked a table."

Kedrov drew out a chair and gestured to Russ to sit down. Russ did, noting that Mriya was wearing the dark blue jacket and skirt and white blouse of an Aeroflot agent, the same as last night. She wore the outfit carelessly, had not bothered to knock the cigarette ash off her lapel. Kedrov carried his years better than she did.

"I like this place," Russ said. He glanced around the elegant dining room. The walls were pale yellow, the woodwork white. Sunlight from the street came through the many windows. Quiet, efficient German waiters hurried from table to table, accommodating every wish of the diners. "I've liked it for a good many years."

Kedrov raised his hand to summon a waiter. "*Schnapps?*" he asked.

The waiter came to the table, and Russ spoke German to him—"An American martini, *bitte*. Beefeater gin, drop of vermouth, twist of lemon peel. Tell Fritz it's for Herr Tobin."

Kedrov listened to this, then grinned. "You are the master of the situation, Russell Georgievich, wherever you are."

"I wish it were so, Nikolai Pavlovich. So, tell me—how is everything with you?"

Kedrov had a glass of vodka before him, which he now lifted and drank. "The world has changed, Russell Georgievich. I have begun to feel old."

"You are a year younger than I am. We are not old enough to retire, either of us. Anyway, it cannot have changed so much, if you are in Berlin. If you were living comfortably in a *dacha* outside Moscow, I would believe the world has changed. But here you are, Nikolai Pavlovich: an old horse, obviously still in harness."

"As are you. Still in Berlin."

"But I think of living out my life here," said Russ. "I live in what used to be *your* zone. And you—here you are, sitting at lunch in what used to be *our* zone."

Colonel Nikolai Pavlovich Kedrov grinned. He was capable of a brittle and artificial fleeting grin, which was what he showed now. "You lived before in the DDR," he said. "And I sat and enjoyed lunch in this dining room. In the old days, when we'd have been killed if we were betrayed."

"If I had a glass, I wouldn't raise a glass to the old days, Nikolai Pavlovich."

"We knew who we were," said Colonel Kedrov.

"I know who I am," said Russ. "I must confess curiosity about who you are now, Nikolai Pavlovich."

"Semiretired," said Kedrov. "What is there for an intelligence officer of an empire in retreat?"

"All empires are in retreat," said Russ. "To one extent or another."

"Thank you for the kind thought, Russell Georgievich," said Kedrov.

The use of the patronymic between them fixed their relationship: casually friendly, not intimate. It did not surmount the overall tone of what Tobin heard in Kedrov's voice: wary distrust, dismay at this meeting, suspicion that it was not fortuitous. They had stymied each other often over the years. Kedrov was not so credulous as to suppose Russ Tobin had just *happened* to walk into the dining room of the Bristol-Kempinski on this particular day.

"You have won your *dacha*, Nikolai Pavlovich?"

The *dacha* Russ was talking about was a country home in a wooded government enclave a few kilometers southwest of Moscow, where the highest-ranking officers of the Soviet Union took most of their vacation time and where they lived when they retired. Built over old earthworks dug out by the Germans in 1941—so close had they come to taking Moscow—the *dachas* varied widely from luxurious to minimally comfortable. Most of them were rugged lodges of bare pine. Having one had long been the ultimate symbol of success in the Soviet world.

Mriya Meyerhold's eyes narrowed on Russ. She had told him last night that the powers had never granted a *dacha* to Kedrov and probably never would. She had not needed to tell him. Tobin knew. What was more, he knew why. She didn't like the cut Tobin made in Kedrov's sensitive hide when he reminded him he did not have a *dacha*. Russell Tobin could be vicious.

"The powers that be may abolish *dachas*," said Kedrov.

"I hope not before you get yours."

"I think sometimes," said Kedrov, "I would rather retire to the Caribbean. I would like to learn to sail a boat. I would like to fish from my boat."

"None of that is beyond the realm of possibility, Nikolai Pavlovich."

Kedrov flashed that quick, nervous grin. "No. Nor has it ever been, I imagine."

"Never impossible," said Russ. "For any of us, ever."

Kedrov nodded. "The market is glutted," he said wearily.

"There is always a market for a quality asset," said Russ.

Kedrov raised his chin. "In the Caribbean waters off Florida, what do you catch?" he asked ingenuously. "I mean, what kind of fish do you catch?"

"Many kinds."

"Are they edible?"

"Most are. You can buy books that tell how to cook the various kinds. Even sharks. A tasty meat."

Kedrov retreated behind his eyes. "Ah..." he murmured. "You sit in the rear of this superb boat, on the blue water, in the hot sun..."

"It sounds like heaven," said Mriya.

"These sharks . . . " Kedrov speculated quietly. "You can actually catch them on a line?"

"Yes."

"Ah. But—you can do this on the Black Sea."

"Not the same," said Russ.

"No," said Mriya wistfully. "It is not the same."

Kedrov shrugged. "Too bad," he said.

When Tobin left the table, Kedrov and Meyerhold remained sitting. Kedrov watched the American cross the room, waited for him to glance back and smile a final farewell, then turned to Mriya.

"*Smert shpionam.*" Death to spies.

"Nikolai!"

"It is no coincidence that he came here."

"He lives here."

"I mean that he came to this dining room, today. It is a warning, Mriya. He is playing a little game, before he strikes."

"Maybe—"

"He is dangerous. He has always been dangerous. I wonder how much he knows."

Mriya sighed. "I would be more concerned, if I were you, about what *he* knows." She indicated who she meant by flashing her eyes only, not turning her head in the slightest. "It is no coincidence that he is here, either."

The man she had glanced at, eating alone at a table near the wall, was Major Ivan Stepanovich Yuryev. Chairman Vyshevskii had made a mistake in assigning Yuryev to tail Kedrov. The colonel had been in the KGB too long not to know who Yuryev was.

Major Yuryev. The Chairman's snake. Prominent in the KGB directorate an American police department might call internal affairs, Yuryev's job was to watch for problems inside the KGB. He was a loner who avoided any form of unofficial contact with the men and women of the KGB. He and the Chairman thought, apparently, that few in the KGB would recognize him, or if they did would not know what he was. In that, they were fools. The craftier ones, the survivors with long experience, knew who Yuryev was and what he was.

Such people tend to be alike. He is the pimply schoolboy with the runny nose who doesn't play games well. She is the young woman who guards her virginity with her life, then becomes pregnant from her first experience. He is the man who seeks out friends he can trust well enough in order to confide that he really admires his superiors and is grateful to be working under such exceptional leadership. He is the man you catch sitting at his desk with his eyes closed and learn that he is praying—after which he shyly yet proudly confesses his total commitment to Jesus.

Ivan Stepanovich Yuryev looked like the late movie actor Peter Lorre. Compact, hunched, with a worried look always on his mousy little face, Yuryev was a chain-smoker. He wore an indifferently tailored double-breasted suit, a poor choice for a short, stocky man; and his lapels were gray with cigarette ash.

"So long as nothing more formidable than *that* pursues us," said Kedrov, "we have little to worry about."

"Don't deceive yourself. He's not here on his own orders."

Kedrov glanced boldly at Yuryev. "Vyshevskii," he sneered. "A politician."

"Fishing for sharks," she said.

"Yes. Tobin was fishing. He's the one who was fishing." Kedrov reached for his coffee cup. "This shark," he said, "is going to pull the fisherman out of his boat, into the water."

"Nikolai . . . The shark is strong and cunning and dangerous. But when he fights a strong and cunning and dangerous man, he invariably loses."

"*Smert shpionam*," said Kedrov.

"I must confess," said Mahmud Nedim.

"Catholics confess," said Kristin Kuniczak. "Please you not to don't."

Mahmud smiled at her fractured English. His own was not perfect, but Anne-Lise's—as he thought her name was—could be amusing in its ingenuous tangles.

"I must confess I have never before done what we are doing," said Mahmud.

"For a man which has never done it before, you do it very well."

"Thank you. It is, I suppose, instinctive."

"No. Many men do it altogether badly. Even after years of experience."

They lay face-to-face on an iron single bed, his muscular, smooth brown body pressed close to hers. She saw efficiency of design in the bodies of Asians. Mahmud, for example, had everything he needed to be a man—and nothing more.

He was spent right now, but his—damn the English, they had no good word for it. His . . . what the Germans called *das männlische Glied*, literally the manly limb, was more than she had expected for so small a man. She'd had almost to force him to expose it to her. He'd wanted to turn off the lights before they undressed. In fact, he had asked if they could not make love without undressing entirely. When she had lifted his *männlische Glied* in her hands and given it a friendly kiss—just with her lips, just on the shaft—he had jerked away and giggled nervously.

Right now he was placidly kissing her breasts, drawing her nipples between his lips, having confessed that this was something he had dreamed of doing for ten days.

"If you not so goddamned timid, you could have done ten days past."

"This is not done at home. Even with his wife, a man may not do this, I don't think. You must understand I have lived my life very differently from the way you have lived yours."

"Be thankful you are not at home, then."

"I am," he said simply.

Kristin punched the single pillow into the angle between the bed and the bars of its head. She lifted herself on her elbow and settled back on the pillow. She meant to display herself to Mahmud, but immediately he lowered his face and began to nuzzle her belly. For a moment she thought he was about to bury his face in her crotch, until she realized such an idea would never occur to him.

The room where they lay was modest. Besides the bed, it contained a small yellow-oak dresser and a small square table to the right of the bed. A mirror in a dark wooden frame hung on the wall opposite the door into the living room. All the light was from the one bulb in an old-fashioned bridge lamp, the kind with cast-metal curlicues and an attached ashtray at a convenient height. The bulb in it was powerful, though, and filled the room with light only a little subdued by the pleated paper shade.

Besides the bedroom, the flat consisted of a living room, a tiny kitchen, and a bathroom.

"I shame you see how I live," she had said to him when they came in.

"It looks comfortable," he had said politely.

"I suffer problems. Must send money to family. My brother has stolen from me, also."

That was what they had said when they came into the flat. Now Mahmud chuckled and said, "You smell good. You know? No sour smell. No sweat. Talcum powder, no?"

"Is good for everybody," she said.

He nodded emphatically. "For me. I know you mean, for me, too."

"You live comfortably, Mahmud?"

"My flat—" He smiled weakly. "—is a bit larger."

"Nicer. You have television, no? Refrigerator, no?"

"Well . . ."

"You like me, Mahmud?"

"Yes. Very, very much."

Kristin stretched, throwing her breasts forward, suggesting he kiss them again. He did not catch the suggestion. She prompted him. "Kiss, my lover! Nibble!"

He did.

"Mahmud . . ."

"Yes?"

"We could live together? Do like so every night?"

"That would be heaven, Anne-Lise."

"Ah. This little bed. The couch of love."

"Or *my* bed. In my flat. More room. Television. Refrigerator. Microwave oven!"

"Your flat? Your beautiful flat? You would do this for me?"

Kristin laughed. She bent over, grabbed his penis, and shoved it into her mouth. For a moment, only a moment, she sucked on it and licked it. "Ah . . ." she whispered. "I will teach you what you don't know!"

"It is difficult, you understand. The diplomatic situation makes it most difficult for us to treat the man as a spy. We must be circumspect."

Speaking was Erich Voss, Berlin chief of the German security service, BND. Tobin had come to his office, and they sat in a severely modern room, furnished with a Herman Miller zebra-wood desk and credenza and Le Corbusier chairs. The office was equipped with computers; screens glowed on the desk and credenza.

"Colonel Nikolai Pavlovich Kedrov *is* a spy," said Tobin. "Circumstances have changed. Kedrov hasn't."

"I know," said Voss. "Unfortunately, some very prominent people in the German government refuse to believe there are spies or any need for them anymore. Not in Europe, anyway. How fortunate you are to represent a chronically paranoid nation."

Voss smiled as he spoke the final sentence, and Tobin nodded and grinned.

Erich Voss was an aging veteran of the *Bundesnachtrichtendienst*. Liver spots mottled his loose, wrinkled, and pallid face. His blue eyes watered. His lips trembled and made his cigarette wobble.

"What can I do for you, Russ? Legal or not."

"I'd like to have some good, inconspicuous people keeping an eye on Kedrov. I need to know who he contacts. He has people here from Zagorsk. I don't know who. I'm not sure we'd know them even if we had their identities."

"The story is, he spent an afternoon at Zagorsk not so long ago," said Voss. "That visit was hardly likely to have been an inspection tour. Who left there immediately after his visit? Whoever did would be his agents."

"Good thinking," said Tobin. "The problem is, twenty students graduated from Zagorsk within five days after Kedrov was there. Our source there did not know the names of more than a few of the graduates. I see no choice but to try to find out who he sees and maybe photograph those people."

"Mriya Meyerhold is with him in Berlin. Whose side is she on now?"

"Her own, of course," said Tobin. "She still has the problem. Nothing has changed."

"She's still bitter, then?"

Tobin nodded. "Bitter, discouraged, and afraid."

Voss touched the flame of his lighter to a fresh cigarette. "Perfect," he said.

"Might be. Except that Kedrov knows what she did to Reuss. In fact, the more I think of it, the more I wonder if Kedrov didn't order the destruction of Otto Reuss."

Colonel Kedrov spoke to Kristin in Russian. "You little devil! You knew I'd have to watch this. Damn!"

Kristin reached over and touched the Stop button on the VCR. "There is nothing more of interest," she said. "You can watch the rest of it whenever you want to. Alone. It is erotic, not informative. I let the camera run so you can see everything."

"Devil . . ."

"It was your choice, my friend."

"A nigger," he said, using the American word.

"That, too, was your choice."

Kedrov blew a noisy sigh. "So. Are you going to move in with him?"

She nodded.

"And?"

"It will not be possible, I think, to install a camera there. Microphones, yes, but no camera. Have the microphones installed in his bedroom. That is where I will encourage him to talk."

"Will he talk?"

Kristin smiled provocatively. "What is your guess, Nikolai Pavlovich? Will he?"

Kedrov regarded the interview as over and was at the window, checking the street for anyone or anything suspicious. He let the curtains fall together and went to the VCR to remove the tape.

"There's a newspaper to read," he said. "Don't leave for an hour. At least an hour. Take a nap if you want to. The longer you stay here the better."

"Next time we meet, I'll dress as a man," she said.

"Please do."

7

IN ALL HER LIFE, Debora Benson had owned only one automobile. It was a gift from her father, one of his own most prized possessions: a 1969 MGB with left-side controls, lovingly maintained by him until he gave it to her on her twenty-fourth birthday, lovingly maintained by her for the ten years since. It was a classic, British racing green. On a long run down I–95 or the *autobahn*, not only did half the cars on the road outrun it, but the driveshaft tunnel got so hot you could barely put a hand on it. The top leaked and you had to replace it every year or so. The fenders rusted and required constant metalwork. The red battery light came on whenever you switched on the ignition and remained on, always; and when occasionally the battery did run low, it surprised you. The car was noisy, shaky, and sometimes refused to start. But Debora loved it and was determined to drive it as long as she could keep it alive.

She was horrified when she came out into the parking lot in a small shopping mall near the Gatow Airport and found an ugly crease in the left rear fender. She stood staring at it for a full minute, tears filling her eyes. Wear and tear, yes, but . . . *violation?*

When she opened the door she found a note lying on the passenger seat. It was in English and it said:

I regret that the wing of my car brushed that of your marvelous MG as I backed from my parking space. If you will be so good as to ring me at 29–324–1111, I will arrange to have expert repairs done at my expense. My apologies for the inconvenience.

Michael Ormsley

The note did little at first to assuage Debora Benson's vexation. She returned to her fender and stood staring at it mournfully. Then she glanced again at the note. It was polite. It was written on a small sheet of blue notepaper embossed with the initials MGO. She tucked it in her handbag. Tomorrow she would decide whether or not to telephone this Michael Ormsley.

Tomorrow. That would be soon enough. Debora Benson was not sure she wanted to speak to a strange man on the telephone, even to get him to pay for her damaged fender. He was British, obviously—he called the damaged part a wing, not a fender. Maybe—well, maybe she would call him. He might be a decent sort of Britisher.

He might be.

He might be very different from her usual experience with the male sex. Not likely, but he might be.

When she was twelve years old, Debora and two friends, Lynda and Susan, had taken a canoe out on the upper reaches of the Connecticut River. Their parents had rented cabins on the riverbank for a week for the cheap fishing-and-swimming-camp vacation prep-school teachers could afford. Lynda's father taught at Choate, Susan's at Groton, Debora's at Litchfield.

They did not canoe alone. Three boys came along in an aluminum canoe. At midday, with muscles aching from paddling upstream, the three girls ran their canoe up on a willow island. They built a fire to roast wieners on willow spits. The three boys, who had been half a mile or more ahead of them, returned as the fire began smoking.

The boys had beer, which they drank. Two of the girls did, too. Debora did not, in spite of the derisive things the others said. When they had drunk two or three cans of beer apiece, the boys took off all their clothes, exhibiting stretched-out, bony bodies, without much muscle and entirely without hair, but with dark male parts engorged. Debora had never seen a naked boy before and provoked raucous laughter from the others when she turned her eyes away.

Then the other two girls took off their clothes, showing tiny breasts and hairless pudenda, leaving Debora looking and feeling miserable in her blue schoolgirl shorts and white T-shirt.

Cruel talk. Twelve- and thirteen-year-olds are capable of a sadism unique to them, to which very few other normal human beings can descend. Under the lash of their scorn, Debora, too, finally undressed, only to hear their savage jeering directed at her naked body. Hers was as good as theirs, as mature as any twelve-year-old girl's, but because she had been the last to expose it, they laughed at her.

She cried. She sat down in the mud, bent double, and sobbed.

After a minute or so, she felt a gentle touch alongside her neck, in her hair, and on her throat and shoulders. On the right. Then on her left. She drew in breath and accepted those kind caresses. They—oh, they had stopped laughing at her! She straightened and smiled.

Then she heard a snicker. She glanced to the left and right.

Two of the boys were rubbing her neck with their penises!

Debora shrieked. Then she threw herself face down in the mud and sobbed. She cried until the others became alarmed, and the other two girls became angry at the boys for having caused agony they might wind up having to explain.

Disgusted, the boys dressed, climbed into their canoe, and shoved out into the water. Not until two hours later did the girls venture downstream. Lynda and Susan did not invite Debora to do anything with them again, not all summer.

The next time, with other boys and girls, Debora was the boldest of them all. The result was no more comfortable. Whatever she did, it was graceless. A few years later she surrendered her virginity, not because she wanted to but because it made her such a *freak* to keep it. She did it, but she found in the act no great inspiration.

* * *

"Mr. Ormsley? This is Debora Benson. I found your note in my MG last evening."

"Oh, I am glad you rang. Very glad. I was so distressed to have marred your really extr'*ord*'n'ry car. Please do let me see to the repairs. I've made some calls today, looking for the best garage to smooth out the wing of a classic MGB. I think I've located someone who can do it well—unless there is another chap you'd rather have."

"I, uh . . . I, uh, have no one special in mind."

"Well, then, Miss Benson—is it, *Miss* Benson, I'm sorry. *Miz* Benson, hmm? Uh, how shall we arrange it? You will be without your car for a day or two. Please let me drive you from the garage to wherever you spend your day and drive you home after."

"That won't be necessary. I—"

"Well, we may be soulmates about automobiles, Miss Benson. You see, I drive an E-type Jaguar myself. I should consider it a privilege to drive you from the garage to wherever you want to go."

It was settled. She would take her MG to a small neighborhood garage in the Spandau district. He would meet her there and drive her to Dahlem. Day after tomorrow.

When the grimly efficient Max Wenzel, director of the Dahlem laboratories of NSI, asked if Tobin's evening were free, Russ expected an invitation to dinner at home, with wife and children. He said his evening *was* free, and Wenzel surprised him by saying he would pick him up at his flat at eight and they would have dinner in a club he favored.

Wenzel came on time in his chauffeured limousine.

The club he favored was on the Kurfürstendamm, some twenty blocks southwest of the Kaiser Wilhelm Church. The club was called Cantina and had been styled to resemble the cantina in *Star Wars*, where Luke and Ben first met Han Solo. It was a large, dark place, divided into discrete areas by thick artificial-stone columns. The headwaiter who checked their reservation and led them to their table wore a Darth Vader costume. One of the bartenders was Chewbacca, the other C3PO. The musicians wore costumes based on various grotesque aliens. Wax figures, some of them seated at tables, represented more aliens.

The young women who carried food and drink to the tables provided titillation. Except for plastic calf-high boots in various colors and belts slung around their hips, from which hung "blasters" in holsters, they were naked.

Their table afforded a clear view of a square stage, where a comely young woman was sinuously stripping—though why she should when the waitresses were all naked, Tobin couldn't guess. She was, he had to grant, exceptionally beautiful. What was more, she was a rare bird: a talented stripper, with a sure sense of the erotic. Seeing her gradually uncover her alluring body was, he had to concede, far more sensual than looking at the already-naked waitresses.

"Believe it or not, you can get a good meal here," said Wenzel. "Limited menu. Steak or fish. But it will be good."

Their waitress, a dark-haired girl with generous breasts and thick curly pubic hair, came to the table and in a soft voice asked what they would like from the bar.

"Whiskey?" Wenzel asked Tobin.

Tobin nodded, and Wenzel ordered a bottle of Johnnie Walker Black brought to the table.

"A little business talk," said Wenzel. "I've been watching my staff very closely, and I've seen nothing unusual. No one has missed a day's work in two weeks. No one seems nervous or upset. We've instituted some new security precautions, and no one has objected." He shrugged. "I have an uneasy sense that we are a target, but I can't discover anything specific."

Tobin clasped his hands on the table and leaned a little toward Wenzel, so he could speak and be heard over the music. He kept an eye on the stripper but glanced often at Wenzel. "Reminds me of a story," he said. "A man worked in a lumber and building-supply warehouse. Every day when he left work he took with him a wheelbarrow loaded with sawdust. This was allowed; sawdust was a nuisance there, and they were glad to get rid of it. But the man had a reputation for being a very clever thief. The guards at the gate were instructed to sift through his sawdust every day, to make sure he wasn't stealing tools or something else by hiding it in the sawdust. This went on day after day, and they never found anything in the sawdust. It worried the owner of the sawmill. Like you, he had an uneasy feeling that something was happening, but he couldn't put his finger on it. Finally, he called the man in his office and said to him, 'I know you're stealing something. I just know you are taking something away. It is driving me crazy. If you will tell me what you have been stealing, and how, not only will I not prosecute, but you may keep your job and I will pay you a bonus of five hundred dollars for the information. So, tell me. What are you stealing?' The man shrugged and said, 'Wheelbarrows.'"

Wenzel laughed. Perhaps courtesy inspired a more hearty laugh than the story deserved.

"Intelligence work is often like this," Tobin said. "Right now, just about all we can do is watch and wait. To use an American expression, right now the ball is in Kedrov's court. We can't move until he does."

"But maybe he is moving already. Like your man with the wheelbarrows."

"Then we have to find out what he is doing."

Wenzel fixed his eyes intently on the stripper, who was now near the end of her act. "What if Colonel Kedrov were to be the victim of an accident?" he asked.

"Then they'd send someone else, someone we don't know," said Tobin. "In fact, we have to keep in mind the possibility that Kedrov's presence in Berlin is a diversion to capture our attention while someone else moves against us. Anyway, we are supposed to have achieved a higher plateau of civilization and put behind us the old habits of killing each other."

"Have we really?"

"In theory, anyway. All the intelligence agencies, with maybe an exception or two, have revised their standing orders. Murder is out of favor. Out of style."

The stripper left the stage. Wenzel applauded. So did Tobin.

Their waitress returned, bringing the bottle of scotch, glasses, ice, water, and soda. She described the menu: steak or fish, as Wenzel had said. He told her they would order later.

"Two charming young ladies will soon approach and ask if they can join us. Do you object?"

"I don't object."

"One of them will go home with you later, if you like."

"I'll pass on that privilege."

"Nice girls," said Wenzel. "Not the usual sort."

"But they work here."

"Oh, yes."

"I don't really care to take one of them to bed, Max. I'm not judgmental about it. I used to do it. But—"

"No problem. You do live alone, though, don't you?"

"I do."

"Maybe you should think of establishing a friendship with one of the pretty young women on my staff. It would give you a reason for being around the laboratories more. She might also become a source of information."

"Sounds like a good idea."

"I've one in mind. An American. A computer genius. Not a great beauty, but I think you will find her attractive and interesting. You might want to run a security check on her before you meet her. I mean, you might want to find out what your agency and the FBI know about her. Her name is Debora Benson."

Tobin was feeling his liquor when he pulled his Porsche to the curb in front of the brick house he shared. He didn't quarrel with the new obsession about driving after a few drinks but had formed his own habits in the old days when it was supposed an intelligent person would act on good judgment. He had driven carefully. He was home.

"Russ . . ."

He spun. He didn't carry a pistol anymore, but his hand went to his chest and inside his jacket, instinctively, as if the little Walther PPK were still there.

"Извинйте!" ("Excuse me!")

Mriya.

She had climbed out of a car just as he arrived. Her cigarette flew across the street, an orange arc of fire that splattered tiny sparks when it hit the pavement. Wearing boots not unlike those he had seen at the Cantina, a short black skirt and jacket, she smiled as she approached him.

"I made you wait the other night," she said in Russian. "Tonight, you've made me. I'd like to come in and talk to you."

He nodded and turned a hand toward the gate. "Nikolai Pavlovich?"

"Moscow. The early evening flight. Called back for a meeting with Vyshevskii."

"Any idea why?" Russ asked as he unlocked the door.

"Maybe to schedule the date of his execution."

Russ chose not to respond to that and turned his attention to switching on the lights in his living room. "I am fresh out of vodka," he said.

"I've lost my taste for it anyway," she said. "I've developed a taste for English whiskey."

"Scotch."

"Yes, what they call scotch."

She tossed her coat on a chair and sat down on the sofa. He went in the kitchen and poured two scotches, each over a single small ice cube. When he returned she sat with her legs stretched out before her, rubbing the muscles of her calves. Then, maybe impulsively, she kicked off one boot and then the other.

"Sharks," she said. "I want to fish for sharks."

"Mriya Aronovna . . . you are not going to betray Nikolai Pavlovich. Don't try to tell me you are."

"He and I have two choices," she said quietly. "Nikolai Pavlovich still thinks he can earn his *dacha*, still thinks he can win the respect and confidence of the chairman, Vyshevskii and Andronikov—if he just does his work well enough. I know better. I favor the other choice."

"Come over to our side," said Russ.

"I have destroyed Nikolai Pavlovich, as you well know."

"He destroyed himself," said Russ. "At the very least, he was an equal partner in his destruction."

"He is followed. They sent a spy to watch him. They don't trust him."

"In our line of work, nobody trusts anybody."

Mriya drank her scotch in two noisy gulps. "You know what I mean. Don't play conversational games with me, Russell Georgievich."

"Why are you here?"

"I want to fish for sharks."

"What would you bring for bait?"

She raised her glass, indicating she wanted another drink. "Once I might have offered you me."

"I'd have accepted," he said as he reached for her glass. "I'll accept right now. But what you offer isn't worth what you want."

"Oh, thank you, gallant gentleman."

"Stakes are too high. Always have been. No woman—no man either, for that matter—is worth the stakes."

"You've proved your attitude on that often enough."

Russ went to the kitchen. He poured her a double and refreshed his own. "We are survivors, Mriya," he said. "Both of us must have a sharp sense of worth."

When he returned to the living room, she was bent forward, elbows on her knees, staring into the cold fireplace built only to burn coal, which he had never lighted. She took her drink from his hands and took a quick swallow.

"I can't win, you know," she said. "It has never been possible."

"Nothing has changed."

She shook her head.

"Nikolai Pavlovich—"

"Should go fishing for sharks. Should. And won't. Never will. He's a Russian. He's a Bolshevik. Unreconstructed. Gorbachev, Yeltsin..." She shook her head. "They mean nothing to him."

"He loves his country."

"The Motherland. He will die for it. Or he'll let it kill him. And don't ever mention the *dacha* to him again. When you mention that you are putting a knife in both of us, him and me."

"You and him."

She shook her head mournfully. "His *dacha* he will never have. They know he would bring me there. So he will never have it. The wives... not just the wives. The men. I make a fit servant. If I scrubbed the floors, that would be all right. I spy for the Motherland, and that's all right. But—"

"But they don't want to know you."

"If I went into a temple and pissed on the Torah, it would make no difference. I have betrayed...that. For them. And still they don't want to know me."

"I understand."

"You could not understand."

Russ stared at her for a few seconds. "What do you want? Why are you here?"

"I want a chance. For him and for me. I want to go fishing for sharks."

"Nikolai Pavlovich doesn't want to go fishing for sharks."

"Rather than be shot."

"Is it that bad? Really?"

"It is that bad."

"The sharks come at a price," said Russ.

"Which is?"

"I want to know what you and he are doing in Berlin."

She finished her second drink in one gulp. "From the back of a fishing boat off the Florida Keys, I will tell you."

"Pay first, perform later? You know better."

"I will have to convince him. Promise me that the fishing boat is possible."

"You have my word on that."

"Possible. Only possible?"

"Specifics for specifics, Mriya. Refuge for both of you. For a price."

She nodded. "Ummh." She glanced toward the stairs that led to the upper floor of his flat, obviously to his bedroom. "We never learned to know each other very well. Would you like to know me better?"

"That's the best offer I've had tonight, Mriya," he said.

Kristin Kuniczak tossed a small, cheap suitcase on Mahmud's bed. She had carried that. He had carried two heavy duffel bags. All her possessions, she said.

"Paradise!"

He grinned. "Not paradise, my dearest love," he said. "But the best I can afford."

He could afford it perhaps because it lay on one of the glide paths to a main runway at Tempelhof Airport in a building not yet built in 1948 when the American transport planes had swept a hundred meters above the rooftops, two or three a minute, carrying in the food and coal that had kept Berlin fed and warm that winter of the blockade and airlift. Here and there in the neighborhood, monuments stood to the crews of C–54s that had crashed—and to the people whose lives and homes had been destroyed by those crashes.

Mahmud Nedim knew nothing of this. It was not a part of the history the schoolmasters had taught in Rawalpindi, where the instruction concentrated on the magnificence of the Prophet's empires and not on the squabbles of the unbelievers. He had not bothered to read the inscriptions on the monuments. The monuments he had looked at proclaimed the glories of men and things not glorious, so why look at monuments?

Glorious was this exquisite Western woman who had agreed to live with him and give him ecstasy every night. Anne-Lise Hein. He could not write home and tell about her. A daughter of the heathen. God-sent to him to prove him a man! His father would spit at his feet if he knew.

She capered around his rooms, exclaiming over everything: the television set, the radio, the rangetop and oven in the kitchen, the microwave, the dishwasher, even the telephones! All of it was marvelous; she had never seen the like.

"We didn't have these thing, you know," she said soberly. "In the old DDR, we lucky we have the electric toast-the-bread. We have television, but what to watch—the speeches of the seniles called leaders? We *must* have the television. Otherwise, you maybe missing the latest word from the seniles. Ah! And since I haven't been able to afford . . . !"

She threw her arms around him and kissed Mahmud.

Later, she soaked for an hour in his tub. He poured drinks for them, and she let him sit beside the tub and wash her! She let him run his hands and a wet, soapy cloth over her lithe naked body! And eventually she told him to undress and come into the water with her. Together in the tub, they made it overflow, sloshing gallons of water on the tiled floor, and she only laughed!

They went out for dinner. She ate pork! She picked up a morsel of it on her fork and pushed it between his lips. God— He murmured the word, and Anne-Lise tittered and said, "God is a silly old man. Old men, they silly. So he, the oldest of all, the silliest of all! No? Is not so? Silly."

It tasted good.

In bed she gave him experiences he had never dreamed of. He asked her how she had learned all this. "How have you not?" she answered simply. "The person... how you say? The—"

She ran her hands over her body, and he prompted her with the word: *body*.

"The body... is like fine violin. You play. You play not good, you not enjoy. Is what worse than bad-played violin?" She grinned. "Is what better than good-played violin, good-played body?"

He was awake after midnight. The green light from the digital clock disturbed him, but he did not turn away from it because to turn away from it he'd have had to turn away from her.

He lay cuddled against her back, conscious of her extraordinary warmth.

She woke.

"Mahmud..."

"Anne-Lise."

"I dream you work in laboratory and something explode and kill you! You not have nothing there that...?"

"No. Nothing like that. Only computers. Computers and the machines that engrave circuits on silicon wafers."

She yawned. "'Engrave circuits on silicon wafers.' What is this? How does this work? You know, I use the computer in my work. I not... ignorant of this."

"It may be the supreme technology of the nineties," he said, glancing at the clock, astounded that she should waken and begin to talk about this after three in the morning. Still, he was happy for the chance to communicate some of his enthusiasm for his work. "There are other techniques for etching extremely fine circuit patterns on silicon—X-ray, for one—but we believe we are developing the next generation."

She ran her hand down his chest and over his belly and gently closed it around his penis. "My genius," she said. "I have heard of the X-ray way of doing this thing. Why is your way the better?"

"Extremely precise," he said. "Very fine etching. We send a very fine stream of electrons onto the silicon material. A human hair is seventy-five microns to a hundred microns wide. Think of dividing a human hair into five or six hundred parallel lines. That is our machine."

"Reliable? Fast?"

"Yes. We are working on both aspects."

She yawned again. "I lucky to be in the bed with so a genius," she said. "Is not dust in such a machine? Dust must look as big as an automobile in such process. How you keep away the dust?"

"Magnetically, for the most part," he said. "High voltage attracts dust magnetically. High-voltage collectors draw the dust away from the electron-stream projector."

"How you can aim the stream of electrons with so precision?"

"Magnets."

"So precision?"

"Anne-Lise . . . I have said too much already. I cannot tell you more. It is all a very big industrial secret."

She rolled over to face him. She kissed him. "You must trust Anne-Lise, my friend," she whispered. "I interest what you do. You genius. I know. I interest what you do. How you do. Do not be mysterious with Anne-Lise."

"Oh, no. I do not mean to be—"

"What good is six hundred lines on a hair?" she asked.

"Cram more circuits on a chip," he said. "More efficient computers. More memory. It is extremely important."

"Can you show me this thing?" she asked.

"Show you what?"

"This machine. What my genius has invented!"

"I didn't invent it, Anne-Lise. I'm only one of many scientists working on it."

"Even so. I want to see what you do. I want to see this thing make a chip."

"It's secret. I couldn't possibly show you."

Abruptly, she sat up. He rolled on his back and frowned up at her. She crossed her arms and stared at him.

"You don't trust me," she pouted.

"I can't show you. They won't let me. I couldn't take you inside the laboratory."

"Then let me see picture of this machine," she said. "I want to have in my mind a vision of what my lover does all day."

Mahmud turned down the corners of his mouth and shook his head. "All you would see is a picture of the cabinet. And even that I am forbidden to take from the laboratory."

"So," she said. She lay down again, with her back to him.

Coded and scrambled, then unscrambled and decoded, a five-page confidential file arrived at the CIA station and was locked in a safe. It was eyes-only for Mr. Tobin, and when he came in on Thursday morning, Jane Mahoney told him it was there.

The cipher clerk had sealed it in an envelope. Russ sat down at his desk and slit the envelope open.

CENTRAL INTELLIGENCE AGENCY CONFIDENTIAL
FROM: FEDERAL BUREAU OF INVESTIGATION

Subject: Debora Clark Benson, re security.

The subject person was born in Cambridge, Mass., in 1958. She graduated magna cum laude from M.I.T. in 1981 with the degree Bachelor of Science. She was awarded a doctorate (Ph.D.) in mathematics at Harvard in 1983. The subject is, as of the date of this report, unmarried. She has no children. She has held positions in the research and development laboratories of IBM and, currently, Laser Solutions, Inc. (LSI). <u>Except as below noted,</u> the Agency is in possession of no information that would suggest she is a security risk.

***

The subject person is the daughter of Willard F. Benson and Amanda Clark Benson.

Willard F. Benson was born in 1926 and is a graduate of the University of Chicago (B.S., 1948 and Ph.D., physics, 1951). Granted AEC security clearance, 1949.

Willard F. Benson was a student of Dr. Edward Teller at the Institute for Nuclear Studies of the University of Chicago. Was employed by the AEC at Los Alamos, 1951–52 and was one of the extended team of scientists who witnessed the detonation of the first thermonuclear bomb on November 1, 1952. Resigned AEC, May 1953, appointed associate professor nuclear physics, Princeton. Continued research on thermonuclear devices.

On March 8, 1954, Willard F. Benson was summoned to appear before the Committee on Un-American Activities of the United States House of Representatives. During that appearance he refused to answer the following questions—

(1) Whether or not he had ever been a member of the Communist Party or of any organization named on the Attorney General's list of subversive organizations.

(2) Whether or not any of a list of eight individuals known to him were members of the Communist Party or any such organization.

(3) Whether during his association with the eight named individuals he had ever heard any of them express criticisms of the Constitution of the United States, the American form of government, and so on.

He refused, further, to deny that he had been heard to say—

(1) That Alger Hiss was not guilty and was the victim of a conspiracy.

(2) That the House Committee on Un-American Activities and the Permanent Investigative Subcommittee of the United States Senate were greater threats to the freedom of Americans than was the Communist Party.

(3) That he did not trust the president of the United States with a weapon as powerful as the hydrogen bomb.

(4) That it was advantageous to world peace for the Soviet Union to possess the hydrogen bomb.

Willard F. Benson was subsequently charged with contempt of Congress, was convicted, and served seven months in a federal reformatory. His security clearance was revoked. He was dismissed from his professorship. During the years 1955–67, Willard F. Benson sold shoes, first in a store in Boston, subsequently as a traveling salesman, selling wholesale. In 1968 he was offered a position as an instructor in mathematics and physics at Litchfield Academy. As of the date of this report, he remains a ''master'' of those subjects at that school.

The subject person was born while her father was a shoe salesman. She often expresses extreme bitterness about what she considers grossly unfair treatment he received at the hands of his government. She is a member of Americans for Democratic Action, the American Civil Liberties Union, and People for the American Way—these memberships in addition to the usual professional memberships appropriate to her profession.

The subject person has exhibited a degree of emotional instability.

It is suggested that she be denied access to information classified ''top secret'' or ''secret,'' but there would appear to be no need to deny her access to ''confidential'' information on a need–to–know basis.

8

SHE HAD NOT thought he would really show up driving an E-type Jaguar. He did, though. She was a little disappointed in it, a 2 + 2 with a backseat, but still it was a fine example of its type, with the characteristic long engine compartment and hood almost half the length of the car. It was shiny black, with a dent on the fender corresponding to the one on the MG. The leather upholstery was in mint condition or had been replaced. The mahogany dashboard was intact. The driver sat on the right. The license plates were British.

And so was Michael Ormsley, as British as he could be: an uncommonly handsome man, youthful, affable, openly straightforward. He wore a tweed jacket, dark slacks, a tweed cap. He apologized profusely once again for having dented her fender—her wing, as he called it.

The German mechanic was expecting the MG. Ormsley spoke to him in rapid, idiomatic German, a little of which was lost on Benson, whose college German served well enough but was still weak on slang and specialized terms.

"Well," said Ormsley as they settled down in the tan leather seats of the Jaguar. "To Dahlem."

"To Dahlem, with many thanks."

"You are, of course, American. You sound it. I'm sorry I've never had occasion to visit America. Often thought of it."

"I'm not sure you've missed anything much," she said.

"That doesn't sound patriotic."

115

"I suppose I'm not patriotic. In fact, I think it's idiocy to commit your loyalty to a piece of geography. I could live anywhere. Or . . . almost anywhere."

"London?"

"I love London."

"I've become rather fond of Berlin," he said. "For you and me it has no evil memories. Even my dad, in fact, had no evil memories. But my grandfather—" He grinned. "He was a bomb aimer. All he regrets is that a single building is left standing."

Ormsley drove with skill and confidence. She liked the way he handled the Jaguar, projecting his will through the controls, utilizing everything the car was capable of. He steered and shifted with practiced precision, though he seemed unconscious of what he was doing. Like anyone with talent, he made his art look easy.

"If it's not intrusive of me, may I ask what you do at this address in Dahlem?"

"I'm a computer systems analyst and designer. For a company called Laser Solutions, Incorporated. It's an international venture: British, American, German, Japanese."

"How very interesting! You must have a rather good education."

"Rather good. American."

"What I do is a great deal simpler," he said, glancing away from the street ahead and smiling at her. "I sell a line of sportswear called Sportivi. Travel about Europe. Sell to the big chains mostly, though also to the smaller shops. Not very intriguing work, I'm afraid."

"You have the Oxonian accent."

"Legitimately so. I took a degree at Oxford, yes. But . . . only in English literature. Nothing so futuristic as computers. Indeed, I'm afraid I'm almost computer illiterate."

Debora Benson turned and fixed a dubious eye on this young man (for she judged him younger than herself). "Actually," she said, "I'd like to know someone who is, first, intelligent and, second, *really* computer illiterate. You will never believe how tiresome logic becomes."

He looked at her for a moment, with an eye as dubious as her own. He saw in her face an idiosyncratic innocence, maybe an entreaty for sympathy. She was a handsome young woman, but he doubted she knew it. Her face was bland but pleasant. He decided he liked her.

"Uh . . . you see, Mr. Ormsley—"

"Please. Michael."

She nodded. "Then Debora."

"Good, Debora. You were saying?"

"Sometimes cold logic is just overpowering. Sometimes you wish a computer could scream. Does that make any sense?"

"A great deal of sense."

"Sometimes the damned thing is like a corpse that's come to life and can think but can't feel. There's so much that computers can't do, you know. People talk about computers being like humans. Ha! They're *not* like humans. And . . . well, actually, sometimes that's an advantage, I guess. They can't hurt you. They can disappoint you, but—"

"Like driving a racing car," he said.

"Yes. Yes, that's a very good analogy. If your car fails you, it's not because it wanted to. A machine's not spiteful."

"Debora . . . what time do you leave your laboratory? I will pick you up and drive you home."

"Not necessary. There are people at the lab who can—"

"I have another motive. I'd be grateful if you'd let me take you to dinner on the way home."

Russ did not sleep with Mriya. He hadn't wanted to. He had poured scotch for her instead, until she began to yawn, slur her words, and finally doze off. He put her to bed and slept on the sofa. In the morning, when she awoke to the smell of coffee and of bacon and eggs frying in the kitchen, she was initially uncertain if they had slept together or not.

What was more, she was not going to ask.

The birds were at it again, whirling over Joachimstrasse outside his windows, squawking. A dismal early-spring rain did not discourage them. Mriya ambled into the kitchen. Last night she had made herself comfortable by taking off her skirt and stiff, heavy sweater; this morning she was wearing what she had been wearing when he led her into the bedroom and gave her a gentle shove toward the bed: a white half-slip and a sturdy brassiere.

She sat down at his kitchen table. Without a word he poured a cup of coffee and pushed it in front of her.

"Thanks, Russell Georgievich," she said sarcastically, in Russian.

"For . . . ?"

"You put me to bed. I wasn't sure at first, but now I've decided you didn't join me. Thank god Nikolai Pavlovich doesn't find me so drab."

"I don't find you drab, Mriya Aronovna. I find you an adversary."

"A gallant adversary could have endured a fucking," she said bitterly.

"Right now, then," he said. "You're sober and know what we're doing. Right now, Mriya."

She focused her eyes for a moment on the wheeling birds outside his kitchen window. "Oh, you are safe, Russell Georgievich," she muttered. "As you well know."

"It's one of two ways," he said. "You tried to hedge once— or I thought you did. No longer possible, Mriya. Either you are a fisherman or a shark."

"Sharks rise to bait," she said.

"What bait should the fisherman dangle?"

Her eyes narrowed as she stared at him across the cup of steaming coffee that she held just under her nose. "The boat," she said. "The beachfront villa."

"They come at a high price."

"So does the shark."

Erich Voss had aged badly. At sixty-seven, he should not have been in such bad shape. Tobin wondered if in another seventeen years he, too, would have watery eyes and lips that fluttered.

But the man's mind was as sharp as ever. And that was very sharp, indeed. He was one of the few people Tobin had ever seen outwit André Guyard. He had done it in a very simple way, just by paying a handsome bribe to the military attaché at the Spanish Embassy in Paris. Guyard had been working for weeks on an elaborate scheme to involve the attaché in a homosexual liaison. He meant to get from him some information about weapons Franco planned to buy. He tried to blackmail the man, but Voss had bought the information ten days before. The West German government had already acted on it. Guyard's intelligence was too late.

"I am going to hand you an envelope with a photograph in it," said Voss.

They were in a small brick-cellar restaurant on the Kurfürstendamm or Ku-damm, as Berliners called it. The place was crowded, almost exclusively with men. The air was dense with tobacco smoke and the smell of wet raincoats. Voss was drinking beer. Tobin had a scotch on the rocks.

"Who is she?" Tobin asked after he had examined the photograph.

"You don't know? That surprises me. Kristin Kuniczak. You've heard of her, likely."

"I have heard of her."

"Your source at Zagorsk gave you six names. You gave those names to me—the names of students who graduated from Zagorsk within the ten days after Colonel Kedrov's visit. I ran those names through several data banks. The only match we found was a report that a narcotics officer spotted her in the Frankfurt airport about three weeks ago. Since we've abandoned virtually all immigration control in the new Europe, we have little idea who enters the country, but—"

"She wouldn't have been carrying a passport in her own name, anyway," said Tobin.

"Maybe. Well, we do watch out for drug traffickers. Since her flight was from Rome, she could have picked up something in the south of Italy, so our narcotics people took a close look at her as she recovered her luggage and so on. One of the men was sharp enough to think he remembered her face from somewhere. Not only that, he was dutiful enough to follow up."

"Lucky," said Tobin.

"You know, we have our files computer-crossindexed a thousand ways. You can look for people by personal appearance—female, thirtyish, small, slight, dark-brown hair . . . you can search by the source of our interest—drug traffic, common criminal, espionage, victim . . . and since our man had worked only in Frankfurt for the past ten years, whatever might have caused him to think he remembered her had to have happened in Frankfurt. The computer search tagged a dozen dossiers. They were faxed to Frankfurt. The agent looked at the dozen dossiers and the photographs in them, and he identified her. Kristin Kuniczak."

"Why was there a dossier?"

"One of those stupid things that can foul up the finest of agents. Coming through Frankfurt in 1986, she was carrying in her handbag some suspicious-looking tablets. Our customs agent called over a narcotics agent, and he took her into custody. She had a prescription, it turned out, for three-milligram reserpine tablets. Reserpine is a potent tranquilizer. The prescription had been written by a Warsaw physician. The narcotics agents accepted it as valid. But while she was being held, Customs and Narcotics searched her luggage thoroughly. They found a second passport in a different name. That brought her under the jurisdiction of the BND."

"What were the names on these passports?"

"Kristin Kuniczak on the one she was using. Kristin Sempinski on the other. They took her from the airport, downtown to the Frankfurt office. She said she was recently married and the extra passport was just her old one, in her maiden name. Our agents called the Polish consulate, the consulate called Warsaw, and in a couple of hours Warsaw called back and confirmed her story. At that time the name Kristin Kuniczak meant nothing to us, so we released her. But we established a dossier with her photo and fingerprints. I doubt she ever told her control that she had been photographed and fingerprinted."

"One suspects the tranquilizer was not for her," said Tobin.

"No. The stuff has a lot of uses. And of course the then Polish government was all too ready to back any cover story she offered," said Voss.

"As I recall, she is what we Americans call a hitter."

"No," said Voss. "She is not sent out to kill. She is not given a target and assigned to murder that person. We think she killed Friedrich Valentin, though. You remember the Valentin case? Valentin was not smart."

"Shot him in the back," said Tobin.

"Somebody did. In Hamburg, in 1987."

"The Colin Gray deal—"

"More likely. The story is that she was pregnant by Colin Gray, too. MI6 would like to be sure she's the one who shot him. If they were, I think they'd track her down and nullify her."

"A nice young lady. Gray took his bullet in the back of the neck, as I recall."

"Professional," said Voss. He lifted his tankard and drank beer. "Very neat."

"A stone killer."

Voss nodded. "We don't know for sure that Kristin Kuniczak killed either of those men. We do know, for sure, that she was the dark-haired charmer behind the suicide of Gerhard Weyrich."

Tobin glanced at the photograph one more time. The young woman in the mug shot was no great beauty. Yet even in this kind of photo, she exhibited an evocative charm. If she had been afraid when this picture was taken—and she had good reason to be terrified—she had concealed it. His impression was of a skillful adversary.

"Have you circulated this picture in Berlin?"

Voss nodded. "Every police officer has seen it." He shrugged. "Of course, they see a hundred each week. It is difficult to put much stress on the matter when all we know is that she passed through Frankfurt Airport some weeks ago."

"The connection between this young woman and Colonel Kedrov is more than tentative," said Tobin.

Erich Voss bumped his beer stein down on the heavy oak table. "If we were to locate this one, we would be under no obligation to play diplomacy. If we find her, I'll subject her to rigorous questioning."

"Change the subject," said Tobin. "What obligation do you feel about Mriya Meyerhold?"

"My government would like to hang a gold medal around her neck—then choke her with the ribbon."

Tobin chuckled. "She got you Reuss. But it may not have been as great a favor as we thought it was. She's talking about defecting. How could we encourage her?"

"What good would it do us?"

"It would be the end of Colonel Nikolai Pavlovich Kedrov. He can't have his *dacha* because he would want to take a Jewish woman there with him. What if she then defected? I mean, what if she came over with a big public confession?"

"Do you want to do this to Kedrov? I supposed he was one of the better types."

"He is. But he's loyal to the Motherland. He's an enemy, Erich. Let's not lose sight of that. He is one of the better types. I respect him. I think he has a certain sense of... propriety. Honor. But he'd kill you or me in a moment, for any number of reasons."

"He's in Moscow."

"I know. When will he be back?"

"He bought a return ticket when he left Berlin. He won't be back until Saturday."

"You have any reason to take her in and sweat her?"

Voss smiled. "I can find one."

"Twenty-four hours. Rough. Then let her go before he comes back. Ten to one she won't tell him."

"What good will this do us?"

"I don't want her to think she's safe, invulnerable. If she defects—I mean one hundred percent and for sure—"

"You want to be her savior?"

"Why not? Thanks for the idea."

"You put a good deal of emphasis on this, Russ. Are you going to tell me why?"

"I'm sorry. Let's order something to eat, and I'll fill you in on every last detail."

Voss grinned. "Only what I need to know," he said. "Which is of course all you'll give me."

Tobin put his hand down firmly on Voss's. "All I'll give you. All you'd give me. Mutual respect."

Voss lifted his chin high. "Did you ever think you could give mutual respect to Kedrov?" he asked.

Tobin pondered that question for a moment. "In the right circumstances... but not the same way. Yes, Erich. If it matched. But only as much respect as he would give me. A touchy question. What kind of respect do you give a man you know would kill you if he saw reason?"

"Do you trust his reasoning?" Voss asked.

Tobin nodded. "Yes. I trust him to reach a rational conclusion about killing me. I trust he wouldn't do it irrationally. And he understands the same of me... don't you think?"

"Honor... we talk about it."

The wipers labored across the windscreen as Michael Ormsley steered his Jaguar out of the parking lot beside the LSI lab building in Dahlem.

"I hope you made a great breakthrough in computer science today," he said, "because I sold nothing. Our clothes are high quality but not cheap. The stuff from Spain *looks* like ours... Actually, it looks like ours for about a month, then—well, I'm sorry. What right have I to impose this on you? Will you redeem an unendurable day by allowing me to take you to dinner? The thought of dining alone simply appalls me. Please, Debora. I should be grateful."

She had decided during the day that she would not go to dinner with him tonight. She would accept an invitation for dinner another night, a few nights hence. To go tonight would imply ... well, what? That she was lonely? That she was eager? Or that she was easy? Experience had taught her that she should strike a careful balance between too quick and too slow. She had suffered hurt both ways.

Yet... the heavy atmosphere. The dispiriting rain that had turned from drizzle to downpour during the day. The powerful appeal he made. The prospect of an evening alone, even if she had planned to listen to a broadcast of the Berlin Philharmonic, while eating a dinner of salmon steak and pea pods . . . The prospect of an evening with this alluring young Britisher . . . What could happen?

"How can I refuse such an appeal?"

"I had hoped you couldn't."

"That's honest."

"Debora . . . I do mean to be honest."

Mriya Meyerhold knew her life was over. Whatever happened, whatever the meaning of what was happening, it was over. In all her years, through insane assignments, through struggle to achieve the impossible, more than once, and through gleaming success and dark failure, she had never been arrested. Now, in an unmarked van, with her hands locked behind her back, she was a prisoner for the first time in her life.

She had been trained for this eventuality, so she was saying nothing, asking nothing. She had not asked why she was seized, why she had to be handcuffed this way, where they were taking her, for what reason, for how long, or on whose authority. The arresting officers, a man and a woman, had stopped her on the Ku-damm half a block away from the Aeroflot office; apart from showing her their indentification and ordering her into the van, they hadn't said anything either.

They drove toward the Spandau district. She wondered if they were not taking her to the old Spandau prison; but they were not; they took her instead to a very new prison in Siemensstadt, a group of connected single-story brick buildings inside a fence topped with razor wire.

Everything was quite correct. They took her passport and put it in an envelope. They told her to count her money, write the amount on another envelope, then seal it inside. They took her fingerprints and photographed her. Two women ordered her to strip, and they performed a humiliating body-cavity search. They handed her a pair of short-sleeved orange coveralls, and when she was dressed in those they led her barefoot through several corridors and finally along a row of cells. Still without a word to suggest why she was here, they locked her in a cell numbered 17.

It was a simple, bare cell, clean and brightly lit, with steel walls painted light green. It was about three meters wide and five deep—ample room for the cot, a toilet and basin, a little wooden table, and a straight wooden chair. A window at the rear of the cell was blocked inside the glass by a thick steel mesh, outside by steel bars. Through it she could see the rain falling on a plot of green lawn between this building and the next. She could see sheets of wind-driven water falling through the harsh lights that glared on the prison compound. Through a barred square window in the steel door she could see nothing but the wall on the opposite side of the corridor. On the table lay four books, all in German: a Bible, a history of Europe in the eighteenth century, a biography of Konrad Adenauer, and what appeared to be a novel about American cowboys.

Mriya sat down on the cot. If any strength remained within her, she had to gather it for the rigorous interrogation she was sure she would face within the next few hours.

No one came. She lifted her feet and lay on her back on the cot, staring upward. The ceiling of the cell was a tight steel mesh. The lights were mounted above the mesh, out of reach of the prisoners.

She did not see the television camera focused on her.

She wanted a cigarette. No. She *needed* a cigarette. She realized abruptly, with tightening dread, that she would be without cigarettes for . . . for how long?

Mriya broke into a sweat.

Her mother had kept a family album. She kept it hidden in a box, not just under the bed, but beneath the floor under the bed. To take it out, she had to move the bed and lift loose floorboards. But she did take it out from time to time and show the old photographs to her sons and daughter, lest they forget who they were.

Her mother had been especially proud of a cracked old picture of her own grandfather, Mriya's great-grandfather. The photo was of an aged, patriarch with a white beard but dark mustache, high cheekbones and hollow cheeks, and old, wise eyes filled, as Mriya read them, with a rare mixture of contented faith and cynical skepticism. Over his head and around his shoulders he wore a striped prayer shawl. On his forehead he wore a *shel rosh*, a black leather cube containing bits of inscribed parchment: "Hear, O Israel, the Lord our God is one Lord . . ." He sat at a scarred wooden table: a poor man, obviously, but a proud man.

Another photograph was of two uncles of her mother. Wearing boots, they stood in mud and melting snow before a building her mother said was a synagogue. Each also wore a *shtreimel*, flat fur hat, and the black caftan and a prayer shawl. Mriya remembered reading in the faces of those two men a wariness that could come only of fear and fear that had come only of experience.

These pictures were evidence of life before the Revolution. By the time Mriya was born, hardly anyone dared wear anything that suggested religion. She had been reared in a home in which faith and tradition were kept sagaciously hidden.

Hiding made little difference, though. She had been called bad names. She had been treated badly: as an alien, as a person not to be trusted. Only her outstanding performance in the schools she attended, plus frenetic activity in Komsomol, had enabled her to break through centuries-old barriers the Revolution of the Proletariat had not only failed to abolish but had in many ways hardened. The KGB had accepted her for training chiefly because she was a linguist, but they had demanded her unqualified assurance she was a committed atheist. Someone in the KGB had erred, she suspected, but by the time the error was found she had learned too much to be expelled. Even so, if she had not fallen under the protection of Nikolai Pavlovich, she might either have been discharged or made a file clerk.

She needed a cigarette. *Needed* it! She lurched to the door and pressed her face between the window bars, as far as she could, to find out if she could see anyone. She saw no one. She was afraid to yell.

* * *

Mahmud Nedim did not know how to drive a car. Anne-Lise did, and tonight she was driving a BMW she said belonged to Deutsche Handelsbank. Tomorrow morning early she was to go to Leipzig to translate at a conference, and they had assigned her a car so she could meet the appointment. She would drive! Drive an automobile! Anne-Lise was one of those young women the Westerners called liberated, who knew everything, could do everything.

Liberated. Free. Free of all inhibitions, certainly. Free of reverence. Frivolous. Flippant. In fact, she resented any restriction on her whims.

That troubled him. Life was, after all, hedged about with restrictions and limitations. Rational curbs on his will and wishes separated man from the beasts. God's laws, man's laws; it made no difference; man lived with laws. He himself had lived with them always; and until he met Anne-Lise Hein, he had been proud and glad that he did. But she laughed at the laws and laughed at him, and he was growing painfully apprehensive.

It was as the Prophet said. Ecstasy came at a price.

"You have brought it?" she asked as they drove away from the LSI laboratories in Dahlem, after she had kissed him fervently before he had even pulled shut the door of the car.

"Yes."

"I am interest."

He did not understand her interest. She had explained last night—explained and explained and explained—and still he did not understand.

"Lifes together," she had said. "All shared. Nothing hiding. No secrets."

Then this morning she had said something startling. "What if we going to have child? Is maybe."

"Anne-Lise . . . " he had whispered. "Is this possible?"

"Possible! You know it is possible. So . . . lifes together. Hmm?"

Could it be true so soon? If it were true, he could never go home. His father would spit on him and on her. If it were true, he had to learn to live this new kind of life and much of what she said defined it.

Share "lifes." He had thought about it all day. A child—he could hope, a son—with this European gamine. Never to be recognized by his family. Could he live her way, the Western way?

It *was* better! They were *happier*, Europeans. They had thrown away everything and created a new kind of life dedicated to satisfying their appetites. That was how they lived. They cared nothing about God, nothing about God's plan and law, nothing about tradition—

Tradition. They created it as they went along. If God didn't like it, they banished Him and made for themselves a new god. And still they prospered in defiance of law, tradition, morals. They defied old rules, made new ones, then defied those, too.

So he had done what she urged him to do. Leaving the laboratory this evening, he had folded into the pockets of his raincoat some engineering drawings and schematics of the e-beam device. Enough so he could explain it to her.

Lifes. All shared.

No matter that he had sworn not to take anything from the lab. No matter that his contract said he wouldn't. No matter that the company and all his colleagues depended on him not to do it.

Lifes. Shared.

Innocent curiosity. She wanted to know how he spent his days. She knew little of the concepts behind electron-beam lithography. What harm could it do to show her in general terms how the thing worked? She wouldn't understand. But she would know that he was sufficiently devoted to her to break every rule. That was what was important.

She couldn't be pregnant already. Could she? Was it possible? If she was missing a period. He had—

"We eat at home?" she asked. "With the car so handy, maybe—"

He did not know Berlin as well as she did. She drove to a restaurant near the Gatow airport, where their table overlooked the Wannsee. They drank Rhine wine and ate noodles in cream sauce, a dish for which she had a name that he did not remember.

"Not to eat heavy," she said playfully. "We going to do hard work in bed. No?"

Yes. The suggestion of it aroused him.

When they left the restaurant, the rain had stopped at last. She drove home, going a little faster than he would have liked; and they ran up the steps to his flat like two children.

"Bed first, bed," she whispered breathlessly. "Then you tell me about the machine. I interest."

An hour later he spread the drawings and schematics on his coffee table and tried to explain to her the general principles of electron-beam lithography. He was surprised at her quickness in grasping the concepts and the perspicacity of her questions.

Later still they returned to bed. He lay his hand flat on her belly and asked her if she actually thought she was pregnant.

"Is maybe," she said with a warm smile. "Not sure. We hope, no?"

"Does it bother you," he asked, "that we are of different races?"

She smiled. "What is races? I hardly notice difference. I love you brown skin. Is very pretty, Mahmud. Child would be mix of us, lighter as you, darker as me. Beautiful."

At three he woke and squinted at the clock. She was not beside him.

He had wondered if it would happen, if he would waken some night and find Anne-Lise gone. They had drunk brandy—he'd had a great deal—before they went to sleep. If she wanted to leave, he was not likely to waken.

But—the living room was bright. The lights were on there. Confused and still half asleep, Mahmud rolled out of bed and walked, naked and stumbling, to the door.

She was naked, too. She had not bothered to cover herself. The drawings of the e-beam machine were spread on the table again, and she was photographing them.

"*Anne-Lise!*"

She spun around, her eyes flaring with a fury he could not believe.

"Anne-Lise, what are you doing? This is—"

Her face softened. "Is tomorrow you take back to lab," she said. The effort she needed to control her voice was obvious. "Then I get never a chance again to learn more of this. I interest, but I ignorant. You want me ignorant of your work, my love?"

"But Anne-Lise, to photograph those documents is . . . it is a *crime!* It—you must not do it!"

Gradually she regained her aplomb. "Well . . . this is wrong? I must not? I have done wrong?"

"Anne-Lise . . ."

She smiled. "If so—" She opened the camera, jerked out the film cartridge, and pulled the film out of it, into the bright light. "You see? I not want to do wrong."

He stood open-mouthed, unbelieving. The film cartridge dangled on the end of the strip of film, swinging back and forth. It swung back and forth across the exquisite body of this extraordinary young European he had learned to love. She grinned at him playfully. Obviously the film meant nothing to her. All she wanted was to learn more about his work.

"Anne-Lise. I'm sorry."

She shrugged and turned down the corners of her mouth. "You feel very wrong you have taken these papers from the laboratory," she said.

"Yes. Tomorrow I will confess it. I will say why. They will understand that you are innocently curious."

She frowned. "You tell them?"

"Then our consciences will be clear, Anne-Lise. They will make their inquiries, but it won't make any difference. They will understand. My company employs many people who . . . who are, as you might say, eccentric. They will understand, and you will become, in a real sense, a part of the company family. When we say we are going to marry and have a child—"

She smiled. "Of course," she said happily. "That will explain. They will understand I only want to know what my lover, my husband, the father of my child, does all day every day. What kind of people would not understand? They will understand."

Mahmud nodded emphatically. "I am sure they will. Maybe not at first. They will make their inquiries. And they will learn that my beautiful girl is as loyal to my company as she is to me."

Anne-Lise glanced down at the documents still exposed on the coffee table. "They miss these?" she asked. "They might discover missing, yet tonight? Send police?"

He shook his head. "No. I will take them back in the morning."

"No, Mahmud! We take them back now!"

"Not now, Anne-Lise. It is—"

"Now! I feel like they catch fire, burn down building. Burn lifes. No. I cannot sleep with them here. I sorry I beg you to show me! We take them back now! Now, Mahmud! Is open all night, your laboratory. I know is. Back now!"

"Anne-Lise . . ."

"Please!" she whispered tearfully.

Ten minutes later they left his flat. The night now was cold and dry. She drove across Berlin, grim and purposeful, and he tried to assure her they had done nothing terribly wrong, that the security department would understand. She nodded, but he could see he had not convinced her. She breathed through her mouth, and her lips remained parted.

He was fully dressed: suit, shirt, tie. She had pulled on her raincoat over nothing much. He wasn't sure. Maybe she was naked under it.

Suddenly she gagged, as if she were going to vomit. Could it be . . . ? No, not so soon, not from pregnancy.

"Darling . . ."

She turned right and drove into the Grunewald, the wooded park that dominated the southwest quarter of Berlin. She gagged again.

She pulled the car to the edge of a road and stopped.

"Mahmud—some fresh air. Mahmud . . ."

She opened the door, got out, and walked across rain-squishy grass toward a grove of trees. He followed her, conscious that his shoes were sinking into the mud. He felt the water inside them.

"Don't look!" she grunted as she bent over.

He turned away.

He did not feel what happened. If she was capable of kindness, she was kind toward him. Her aim was sure. The first .25–caliber bullet from her pocket Beretta hit him where his spine joined his skull. He was instantly dead—unconscious anyway, and unfeeling. When he lay on the ground, she put the pistol to his ear and fired again.

A little pistol like that didn't need sound suppression. The two shots had made only two dull pops.

The drawings and schematics lay on the back seat in the car. She took them from there and locked them in the trunk. She drove out of the Grunewald and west toward Potsdam and Brandenburg. Her drop was north, at Rathenow.

9

DEBORA BENSON'S EYES filled with tears. Her face was flushed. She choked on her words.

"Who . . . ? Who, for God's sake? Such an innocent!"

"Not so innocent, I'm afraid, Miss Benson," said the man who had introduced himself to her as Russell Tobin. "Some highly confidential documents are missing from the files of the e-beam lab."

He had introduced himself by name only, without a suggestion of his interest in the murder of poor Mahmud. He spoke with an American accent. CIA? Very likely.

The other man . . . Voss. BND. *Bundesnachtrichtendienst*. The German intelligence agency.

What a pair. The German was an old man, yet obviously very much in control of himself and what he was doing. The American exhibited complete self-assurance, a mastery of the world around him. He was handsome, perhaps fifty years of age. He was artificially affable. He was the kind of American she could not abide.

"We haven't the slightest thought, Miss Benson," said Tobin, "that you have anything to do with the murder of Mahmud Nedim. We understand you were a friend of his. We know he has been seeing a young woman. We'd appreciate it if you would look at some photos and tell us if you have ever seen any of these young women before."

Debora Benson glanced at Max Wenzel, the director of the

laboratory. They were meeting in his office. Wenzel had summoned her there. The director nodded at her. His nod was meant for assurance. She was in no trouble, he was saying.

Voss handed her a manila envelope. She opened it and pulled out half a dozen photographs.

"This one," she said after a moment. "This is the one Mahmud was seeing. I think he had decided he was in love with her."

"Who is she, do you know?" asked Tobin.

"A language expert. A translator for Deutsche Handelsbank. She translates Russian and I think Polish into German. Her English is not very good."

"What is her name?"

"Anne-Lise Hein. Has anyone notified her—oh, my God! Do you think she . . . ?"

"We don't know, Debora," said Max Wenzel. "It is just one possibility."

She stared at the mug shot. Apparently Anne-Lise Hein had been arrested somewhere, sometime. Even in this grim official picture you could see the vivacious little chippy who had so stricken Mahmud. Seductive eyes. Defiant half-smile. And poor Mahmud had doted on her.

Max Wenzel spoke. "Some engineering drawings and some schematic diagrams relating to electron-beam lithography are missing from Mahmud's files. We have to assume he took them. There is no other rational explanation."

Debora Benson stiffened. "I have never known anyone as honest."

"And maybe you've never known anyone as seductive as Anne-Lise Hein," said Tobin.

"Mr. Tobin, that's offensive."

"Not meant so, Miss Benson."

"Because he was an innocent young boy—"

"Not so damned innocent and not so damned lost, if he lifted confidential data worth tens—no, hundreds—of millions of dollars from company files. Let's just be realistic."

"He's *dead*, Mr. Tobin. How many millions is that worth?"

"I'm sorry, Miss Benson. When he left the lab last evening, he must have been carrying the secret documents. Someone killed him before he could come back. What are we supposed to think?"

"That a very fine, honest young man is dead," she said, shaking her head. "I don't know how and I don't know why. If I can help you find out, please call on me. Right now, I think I've probably told you all I know."

Two hours later Russ knocked on the door of Debora's office and then opened it.

"I'm very sorry we got off on such a negative start this morning," he said. "I accept responsibility for it."

She sat behind her desk in a spartan office, with an immense chart—to him unreadable—spread across the entire expanse of the desk. She had been marking entries on a diagram with a red pen.

"It doesn't matter, Mr. Tobin," she said. "Whether or not we like each other is beside the point."

Russ smiled. "I hope not. Will you call me Russ? May I call you Debora? We're two Americans in a foreign country. We're not tourists, either; we're doing our jobs. Our two jobs happen to have brought us together this morning. I didn't mean to make you dislike me."

She put her pen aside. "I don't dislike you. I only said that our circumstances do not require us to like each other. I might in fact come closer to liking you if you would tell me what you're doing here."

"CIA," he said. "Not a secret. It's been a long time since I was a secret agent."

She gestured toward a chair. "Please. Why was Mahmud killed?"

Russ sat down. "We don't know for sure. We have to assume it was for the papers that are missing from his office."

"Industrial espionage . . . "

"Yes."

"For a competitor?"

"More likely for the Soviet Union."

"Because they need the technology," she said.

"They need it desperately."

"Then if Anne-Lise Hein . . . "

Russ nodded. "KGB."

Debora sighed. "I thought we were beyond that kind of thing. I mean—"

"I know. You thought a man like me had become obsolete. I'm afraid that perfect world hasn't come along yet. I'm like a doctor. Discovery of the cure for one disease doesn't put me out of business."

"Don't try to read my mind. I don't think we've achieved a perfect world or that you've become obsolete. What I thought we might have progressed beyond is killing. Are you sure you haven't assumed Mahmud was murdered by the KGB because that's your old obsession?"

"It's possible. But do you have another idea? Mahmud Nedim is dead. The woman you identified is a KGB agent with a record of killing men by shooting them in the back of the neck."

"Is that how he died?"

"Instantly and painlessly," said Russ.

"He's just as dead."

"Exactly. Everyone who works here should understand you are working with something someone is willing to kill for."

"They got what they wanted."

"Maybe not all they wanted. In fact, Max Wenzel tells me Mahmud Nedim's documents did not include enough information to make it possible for someone else to build the machine. Nor is the e-beam machine the only top-secret project LSI has here. You yourself are working on massively parallel processing. They might want to know about that, too. What I want to say to you is: Be damned careful."

"I *am* damned careful."

"Good. Well . . . one more thing. I wonder if I could take you to dinner this evening? Or tomorrow evening?"

Debora could not conceal her surprise. For a moment she stared at him, her blue eyes communicating nothing. Then she shook her head. "I don't think so. I can't see any point in our seeing each other except strictly in the course of your investigation. We . . . have little or nothing in common. Frankly, we're not of the same generation. I'm not sure we share the same ideas. No. You are kind to ask. But no."

Russ smiled. "Plain enough," he said. "So . . . remember what I said about being careful."

An hour later Tobin sat in the office of the governor of the prison where Mriya Meyerhold was spending her seventeenth hour in a cell. He and Erich Voss and the governor watched her on a black-and-white television screen. They could hear her movements. She paced, sat down, got up and paced some more, sat down again, checked the corridor through the window in the door, paced, sat down, got up . . . Her bare feet made no sound on the concrete floor. They heard her cough once, nothing more.

"Nervous," said Voss.

"She was given breakfast this morning," said the governor of the prison. "Except in handing her her tray and later recovering it from her, no one has spoken to her."

"She's expecting interrogation," said Voss.

"She's quite agitated," said the governor. "Was all night, I'm told. Terrified, I suppose."

"Maybe," said Tobin. "I'm more inclined to think she's suffering nicotine withdrawal."

"You said twenty-four hours," said Voss.

"This is enough," said Tobin. "I'll talk to her alone if you don't mind. And, as you suggested, I'll be her savior."

They brought her into an interrogation room with a table, a chair for the prisoner, two chairs for the interrogators. After she had sat there alone for five minutes, Russ came in.

"Mriya Aronovna . . . "

"Russell Georgievich!"

"They told me you were here. Why? Do you know?"

She shook her head. "No one has spoken to me."

Orange coveralls had become standard international prison

garb. In hers, Mriya looked like a prisoner, subdued and help-less. She clasped her hands so tightly on the table that her knuckles were white.

"Why, Russell?" she whispered. "You know, don't you?"

He shook his head. "Did you ever hear the name Kristin Kuniczak?"

"No."

"How about the name Zagorsk?"

Her face hardened. "I know what it is."

"Kristin Kuniczak was trained at Zagorsk. Last night she murdered a man in Berlin. There is new excitement."

He did not tell her that Kristin Kuniczak had killed Mahmud Nedim hours after Mriya was locked in her cell here in Sie-mensstadt. She would probably find out sooner or later.

"If this Kuniczak woman killed someone . . . she did it without my knowledge . . . and without the knowledge of Nikolai Pav-lovich."

"Then with whose knowledge did she do it? She is twenty-eight years old. She is not running her own operation."

"Russell, I don't know!"

"Who runs her, Mriya?"

"I told you I never heard the name."

"You stick with that story, you may be in this place a long time."

Mriya looked away from him for a moment, then asked, "Did you bring any cigarettes?"

"No."

"Russell . . . I'll die without—"

"No you won't. Nobody ever did."

She looked stricken. This was not the first time Tobin had used cigarette denial as a minor torment. Anything an inter-rogator could withhold gave him an edge. Tobacco addicts be-came pathetic.

She closed her eyes. "I can't understand why I've been ar-rested."

"It's just a move in the game. You've been making moves. Now the BND has made one."

"If they think they can turn Nikolai Pavlovich by—"

"They're not stupid."

Mriya opened her eyes again. "What are they going to do to me?"

"Let you go."

"Why? When?"

"I have asked them to already. The governor of the prison is waiting for written authorization to release you in my custody."

"Your custody?"

He shrugged. "I have no intention of keeping you in custody."

She pushed back her chair and stood. She glanced around the square room. The walls were white. It was psychologically difficult—for some, impossible—to stare at white walls and not look at the interrogator.

"It's a cruel game, Russell Georgievich."

"It certainly is."

"No, I mean what you've done to me. I understand it now. You had me arrested, and you can free me. You wanted to frighten me. Fine. I was frightened."

"I can leave you here. I can let Nikolai Pavlovich come and get you out, when he flies back from Moscow."

"No."

"No. You don't want him to know you've been here."

She drew in her breath. "I won't talk to you here. There are microphones."

"We can talk over lunch. I'll take you to the Bristol-Kempinski."

"No. I will tell you why later."

The other patrons of the restaurant in Pankow glared resentfully at the woman in the Aeroflot uniform—also at the man with her, once they heard him speaking Russian to her. The Pankow district had been in the Soviet Zone, east of the Wall, and bitterness had not subsided. For forty years the people here had been forced to refer to the Russians as "our friends," and now they were not subtle in letting Russians know they were not friends.

Hostility was so heavy that Russ decided to do something

about it. When the waiter came to the table, he said to him, *"Ich bin Amerikaner. Bitte geben Sie mir ein Amerikanischer martini, mit viel Eis. Viel Eis, Sie verstehen. Und für meine Freundin, ein Glas Weisswein, bitte."*

Mriya sucked raptly on a cigarette. He had stopped in Siemensstadt, only a couple of blocks from the prison, to buy her two packs. The store did not carry the harsh Russian cigarettes she craved, so he had bought her unfiltered Camels instead.

As the waiter moved away from their table, she leaned closer to Russ and spoke to him quietly in Russian. "Have you ever heard of a man named Yuryev?" she asked. "Major Ivan Stepanovich Yuryev?"

Russ shook his head.

"Every agency has its internal police," she said. "You have yours. Yuryev is an internal spy."

Russ wondered why she was telling him this.

"He is in Berlin."

"Why?"

"Spying on somebody," she said. "Ready with a knife to shove into someone's back."

"Nikolai Pavlovich's."

She nodded. "Very likely."

"Are you suggesting someone do you a favor?"

"You might be doing yourself a favor, Russell Georgievich. You don't know Yuryev, but Yuryev knows you. He sat in the dining room at the Bristol-Kempinski the day you had lunch with Nikolai Pavlovich and me. He had a long look at you. I am sure he knew who you were. I am certain also that he reported our meeting to Vyshevskii. That is why we can't see each other at the Bristol-Kempinski anymore. Or at any other prominent place."

Ivan Stepanovich Yuryev...

Erich Voss shook his head. "I've never heard of him. I'll run a computer check."

"Suppose she's right—and telling the truth. That puts an interesting little twist on things, doesn't it?"

"Their most trusted man."

"No. He never was. Or hasn't been since he made the Mriya Meyerhold connection. With the resurgence of anti-Semitism in Russia, I'd guess he's in distinctly bad favor right now. The chairman, Vyshevskii, is from the old right-wing of the Party and is reputed to be violently anti-Semitic. She's afraid. She's told me. I believe this part of what she says."

"I think we had better apprise André Guyard of this," said Voss.

"I have no objection, but what do you have in mind?"

"Otto Reuss. We've wondered if Meyerhold betrayed him to us because the HVA and the KGB had decided to rid themselves of him and used her as a convenient tool—while making us believe she was genuinely turned. I'm thinking now that it's possible she fingered him for her own reasons, that maybe even Kedrov didn't know what she was doing. And maybe he doesn't know yet. Maybe she acted independently."

"Why?"

"Reuss was a vicious Jew-baiter. There were never more than one or two Jews in the HVA, but Reuss made it his business to destroy them."

"Guyard?"

"Guyard is a Jew," said Voss. "Didn't you know?"

"And Guyard—"

"When Reuss died, we were trying to work out ways to use him as a conduit for disinformation. We were furious, you remember, when Guyard killed him. We accused the French of non-cooperation. Maybe Guyard operated more independently than we guessed. Maybe he operated independently of his own government."

"Not impossible," said Russ.

"If Mriya Meyerhold is afraid, then maybe Guyard has reason to be afraid. And it could be, too, that Guyard will move on this Yuryev the way he did on Reuss. What do we have to lose?"

"What do we have to gain?"

"At the very least," said Voss, "we will spread confusion among people we would like to have confused."

"A good enough motive."

Olga Chernov poured scalding tea into a glass. They were in her office at the Institute, and she shoved some papers aside to make room for the tea. Kedrov glanced at her blackboard. Once again she had been scribbling, diagraming, covering the board with scrawls that were indecipherable to him. Her clothes were dusty with chalk.

"I have had enough time to give these documents only the most cursory examination, Colonel Kedrov," she said.

The engineering drawings and schematic diagrams Mahmud Nedim had taken from the LSI laboratory in Dahlem had reached Moscow in mid-afternoon, in the map cases carried by an Aeroflot captain and his first officer. Kedrov had ordered them delivered immediately to the Institute and personally to Olga Alexandrovna Chernov. Now, in early evening, he had driven to the Institute to hear her preliminary evaluation.

"I hope they are worth what they cost us," he said.

"At first glance they appear invaluable."

"I hope so," he said. "They came to us at a high price."

"I understand the technician was killed."

"That is not the high price I was thinking of, Olga Alexandrovna. The death of the Pakistani technician may have compromised all the rest of our enterprise, may have made our other goals far more difficult to reach."

"That would be a high price," she said. "This information appears to be excellent, but it is of course only the beginning of what we need. Is the matter of the technician really so important?"

"If their security was tight before, think how tight it must be now. What is worse, people who were inclined to be careless, as the Pakistani obviously was, are now frightened and careful."

"Why did your agent kill the man?"

"I don't know. I haven't talked to her."

Olga Chernov slapped the little pile of drawings and diagrams.

"This information may save us months of experimentation. But at the end of those months we will still be a year behind the West in the development of this machine. We need more."

"It's going to be difficult."

"Also, I understand you are making some progress toward acquiring information about massively parallel processing. Please regard that as even more important."

"The agent assigned to that is working much more subtly. Of necessity. His target is far more clever than was the Pakistani."

"Let us hope the agent is far more clever than was the one who killed the Pakistani."

Leonid Ivanovich Vyshevskii, Chairman of the KGB, was five years younger than Colonel Kedrov. His office was modern, in a modern building, wholly unlike the offices in the Kremlin that smelled of decades-accumulated dust and of the oil used on the old wood floors. He faced Kedrov across an immense desk bare except for a pen-and-pencil set, a small brass clock, and a note pad. Kedrov knew what he was not supposed to know: that the Chairman's adjoining private office was as cluttered as any man's, that this uncluttered office was a little psychological ploy that did in fact intimidate some people who sat facing the desk. Maybe, Kedrov reflected, the Chairman needed a few little tricks to overwhelm visitors, since he was a decidedly unprepossessing man.

He had the head of a Siamese cat or, more unkindly, that of a boa constrictor: a strangely flat head awkwardly thrust forward from his shoulders, as if to stretch his intent blue eyes out closer to whatever he was looking at. And, like the head of an alert snake, his bobbed up and down slowly, as though constantly gauging the distance between him and his prey.

"There is an explanation, I suppose," he said.

"Not until I talk with her."

"What can she say? She killed the man."

"Can we be sure he wasn't about to—"

"Wasn't about to kill *her?* Come now, Nikolai Pavlovich!"

Chairman Vyshevskii opened a drawer and extracted a long,

thin, green-paper cigarette. He lit it with a butane lighter from the same drawer. Western manufacture, Kedrov observed. The Soviet Union could roll green cigarettes but could not manufacture and distribute an effective lighter.

"I can say nothing until I talk with her."

"Nikolai Pavlovich... who said the old world is gone and gone with it are the old techniques? Who said we had to learn new ways? Who, more than any other man, sponsored the new training center at Zagorsk? *And who, just now,*" the Chairman barked angrily, "*has sent out a Stalinist agent who seems to have learned her techniques from the likes of Lavrenti Beria?*"

"She has served effectively, Leonid Ivanovich," said Kedrov, using the first name and patronymic that few dared use in addressing the Chairman of the KGB. "She was to be trusted. She *is* to be trusted."

From the drawer from which he'd had taken his cigarette and the lighter, Vyshevskii now took a tiny ashtray that sat on a red velvet bag. He flicked ash with finicky precision. "Your protest would be more meaningful, Nikolai Pavlovich, if you had not enjoyed the body of your agent Kristin Kuniczak. You are a handsome man, my friend, and you have an unfortunate proclivity for establishing intimate relations with young women who are impressed with you. Once you have experienced their carnal charms, your judgment of them is imperfect. I wonder how you would judge Kristin Kuniczak if—"

"Being a good and effective officer does not require a man to be a monk," said Kedrov.

"A monk's judgment is focused where it should be: on his life's work. When a man's focus is on the place where a woman's legs come together, his judgment is questionable.

"What do you want of me, Leonid Ivanovich?"

"Nothing more than you pledged."

"I remember my oath."

"Good. Review it, Nikolai Pavlovich."

"What do you want me to do about Kristin Kuniczak? Be specific."

The Chairman crushed his half-smoked cigarette in the precious little ashtray. "Use good judgment, Nikolai Pavlovich. Do you deny that the murder of the Pakistani was a disaster for us?"

Kedrov shook his head. "When the bell rang, Pavlov's dogs salivated. Conditioning, Leonid Ivanovich. We conditioned them to react in a certain way. Reconditioning is not the world's easiest process. So I've got a bitch who still drools when the bell rings. She's a problem. I can't deny that she is a problem."

"Do I have to tell you your duty?" the Chairman asked indignantly. "Really, Nikolai Pavlovich, you ask too much. You know what you have to do. Do it."

Kedrov felt an unaccustomed tightening in his upper chest and in his throat as he walked out of the building and into the Moscow night.

Damn! Kristin Kuniczak... Vitality and spirit personified in one taut little body. The Chairman hated her.

On the other hand... what if Steiner had botched his assignment as badly as Kristin had botched hers? What if Steiner had damaged this whole mission?

What if Steiner had provoked the Chairman's anger? How would he, Kedrov, have reacted to that?

Damn her! She'd endangered all their lives! His, Mriya's, Steiner's...

Well—he had his orders.

Tobin returned to his flat early, intending to eat a light meal from his own kitchen. He found a wire from the States:

WILL ARRIVE TEMPELHOF TOMORROW AFTERNOON AT 11:40 BERLIN TIME BRITISH AIRWAYS FLIGHT 602 IF INCONVENIENT I WILL ENTIRELY UNDERSTAND PROFESSIONAL VISIT TO BERLIN CAN BE SOCIAL ALSO IF YOU HAVE TIME WILL BE AT SCHWEIZER HOF IF NOT WITH YOU

AUDREY

"Michael . . . I'm afraid I won't be much company. This has been a wretched day."

The dent on the fender of her MG had been repaired, and Michael Ormsely had come by the LSI labs to pick up Debora Benson and drive her to the garage in Spandau. He was suggesting now that they have dinner together.

"If you've had so wretched a day, p'raps it's the very best evening for me to take you to dinner. I should like to prove helpful."

"You have, Michael. About the car. I have no right to impose on you."

"*Impose?* I'm asking for the pleasure of your company."

Didn't having dinner with him two successive evenings imply something? A quick-blooming affinity? Debora wasn't sure she wanted anything like that. Still . . . Michael was maybe the most pleasant man she'd ever known. His talk was salted with wit. He laughed easily and genuinely at her little jokes. He was undemanding. He asked no personal questions. His conversation was wide-ranging, about all kinds of things; and if some of his opinions were not well thought through, they were not offensive or rigidly held. When she had said to him, for example, that he was wrong in supposing John F. Kennedy had been one of the best presidents the United States had ever had, he had just shrugged and said she would of course know better than he.

He was a handsome man. She saw a strange contrast in him, though. Nothing flawed his happy, innocent face. His eyes shone with untroubled optimism. He had not a scar, not a wrinkle, nothing to suggest he had known a single misadventure from the day of his birth. Still, he carried himself with a stiffness that suggested apprehension, as if he were constantly alert, tense, ready to react to some threat.

Sitting behind the wheel of his Jaguar, smiling at her as he offered her dinner a second evening, he was difficult to refuse. He was wearing his flat tweed cap—and a tweed jacket with leather patches on the elbows.

She wondered if he was attracted to her. In her experience, a man who approached her had forsaken hopes of enticing more alluring women. She was the best he could do. Too often men had been less than successful in concealing their lack of enthusiasm over her.

She could not say she saw enthusiasm in Michael. But somehow he made her feel enthusiasm was no essential of what he was suggesting and offering. He was not playing the old game. He seemed too open for that kind of thing, too forthright.

"It's important to be able to talk about troubles," he said earnestly.

"Michael, I . . . if I'm not imposing on you."

"Last thing in the world that should occur to me, Debora."

An hour later, driving her MG, which had been beautifully repaired, she followed the Jaguar to a restaurant on Unter den Linden. And maybe he had been a little less than ingenuous, since he had booked a table.

They sat side by side at a cozy banquette. Without asking what she wanted, he ordered *heisse Biersuppe*, hot beer soup, a dish she had heard about but had never tried.

"It is good to have a nourishing hot soup before these Germans begin pushing *schnapps* at us," he said.

"You know the country well, don't you, Michael?"

"I sell more merchandise here than I do in any other country. That means I spend more time here."

While they ate the soup, they talked about Berlin. They agreed it had become a dominant city: economically, politically, and culturally. Debora told him she was glad for the opportunity of living amidst it all.

Then they ordered drinks: he whiskey, she gin. When the glasses were on the table before them, he asked, "Wretched day, you said. Would you like to talk about it?"

She looked up into his steady blue eyes. "A man who works for our company was murdered last night," she said quietly.

Michael shook his head. "That's terrible. Why? Do you know?"

"He was a Pakistani. He was involved in highly confidential work. A young woman . . . she seduced him. When he left the office yesterday evening, he carried with him some secret documents. He was found dead in the Grunewald. The papers are missing."

"That's appalling!"

"The investigation involves not only the German police and the BND, but also the CIA."

"CIA, indeed? What in the world would the Americans have to do with it?"

"Our company is an international joint enterprise. Americans hold a large part of the stock. Americans are prominent in the management. And being the CIA, they assume everything has national security implications."

"I suppose our chaps would take the same attitude. MI6 would assume such an affair involved espionage."

"The CIA apparently thinks I might be the next target of some effort by the KGB to steal technology for the Soviet Union."

Michael smiled. "They *do* steal technology. My company manufactures a pneumatic running shoe. I suspect you've heard of it. You inject air and so adjust your shoe to your weight and the kind of running you do. Clever little device. A Moscow company now manufactures shoes with the same device as the Sportivi shoe. They stole the technology. A minor thing compared to what you do, but—good lord, Debora, you don't mean this murderer might target *you?*"

She shrugged. "All of us at LSI work on projects that may produce valuable software or hardware. Some of what we do may turn out to be immeasurably valuable—make-or-break innovations for entire industries."

"Worth stealing."

"Yes. Of course. And worth killing for, apparently."

"Then you must be damned careful, Debora."

"I'm involved in something called massively parallel processing."

"I don't want to know. I only want you to be careful."

She picked up her glass and sipped. "The CIA man asked me to have dinner with him tonight."

"Ah. A handsome American?"

"Uh . . . yes, I suppose he is handsome. Old enough to be my father."

"Well . . . what did you say to him?"

"I didn't say much. But he's everything I hate in a man. Far too self-confident, to start with. Too old. And, on top of that, a spook."

"Spook?"

"A spy. An intelligence officer for the government of the United States."

"Do you dislike all spooks?"

"Michael, if you tell me you're an agent of MI6, I think I'll vomit."

He put his hand on hers on the table. "Debora," he said solemnly, "I promise you I am not an agent of MI6."

"Thank God. I can't stand government agents and people who want to call me Debbie."

"I'm glad you warned me. And, Debora?"

"Yes?"

"I'm glad I damaged the wing of your MG. If I'd imagined it would result in our meeting, I'd have done it purposely."

10

AUDREY STRODE ALONG the corridor from the British Airways flight. Because her legs were so long, she walked faster than the other people hurrying toward the exit gate. Russ had spotted her far down the passageway and watched her as she came. She was unmistakable, even when she was still fifty yards away: the tall redhead with the long, confident stride, wearing a black cashmere turtleneck sweater and a short houndstooth-check wool skirt, proudly showing a lot of those lovely long legs in dark stockings. He smiled as he watched men slow down so they could walk behind her and stare at her legs and her hips.

Immigration and passport controls were perfunctory, though clearing an American passport took a moment longer than a European passport. He used that extra moment to admire his striking second wife. So did the immigration officer, who also saw fit to give her a cordial salute, probably because he had discovered she was *Frau Doktor* Audrey Tobin.

"Good of you, Russ," she said as she embraced him and gave him a warm kiss full on the mouth. "I hope I'm not imposing."

"You've arrived in the midst of a struggle to save the world, Audrey," he said, "but I'm happy to put that aside long enough to meet you and welcome you to my humble digs. What brings you to Berlin on short notice?"

"Dr. Heinrich Draeger is what brings me. Remember him? I studied under him when we were here together."

"I think I recall. You studied under Draeger, who studied

under Jung, who studied under Freud—which puts you on the genealogical chart of the profession."

He did not intend sarcasm, and she knew him well enough to know that. *"Herr Professor Doktor* Draeger is chairman of a conference on using psychopharmacology to break drug addiction. I have myself used this treatment on patients—I must say with indifferent success—and I hadn't intended to come to the conference. But one of the conference sessions is based on a panel discussion, and last Friday one of the panelists died. Professor Draeger was desperate for someone with experience in the field who can also speak German. So here I am."

"I'm glad. When does the conference start?"

"Monday. I'm supposed to have dinner with Professor Draeger and the panel members this evening. I meet with them again on Sunday afternoon. The conference itself begins with a Sunday evening dinner. Real work sessions start Monday."

"You can drive my car while you're here. I'll have the station assign me one from the motor pool."

"That's nice of you."

"Since you're having dinner with the professors, maybe we should have lunch."

"I'll make a point of getting away from tonight's dinner as early as possible," she said with a seductive smile.

Forty minutes after Russ and Audrey left Tempelhof, the Aeroflot flight returning Colonel Kedrov to Berlin arrived, a little late. Mriya met it.

As always, she found exhilaration in her first sight of him when they had been apart a little while. Nikolai was such a handsome man! He had such commanding presence! What was more, he loved her. And she loved him. That was more important than anything else. Every time she thought of that, she was moved to renew her commitment to what they shared and hazarded together.

On the other hand, they did not share everything. She had decided not to tell him she had been arrested and held overnight in prison. Nor would she tell him of her talk with Tobin.

She would say nothing more for now about fishing for sharks in the Caribbean. Maybe Nikolai had thought about that and would bring it up himself. She hoped so.

In the taxi she spoke Russian to Nikolai and asked him if he'd heard about the death of the Pakistani.

"Yes. Where is Kristin Kuniczak?"

"She made the drop at Rathenow. Did the papers reach you safely?"

"Yes. But where is she now?"

"I haven't seen or heard from her. No one I've talked to has, either."

"I want the word circulated to all our people. I want to see Kristin Kuniczak."

Mriya decided she was glad she wasn't Kristin Kuniczak. Only once or twice before had she heard this tone in Nikolai's voice.

"It was a piece of damned foolishness, wasn't it?"

Staring ahead, his face rigid, he nodded curtly, just once.

"Michael. . . . I just called to tell you I'm thinking about you."

"I am so pleased."

"Michael, I . . . I've thought about you all morning. Please accept my apology."

"For what, Debora? I can't think of a single thing you need apologize to me about."

"Michael. If when we are again together, you want to kiss me goodnight . . . I'll *welcome* it. I'm sorry to have been so awkward. I just—"

"Debora. I'll come by your flat and kiss you goodnight right now—even if it *is* noon—and be gone in one minute. Or I'll take you to dinner tonight. And if we kiss . . . it will be splendid. If we don't, I shall still think myself privileged to have been with you. Say we'll have dinner this evening."

Holding the telephone instrument in her right hand, Debora ran her tongue over her lips and imagined she was feeling his kiss. What a fool she had been!

"Are you sure you want to? I wasn't very—"

"You are *wonderful*, Debora! Please say you'll let me take

you out tonight. Do you enjoy cabaret? We'll go where there's a show!"

"Actually, I'd rather just be with you. I enjoy talking with you, Michael."

After his lunch with Audrey, Russ gave her the keys to his car and his flat. She knew Berlin well enough to find his address.

He went to his office briefly and arranged for a car. Then he went to BND headquarters to meet with Erich Voss and Max Wenzel.

When he entered Voss's office, he found that Wenzel was late. Voss was talking on the telephone, nodded to him, and handed him a file folder.

Inside was a report, in German. It read:

YURYEV, IVAN STEPANOVICH
   The subject is a major in the KGB. Very little is known about him. All information is secondhand, and most of it is based on rumor and speculation. No photograph is available. He is believed to be about 40 years old. He was originally assigned to the Second Chief Directorate—internal security—but has for some years worked directly for the administrative office of the Chairman. He is the subject of rumors, none confirmed, that he has personally eliminated at least half a dozen KGB defectors. He speaks only Russian with any fluency, though he is said to be able to understand and make himself understood in German and English. Because of his want of facility with languages, and also because he is indifferently educated, he rarely leaves the Soviet Union. It is believed that when he does travel, he is on assignment to kill a defector.

Not much information, if the man was important. Tobin wished he had noticed him, had paid him a little attention that day in the Bristol-Kempinski.

Voss ended his telephone call, and at almost the same moment Wenzel came in.

"Well, gentlemen," said Voss. "We have no idea of the whereabouts of Kristin Kuniczak. It is my guess that she has left the country. She was driving a car and could easily have driven across the Polish frontier hours before the body of Mahmud Nedim was found. By the time we notified authorities that we wanted her for murder, she could well have driven across the Soviet border. Or she could have abandoned the car and taken a flight or a train from Poznan."

"I suppose Deutsche Handelsbank never heard of her," said Wenzel.

"No, of course not. That was just her cover story, which Mahmud Nedim was too gullible to check."

"You are certain she is an agent of the KGB," said Wenzel.

"Absolutely," said Voss. "She was once with Polish Intelligence, but she has been with The Committee for several years. Recently she was retrained at Zagorsk."

"The retraining didn't have much effect, apparently," said Tobin. "She handled her assignment the same way they handled them under Brezhnev, the same way they handled them under Stalin."

"Certainly she wasn't very subtle," said Voss.

"The drawings and diagrams Nedim took from the laboratory were not the only copies," said Wenzel. "We know what he took, and we've evaluated. This theft is a disaster."

"Are you saying the Russians could now build an e-beam machine?" asked Tobin.

"No. But those drawings and diagrams reflect years of thought and labor. Experimentation. An immense investment in money."

"Still, you say they can't build a machine."

"Neither can we, in a practical sense. The machine remains experimental. We have many problems to solve before it becomes practical, economical."

"They'll try again," said Tobin.

"I don't think they'll penetrate us again."

"Yes, they will, sooner or later. I'm going to ask you to cooperate in something," said Tobin. "It will have to be done very ingeniously, and you will have to make an investment. But if you do what I ask, and do it successfully, we might even manage to make their theft worthless to them."

"You're thinking of feeding them false data," said Wenzel.

Tobin nodded. "What we call disinformation. We could send them off on the wrong track and cost them years of delay. But don't underestimate them. Unless the thing is very shrewdly done, they'll see it for what it is."

"I will put people to work on it."

"Look at your people very closely," said Voss. "Watch for departures from old habits. Look out for new friendships. Anyone who has a new friend, especially an intimate new friend, is to be observed."

"We will watch closely," said Wenzel.

Debora had decided she was happy—a feeling she did not often have, an acknowledgment she did not often make. Michael held her hand as they dodged their way through the jostling sidewalk crowd on the Kurfürstendamm. The street exhilarated her. The bright lights in the fine stores, the cars racing along the street, the big hotels, the attractive restaurants—even the looming *Denkmal*, the fire-blackened Kaiser Wilhelm Memorial Church, gladdened her.

They walked a little faster than most people, swinging their arms. He led her into the tallest building in Berlin and into an elevator that carried them to the top, where he had booked a table, where they sat side by side on a banquette on a riser, with a view of the Tiergarten, Berlin's great central park, the Brandenburg Gate, the restored Reichstag building, and all the northeast quarter of the city.

"Michael . . . this is too much! I insist on paying the check, at least half of it."

He grinned. "You are of course a buyer who might give me an order for a hundred thousand pounds worth of Sportivi sportswear. Don't worry about it."

"I don't want you to—"

"Debora. Don't think about it." He put a finger under her chin and tickled her gently. "Sobersides."

"Michael." She glanced around to see if anyone was watching them "Michael, kiss me the way you wanted to last night."

He leaned over and kissed her on the mouth. "The goodnight

kiss we didn't share last night," he said. "And think. The evening has just begun."

Colonel Nikolai Pavlovich Kedrov sat on the brown plush-covered sofa in the modest living room of a small stuccoed house in Köpenick. Mriya sat on the floor. She had just finished giving him oral sex, and both of them were meditative. She was naked. He was not.

For a full five minutes they sat without moving, without speaking. Then she broke the silence.

"It is foolish of us to suppose they won't kill us."

"The whole world has fallen apart."

"There is an English rhyme the children chant:

> Humpty-Dumpty sat on a wall.
> Humpty-Dumpty had a great fall.
> All the King's horses, and all the King's men
> Couldn't put Humpty together again.

"Which means?" he asked brusquely.

"Which means that the old world of certainties, when dictators ruled, when The Committee ruled the dictators, when— Nikolai, my dearest love, that world is gone. Gone forever. Nations will crackle under the radioactivity of atomic fires before we can put it together again. Humpty-Dumpty was an egg, Nikolai, and no one can put a broken egg together again. We have to live in the new world."

"You are talking again about defecting."

"I am talking about living."

Kedrov tossed his feet up on the couch and put his head back against the pillows. "My loyalty to the Motherland—"

"The Motherland is people," she interjected harshly. "Right now, for us, it is Vyshevskii and Andronikov—and Yuryev. That's what it is, Nikolai. It is not the black soil. It is not the vistas. It is not the mosaics of the Moscow underground. It is the men who live and control. I want to live, Nikolai, and I want to fish for sharks."

"I've thought about it," he said. "Fishing for sharks ... I do think about it. But—listen. I make a picture. Understand? I can see it in my mind. But I can't see myself in it. Do you understand? I'd be a man without a country. I could never be an American."

"I am not sure the Russians are going to let you be a Russian much longer," said Mriya. "They've never let me be one. And you ... you are tainted by me."

Kedrov shook his head. He changed the subject. "I know where Kristin Kuniczak is," he said.

"I don't give a damn about Kristin Kuniczak," she snapped.

"You had better care. We are meeting her tomorrow in Potsdam."

"Why?"

Kedrov's eyes narrowed, and his face hardened. Then he dropped his chin. "We are going to carry out an order from the Chairman," he said.

"That's not the sort of kiss I want to give you," he said after kissing her gently once again, in response to her timid invitation. "If I gave you that here and now, they would probably ask us to leave."

"What kind of kiss is that? Tell me."

He put his hand on her left breast. "A kiss there," he said. He touched her belly. "A kiss there." He touched the inside of her thigh. "And there. Don't say I didn't warn you."

"Oh, *Michael* ... "

"We could leave," he said. "We don't have to eat. But you know something? Anticipation ... thinking about what we might do later—"

She nodded. "Yes! It will be wonderful."

They ordered more drinks. Debora drank straight gin, Beefeater, on the rocks. She could hold it. In this respect she surprised many people. And two or three drinks had no apparent effect on her.

When their second round of drinks was on the table, Michael

grinned and asked, "Has your CIA agent been back to annoy you?"

"Thank heavens for small blessings, no."

"I'd rather imagined he might be an interesting sort. Did you mention his name?"

"I don't know if I did or not. It's Tobin—Russell Tobin."

"Except that his presence would distress you, I might enjoy having a drink with the fellow sometime."

Debora shook her head. "I don't like that kind of man," she said. "Or what he does."

"Oh? Has the CIA given you trouble?"

For a moment she drew her lower lip between her teeth, and she frowned and hesitated. "Not the CIA. Just what it represents. Super-patriotism. Maybe I'm wrong about what I see in Tobin, but what I think I see is too much certainty—I mean, too much unquestioning confidence. I . . . " She faltered. "I'm not saying this right. Michael—the worst thing in the world is belief. Do I make any sense?"

"What do you believe in, Debora?"

"In nothing. Nothing whatever. To me, the word *belief* means you embrace something without examining it. That's what religionists do. That's what ideologues do. And it's the worst thing in the world, because it infuses them with the presumption of their own infallibility." She lowered her eyes. "I'm sorry, Michael. I'm making a speech."

He nodded thoughtfully, and she was sorry she had spoken so intensely, because she could see she had disturbed him.

"Michael . . . what do you believe in?"

He rubbed his hands together before his chin for a moment. "I suppose I'd like to believe in myself," he said soberly. "I mean, I'd like to think I can achieve at least something of what I want to achieve."

"That's not belief, Michael," she said. "Not in the sense in which I mean the word. When you believe in yourself, it means you have examined yourself and reached a conclusion, at least a tentative conclusion. You don't think you're a god."

"Does this man Tobin think he's a god?"

"I think he imagines he serves one. Not any religious god.

The great god he would call American democracy."

Michael Ormsley smiled. "There'll always be an England," he sang under his breath. "Always a king or queen. Always two great universities, no more. Always—well . . . and never let the facts begin to persuade us otherwise."

That night it rained again in Berlin. Rain somehow sharpened the contrast between the east and west halves of the city. Much of the western city was new, and the rain fell through the gleaming light from new buildings and glistened on broad, straight streets. In the east sector, the rain fell in the darkness of old streets, contributing to a gloomy, sullen mood. The best of East Berlin was like some neighborhoods of London—Belgravia and Kensington, for example, quiet with age and tradition. But some of it was as grubby as Camden Town or Bow.

Audrey was influenced by this contrast. When she had lived in Berlin, you had to go through a formidable checkpoint to cross the Sector Border. Now you drove across without so much as slowing down, on any street. They had so completely demolished the Wall that across much of Berlin you couldn't tell where it had been. But you didn't have to drive many blocks past where the Wall had been before you were acutely conscious that you were east or west. She could not understand why Russ had chosen to live in the east.

She'd had to walk a block in the rain to reach the car and was chilled as she trotted from the street to his door. When Russ arrived, she was soaking in hot water in his bathtub. A snifter of brandy sat within reach on the bathroom stool.

"A successful preconference planning session?" he asked.

She nodded, but added, "People age."

Russ's clothes were damp, and he went into the bedroom to change, leaving the doors open so they could talk.

"Tell me something, Russ," she said. They could hear each other without raising their voices. "Do you by any chance keep a gun around here?"

"Why? Did you find the one in the car?"

"No. As a matter of fact, I didn't."

"Good. It's not easy to hide a gun inside a Porsche—I mean, hide it and have it within quick reach. There's an Uzi machine pistol under the passenger's seat. It's loaded with thirty-two rounds and spits them out at nine hundred per minute. You can't fire a long burst."

"Have you ever fired it?"

"Not that one."

"'The one in the car,' you called it. Does that mean there's another one?"

"In the bedroom closet," he said. "In a holster. I carry it occasionally."

"Nothing's changed," she said.

"Hey, Audrey! Gary Cooper or Gregory Peck, I ain't. Once in a very long while it's a good idea to be able to shoot back."

"You have never given me a straight answer to a straight question."

"Time I should, then."

"I know you killed a man, Russ. When we were in Berlin together and you went across the border. But—how many?"

"None since you last asked me."

"Don't be flippant. Please."

He stood at the bathroom door, stripped but for a pair of bright red French slingshot underpants. "I am not flippant on that subject, Audrey. Not flippant. Not at all."

"Then?"

"Why do you bring this up again?"

"You never answered the question. You've ducked it for years. I just want to know what kind of guy you are."

"I think you know already, Doctor—better than anyone else who's ever known me. Why do you want to know? Do you really care, or is it just something for cocktail-party conversation?"

"You son of a *bitch!* Do you think I'd do that to you? Trivialize your work, trivialize you? No, Russ."

He stepped into the bathroom and sat down on the closed lid of the toilet.

"Sometimes I thought you didn't trust me," she said quietly.

"Does it count? What about the guy who's twenty-eight?"

"He's twenty-eight."

"Audrey . . . I became an intelligence officer about the time he was born—"

"And the son of a bitch dared to scorn you!"

"And you care?"

"Hell, yes! What do you think?"

He knelt beside the tub and ran his hand through her hair. "Audrey. In my years as a CIA agent, I've caused deaths. I don't know how many. Most of them I caused indirectly—like a reconnaissance pilot who identifies a target, knowing it will be bombed and people killed. Others I caused more directly, like an artillery spotter who calls in shots on a farmhouse and sits there watching while the shells fall. What you want to know—"

"How many times did you see their eyes?"

He hesitated for a moment, then said—"Three times. Is that what you wanted to know?"

He could not have been more surprised when Audrey began to cry.

Michael removed his hand, which had been on Debora's and put it beneath the table, where he began to stroke the inside of her thigh, halfway between her knee and crotch. She started. Then she relaxed visibly.

"Did you say you've been a victim of super-patriotism?" he asked.

All her life Debora had tensed with alarm when a boy or man touched her where Michael was touching her now. It had always made her uncomfortable, at the very least. But his touch was soothing. She put her hand gently on his, to encourage him.

"Long story," she said quietly.

"I've nothing better to do than listen."

She looked up into his face and could find no suggestion that he hadn't meant exactly what he'd said.

"When the United States detonated the first hydrogen bomb, in 1952, my father was one of the scientists aboard a ship, watching the explosion. They had set the bomb up on an island in the Eniwetok Atoll, island called Elugelab. When the device exploded, Elugelab simply vaporized. A whole island . . . my father saw it. And he realized that bomb could have killed every living person in New York or London or Paris—or Moscow, which was exactly what they had in mind—in seconds."

"What was your father's role?"

"He was a nuclear physicist. He was just twenty-six years old at the time, and his contribution to the development of the bomb had been minuscule. But he had witnessed the detonation. That is, he had witnessed it as much as anyone could, from fifty miles away. It frightened him."

"I should think it would."

"What frightened him most was that science had put such a weapon in the hands of people he could not trust. He knew he could not trust President Truman not to use the thing. He trusted Eisenhower even less—Eisenhower and John Foster Dulles and Charlie Wilson and Sherman Adams. Oddly, he trusted Robert Taft, the senator? You ever hear the name?"

"I believe so. Yes. Yes, indeed."

"But Taft died, and he was succeeded as Republican leader in the Senate by that cretin, William Knowland. Then there was Dirksen and Bricker . . . and McCarthy. These were the leaders of the Congress. My father despised them. And he said so."

"Not wise."

"Nine months after the United States detonated the first hydrogen bomb, the Soviet Union detonated one of its own. My father said that was the best thing that ever happened, because now both major powers had this nightmare weapon and neither would dare use it."

"A popular point of view in the States, I imagine," said Michael.

"Yes. My father was summoned before the House Un-American Activities Committee." For a moment she closed her eyes, and she tightened her hand around his hand beneath the table. "They asked him the standard questions: had he ever been a member of the Communist Party and all that. I've read the transcript. Have you ever read the accounts of trials for heresy, during the Reformation? People were brought to trial on charges of having *said* something or other."

"Yes. People were put to death for saying there were no such persons as witches."

"Precisely. Well, my father had said that he welcomed the Soviet development of their own bomb, that the House Un-American Activities Committee was itself the most un-American thing in America, and so on."

"So they condemned him."

"No. They couldn't have. The Constitution of the United States still meant something, even in the fifties. But my father refused to answer their questions. He refused on principle to tell them whether or not he had ever been a member of the Communist Party. He could easily have said no—because he was never a Communist. He refused to say if any of his associates in nuclear research were Communists. The truth was, he didn't know if any of them were or not; so he just refused to talk about it. And so on. Refusal to testify is called contempt of Congress, which is a crime. Because he spoke so defiantly, they had him indicted for contempt of Congress. Michael . . . my father was sent to *prison*."

"Debora."

"When I was born, my father was selling shoes for a living. He was a brilliant physicist, but he had spent seven months in prison for contempt of Congress. He had lost his faculty position at Princeton University. They had, of course, taken away his security clearance, which meant he could not work at anything that conceivably involved national security. He is a pariah to this day in any research establishment, in academia or industry, where he might have anything to do with weapons development or analysis. Besides which, a university that employed Willard Benson would risk losing its government grants. It would be denounced sooner or later in—"

Michael had turned his hand over and was squeezing hers. "My darling . . . " he whispered.

"My father is as capable a man as any research scientist working on any weapons system the United States is trying to develop," she said grimly. "He teaches mathematics and physics at a secondary school, a private academy, for very little money. I earn five times his salary."

"Disgraceful."

"Well . . . the headmaster and board of the academy have to be respected for having dared to hire him. A few alumni didn't like it. But—actually, I think he and my mother have found some satisfaction in what he does, in where and how they live. Maybe *I'm* the repository of all the resentment."

Michael released her hand and turned his over, resuming his stroking of her thigh. "The world is an unfair place, Debora," he said quietly. "I know I don't need to tell you that."

She looked up at him once more, this time through narrowed eyes. "Maybe it's not entirely unfair," she said. "Alcoholism, suicide, senility, plus exposure as cheap embezzlers, soon ruined most of the peanut politicians my father despised. You won't find any statues in Washington commemorating the services of Knowland or Dirksen or Bricker or McCarthy."

"But your father has found some peace," said Michael quietly.

"Yes, and I'm ashamed of my bitterness."

"Don't be! Sometimes bitterness brings about good things." He looked up. "Our waiter wants to know if we want another drink."

"Yes, please," she whispered.

Major Ivan Stepanovich Yuryev was glad he had come to this nightclub, glad to see what he was seeing. It confirmed his long confidence that the West would eventually collapse of its degeneracy. He had always known that in Western Europe and America, even in Japan, young women exposed their breasts to debauched audiences in dark, smoky rooms. (Even in Moscow a few months ago a club had opened where girls bared themselves above the waist, briefly and in subdued light. The club had closed without police intervention. Soviet citizens found the display embarrassing. They came once, out of curiosity, giggled nervously at the show, hurried away, and never returned.) But here—what he saw here was disgusting.

A dozen young women frolicked about the stage, in the glare of painfully bright lights. They did not quite dance, though they moved to the rhythm of blaring music. Rather, they postured, shrieked, sang raucously, and laughed. They wore black leather harnesses that crisscrossed their bodies and pinched and distorted their breasts. Otherwise, they were naked.

The waiter had mistaken his accent and guessed he was an American. That was why he was drinking an American drink called a martini. He found the taste rather heavy. Even so he pretended to like it. He pretended to be enjoying the show. To do otherwise would have marked him as an odd, even suspicious, person.

He understood why the German had suggested this place for their meeting. This nightclub was expensive, and the German thought he was going to see the spectacle at the KGB's cost. Well, he had a surprise coming. When he was paid for his services, he would find the amount reduced by the cost of entering this place and drinking here.

The German appeared abruptly, as if he had materialized out of the tobacco smoke. He sat down and raised a finger to summon a waiter.

Surprisingly, the German didn't look at the stage. He stared at Yuryev, as if memorizing his face.

"You work alone," said Yuryev, using his accented German. "That's a condition. If anything goes wrong and you are arrested, you say you were trying to commit a robbery. Go to prison if you have to. We will get you out. It may take a while to arrange, so you will have to be patient. We will supplement your money by five hundred marks a day for every day you are in prison."

The German nodded. He was an ugly fellow. His face made Yuryev uncomfortable. A reliable, experienced agent had recommended him, giving unqualified assurance that the man would do the job. According to the agent, the German had been an officer of General Wolf's HVA.

"I have fifty thousand marks in the case under the table," said Yuryev. "When you leave, take it. I will meet you and hand you the balance when I am satisfied the job has been done."

"You will meet me when and where?"

"The story will appear in the newspapers. That's how I will know the job has been done. The next day, at ten in the morning

I will be in the Kaiser Wilhelm Church, sitting a few rows from the back, with another case beside me. You sit down. I'll leave. The balance of your money will be in the case."

The German shook his head.

"What's wrong with that plan?" Yuryev asked.

"I want to see the money before you leave."

"Very well. I will put a newspaper in the case. I will open the case on my lap and take out the newspaper. You will be able to see the money."

The German nodded, and now, apparently satisfied, he looked up at the stage and the naked girls.

Michael ordered their dinner. For a long moment, Debora closed her eyes. Michael slipped his hand down her leg and began to push back her skirt. She was wearing stockings and, under the table and hidden by the tablecloth, he caressed the bare skin of her inner thigh.

"Michael . . . "

"Debora."

"I think I'm falling in love with you."

Colonel Kedrov sucked his cheeks between his teeth. He sighed, frowned, and looked away from Kurt Horst Steiner. Steiner, always pathetically anxious to receive approval, and a word or two of praise as well, from his superiors, stared intently at the changing expressions of the colonel's face. He tried to read them. He would adjust his own expressions, and his narrative, in reaction.

It was 4:00 A.M. Both men had driven to the house in Köpenick. Kedrov wore a crisp suit and smoked a cigarette. Steiner was still dressed in the tweed jacket and dark slacks he had worn the evening before. They sat in the little living room of the modest house, both annoyed that there was nothing to drink. Kedrov had resolved to give orders that vodka and other liquor should be kept available in the house. He might, after all, want to loosen up someone he met there. He might even find need to loosen himself up.

"You should have stayed the rest of the night," said Kedrov glumly. "To leave after—"

"Comrade Colonel! She asked me to leave! She did not want people to see me leaving her flat in the morning light."

Kedrov laughed. His eyes flicked back to the anxious young man, and his smile remained after the laugh. "So—have I sent an innocent to seduce an innocent?"

"No, Comrade Colonel."

"Steiner! Stop calling me comrade. I warned you. The habit must be dropped."

"Yes, sir."

"Now, then. I want you to tell me exactly what you did. What you said and did, what she said and did, in *detail*."

"Sir, I did the usual things. What I suppose are the usual things."

"Beginning. What first?"

"Well, of course, beginning by establishing an acquaintance, then a friendship. Friday night I tried to kiss her goodnight. She could not allow that. Then on the telephone she apologized and said she would let me kiss her the next time I wanted to. So, this evening—that is, last evening—I took her to dinner. In the restaurant I did kiss her, and she allowed me to touch her intimately under the table."

"'Intimately.' What does this mean?"

"Well, I—we were sitting side by side, you see, and the tablecloth concealed everything. I pulled her skirt back and petted her on her bare legs, above her stockings. She liked that. She confessed she did. She said she was falling in love with me."

"Good. Then what did you do?"

"I rubbed her crotch. I did so until her panties became quite moist."

"When did you suggest the two of you go to her flat and go to bed?"

"I didn't, actually. It was just . . . understood. I mean, I would have raised the subject, Colonel, but I didn't have to."

"She talked?"

For the first time, Steiner allowed a tiny smile to flicker over his face. "Constantly," he said.

"In a few minutes I am going to switch on a tape recorder. We will go over everything she said, in the greatest detail, while your memory is fresh."

"Yes, sir. She talked about her own life, mostly—about her father, especially. He was—"

"I know what he was. For the moment I want to hear more about the personal and physical aspects of this relationship. You know what Kristin Kuniczak did. I want to be sure you are not pressing too much, too rapidly. I want to know you are being subtle. You aroused her too much, too soon, in the restaurant. She might have decided you were far too bold. She might have experienced a revulsion against what she was feeling, because she was feeling it in a public place where she could do nothing about it."

"She *wanted* it, sir! She put her hand on mine and encouraged me to continue."

"Even so. Do not forget what you have to do eventually. The relationship must be cemented so firmly she will accept even that."

"When I left her this morning, she was declaring her love repeatedly. Tearfully."

"A woman who falls in love fast can fall out of love fast. Our information on her suggests she is not a loose woman."

"She isn't, I am sure. She wears very ordinary white underclothes. I was thinking I might buy her something more... glamorous, as a gift."

"Do that. Something not too daring. Something not very expensive. Leave something more daring, more expensive, to be given later. So. You went to her flat?"

"Yes. And I detected a bit of hesitation. So I treated her very gently. I suggested maybe she would rather not go to bed with me. She asked if I'd be disappointed if we didn't. I said I would but that I'd be more disappointed if she went to bed with me when she hadn't really determined she wanted to."

"Clever."

"Thank you, sir," said Steiner, not detecting the derision in Kedrov's voice. "Well. She was reluctant to undress in front of me. She made some comment about her underclothing: that she buys it at the most proletarian shops. She is rather tall. Her figure is somewhat spare. She is obsessively self-conscious about it, doesn't think her breasts are large enough. She—"

"Did you have to overcome any more reluctance?"

"No, sir. Once she was undressed, she wanted to get into bed immediately and cover herself with the sheets. From that point on, sir, it was all rather . . . normal. The usual thing. She was no longer hesitant. She seemed to enjoy it."

"You've no sense that you deflowered a virgin, I take it?"

"I . . . I don't believe so. She didn't say so. Or act as if . . . No. No, I'm confident she wasn't."

"But if she was, she was well and fully deflowered, hmm?"

Steiner grinned. "Yes, sir. I think I can say that, sir."

11

RUSS AND AUDREY slept until after ten. They bathed together and then repeatedly stumbled into each other in the kitchen as both of them tried to make breakfast. They drank coffee and ate toast and eggs, read the Sunday morning Berlin and London newspapers, and took the coffee pot and some sections of the papers to the bedroom, where they lay comfortably together for two more hours.

She left his flat a few minutes after two, allowing herself plenty of time to drive to the Free University of Berlin by three o'clock, when the final planning session of her conference opened. She pulled the Porsche into a parking garage a block from the building where the conference was meeting, took a ticket from the machine, and found a space on the second floor.

She paused for a moment before leaving the car, to check the state of her hair and makeup in the rearview mirror. Impulsively, she reached under the passenger seat and felt for the gun Russ had said he kept there.

She touched it immediately. It was just far enough back under the seat to be out of sight to someone who didn't know or suspect it was there, yet within instant reach. It was wrapped in a bit of fabric, like a handkerchief, and when she pulled on it the fabric pulled away, and her hand was on the steel of the pistol. She glanced around to be sure no one was watching, then dragged the gun out.

An Uzi, he had called it. The stubby barrel protruded no more than an inch or so from the square body. She knew little about pistols but recognized this one as dangerous. It had no safety, though she saw that a sort of rear trigger on the back of the grip would be depressed by the heel of your hand when you pulled the trigger. Maybe that was the safety; the pistol would not fire until there was pressure on both triggers.

He'd called it a machine pistol and said it fired hundreds of rounds a minute. Audrey stared at it for another minute, then rewrapped it and shoved it back under the seat.

The Sans souci palace was built in the middle of the eighteenth century by Frederick the Great, King of Prussia. Voltaire was his guest there, as was Bach. Built in the style of Versailles but on a much smaller scale, it is a gem of eighteenth-century architecture. Allowed to fall into disrepair after the Prussian kings and emperors moved into a pretentious palace nearby, it was restored by the government of East Germany and made a tourist attraction. With the disappearance of the Sector Border and the oppressive checkpoints, Potsdam and Sans Souci became more popular with tourists.

Especially on Sundays.

Kristin Kuniczak had specified it as the place where she would meet Colonel Kedrov. On Sunday afternoon.

He understood. She wanted to meet him in a place where they would be surrounded by hordes of people. She was being cautious. Kristin had a finely honed instinct for survival.

The handsome palace sits on a low, landscaped hill. Without the grandiosity of Versailles, it welcomes visitors as it welcomed Frederick's guests. One of its features is its superbly designed parquet floors. To protect the parquet against scratches, visitors are required to wear grotesque oversized felt slippers over their shoes; and they shuffle through the rooms and corridors, polishing and dusting as they go.

As always, guides led groups of tourists through the rooms, lecturing inaccurately to them in various languages. Though most tourists were stunned by the unexpected beauty of the place, few of them had ever heard of it before their hotel desks recommended it, and the guides were never contradicted.

Kedrov arrived at two o'clock with Mriya. It was their second visit of the day. They had come at ten o'clock to refresh Kedrov's memory about the room layout. Now they separated; Mriya went her own way.

With the ludicrous felt slippers over his shoes, Kedrov shuffled across the floors with a gliding motion, not unlike that of a novice ice skater. Some Americans doing the same made it the inspiration for giggling.

He found Kristin Kuniczak staring thoughtfully at a musical instrument. A harpsichord? Clavichord? Pianoforte? The guides would tell their charges. It had been played by Bach or Mozart, both of whom had been guests at Sans Souci.

She wore soft black leather boots, a short black skirt, an off-white cableknit sweater.

"Did you have to kill him?"

She nodded. "I had no choice, Nikolai Pavlovich."

"There is always a choice, Kristin. Your orders were very specific. You were not to kill him."

"He was going to his company security men. He had a hyperactive conscience. He was going to confess all, even that I had photographed the papers he brought me. Honesty, he insisted, would correct everything. He was going to *confess*."

"How could you have been so stupid as to put yourself in that position?"

"Put myself— Nikolai Pavlovich, you blame me?"

He walked away, out of the music room, along a corridor that led toward the magnificent library of the palace. She followed him, sliding along in her felt slippers as he was doing.

"Everything has become far more difficult," he said to her. "Security has been tightened, not just at LSI, but at every high-tech company in the West. You saved yourself and damaged the mission. *Damaged*. Not just a little."

"I have served—"

"You have killed before when you were told not to."

"Save myself, save the mission. If I had been arrested—"

"What? You would have talked?"

"How could I not? They would have drugged me."

Colonel Kedrov shook his head. "Very doubtful. Anyway, you had your means, did you not?"

"The capsule?" Her back stiffened. Her shoulders jerked.

"Short of that, you might have done many things. Why couldn't you simply have walked away from him?"

"He might not have allowed it."

"You had the pistol, didn't you? I don't believe the Pakistani had one."

"Nikolai Pavlovich—"

"You've made a mess of it. Not just of your job. Of my mission. Of the larger mission. A mess."

"What can I do?"

He walked on. Reaching a flight of stairs, he mounted them and shuffled to the top. She followed. He turned along a corridor on the upper floor and walked down a row of doors leading into bedroom suites.

A gaggle of tourists shuffled toward them. Kedrov glanced at Kristin Kuniczak and turned into a bedroom—his glance suggesting to her that he did not want to confront that crowd of tittering Americans. She followed him into the bedroom.

"Nikolai Pavlovich—"

He spun around and faced her, and his features contorted with anger monopolized her attention. She did not see or hear Mriya Meyerhold. She did not realize anyone had suddenly stepped from behind curtains and was behind her.

Mriya held two short dowel rods in her gloved hands. The wooden rods were joined by thirty centimeters of fine, strong steel wire. Bringing the wire down over Kristin's head, she jerked on the wire with all her strength.

Kristin Kuniczak did not die of strangulation. The fine wire, yanked violently against her throat, cut through flesh, muscle, and cartilage. Mriya sawed on it. Kristin gurgled as she tried to draw breath, then coughed and blew blood through the thin cut. She slackened, then slipped to the floor, great gouts of blood erupting from her cut throat.

Mriya let go of the dowel rods. She pulled off the gloves and tossed them down on the body of the dying young woman.

Kedrov led the way out of the bedroom and along the corridor, where the guide had led the tour group into one of the major bedroom suites, as he had known she would. He and Mriya walked past them and on to the main staircase at the front of the house. They had reached the orangerie before they heard the first screams from inside.

Audrey shook the last hand, smiled her last smile, and finally got away from the dinner and the *professor-doktors* of the conference on the possibilities of treating narcotics addiction with psychopharmacology.

The Porsche was in the garage where she had left it this afternoon. She was annoyed at how difficult it had been to break away. She had come to Berlin for this conference, had not come—and would not have come—just to be with Russ. Yet she had promised to return to his flat early enough for them to go out for dinner. You could find a good meal at all hours in Berlin. It was one of the attractions of the city, something London would do well to emulate. Even so, she thought of him waiting for her at the flat. His work was as important as hers, and he had made a point that absent the start of World War III, he would be at the flat by seven. It was almost eight, the sun had set, and she began to shove the smooth Porsche transmission through its gears, watching the tach as he had taught her to do so many years ago, getting the best out of the engine and transmission, determined to get to the flat as quickly as possible.

Running through the streets of Berlin, she tried to make a fast transition: mind turning from the medical questions of the conference to the evening with her ex-husband. Life sometimes demanded this: movement from one mode into another. When she left an airplane in the misty dawn at Heathrow or Charles DeGaulle or Tempelhof, was she the same person who had left her house in Chevy Chase yesterday afternoon? Not quite. Not exactly. For her, a professional student of the mind, this posed intriguing questions, issues.

But not now.

Russ could have driven the distance in less time. He knew the city, particularly the eastern part, far better than she. She took the most obvious route, maybe not the most direct.

She missed the next-to-last turn. Within half a minute she knew it. She turned, made the correction, and reached Joachimstrasse at exactly eight-eleven.

She looked up and could see the light in his windows. Russ was a man who understood the demands of duty—she had certainly waited for him times enough—and would forgive her being late. She pulled the Porsche to the curb, glad to have no problem in finding a parking place, and switched off the lights and the ignition.

She paused. Maybe she should switch the lights back on and check her face in the rearview mirror. But couldn't she just turn on the interior lights? She bent forward to stare at the knobs to the left of the steering wheel—

The windshield blew in in a hailstorm of glass shards. Her left shoulder erupted in fiery pain. The shock against her shoulder threw her back against the door. Blood—that thick, warm gushing fluid couldn't be anything else—spurted from her arm and shoulder.

Audrey slumped forward. In an instant she understood she had been shot. Why? *Jesus Christ!* She was still alive, but—

She saw the figure. A man. It *was* a man. Outside the car. Moving toward it. Moving toward *her*. God! He was coming to make sure of it, to be certain she was dead.

Audrey grabbed for the wrapped pistol under the passenger seat. The Uzi. In a trembling, fumbling motion, she tore away the fabric and gripped the machine pistol.

The man! He was there! Above her! His head moved. He was searching for her in the dark inside the car.

He saw her. She saw him step back a pace and aim a pistol with both hands.

Audrey squeezed the triggers of the Uzi.

The gun exploded. Exploded. The right half of the windshield blew away. A blast of blue-and-orange fire and a torrent of bullets lifted the man off his feet. The slugs, twenty or thirty of them, raised him in the air, and for a full two seconds he hung there on the impact, shaking violently like a marionette on jerking strings. He blew apart. Literally, he blew apart.

The roaring explosion stopped. She had relaxed her grip on the triggers, but that was not what stopped the firing. It had stopped because the magazine was empty. Pain and horror overwhelmed her, and she dropped the machine pistol and slumped backward against the seat of the Porsche.

Russ rode with Audrey in the ambulance, a van without windows. She lay on a wheeled cot. Russ sat to one side of her, a medic to the other. The van was filled with the sound of its emergency horn—*ee-aw-ee-aw-ee-aw-ee-aw*. Audrey opened and closed her eyes. Russ was not sure how much she was aware, how much she was drifting.

He had shown his diplomatic passport to the first police unit that arrived and had asked to use their radio to relay a quick message.

"*Wem?*" To whom?

"*Der Bundesnachtrichtendienst.*"

The first BND agent had arrived before they loaded Audrey in the ambulance, with word that Herr Voss would meet Herr Tobin at the hospital.

Audrey would not die, of course. Russ had been sure of that the moment he knelt beside her and saw the wound. But she had lost too much blood, she was in shock, and the harm done her was significant. He held her right hand, gently squeezing when she opened her eyes, knowing it was unlikely she saw him or that she understood anything of what he said to her: that she was not dying, that she was going to be all right.

The sympathetic and efficient medic monitored her all during the run to the hospital. Efficiency, competence, thoroughness— all part of the German ethos. The sympathy was an appreciated extra.

Back on Joachimstrasse, efficiency, competence, and thoroughness were also in evidence. The BND agent had taken charge of the investigation. Russ had quickly explained the situation, and the man had immediately begun snapping orders at the Berlin police officers.

Russ had taken only one quick look at the man lying on the

street. He was a grisly demonstration of what a 9mm submachine gun, fired at close range, did to the human body. His upper chest had been torn apart. Shreds of his flesh lay scattered on the pavement.

Russ was sure of one thing. He didn't know the man.

Audrey gasped. "'E troid t' kill me!" she whispered.

Russ squeezed her hand. "We know, honey," he said. "But he didn't."

She drifted back into the retreat the wounded human body makes for itself, a kind of haze. In this instance, the retreat was fortified with a sedative the medic had administered. There would be no question of her having to justify her actions. She would not even be interrogated. The BND would take care of that.

Her assailant had shot her with a TT–33 Tokarev automatic, a pistol of Soviet design that had been licensed for manufacture in several of the former East Bloc countries and had been standard issue for their security forces. *Stasi...*

Obviously, the man had not meant to kill Audrey. He had meant to kill the man who drove the Porsche. Russ had never considered that possibility when he told Audrey to drive it. All he'd been thinking of was that it was his car and the one he'd get from the station motor pool would belong to the government. So he'd arrived in Joachimstrasse in an anonymous car, and she had arrived in the Porsche marked for the ambush.

The hospital was brightly lighted, bustling, and, determinedly efficient. No one asked if the patient had insurance. No one even asked who she was. They were interested in her wounds, nothing else.

Voss arrived at the hospital shortly after green-gowned attendants wheeled Audrey into surgery. Accompanied by two agents, one a woman, he shook Russ's hand and asked grimly if Audrey was in any danger.

Russ shook his head. "I don't think so. They tell me she isn't. But she's got severe damage to her arm and shoulder."

"I have been on the telephone in my car while on the way here. We have identified the man who shot her."

"Who intended to shoot me."

"I suppose that is very likely. Anyway, the man's name is Albert Heckler. He was a medium-rank officer of *Stasi*. When it was abolished, he did not go to Zagorsk; I would guess he was not offered the opportunity. He has remained in Berlin, eking out a living as best he can. He is suspected in a number of crimes."

Even if you were a National Intelligence Officer of the CIA conferring with the Berlin chief of the BND, you met in a room where the lights were too bright, where you sat on gaudy orange fiberglass chairs, where the corner tables were covered with stacks of well-worn, out-of-date magazines—while you waited for word from the operating room.

Voss did not leave. He spent much time on the telephone, but he waited.

"I have news for you," he said early in their wait, while they were staring into their first cups of coffee. "Kristin Kuniczak was murdered this afternoon. At Potsdam, in the old Frederick the Great palace. She was strangled. Within ten or fifteen meters of where a group of tourists was listening to their tour guide in another room."

"Strangled—"

"With steel wire attached to handles. Most professional."

"Strange place to kill a person."

"A perfect place, if you knew what you were doing and had thoroughly examined the site in advance," said Voss.

"Somehow lured there, you have to figure," said Russ. "A meet. She wouldn't meet anyone except in a very public place. In the middle of a crowd."

"Exactly," said Voss. "But the killer knew the palace better than she did and knew how to find the necessary privacy in a public place. We must suppose, too, that Kristin Kuniczak was a little careless."

"Kedrov?"

"Or someone working for him. Or maybe someone else. The murder of Mahmud Nedim must have angered others besides Kedrov."

Voss waited with Russ the entire three hours that Audrey was in surgery. At last, the surgeon, with his mask dangling around his throat, came to the room. He spoke English:

"Is no danger to life. Is much damage, much pain. Shock. Much loss of blood. But a strong woman who will recover. She say she is doctor. What kind of doctor?"

"A psychiatrist," said Russ.

"Ah. Well, then. No problem with the practicing the profession."

"What does that mean?"

The surgeon was a young man, maybe thirty, with a heavy black shadow of beard. He wore round, silver-rimmed eyeglasses. He glanced at Voss, then went on.

"You know what means the tuberosities of the humerus? Is upmost parts of upper bone of the arm. Is shattered by bullet. We find . . . many splinters in flesh, in clothes as cut away. Some parts gone. Also parts of adjoining bones of shoulder joint." He shook his head. "Will result in much loss of mobility of left arm. We repair as is possible. Maybe later plastic or metal parts can be inserted. But will always be much loss of utility of left arm. We are very sorry."

Russ unlocked the door and walked into the dark living room of his flat on Joachimstrasse. He walked to the window and looked down at the street, searching the shadows for someone waiting to take a shot at him with a rifle. He closed the drapes and only then switched on the lights.

A gift-wrapped package lay on his coffee table. A nightgown he had bought for Audrey to wear tonight.

Instead, a coarse white hospital gown. A half-conscious figure, pallid from loss of blood. Confused. Not sure what had happened to her. Still frightened. He had sat with her until she went to sleep.

Russ went to his bedroom closet to hang up his jacket. He took off his tie and hung it there, too.

He drew a pistol from the shoulder holster that lay wrapped in its harness on the closet shelf. The little Walther PPK was designed to be a pocket pistol that a man could carry hidden in the waistband of his trousers as well as in a shoulder holster, that a woman could carry in a small handbag. He had always been reluctant to carry a gun. And for years he'd had to carry one. In fact, for years he'd had to qualify annually on a target range. He shoved the PPK into his pocket.

The telephone rang.

"Russell Georgievich?"

"Mriya."

"I saw you come home. I was afraid to approach you on the street. I would very much like to come up and talk to you."

"Why not? I'm alone."

"I know. Can I come up to see you?"

"Sure."

She was again wearing the uniform of an Aeroflot ticket agent. Her narrow eyes were all but closed, as if they were swollen. He wondered if she had been crying. She looked tired, too.

"Whiskey?"

"Please."

"To what do I owe the honor of this visit?"

"Nikolai Pavlovich asked me to come to see you," she said.

"The visit is not social, then."

She went to the window, parted the drapes an inch or so, and stared down at the street. "Dammit," she said.

"You've been followed?"

She nodded. "I think so. Maybe not. I don't know."

He smiled. "Maybe Nikolai Pavlovich is suspicious of you and me. After all, you did spend the night here last week."

"Nikolai Pavlovich knows I'm here. He sent me to express to you his sympathy and regret, also his outrage, over the injury to your former wife."

"How does he know about that?"

She lifted her chin high. "We occupied this part of Berlin for forty years. Not everyone hated us. Many still consider it a duty to call and tell us things."

He handed her a glass of whiskey and lifted his own in salute. "His sympathy, regret, and outrage. I am supposed to believe, then, that neither of you had anything to do with what happened to Audrey?"

"Nikolai Pavlovich wants you to know and believe and understand."

"I can imagine."

He sat down without inviting her to sit, and she glanced at the couch and two chairs, chose the couch, and sat down without invitation. "Nikolai Pavlovich invites you to use your brains, Russell. Whoever hurt your former wife was probably trying to kill *you*—though not necessarily. Why would Nikolai Pavlovich want to kill you? Why would he want to kill your ex-wife? You are old adversaries, but you aren't adversaries anymore."

"Why is Colonel Kedrov in Berlin?" Russ asked.

"Why are *you* in Berlin, Russell Georgievich?"

"Fair enough. So why does Nikolai Pavlovich care so much whether I think he had anything to do with what happened this evening?"

"Two reasons. First, I think you should understand that Nikolai Pavlovich holds you in high regard."

"Mriya . . . "

She smiled faintly. "It is bitter respect, as you can imagine. But it is real."

Russ grinned. "Okay, you can tell the old boy he's the toughest bastard I've ever come up against."

"Both of you are alive, Russell Georgievich," she said. She tossed back her whiskey and pushed the glass toward him. She took out a cigarette and lit it. "After a great many years in this profession. That alone should earn each of you the respect of the other."

He took her glass to the kitchen and poured her some more Scotch. "The second reason?" he called back through the door. "The second reason why he wants me to know he didn't try to kill me?"

"To tell you there is a third party in the game," she said.

"Yuryev."

"Yes. I didn't tell Nikolai Pavlovich I had spoken to you about Major Yuryev. He authorized me to tell you tonight."

"What possible reason could this Yuryev have for wanting to kill me?"

"Maybe none. Maybe you weren't the target. It is possible—let us say it is just possible that your former wife really was the target tonight. It's possible that Yuryev wanted to make you Nikolai Pavlovich's executioner."

"You'll have to explain that. It doesn't make any sense at all."

"Suppose your former wife had died tonight. Suppose you thought Nikolai Pavlovich was responsible. You might well arrange a fatal accident for him. That might suit Yuryev's purposes very well. And Vyshevskii's. They would be glad to have you do a dirty job for them."

"Nikolai Pavlovich is in trouble?"

She drew smoke deep into her lungs and nodded.

"Which means Mriya Aronovna is in trouble, too."

"Yes. I am not sure why, exactly. It could be the old anti-Semitism. It could be they've found out—or have known all along—that I gave you Reuss. It could be something else. It could be something Nikolai Pavlovich is involved in that I don't know about."

"So is he going to go fishing for sharks, or not?"

She drank half of her second whiskey in two gulps. She shook her head. "He may be forced to. But unless he is . . . Nikolai Pavlovich Kedrov can't imagine living anywhere but in Mother Russia."

"'Forced to . . .' His trouble goes back a while, doesn't it? It's not just something that's come up the past few days."

"The hatred of Jews—" She shrugged. "Two thousand years. But only eleven years for Nikolai Pavlovich—since he and I . . . " She shrugged again. "Other things. Russ. Other things."

"Who killed Kristin Kuniczak?"

Mriya's face stiffened. She shook her head. "I don't know."

"Who ordered her killed?"

"I don't know."

Russ walked back to the kitchen and refreshed his own drink. "Yuryev again?"

"That's possible."

"A busy fellow, this Major Yuryev," Russ said, not without a trace of sarcasm in his voice.

Mriya drank the last of her Scotch and stood. "I came to tell you Nikolai Pavlovich and I had nothing to do with what happened to your former wife. You can believe us or not believe us; there is nothing we can do about that. But if you are focusing all your attention on us, you may be making a dangerous mistake."

Russ parted the curtains an inch or so and scanned the street. He saw no one and wondered if her suggestion that she had been followed was some little game. Then he saw the man. If he wasn't waiting for Mriya, what was he doing out there at this time of night?

"Can you phone Nikolai Pavlovich?"

"Yes."

"Why don't you do that? Tell him you'll be staying here the rest of the night. We may as well let your friend down there think you are here because you're sleeping with me. That may throw him off a little bit."

Mriya picked up the telephone. "Pour me another whiskey, Russell Georgievich," she said. "Last week you subdued my ardor by making me sleepy with whiskey. I assume you'd rather do that than make love with me."

12

As EARLY AS they would allow on Monday morning, Russ went to the hospital. Audrey was in a grimly modern private room, in a bed surrounded with the buttons and switches that controlled a dozen electric and electronic devices for her comfort. She sat propped against a stack of pillows, wearing a coarse white hospital gown. Her left arm hung in an apparatus suspended from a frame over the bed. Two sprays of flowers lent the room a cloying scent, though Russ himself had not yet sent her any.

"They know I'm a doctor," she said. "Nothing's too good for me."

"Nothing *is* too good for you, Audrey," he said somberly.

"Look what they've given me." She spoke weakly. "In the little plastic box there."

He opened the box. Lying in it was the characteristic bottle-neck slug from the Tokarev pistol, flattened and deformed by its crushing impact against her bones but still recognizable.

"Damned good thing Oi'm not left-'anded," she said, slipping into her childhood accent.

"Yeah. And I can't even avenge you. You blew the guy away. I suppose they told you that."

"They didn't 'ave to. Oi saw. That . . . thing you carried in the car. It tore that man apart."

"And saved your life."

She nodded. "Roight," she said quietly. "It saved me loif."

Audrey's red hair emphasized her pallor.

"He came to kill me," he said to her. "Not you. You're in no danger. Even so, there are BND men watching outside. Don't worry about it."

"What about you?"

He shrugged and tried to smile. "You took care of the man who wanted to kill me."

She looked away from him. "If you won't tell me the truth, then we don't have anything to talk about." Feeling more assertive, she abandoned the Camden Town accent.

"The Cold War is not over," he said. "Just changed. And not even all that much."

"If we're not thinking of aiming the Bomb at each other anymore—and I guess we're not—then it's changed."

"Right. I guess my focus is too personal."

She clutched her left wrist in her right hand and gently flexed the wounded arm. She winced, then gasped. "In Washington last month you told me you're entitled to retire. Will you ever? I mean, before someone retires you another way? Don't you think it's time to let younger men shoot at each other?"

"I have to finish what I'm doing right now," he said. "You're right about the man last night. He wasn't operating on his own orders. And what they tried to do gives you a small idea of how important this deal is."

"They're all important."

"That's true. They all are."

Audrey sighed. "I lay here in this bed this morning thinking about you. What is this? I asked myself. *High Noon?* What am I, Grace Kelly trying to talk Gary Cooper out of his shootout? What a goddamned cliché, Russ! I won't be a part of it."

"Me neither," he said. "But I've been thinking about chucking it. I really have. I'm entitled. I've got my years in. I've thought about living here in Berlin. Hell, it's home to me, Audrey. I'm not at home in the States anymore. You know, I counted it up. I've spent something like nineteen months in the States in the past twenty-seven years. I'm not sure I'd be comfortable there anymore. Berlin . . . London, maybe. Go fishing for sharks."

"Fishing—what does that mean?"

"It's another way to say retire when the real word bothers you."

"Chevy Chase?" she asked quietly.

He opened his mouth and drew breath to answer her. Then he hesitated. "I've never stopped loving you, Audrey."

"Well, think about it," she said.

He drove from the hospital to Dahlem.

The *Versuchsräume* in the LSI building were hardly laboratories in the traditional sense. Mostly, they were cubicles where people tapped keys and frowned at screens, plus conference rooms where they sat in groups, drank gallons of coffee, and covered greenboards with messy diagrams. Only a few rooms had equipment in them.

There was one big computer room on the second floor, where a mighty mainframe shot electrons through labyrinthine circuits, invisibly and soundlessly opening and closing millions of electronic gates at speeds that were almost beyond human comprehension. The mainframe was attended by technicians, not by engineers and designers. They monitored it vigilantly, alert for anomalies and vagaries; but the commands it obeyed came from the terminals in the cubicles.

Jane Mahoney was with Director Max Wenzel in his office when Russ arrived. "Oh, Russ, Jesus!" she said. She got up from her chair and threw her arms around him. "My sympathies—I don't know what to say."

"Nor do I," said Wenzel. "If there is anything we can do . . . I mean, if any facility can be offered—"

"I'm grateful to you both," Russ said. "She's getting the best of care. I know I can count on you if I need any help. For now, I'd like to walk around a little. I was just thinking as I came in. These rooms seem an unlikely place for—"

They left the office and walked along a hall, glancing into the rooms to either side.

"It does not look like a fortress under siege, does it?" commented Max Wenzel. "It is difficult for me to believe it is."

"You would have found it even more difficult the day before Mahmud Nedim was murdered," said Tobin.

"True. I don't doubt you, Russ. But I walk through these rooms every day. I stare at the faces of the people. I see nothing in their eyes, nothing different."

"I wish it were that simple," said Tobin. "If it were, the CIA and BND could be staffed with ophthalmologists."

Mahoney grinned, but Wenzel didn't catch the attempt at wit and said, "As you asked me to do, I've made a list of the people doing the most sensitive work."

"Would Mahmud Nedim have been one of them?"

"Definitely."

"I'd like to look at that list."

"Yes. Jane has brought it up on the computer screen. I'll print you a copy. I've looked at the people on it, trying to see anything different in their lives. I see nothing."

"If anybody is doing something different, they'll try to prevent your seeing it."

They paused at the door of a small conference room, where Debora Benson stood at a greenboard and scrawled a diagram, stabbing the board with her chalk, breaking it, grabbing up another piece, and scrawling on, gesturing at and lecturing two men who nodded and grunted their agreement.

"Max?" she asked, interrupting herself and taking one step toward the door.

"Just walking by, Debora."

She nodded. "Mr. Tobin," she said crisply.

Tobin smiled at her and walked on.

"Mathematically brilliant," said Wenzel. "Personally prosaic. I had hoped you might find out something through her, but I'm afraid you frightened her. She's easily frightened."

"University type," said Tobin.

"To what extent are you interested in people with . . . how shall I say . . . aberrant lifestyles?"

"Like what?" Tobin asked as they reached the end of the hall and faced the door into a canteen where employees could take drinks and food from an array of vending machines.

"Like, for example, homosexuals."

"The old obsession with homosexuals as security risks died with a lot of other canards. You can hardly blackmail people for being what they want to be."

Max Wenzel cast a dubious glance at Tobin, then shrugged and said nothing.

They walked on, returning eventually to Wenzel's office, that sanctuary of neatness. Wenzel turned to his computer keyboard, punched a few keys, and brought up on the screen a structured document. He peered at it for a moment, then punched other keys that started a printer. He lifted the printed sheets from the tray on the printer and handed them to Tobin.

The document was the list he had mentioned, of the men and women doing the most sensitive work in the LSI labs.

"Most of them," said Wenzel, "are married, have children, live ordinary lives. I've added some personal observations, which I should appreciate your regarding as absolutely confidential. You will see why when you read them. I can provide a copy of the personnel file on anyone who interests you."

In Voss's office an hour later, Jane Mahoney handed over the list and suggested Voss have a copy made. "Russ has gone back to the hospital," she said.

Voss glanced down the list. A wry smile twisted his thin lips and tilted his cigarette. "Methodical man, Wenzel," he said. "You can also see how his mind works."

The comments Wenzel had added to the list dealt exclusively with sexual habits and preferences. Tobin's comment that he had no special interest in homosexuals must have been a disappointment to Wenzel, who had apparently given some thought to his description of them.

Of Debora Benson he had written, "Her disaffinity for the companionship of males may suggest an eccentric sexual orientation. It may be useful to pursue this line of inquiry."

She was not the woman Wenzel had identified as definitely homosexual.

"There are eighteen people on the list," said Mahoney to Voss.

"Russ would appreciate your cooperation in checking their tax and financial records. You know what we're looking for, of course."

Russ returned to the hospital in the afternoon, carrying flowers and some books he hoped Audrey would enjoy. She had accepted the loss of at least part of the mobility of her left arm, but she felt violated, angry. She had not telephoned her mother. Russ offered to do that for her, and he placed the call from the hospital room. Mrs. Tickhill insisted she would catch the first flight for Berlin, but Audrey got on the phone and begged her not to come until they could travel around Berlin together and enjoy the flowers that would be blooming wildly in a few more weeks.

"It's a lovely city, Mum," she said. "I may decide to live here."

Later in the afternoon, Tobin drove south to Marienfelde, a neighborhood on the south edge of Berlin. He knew where Ulrich Vogel lived, but he guessed that at this time of day, late afternoon, Ulrich would not be at home. More likely, he would be at Strassenbahnhof Bierstube, his favorite bar; and likely, too, he would already be full of beer.

Both assumptions turned out to be correct. Vogel sat at a table near the window, a stein of beer before him, his huge pipe clamped between his teeth, engaged in a grumbling conversation with another man.

Tobin picked up a stein of beer at the bar and stepped over to Vogel's table.

Vogel noticed him coming when Tobin was still a few paces away. He slammed his stein on the table and stood. *"Ich kenne Sie nicht!"* he said. *"Ich errinere Sie nicht!"* (I don't know you! I don't remember you!)

"Es macht nichts aus," said Tobin with an amused smile. (It makes no difference.) *"Ich kenne Sie gut, mein Freund."*

"Der Mann ist verrückt," Vogel said to the other man at the table. (The man is crazy.) *"Aber . . ."*

With that final word and a gesture he dismissed the other

man, who cooperatively got up and left the table.

Vogel blew loudly between fluttering lips.

They spoke German.

"Why can't you be satisfied with your goddamned triumph?" Vogel asked.

"Were you ever satisfied with any of yours, Ulrich?"

Ulrich Vogel was not as old a man as he looked. He was the same age as Tobin, fifty. His hair was white, though, and his face was deeply lined. He had been, as Tobin remembered, a bulky, beefy man, clumsy in his movements but deadly to people who underestimated him. He had been like a hippopotamus: a creature who could, when he wanted to, lift his ponderous mass and move amazingly fast. He sat here now, bulkier for the beer he drank, sluggish for inactivity: a forlorn figure.

He stared at Tobin with watery blue eyes.

"Heckler is dead," said Tobin.

"I never heard of a man named Heckler."

Tobin put his hand on top of Vogel's stein, firmly interdicting another sip of beer. "You can't drown in steins, old man," he said. "You know me. You knew Albert Heckler."

"The past," said Vogel. "Ghosts."

Tobin took his hand off the stein, and Vogel lifted it and took another sip of beer—a small one.

"How would you like to go fishing for sharks?" Tobin asked.

Vogel frowned. "Which means what?"

"Nikolai Pavlovich is thinking about going fishing for sharks. In the Caribbean. Retirement. An honorable retirement. I can't offer you a fishing boat off Key West. I can offer you a better retirement—on condition."

"Meaning?"

"A mob rampaged through your offices, tossed your desks and telephones out the windows, burned your files, smashed your computers . . . "

"And put *us* on the streets."

"You didn't come to me."

"I expected something—"

"Something from the other side. Something you didn't get.

If you had come to me, we might have reached an accommo-
dation."

"We've been through this, Herr Tobin. I had nothing—"

"You had once. You waited until it was no longer timely."

"Who could have believed—"

"That the change was permanent? Maybe it wasn't."

Vogel lifted his stein, then lowered it without taking a drink.
"What could I possibly know that you want to hear from me?"

Tobin glanced around the *bierstube.* "Last night," he said,
"Albert Heckler tried to kill me. Instead, he crippled my former
wife, who was driving my car. Fortunately, she knew where I
kept an Uzi in my car, and she used it. She blew Albert Heckler
to pieces—which may be the most fortunate thing that ever
happened to him, because I'm not quite sure what I'd have done
with him if I'd got my hands on him. I might even have taught
André Guyard a new trick or two. I have one or two tricks like
that in mind. For the man who gave Heckler his orders. I *want*
that man, Ulrich. You help me find him, you may yet go fishing
for sharks."

"And if I don't, I may wind up like Albert."

"If you're lucky."

Vogel licked his lips as he pondered. "What do you want?"

"There are a thousand men like you in Berlin. Five hundred,
anyway. Whatever. You network, as they say in the computer
business. Don't tell me you don't. I want to know who contacted
Heckler, who sent him to kill me. It may not have been Colonel
Kedrov. It may have been somebody else."

Vogel lifted his stein. "I am retired."

"You're alive."

Vogel put down the mug. He stared at Tobin's face for a
moment. His own face collapsed, every trace of grit fading.

"You don't kill—"

"Heckler did. For somebody. If somebody can, why can't I?"

Vogel drew a deep breath and let strained words out on it.
"Nothing's different. The same—"

"A lot of things are different. But not men. Not our kind of
people."

Vogel stared into his stein for a moment. "Heckler couldn't change," he said. "He couldn't even be cynical. You know that's what keeps some of us sane, Tobin. Being cynical."

"Cynicism is what kept a lot of us alive."

Vogel nodded. "I thank God I was able to keep my cynicism. Always."

"That's why I can trust you, Ulrich. That's why I came to see you."

"I don't have the answer. I don't know if I can find it."

"There's some money available," said Tobin. "A cynical man will know how to put his hands on it and what to do with it."

"No promise. No commitment."

"The promise is on my side," said Tobin. "You know I keep my promises."

"You have that reputation."

Tobin was newly cautious about returning home. The government car he was driving had only one advantage over his damaged Porsche: It was inconspicuously anonymous. Even so, when he drove through Joachimstrasse for a look, he had the Walther PPK lying on the seat by his right hand. When he went to his door, the little pistol was back in his shoulder holster, but his hand was inside his jacket and his finger was looped through the trigger guard.

Two telephone messages were waiting on his recorder. One was from Erich Voss, who had called to say he had already obtained some interesting information from the BND check into the finances of the people on Wenzel's list. The other was from André Guyard, who had arrived in Berlin and asked Tobin to call him at his hotel, the Potsdamer Hof.

He returned Voss's call. Voss was out of his office. He called Guyard. Guyard inquired after Audrey, then asked Russ to join him for dinner.

They met an hour later in a Swiss restaurant. Guyard said he liked Swiss cuisine.

Why André Guyard liked any food better than any other was a mystery to Tobin. The man's obsessive cigarette smoking must surely have long since destroyed the last remnant of his sense of taste. Nonetheless, he was precise in ordering his drinks, wine, and food—discussing with the bemused waiter the way the chefs here prepared certain dishes on the menu, rejecting one or two with a disdainful shake of his head after he heard the waiter's description.

"This thing . . . the last night's shooting. It is the outrage."

"If I find out who did it, somebody's going to find out just how much of an outrage it is."

Guyard smiled a carefully measured little smile under his great black mustache. "Am I to understand I see anger in the ever-cool Roos-ell Tobin?"

"You can understand it that way."

"Be careful then, my friend. The ever cool has kept you alive. The man with the calm, analytical mind, the one who never loses sight of the key things, of the underlyings—he has been a success, this Roos-ell. An angry one might fail."

"Anger is a luxury," said Tobin.

"All emotions are a luxury."

Their drinks were put before them. Then Tobin asked, "What brings you to Berlin, André?"

"The word you sent. Voss sent. That Major Yuryev is in Berlin. If Yuryev is in Berlin, Colonel Kedrov and Mriya Meyerhold are in danger. I suppose we don't want to lose Nikolai Pavlovich and Mriya Aronovna."

"I am not their keepers."

"You don't suspect *they* ordered the last night's shooting?"

"Nikolai Pavlovich sent Mriya to me to assure me they didn't."

"So? You believe it not?"

Tobin tasted his martini. Gradually over the years, European bartenders had learned to mix an American martini. You didn't have to go to Harry's Bar anymore to find one.

He didn't answer Guyard's question. "Why would Vyshevskii send Yuryev to Berlin to kill Nikolai Pavlovich and Mriya?" he asked. "If he wants them dead, why didn't he kill them in Moscow?"

"They are here on a mission," said Guyard. "If they fail, they die. The death of the Pakistani was a failure. Kristin Kuniczak died for that failure. One of them, or both, will die for the next failure."

"You speculate."

Guyard nodded. "I speculate. How do you say? An educated guess."

"That would mean Kedrov or Meyerhold ordered Audrey shot. They were trying to kill me, to prevent my interfering and causing a failure."

Guyard shrugged. "I would not omit such an idea from my catalogue of possibles."

For a moment Tobin stared into his martini, watching the melting ice swirl visibly and gently, mixing with the gin. "You still haven't told me why you came to Berlin, André."

"I am thinking maybe I'll kill Yuryev," said Guyard.

Debora Benson stood before the mirror in Michael's bathroom, combing her hair. She gazed at it critically, wishing it were longer, wishing she had let a hairdresser give it a more vivid color. Since her fourteenth or fifteenth year, her girlfriends had heckled her about her hair. Let it grow longer. She'd done that. Cut it shorter. She'd done that. Have it curled. No. Have it teased. No. Bleach it. She did that, did it herself, and it was unevenly lightened. Give it a better color. Let a pro work on it. Put yourself in the hands of someone who'll know how to— Until she had grown to resent the whole idea of having to give it any thought at all and had determined to do the very least she possibly could with it. She bleached it and kept it cut conveniently short.

The same with makeup. She acknowledged that her face looked better—not so bland, not so vapid—if she colored her lips a little and darkened her lashes and eyebrows. A little eyeshadow, the same friends insisted. She didn't want to have to waste more than five minutes a day on makeup. So she wore a little pink lipstick and put a little mascara on her lashes. Very little.

She'd never given a damn, really. After all, what they saw was what she was. If that wasn't good enough...

Now she was sorry. She wanted to look good for Michael. She had come here directly from work and was dressed as she had been all day, in a white blouse, a knee-length tailored brown tweed skirt, and a jacket that matched the skirt. She decided to hang the jacket on the back of the bathroom door. It was really *too* severe.

He was in his kitchen, pouring drinks, slicing cheese. She had insisted he was not to take her out to a restaurant every night, so he had suggested they eat here, in his tiny suite in a residential hotel on Emserstrasse. He would order something delivered, to which she had agreed only if he would let her pay. That was the deal. You could order Chinese food in Berlin, the same as you could in any city. It would be delivered at eight. He had picked up a liter of Beefeater so she could have her favorite gin.

She sat down on his sofa. It folded out into a bed and was very comfortable, he assured her—as comfortable as a regular bed. In fact, the whole arrangement looked comfortable. The furniture was all new or almost so: a reclining chair as well as the sofa, a second armchair, a small dining table with two chairs, a large console television set.

It was quite serviceable for a man who traveled a good deal, he said. The only trouble with it was that a suite like this could never be called a home. "You see, there's nothing personal here," he had said immediately as they came in. "I mean, from the look of the place, you couldn't tell who lives here, could you? It could be me or any of fifty other fellows. Or a woman."

But he was obviously comfortable with it. He had pulled off his jacket and necktie. His charcoal gray slacks were taut across his behind, she noticed.

"Will you be going away soon, Michael?" she asked. "Traveling?"

"Not for several weeks yet. Just day trips for a while. Hamburg. Dresden. Leipzig. Prague. I'll drive those. Then I've got to get down to Munich for a few days. Might fly. Might drive. Could you get a few days off and go with me?"

"I'd like to."

"Romantic country down in Bavaria."

"Yes. And Switzerland. I love the mountains."

"Do you like to travel?"

"More than anything," she said.

"I travel all over in my business. Maybe I'd chuck it for something more—well, something else. But I've loved the traveling. I've been everywhere in Europe."

"Working in Berlin has given me chances to go places I've always wanted to see," said Debora. "Venice. Florence. Rome. Budapest. Prague. Athens..."

"St. Petersburg? Moscow?"

She shook her head. "No. I haven't even gone as far east as Warsaw."

"You should. Fascinating cities, St. Petersburg—what they used to call Leningrad—and Moscow. I've been to Kiev and really all round the western part of Russia."

"Business?"

"I should hope so. When the Iron Curtain came down, people in the East couldn't wait to blossom out in clothes like the Sportivi line. Drab we're not, my dear. Sport clothes with what they call the Italianate flair."

"Do you spend much time in Russia?"

"Not much. Two weeks a year, maybe three."

"Can you speak the language?"

"I've picked up a little. Very friendly people. Helpful to foreigners. Warm and friendly."

Debora drew a deep breath. "There was a time in the States when you could have got yourself seriously abused for suggesting that the Soviet people were warm and friendly."

"That's unfortunate."

"It's true," she said.

"The Russian people I've met have a sense of community, a sense of family, sort of, that we don't have in Britain and they surely don't have in France and Germany."

"Or in America," she said.

"Surely not. And I'm afraid our countries are characterized by a certain niggardliness. I mean, we have been asked of recent years to aid the Russian people in their economic distress; and we've done so, but only grudgingly. We've sent them food and

medicine but have not aided them in developing the means of
improving their own abilities to produce food and medicine. It's
as though we wanted to make them clients of a new sort of
imperialism."

"That's a very insightful way of looking at it, Michael."

"Well, I don't mean to make the conversation too heavy. Those
are just some random thoughts."

"I'm impressed," she said.

"My ideas wouldn't make you suspect I was too sympathetic
to the old Cold War enemy?"

"Me? Hardly."

Michael Ormsley chuckled and reached for her glass. He took
it into his little kitchen, filled it with ice, poured Beefeater over
the ice, then pared a bit of peel off a lemon and twisted it into
her glass.

"My CIA friend was in the labs again this morning," Debora
said when he returned.

"Is he making a nuisance of himself?"

"Actually, he only walked past an open door and saw me
outlining an idea on the board. He said hello, but that was all
he said."

"Difficult to think he's up to any good."

"Oh, Michael, I . . . Sometimes I think I would be better off
working for McDonald's, developing more efficient methods of
marketing hamburgers. When I was a student, I found out that
the university was doing research on ways of freezing shrimp.
Why? Because a company that marketed millions of tons of
shrimp each year had made a big grant of money to the university, in return for which learned professors were exploring
ways of preserving the flavor of shrimp after freezing. I was so
scornful! Now— What the hell, what am I doing? Is mankind
going to be any better off for anything we do at LSI? Or are
we busting our butts for big business?"

"So what—philosophically—is the difference between developing a massively parallel processor and selling Sportivi
clothes?"

"What *is*?"

Michael grinned. "If you don't know, I'm sure *I* don't."

"Forgive me, Michael. What you do may make the world *look* different. What I do may make it *be* different."

He laughed. "I'm glad you have answered the question, Debora. And I agree with you wholeheartedly. I—I've bought you a little present. May I show you?"

"Michael . . . I hope you—"

"Let me get it. It's in the closet."

He went to one of the closets and returned with a box wrapped in foil and tied with ribbon, like a Christmas or birthday present.

"Michael . . ."

"Open it. I hope you'll like it."

She slipped the ribbon off and carefully removed the foil, tearing it as little as possible. That was the way she had always opened packages, in contrast to her friends, who ripped away the wrapping, no matter how pretty, in their rush to see what was inside. She broke the tape and lifted the lid from the box. She folded back the tissue paper.

"I hope you like it."

She lifted it out. It was a white silk satin chemise, with a bodice of white lace. Also in the box was a pair of white satin slippers, with high heels and fluffy pompoms.

"Michael. I've never had anything like it! I've never had anything so beautiful!"

"Put it on, Debora," he said quietly. "Go in the bathroom and put it on."

She closed the bathroom door and latched it; and for a full minute she stood before the mirror, perplexed and dubious, holding the chemise up in front of her. A week ago she would have curtly refused to exhibit herself in such a garment. She would have called it demeaning. Besides, it would only make her look foolish. She was not the right kind of woman for this sort of thing—she, with her awkward, tall figure, her pathetic little boobies.

Michael wanted her to wear it. Did he really think . . . ?

She undressed, hanging her tailored clothes on one of the towel racks. She'd made a self-deprecating little joke about her underwear: that she bought it at J.C. Penney's; but it really was true that she'd never had anything so exquisite.

She pulled the chemise over her head, settling its two spaghetti straps on her shoulders and shrugging the lace and silk over her body.

It was even more daring than she had guessed. The silk fitted snugly around her ribs, and her breasts were provocatively displayed in the delicate floral lace. The skirt was shorter than she had supposed, covering little more than her behind. She stared at the mirror, apprehensive and ambivalent, unsure if she was alluring or a bizarre oddity.

Oh, Michael...

She pushed her feet into the satin slippers.

She opened the door. "Michael, I—" she whispered.

"You *are* an angel! I knew! I knew it would flatter you. Debora ..." He smiled and shook his head, then he rose and strode toward her to take her in his arms. "Gorgeous!" he said before he kissed her.

"I like this very much," said Nikolai Pavlovich Kedrov to Mriya Aronovna Meyerhold. "Listen—"

He pressed down the key on the tape player.

"The Russian people I've met have a sense of community, a sense of family, sort of, that we don't have in Britain and they surely don't have in France and Germany."

"Or in America."

Steiner had delivered the tape to the Köpenick house after he dropped Debora Benson at her flat, at about two-thirty in the morning. Kedrov had gone to Köpenick to pick it up so he could listen to it tonight. He had wakened Mriya so she could hear it, too.

"... we have been asked of recent years to aid the Russian people in their economic distress; and we've done so, but only grudgingly. We've sent them food and medicine but have not aided them in developing the means of improving their own abilities to produce food and medicine. It's as though we wanted to make them clients of a new sort of imperialism."

"That's a very insightful way of looking at it, Michael."

"You hear? Only now does he talk this way, and only this

much. If Kristin Kuniczak had been so subtle—"

"Mahmud Nedim might still have become angry when he realized what she really wanted from him. And so may Debora Benson. And she may threaten to expose Steiner, as probably Nedim threatened to expose Kristin. And if she does, what will Steiner do? What will *you* do, Nikolai Pavlovich?"

13

Erich Voss swiveled in his chair and pecked on his computer keyboard. "*Ach...*" he said. "You see here what it says?"

Tobin stood and leaned on Voss's zebrawood desk so he could stare at the computer screen.

"You see? It says—"

```
HIRATA, AISUKE
DH 04/1 + DM12,750S–02/1 + DM12,750S–11/2
+ DM42,455K–03/3 + DM12,750S
```

"Meaning what?" Tobin asked.

"It's a record of deposits," said Voss. "I could also show you the record of his withdrawals—of checks he's written—but there is nothing anomalous there."

"*DH?*"

"Deutsche Handelsbank. On January 4 he deposited 12,750 Deutschemarks. That is his salary check from Laser Solutions, Incorporated. You see, he deposited the same on February 1 and March 3. But look at the deposit on February 11. Aisuke Hirata deposited 42,455 marks that day—more than three times his monthly salary. Where did he get it?"

"The number is followed by a *K*. What does that mean?"

"*Die Kasse.* Cash."

"Then the *S* after each other deposit is for *der Scheck*, a check."

"Precisely. On February 11, Aisuke Hirata deposited 42,455 marks in cash. Such funds were not transferred to him from Japan. If they had been, they would hardly have come to him in cash. So, the question is, where did this Japanese computer engineer acquire more than forty-two thousand marks in cash?"

"Twenty-eight thousand American dollars," said Tobin.

"More than fourteen thousand British pounds. Whatever. Where did he get it? We are looking for anomalies in the lives of Wenzel's eighteen people. There is one."

"Good enough. Any others?"

"Among the eighteen there is a Dane who was recently divorced. Which means nothing. Sexual aberrations are more difficult to find. If there has been no complaint, there is no record."

"What else do we know about this Aisuke Hirata?"

"Immigration record," said Voss. He turned and tapped keys on another computer console.

HIRATA, AISUKE (FRAU SUMIKO)—GEBOREN YOKOHAMA, JAPAN, 19/7/48—EINWANDERER—IN DEUTSCHLAND ANKOMMEN 4/12/90—TECHNIKER—LASER SOLUTIONS, INC., BERLIN—VISUM ABLAUSE 31/12/93

Aisuke Hirata, whose wife was Sumiko Hirata, was born in Yokohama on July 19, 1948 and arrived as an immigrant in Germany on December 4, 1990. He was a technician working for Laser Solutions, Inc., in Berlin. His visa would expire on December 31, 1993.

"He has two children, I might add," said Voss. "The little girl came with him and his wife from Japan. The infant son was born here."

"On the record, he doesn't seem like the kind of man who'd—"

Voss interrupted. "Does the name Yukio Mishima mean anything to you?"

"Uh . . . Japanese author. Sort of a cult leader. Killed himself. Big protest."

"Yukio Mishima was a novelist and dramatist, also an actor. He never won the Nobel Prize for Literature, but for several years he was among the leading candidates. As you said, he was the leader of a cult. He founded a fraternity called the *Tate-no-kai*, the Shield Society: an ultra-conservative group of young men who wanted Japan to return to the days when the emperor was divine and the military ruled. In 1970 he made the ultimate dramatic gesture. He knelt, slit his belly with a knife, and slumped forward in agony. A disciple was waiting to hack off his head off with a sword. It required several strokes. Then the disciple slit his own belly, and another one cut off *his* head."

"Aisuke Hirata?"

"Mishima died in the headquarters of the Japanese Self-Defense Force—which is what they call their army. He had invaded the place with a band of followers. One of those followers—disciples—who witnessed his death was Aisuke Hirata. He was twenty-two years old at the time and a student. His father took strict charge of him after that and saw to it that Aisuke finished his education and did what conventional Japanese do: affiliated himself with a corporation. He joined a company that has since been merged into Laser Solutions, Incorporated. Professionally he is a computer engineer. But philosophically . . . who knows what he is."

"Interesting fellow."

"Mishima made a great point of physical fitness. He made himself a sort of Japanese Adonis, a man with exaggerated muscles who went around bare-chested so people could see what a specimen he was. Apparently Aisuke does something of the like. He's a genius, they say; but he's very strange, in German eyes."

"What's your source of that information?"

Voss smiled. "I can't show you that on a screen. That's from Wenzel. I called him after I found the anomaly in the bank deposits."

"What does Wenzel think of that?"

"An interesting reaction. He's reluctant to talk to Aisuke. To be frank with you, I think Wenzel's afraid of him."

"It's a thin thread, my friend: to assume that this odd bank deposit has anything to do with an attempt to steal technology from LSI. There could be a thousand explanations."

"But," said Voss, "we are looking for anomalies in the lives of the eighteen technicians Wenzel identifies as having access to highly confidential information. Here is one."

"What are you going to do?"

Voss shook his head grimly. "I can no longer assume that any deviation from standard conduct by a foreign national brings that foreigner within the purview of the *Bundesnachtrichtedienst*. Our government is firm about that. Our diplomatic relations with Japan—"

"In other words, you expect *me* to look into the matter of Aisuke Hirata."

"Initially. I can't move officially on the basis of a suspicious bank deposit. Add something more. Give the suspicion more weight. Then—but in the meantime I can help you informally. You understand, I continue to keep Colonel Kedrov under surveillance. Unfortunately, I think he knows it."

"Where was he on Sunday afternoon when Kristin Kuniczak was killed?"

Voss shook his head. "He and Mriya Meyerhold left their flat early in the morning and very quickly evaded our men. We did not pick them up again until evening. We have identified a house in Köpenick where he goes at odd hours. Meyerhold has visited *you* at odd hours."

"As I've told you."

"As you've told me."

"Yuryev?"

"The evidence against him is sufficient to justify following him. But he's a shrewd fellow. He goes nowhere an innocent tourist might not go. Museums. Nightclubs—"

"Meets and drops," said Tobin.

"Possibly. We can't identify."

"Why would Guyard want to kill him?"

"André has his own agenda. I ask of him one thing only. If he kills Yuryev, he must be sure he does it so it is plain *he* did it. I don't want it to appear that *we* did it."

*   *   *

As much as possible, Tobin stayed away from the CIA station in Berlin. His connection with The Office was well known. He was the NIO for Central Europe, but he stayed away from the station as much as he could. Over the years he had gauged his people, and he knew what they could—and couldn't—do. They held him in awe. He was a veteran of the years when a man crossed the Sector Border and, as rumor had it, sometimes killed on the other side. Or might be killed on this side.

"We've run those names," she said.

Jane Mahoney was not what you would expect in The Office. Not yet thirty years old, for sure. An attractive young woman. He had noticed that women of late liked to claim offense when men made initial judgments based on appearance—though he'd seen no evidence that women did not still make initial judgments of men by *their* appearance. Even so he had thought that Jane Mahoney was an estimable hand by any standard. Smart. Circumspect. It did not hurt that she was blonde and attractive.

"Names...?"

"The names sent by our contact at Zagorsk."

"Took a while," he said.

"Not so easy," she said. "Something useful came in from *Mukhabarat el-Alam*." She meant the General Intelligence Agency of Egypt. "They don't like to release information."

"What do you have, Jane?"

They sat in his office. He'd ordered sandwiches and beer brought in. As he and Jane Mahoney talked, they unwrapped their sandwiches and regarded them with the usual skepticism people apply when they look at brought-in lunches.

"It goes around and around," she said. "Only one name on your list of graduates from Zagorsk made any real sense. Kristin Kuniczak. And—"

"And she's dead," said Tobin as he used a little plastic knife to spread mustard over his ham sandwich.

"Which does us no good at all," said Jane Mahoney.

"No good at all," Tobin agreed.

She began to spread mayonnaise over her sandwich. "Another name," she said. "Kurt Horst Steiner."

This fellow Steiner, it seemed, had entered Egypt in 1983, carrying an Irish passport and using the name Sean O'Connor. During his stay in Cairo, a renegade KGB agent had died. Nothing linked that to Sean O'Connor, and he had left the country without hindrance. The death of the KGB agent had alerted the tough, effective *Mukhabarat el-Alam*. For several days it had surreptitiously photographed all foreigners leaving Egypt.

All those photographs were sent to Interpol in Paris, where they were scanned by computer. Among those thousands of photographs was a full-front portrait of Kurt Horst Steiner. A computer map was made of the face.

Photographs came in all sizes. People were photographed from all distances. Dimensions were meaningless. *Proportions were not.* Using, for example, the distance from the center of the pupil of one eye to the center of the pupil of the other as a base, the analysis compared that measurement to, for another example, the distance from the tip of the nose to the tip of the chin. Comparing the pupil-to-pupil measurement to a score of other measurements, a computer could create a record of a face that was unique in the same way a fingerprint was unique.

What was more, once a person reached maturity these measurements did not change appreciably. A person might gain weight or lose it, but the dimensions measured for the identification map remained in the same proportions. Still more important, a person could not change the map. Growing or cutting off beards and mustaches changed nothing, nor did wearing or not wearing various shapes of eyeglasses or wigs.

Interpol had matched the photograph from *Mukhabarat el-Alam* to a photograph of a DDR pole vaulter who had competed in the 1979 Pan-European Games. (DDR athletes were routinely photographed by the BND and others. They often turned up later as *Stasi* operatives, even as HVA agents.) The pole vaulter was named Kurt Horst Steiner. That he should have entered and left Egypt four years later with an Irish passport identifying him as Sean O'Connor was evidence enough to fix Steiner as an agent.

This was the kind of thing Interpol did. Contrary to popular impression, it was not an organization of clever international detectives. It was a central repository of information. Once it had been just a giant filing system. Now it used sophisticated computer techniques to retrieve information from its immense information banks. It did not send out agents. It never made arrests. It never, in fact, interfered directly in criminal activity. All it did was supply information to its participating police and counterintelligence agencies.

Kurt Horst Steiner must have been a clever fellow. No one had any further record of him. Until now. The CIA source at Zagorsk identified a recent graduate as Kurt Horst Steiner.

"Do we have a picture of him?" Tobin asked.

"Only the Egyptian picture from 1983 and the pole-vaulter picture from 1979," said Jane Mahoney.

She handed him the two photographs.

He had won a ribbon at the Pan-European games. The photograph was of an exhilarated youth, blatantly handsome, insolently self-satisfied. He was maybe eighteen or nineteen years old. The Egyptian photograph was of a tourist leaving Cairo, standing in the passport line, self-consciously handsome. You could almost see in his face his sense that people were admiring him.

"I want you to do something with this, Jane," said Tobin, handing her the second photograph. "Have some lab work done. Have the guys scan it and put it in the computer. Give Steiner ten years more age. Then make it a mug shot. In fact, make it two or three mug shots. Berlin police, Scotland Yard, and . . . say Brussels. No dates."

Jane Mahoney grinned. "I think we can do that," she said.

"I know you can do it. I'm not sure what I'm going to do with those pictures, but I can think of two or three ways they might be useful."

"Sneaky."

"Whatever we can achieve by sneakiness is better than what we—well, you know the alternative."

Rain was falling again. Debora Benson didn't care. She stood in it, the water running off the brim of her rainhat and over the shoulders of her raincoat. She wept openly. Others frowned and held their lips tightly between their teeth. Only Debora sobbed.

Her friend Aisuke stood beside her. As was typical of him, he had not worn a raincoat or a hat and simply ignored the cold water that was soaking his suit and shirt. He could look grim in a way no one else could. He had a Japanese way of stiffening his lips so it wrinkled his chin. He held his head high.

They were only two of the dozen or so people who had come from Dahlem to Tempelhof to watch the casket put aboard the Pakistani 727. The airplane would be towed away from this area after the casket was secure in the cargo hold. At the passenger terminal, a hundred people would go aboard, none of them aware there was a casket and a corpse in the hold.

No ceremony. No one knew how to conduct one, really. No one knew what Mahmud would have wanted, if anything. No one had any idea what his family might want. No one had come. Mahmud was being shipped home as freight.

And that, as much as anything else, was why Debora cried.

The German authorities had not released the body for two days. For another day or so, no one in Pakistan had indicated any wish to have it returned. Then, as Debora had been told, a curt wire had been received by Wenzel from Mahmud's father, asking to send his son's body home.

So here they were, standing in the rain, watching the canvas-wrapped casket being lifted into the cargo hold of an airplane. And no one knew what to say.

Debora drew in breath and strained to recover her voice. "Aisuke," she murmured. "You'll catch your death out here."

"No," he said. "Do fish die from being in water? No, and neither will I."

"It's ruining your clothes."

"To honor our friend . . . it's worth a suit of clothes."

"Have you a car?" she asked. "I'll drive you back—I'll drive you home to get dry clothes."

"I accept this privilege," he said.

There was no more to do. They had paid respect to Mahmud the best they could. Apologizing for getting her seat wet, Aisuke sat stiffly erect in Debora's MG and stared straight ahead as she drove.

His wife was at home: the diminutive, shy, and very, very beautiful Sumiko whom Debora had met only twice before. Sumiko wore a pink cashmere sweater and a gray skirt, but she bowed repeatedly and spoke in a high-pitched but subdued sing-song voice that suggested the formal kimono.

The apartment, which Debora had not seen before, was Western, even German; but somehow, in the spare way it was furnished, especially in the white vases of flowers that stood on the Western furniture, it suggested the culture of the people who lived there.

Debora was astonished by what happened. As she sat in the living room, sipping a tiny cup of hot sake, which Sumiko said was efficacious for warming the stomach on a cold and rainy day, Aisuke appeared. He was naked but for a white loincloth tied around his hips. He entered the living room and took a cup of sake. His wife showed no sign of surprise or disapproval. When he stood for a moment at the window, judging the rain, Debora had an unobstructed view of his buttocks. She had a view, in fact, of everything but his genitals.

Maybe he was exhibiting his sculptured body. It was said of him that he worked to keep a proud body and was never reluctant to show it.

"He was selling the company's secrets," he said abruptly.

Startled by that sudden affirmation, Debora could only try to conceal her reaction, pretend she hadn't heard it.

"He *was*," said the nearly naked Japanese. "I am sorry he is dead, but that is why he is dead."

The Japanese in the company took a proprietary interest in it, she had noticed: as if they were truly the owners of the company and the technology it developed. The patriarchal company-employee relationship that characterize Japanese business was altogether evident in the way the Japanese technicians related to LSI. None of them had ever worked for another company. None of them expected they ever would.

"He was victimized," said Debora quietly.

"A convenient rationalization," said Aisuke.

"Some of us are strong enough that we don't need rationalizations for what we do. And some of us aren't."

Aisuke nodded. "You find me judgmental," he said.

"Self-confident people tend to be judgmental."

He drank his sake. "I will dress, and we can return to the laboratories."

André Guyard sat on a bench in the Tiergarten, reading a newspaper. As he cracked the shells of peanuts, he ate perhaps every third kernel and tossed the rest to the birds who boldly demanded them. He was smoking, too, as always.

He wore a brown overcoat and a black Borsalino hat. His mustache had been trimmed this morning by a careful Berlin barber. German barbers knew how to trim mustaches, as French barbers usually did not. He was pleased with his trim and with the haircut he had allowed the barber to do—under concentrated observation and persistent suggestion.

They told all kinds of stories about the Tiergarten: of how immense ugly concrete towers, bristling with antiaircraft guns, had once stood somewhere in the park; of how British and American bombers had crashed on its greensward and had been allowed to sit there as *Denkmals;* of how the great park had been denuded of trees in the winter of 1945–46 to provide firewood to help keep Berliners alive. Now it was just what every civilized great city had: a magnificent central park. (The name meant game preserve. The Hohenzollern kings of Prussia had hunted in their Tiergarten just as the Tudor kings of England had hunted in Hyde Park.)

The park was dominated by the 210–foot *Siegesäule,* or Victory Monument, a tower commemorating Germany's victory in the Franco-Prussian War of 1870, which had somehow stood throughout the Second World War and the occupation of the city. To the east, he could see the Brandenburg Gate. Most of what he could see, though, was new construction: the city the Berliners had built since 1945.

Guyard, who loved to sit in the *Jardins des Tuileries* or the

Jardin du Luxembourg, read his newspaper, and toss nuts to the birds, was not annoyed that Mriya Aronovna Meyerhold was late. In fact, she could be later yet for all he cared.

But there she was, walking toward him. She wore some kind of uniform. As she came closer, he saw it was the uniform of the office attendants for Aeroflot. Ridiculous.

She sat down beside him. *"Bonjour, Monsieur le Colonel,"* she said.

"Bonjour, Mademoiselle."

They would speak French, though her idioms were sometimes Russian. She shook a cigarette from her pack and let him light for her.

"Has anything changed?" he asked.

She shook her head. "Does it ever? Will it ever?"

"So . . . Yuryev. What does he have to do with it, really?"

Mriya Meyerhold stared away for a moment, toward the *Siegesäule.* "Who really hates?" she asked. "And who just goes along?"

"A whole damned nation can go along," said Guyard.

"But of course not all the people. Not even all the Germans went along with Hitler. Some do hate. Most just go along."

"So, who hates? Chairman Vyshevskii?"

"Of course, Vyshevskii. Maybe not Andronikov. Who knows? Marshal Malinovski . . . "

"Malinovski," said Guyard, "has not enough intelligence and imagination to be—"

"There's the point, of course," she interrupted. "Vyshevskii for sure. Vyshevskii for damned sure. So Yuryev goes along. Why not? *He* doesn't care. Malinovski doesn't care, so the dear marshal will go along, too. And who else will go along with the head of The Committee? Who wants to oppose him? You have to work from strong principles to oppose the head of the KGB. If you don't give a damn—and who does?—you become a Jew-hater because Vyshevskii is a Jew-hater."

"So we attain nothing by conveniently ridding ourselves of Major Yuryev," said Guyard.

"Nothing."

"Vyshevskii. Vyshevskii, who will never come out of the Soviet Union and expose himself to us. Who therefore must be neutralized for us by his own—"

Mriya interrupted, tears rising in her eyes. "We understand each other, André," she said. "And it is hell for me."

"Leonid Ivanovich Vyshevskii is a poisonous man, Mriya Aronovna. Many lives are at stake. If The Committee recovers its one-time power and that power is held by the hard-liners, they'll close the borders again. Jews won't be able to get out. And God knows what will happen to the ones compelled to stay. There is a hard-right faction in the Communist Party that already talks about the Jews as the cause of the decline of the Soviet Union. They talk exactly the way Hitler talked in the 1920s, saying the Jews are responsible for all the nation's troubles."

"I know. I've heard this talk."

Guyard looked away from her, as if he meant to break off the conversation. In fact, he did to give her time to think through what they were saying. He crunched a peanut shell between the thumb and index finger of his right hand and tossed the two nuts to the birds.

"Nikolai Pavlovich is a key," said Guyard. "If he succeeds at what he is doing here in Berlin, that will be to the very great benefit of Vyshevskii. If—"

"If he fails, Vyshevskii could be in danger," she supplied the final words of his thought.

Guyard smiled. "And that puts you in a difficult position, Mriya Aronovna."

"Shall I deny I love Nikolai Pavlovich?"

"Please don't. I would know you were lying." Guyard cracked another peanut. "How much does he know? How much does he suspect?"

"He is no fool."

"You didn't have to say that."

"And . . . Russell Georgievich—"

"No fool."

Mriya took a peanut from Guyard's bag, cracked it, and cast the kernels on the ground. "I will not tell you what Nikolai Pavlovich is doing in Berlin."

"You don't have to. I know. Tobin knows."

"Then let him defeat Nikolai Pavlovich!"

"Let him . . . ?"

"Nikolai Pavlovich could accept defeat only from an adversary he respects as much as he respects Russell Georgievich. He could accept and . . . and live with it. And maybe then I can talk him into giving up his lifelong work and—"

"And defecting," said Guyard.

"Yes, defecting. But don't ask me to betray him. I can't do that. I can't! Think of what you are asking. It is his commitment to me that has destroyed his status within The Committee. Except for me, he might have become Chairman someday. I ruined him."

Guyard shook his head. "Not entirely. He has other problems. Rivalries. Jealousy. And he has not with every assignment been a complete success."

She shook her head. I can't betray him, André," she whispered. "Defeat him, you and Russell Georgievich. *You* defeat him. Don't ask me to do it."

"What do you think we are doing, Mriya Aronovna? Playing chess? This is not a game! Lives—"

"Save him, André!" she cried. "You and Tobin! Don't force me to choose between—"

André Guyard stared at the woman for a moment, forming a judgment, abandoning a line of persuasion he had ready, changing his mind. "I understand you," he said. "We will do the best we can, Mriya Aronovna. But let *me* not be forced to choose, either. If I am, you know what my choice will be. In fact it *is* no choice."

Patients who face the loss of a part of their body—or the function of some part of the body—vacillate between black depression and bright acceptance. When Russ sat beside Audrey on Tuesday evening, she was on the up swing.

"I can live with it, my friend," she said. "They're talking now about twenty percent loss of mobility. And, Christ, in the left arm! What did I ever do with it?"

"How about practicing psychiatry as *Frau Doktor* Tobin in Berlin?"

"I do—"

She used her right arm and hand to draw herself up a little more erect, tugging on the structure that hung over her bed. As she did that, her mood plummeted. He saw it. Depression returned.

"I do believe I hear a proposal of remarriage," she said.

Russ nodded.

"Not to be considered," Audrey said. "Not even to be thought about. Not while I'm—" She broke. She squinted, and tears glistened on her cheeks. "Only after rehab. I won't hear a proposal directed to a cripple."

"*Audrey!* You have just used a word I don't ever want to hear again. *Cripple.* You're not, and you're not gonna be. I love you, you friggin' *dummy!* Is that so damned tough to absorb?"

"Okay," she said crisply. "When the day comes when I can say to you, 'Love me and be damned, 'cause I don't need you'— and we love each other just the same, and that makes the difference, then let's talk about it again."

"You know the trouble with you, Audrey?"

"Well, you've told me before. What this time?"

"You're too fuckin' smart."

It was odd, Debora said, to have lived in Berlin for a year and never to have driven out to Potsdam. Michael had driven her out, this evening after work, just for a quick look before sunset. They looked at the Sans Souci Palace from outside but could not go in. Then he drove her to the Cecilienhof, where Truman, Atlee, and Stalin signed the Potsdam Agreement in 1945. They ate a light dinner in the dining room there and reached his flat before nine. She agreed during the drive that she would stay all night this time, that there was really no reason why she should insist, as she had done before, on returning to her own apartment in the small hours.

He poured her a drink of her favorite gin. She seemed to thrive on it. Tonight, with no show of reluctance, she changed into her white chemise.

"Debora . . . I'm going to have to go to Prague for two or three days. It would be wonderful if you could go with me. It's a beautiful, romantic city. You could see the sights while I'm keeping my business appointments. And we would be together."

"I'd have to take those days off from the lab," she said.

"Well . . . couldn't you?"

"I suppose I could."

"Aren't you entitled to holidays—what you Americans call vacation?"

"Yes, of course."

"I've been thinking of something," he said. "Two weeks. I can take off two weeks. Why don't we plan to go on holiday somewhere? Somewhere you've never been. Two whole weeks together."

"That would be heaven."

"We'll make it heaven. We can do that, you and I."

"I love you, Michael."

"I know you do. You've shown every evidence of it. So it's about time I told you: I love you, too."

Debora put her glass quickly aside and rushed into his arms. They kissed, and while they kissed he stroked her legs and hips. He pushed the chemise up so he could stroke her bare skin.

"I love you, I love you!" she whispered hotly. "I love the way you make me feel. I love everything you do to me."

He nuzzled her throat. Then he asked, "Where would you like to go for our holiday?"

"Well . . . Paris. But I've been to Paris. Spain—"

"Have you ever seen a white night? I mean a night when it's never dark."

She shook her head. "I've never seen the sun at midnight."

"You have to go to some awfully forbidding places to see that. I'm thinking of interesting cities where the twilight lasts from sunset to sunup, so it's never really dark. St. Petersburg—what the Communists called Leningrad. It's a fascinating city. So much to see there. Then we could take a train to Moscow, which is also fascinating."

Debora smiled. "My company might get a little nervous if I went to the Soviet Union."

"Well—it's just an idea."

14

TOBIN'S TELEPHONE RANG a little after eight o'clock on Wednesday morning, while he was in the bathroom.

"This is Jane. We've got a 'secret' for you, in overnight from Washington. I'm running it through the decrypter right now. I wasn't sure if you are coming in, so I thought I'd call. I can bring it over, if you want. Technically it's not supposed to leave the office, but—"

"Well, I've got some coffee brewing and picked up a bag of danish last night on my way home."

"Be there in twenty minutes," she said.

He took a quick shower, shaved, and had the coffee and danish ready in the living room when she arrived.

She carried a leather briefcase. The decoded message was locked inside. Jane took it out and handed it to him. He glanced over the cover sheet:

SECRET

CENTRAL INTELLIGENCE AGENCY

The information contained in this document is secret. Improper disclosure could reasonably be expected to cause serious damage to the national security. Unauthorized disclosure is therefore a felony.

****

Information contained in this document includes partial contents

of a signals intercept by NSA. It is to be read only by persons
with an ℵ ('ALEPH) clearance.

Tobin looked up from the document, smiling faintly.

"As God is my witness," said Jane, grinning and raising her
right hand. "I don't have clearance for the 'aleph compartment,
and I didn't look beyond the cover sheet."

In addition to classifying information as Confidential, Secret,
or Top Secret, the intelligence agencies of the federal government restricted access by assigning information to "compart-
ments." Only people with the necessary code-word clearance
could see the information in a particular compartment. Russ
Tobin was cleared for 'aleph. Jane Mahoney was not.

He flipped over the cover and began to read the message.

Page One of Two

On 4/02 NSA intercepted a coded computer transmission between the Tokyo and New York offices of Rikuchu Corporation.
Decoded and translated, the pertinent portion of the message
reads as follows—

The information received from Berlin
has proved unfortunately to be of little
value, solely for the reason that we had
already pursued the same line of inquiry
and reached nearly identical conclu-
sions.

No objection is raised as to the dis-
bursements made to obtain the data, but
you should now instruct your agent not
to pay any further money to his contact
unless the contact can assure him of access to certain specific data, as detailed in our instructions to you dated
23/01. Specifically, we must know how
much reduction the Dahlem laboratory

has been able to achieve by phase shifting. Have they broken the 0.25 micron
barrier? We hardly need explain why we
need this information.

Instruct your agent also to consider
whether or not his contact may have sold
him information, knowing that information was without value to us. Why
should we trust a technician a competitor cannot trust?

Apparently Colonel Kedrov is not the only one at-
tempting to penetrate LSI. This may make your present assignment somewhat more complex.

End of Transmission

****
This document should not be filed but should be shred-
ded and burned after it is read.

He read the last sentence to Jane Mahoney. " 'This may make
your present assignment somewhat more complex.' That's the
kind of good stuff they send you in an 'aleph transmission."

"I'm cleared for snark," she said. "But not for 'aleph."

"I know. There are no more than eighteen 'aleph clearances.
And only about fifty snarks. You're in good company."

She sipped coffee and took a small bite from a cinnamon danish. "How is Mrs. Tobin?" she asked.

"Crippled for life," he said grimly. "She'll never regain full
use of her left arm."

"I'm sorry. BND has cooled the investigation. They even
cooled the news media."

"I'm going to find out who did it," said Russ.

She saw the hard determination on his face, heard it in his
voice. "I don't doubt you will," she said.

He sighed. "So how much do you know about the etching of
computer chips?"

"I thought I knew a little something. I've tried to bone up on
it. But this term *phase shifting* is a new one on me."

"And on me," said Tobin.

"It would appear we've got some new work to do."

"It could be done from Prague," said Kurt Horst Steiner to Colonel Nikolai Pavlovich Kedrov.

"How from Prague?" asked Mriya Aronovna Meyerhold.

"I will need a little help," said Steiner.

"But how?" asked Kedrov.

Steiner picked up his sunglasses from the table and settled them on his nose. The sun had come out from behind the clouds and glared on their table just inside a window that faced the Kurfürstendamm. Steiner had been putting on his sunglasses and plucking them off as the sun appeared and disappeared.

"She is enamored of gin," he said to Kedrov. "The flavor is so strong it would disguise anything. Chloral hydrate, for example."

"Oh," said Mriya Meyerhold. "So you knock her out. Then, when she's unconscious, you—what?"

"Drive her to the Soviet frontier."

"A mere six hundred kilometers, by the most direct route. Six hours on the road, with an unconscious woman sitting in your passenger seat."

"Steiner!" Kedrov snapped. "How can you be so stupid?"

Steiner's chin jerked up. "I was assuming I might have a little help. A van. One man driving, another looking after her in the rear. She need not remain unconscious more than an hour. Half an hour."

Colonel Kedrov clasped his hands and pressed them to his chin. "This is crude, Steiner. If, in the end, nothing else promises success, we might have to do as you suggest. Or something like it. For now, I don't want you to give up on the possibility that she will come voluntarily, even that she will voluntarily give us all the information we want."

"It depends on how much time we have, Sir."

"We have time for persuasion," said Kedrov. "I want you to try persuasion first. Listening to your tapes, I hear good progress. Go on the way you are. If I had wanted to kidnap the young woman, I would have assigned someone to do that, and she would have been in Moscow for a week now."

Steiner nodded. "What do I tell her? When do I tell her?"

"You have won her devotion," said Kedrov. "Now reinforce it. When you have reinforced it sufficiently, it may be possible for you simply to tell her the truth, or most of it, and she will still love you and do what you want her to do."

"The young woman is highly intelligent," said Steiner. "And she has strength of character."

"You have played most expertly on her emotions. Continue. We have time."

Max Wenzel, Tobin had decided, took advantage of every opportunity his position might afford to charge a lunch or dinner to his company expense account. He had said this morning that his schedule of appointments was really quite full for today— except that he could meet Tobin for lunch. He suggested Der Löwe. The prematurely warm weather had brought out a few golfers, but the bar was all but deserted at 12:30 when Tobin and Wenzel sat down at one of the heavy oak tables and Hans Günsche came to ask what they would like from the bar.

"The beer is the speciality of the house," said Wenzel.

"Beer, then," said Tobin.

"It was in this place that Mahmud Nedim sat with Anne-Lise Hein—and was, apparently, corrupted."

Tobin glanced around the room. It impressed him as a heavy, somewhat oppressive place, typical of German *Bierstube* and English pubs. It did not impress him as the ideal location for a romantic interlude.

"I need to ask you to define a technical term," he said to Wenzel. "What is phase shifting?"

Wenzel tipped his head to one side, as if he were both surprised and amused by the question. "Everyone," he said, "is looking for a way to etch the circuits that will make possible the 256–megabit DRAM chip. Mahmud Nedim was working on electron-beam lithography. Others—no one at LSI—are working on X-ray lithography. Either one of those may be technology of the future, but they are fantastically expensive. So some companies are looking for ways to wring the last bit of precision out of the old optical lithography. The most promising technique is known as phase shifting."

"Meaning?"

"Glass masks have always been used to etch circuits. Light passes through the transparent parts of the pattern on the mask. Light is blocked by the opaque parts. It's very much like a photographic negative. A phase-shifting mask is *all* transparent. But some parts are thicker than others. Light slows down as it goes through glass. If you can adjust the thickness of the glass with enough precision, you can have light coming out that is 180 degrees out of phase. The peaks and valleys of the waves cancel each other, leaving an extremely narrow dark spot that etches an extremely fine line."

"How fine?"

"At present, maybe zero-point-three micron. Within the realm of practical possibility . . . maybe zero-point-two micron. Beyond that—" He shrugged. "We think the electron beam has to be developed."

"But you are working on phase shifting?"

"In a small way. We are not committing much to it. Uh—you will understand that this is highly confidential."

"You have given me a list of eighteen people working on sensitive technology you consider somebody might want to steal. Is anyone on that list working on phase shifting?"

"I suppose several of them have worked on it from time to time. Mahmud Nedim did. I didn't put any emphasis on it when I made the list. It is nothing of very great importance to us."

Hans Günsche brought their beer. Tobin waited until the German was out of earshot before he continued. "Would you," he asked, "consider phase shifting as a quick and dirty way of doing this year what the electron beam may do two or three years down the road?"

"You could put it that way, yes. Phase-shifting cannot do what the e-beam will do. At best, it is what in English you would term a stopgap."

"But if I were stealing something to give my country a quick shot of progress—"

"Perhaps . . . " Wenzel nodded. "I suppose so. It could be that our Russians want—but what brings it up? Why do you raise this point about a technology you said you didn't know?"

"Rumor," said Tobin. "Just a rumor. I'd appreciate your reviewing your staff and identifying for me the people doing the most work with optical phase shifting."

Wenzel nodded. "I will review the list I gave you. Incidentally—for whatever it means—one of the people on the list is taking a few days' holiday time, starting tomorrow. She is going to spend two or three days in Prague, seeing the sights. She's tired, she says. And tense. She wants to relax a little. She will not return to work until Monday next."

"Debora Benson."

Wenzel nodded. "Debora Benson."

"Is she going alone?"

"I could hardly ask her."

"I find myself compelled to find out."

André Guyard worked alone. He always had. Well, not always.

When François Mitterrand became *Président de la République* in 1981, he was determined to bring France's various police, intelligence, and counterterrorist forces under democratic control—that is, under the firm control of his socialist government. He sensed that these Gaullist services would never accept democratic-socialist control, so he abolished some agencies. He abolished the *Service de Documentation Extérieure et de Contre-Espionage*, better known as SDECE. Specifically, he abolished SDECE's *Service 5*, known by the title *Action*.

Action had been formed for one purpose: to protect Charles de Gaulle against a secret organization of disgruntled army officers who had decided to kill him. It achieved its purpose quite simply and directly: by the brutal murder of any officer reasonably suspected. After that, it was feared not just by army officers, but by everyone who ever heard of it.

Within months of taking office, President Mitterrand was

threatened by a conspiracy as dangerous as that of de Gaulle's army officers. It was based on Corsica and was a combination of Coriscan irredentists, left-wing radicals, and members of *Union Corse*, a centuries-old criminal conspiracy that eclipsed in ruthlessness anything that ever occurred to the Sicilian Mafia. The president's life was in danger.

President Mitterrand had already consented to the establishment of a new counterterrorist organization to replace SDECE. It was known as GIGN, *Groupe d'Intervention de la Gendarmerie Nationale*. He acknowledged the need for it, but he hoped to keep it under control. His hopes were dashed. GIGN was soon as ruthless—and as difficult to control—as *Action* had ever been.

One of its members was the young André Guyard. He quickly came to the attention of Captain Paul Baril, head of GIGN. When Baril determined, with the consent of President Mitterrand, to set up a special Élysée cell—that is, a small elite force to protect the president—his third appointment to the fourteen-man force was Guyard.

Guyard's habit of operating independently was established during his service with the Élysée cell, which worked on the fringes of the official intelligence services, took information from them, and never gave any in return. It reported only to the president, whose confidence in it grew far greater than his confidence in the police force ostensibly responsible for his safety.

Late in the summer of 1983, the cell unofficially and illegally placed a tap on the telephone of one of the editors of *Le Figaro*—though later the office of the president would vehemently deny it. Information developed from the tap led the officers of the cell to conclude that one Alfonsi Bartholdi was the head man of a small team of terrorists plotting the assassination of President Mitterrand.

Bartholdi was a fanatic champion of Corsican autonomy, an intemperate orator, and the organizer of various independence "fronts." His name had been connected to several terrorist outrages, but it was assumed he had not directly participated in them, since he was a member of the Corsican assembly. The telephone tap revealed that he had recruited an assassination team and had procured ten kilograms of Semtex, a plastic explosive, which he had hidden in an apartment in the Nineteenth Arrondissement in Paris.

André Guyard was never troubled by indecision. On October 14, 1983, he walked into a café in the Nineteenth Arrondissement, where Bartholdi habitually drank a bottle of wine between five and six o'clock. Guyard spotted Bartholdi sitting at a table with two friends. He walked directly to that table, pressed the muzzle of a 7.65mm automatic to Bartholdi's ear, and pulled the trigger. He did not know who the two friends were. The one who made a quick move, as if he were a bodyguard drawing a pistol, died from a bullet through the forehead. The other threw himself to the floor, where Guyard left him as he walked out.

In the matter of Reuss, Guyard had acted on information supplied him by The Institute—Mossad. No one in Paris questioned him in the matter. No one would. Except a very few men very close to the *Président de la République*, no one asked what the Élysée cell did. Reuss, for example, had been no threat whatever to the president. No one asked André Guyard why he had decided it was necessary to eliminate Otto Reuss. Who in the government of France could possibly care?

And now, who would care if André Guyard determined it was necessary to terminate Major Ivan Stepanovich Yuryev? If he did it, he had his reasons. Presumably the *Président de la République* knew what he was doing and understood his reasons. That the president had never heard of Yuryev was not suspected.

It would be no great achievement. Tracking Yuryev in Berlin, Guyard had concluded the Russian was a cretin. By extension, Leonid Ivanovich Vyshevskii was a cretin. But not one, Guyard reluctantly concluded, to be lured to Berlin to take Yuryev's place when Guyard put the pistol to the head.

Or should he do Russell Tobin a favor? Would Tobin know how to appreciate a favor?

Yuryev alive might have a lot to say. Yuryev alive might be made to tell many things worth knowing.

Guyard shifted his glance back and forth between the lunch on his plate and the contemptible little Russian at the table by the window. The Bristol-Kempinski should serve the best lunch in Berlin. Well—if it wasn't, it was nothing the hotel should be embarrassed about. Yuryev, with his shifty, apprehensive glance, his conspicuous want of self-confidence, might be embarrassed to be seen in public. Guyard was a chain-smoker, but he did not smoke while eating. Yuryev did.

Yuryev's eyes fastened as long as he dared fasten them on a woman sitting alone at a table in the middle of the dining room. She was wholly unaware of him, and when her eyes shifted so her gaze might pass over him, Yuryev swiftly pretended to be fascinated with something outside the window. He did not dare let her eyes touch his. He looked as if he wanted something of her: to be clasped to her and cuddled like a teddy bear, begging her to understand that anything more intimate would frighten him.

Contemptible!

Guyard finished his lunch, savoring the last forkful with as much enthusiasm as he had the first. Then he lit a cigarette.

Yuryev. Odious little man. It would be a pleasure to rid the world of him.

Tobin spoke on the telephone with Jane Mahoney.

"She'll be leaving in the morning. Let's assume she'll be leaving early. I'd like to know who she travels with. If you can get a picture, all the better."

"I'll take care of it myself."

"You may want a backup. We don't know if she's flying, going on the train, or what. She may be taking a cab to Tempelhof. Or to a railroad station. If so—"

"I know, Chief. Somebody has to tail the subject while somebody else parks the car."

"Sorry. You know your business."

"And I know where she lives. Discretion is the name of the game."

"Okay. I'm on my way to Marienfelde to see Ulrich Vogel. I'll be stopping by the hospital after that."

He found Vogel where he had found him before: in the *Bier-*

stube where the man spent most of his afternoons. As before, he was drinking beer, smoking his pipe, and chatting with two other men who seemed to have nothing else to do.

This time Vogel did not try to dismiss Tobin by grunting that he didn't know him. He told his two companions that he had to talk privately with this old friend. The two left the table.

"I haven't had time to complete my inquiries," said Vogel.

"I didn't suppose you had. But what progress?"

Vogel drew smoke from his pipe. "On Sunday morning Albert Heckler met with—let us say he met with an old friend. He owed that friend eleven thousand marks. He paid him. In cash. When the word came around that Albert was dead, there was a headlong race to the rooms he rented. Someone got there first. When others arrived, the rooms had been torn apart. Whoever got there first probably found something. What do you suppose?"

"Vultures."

Vogel shrugged. "We all have to live."

"Eleven thousand . . . plus what somebody got from his rooms. Does anybody have any guesses about who?"

"Who *has* that kind of money? You asked for guesses. I'd guess this, to start with: that he had a lot more than the eleven thousand. Eleven thousand is not the kind of money you pay for that kind of job. Besides, it's an odd number. Ten, maybe. Not eleven. Or twelve. Fifteen? Maybe. Twenty? More likely. Or twenty-five. That's my first guess: There was more, probably a lot more. So who has that kind of money?"

"The KGB."

Vogel shrugged again. "Not *Stasi*, for damned sure. And I can't think of any reason why the BND would—"

"All right. I've guessed that much myself. Can you make any case for it?"

"They're back in town," said Vogel. "They're hiring errand boys."

"Explicitly . . . ?"

Vogel picked up his stein, looked sadly into it, and shook his head. "I—"

"Call for another one," said Tobin. "One for me, too."

Vogel signaled the bartender. "They recruited a few of us," he said. "From the day when we were thrown out. Younger men, mostly. Not me, for sure. Not Heckler. But as soon as they established their new presence in Berlin, they called for some of us. To be hewers of wood and drawers of water."

"And paid assassins."

Vogel nodded.

"Who's in town besides Kedrov?"

"Lots of them. It's not like it used to be. But they're here. I wouldn't be surprised to see their tanks roll through the streets again! It's the only thing they're good for, only thing they know. Goddamned barbarians!"

"Did you ever hear of a KGB major named Yuryev?"

"No. No, I never heard of him."

"How about a woman named Kristin Kuniczak."

"She's dead."

"What do you know about her?"

"Only that she's dead. When word came around that someone had cut her throat, one or two remembered her. But I never saw her, never worked with her, and know nothing about her."

"How about Kurt Horst Steiner?"

"He's in Berlin. He was a rising young star in *Stasi*—in the HVA, actually—when the roof fell in. The KGB recruited him. Now he's back. Two men have seen him in town."

"Do you know him?"

"Yes. He was an athlete once. A pretty boy. He got some of his promotions, uh... that way. I never could stand the sight of him."

"Where has he been seen?"

"Around. Restaurants. On the street. On the Ku-damm."

"What can you tell me about him?"

"I can tell you two things about him," said Vogel. "The first is that he is capable of killing anyone—and I mean anyone—for any reason, or for no reason at all. He is extremely dangerous."

"And what's the second thing you can tell me about him?"

"He is not very smart. He makes mistakes. Whatever he is

doing in Berlin, he is doing it under someone else's constant supervision. They would never turn him loose and let him operate on his own."

"Can you find him for me?"

"Maybe."

"You do that for me. That will be worth money."

Russ spent an hour with Audrey. He found her in a solarium, sitting in a wheelchair, watching the sun set. Her arm was propped in a frame attached to the chair, but she told him they had made her move it during the morning and again during the afternoon. Also, during the day she had telephoned Washington three times to arrange for other doctors to take her patients for a while.

She agreed she would move into Russ's apartment when she was released from the hospital. Her mother would come to Berlin to help take care of her. She would stay in Berlin two or three weeks anyway, while she continued the therapy the hospital had already begun and while she formed her decision about what to do after those weeks.

Before he went home, Russ stopped at the Potsdamer Hof and called Guyard's room. He thought he would ask him to meet for dinner. He was uneasy about Guyard, unsure of what he might do, how serious he might have been in suggesting he was thinking of killing Yuryev.

Guyard was not in the hotel. Russ left word that he would be in the bar, then in the dining room, for the next couple of hours. He might as well have dinner there. He was in no mood to have it at home alone.

It was nine-thirty when he drove into Joachimstrasse. As was now habit, he drove through the street, checking before he parked the car. When he did park, it was a block away. He walked on the side of the street opposite his building and took the time to gaze into every doorway before he approached his own door.

He glanced around before he unlocked his door. He turned the knob, stepped back, and let the door swing inward. He stared into the darkness of his tiny foyer and the living room beyond, and saw nothing. Then he switched on the lights.

Mriya Meyerhold sat in the armchair facing the fireplace. She was dressed in the Aeroflot uniform she had been wearing in Berlin. Only—

The blouse and jacket were soaked with blood. It hadn't dried. It glistened wet in the light. Her tongue lolled between her parted lips. Blood had gushed through her mouth. Her chin was red with it.

He picked up the telephone and put in a call to Erich Voss at home.

━━━━━━━━━━ **15** ━━━━━━━━━━

DEBORA VENTURED OUTSIDE the glass double doors of their bedroom, onto the little balcony that afforded her a wondrous view of the street and beyond, over some low rooftops, of the magnificent St. Vitus Cathedral. She had not believed the city could be so beautiful; she had come because she wanted to be with Michael, not because she wanted to see Prague.

They had arrived not long after noon, checked into the hotel, and ate lunch in a tavern where you could walk into the kitchen and inspect the brewery that produced the beer you drank with your meal. And the food, whatever it was, was delicious.

Michael had business to do in the afternoon. He had promised to return to the hotel by six. In the meantime, she could explore the city. Memorable sights were within easy walking distance of the hotel. She had walked across the Charles Bridge, had visited St. Niclas's Church and then the gardens of the Valdštejn Palace. She had decided to save the Hradčany Castle and the St. Vitus Cathedral until tomorrow. She stood on the balcony, looking toward them, wondering if Michael might find time to go with her tomorrow. It would be so much more exciting to see the castle and cathedral if he were with her.

Debora glanced at her watch. Five after six. He had promised to be back at six.

* * *

"You know I couldn't just walk up to the guy and shove a camera in his face," said Jane Mahoney. She waited for the reaction of Russell Tobin, not sure what it would be. "I—"

Tobin shook his head. She couldn't have faced the man and taken his picture. Yet the picture she had taken of the man who had picked up Debora Benson that morning showed only a rear quarter-profile of his face. It wasn't the kind of work she liked to hand to Tobin, especially not today of all days.

"It looks like mousy little Debby has captured herself a real beau," she said to him. "Picture or no picture, I can tell you for sure. I got a good look at him. The guy's a hunk. Not only that, off they went in a beautiful Jag."

She knew that Tobin had spent most of last night and most of the day with Erich Voss and other agents of the *Bundes-nachtrichtendienst* and with detectives of the *Kriminalpolizei*, trying to make some kind of sense of the murder of Mriya Meyerhold. She knew they had finally managed late this afternoon to locate Colonel Kedrov to tell him the news. He had agreed to meet Voss and Tobin for dinner. They had much to discuss, Tobin had said wearily.

This was the first time Tobin had been able really to focus on the Debora Benson problem.

"The Jag is registered in the name of Michael Ormsley," she said. "British registration. The address is a flat in Belgravia. MI5 is checking that out for us."

"I hope we aren't putting a full-court press on Debora Benson's innocent affair."

"I contacted the Prague station. They located the Jag this afternoon. It was easy enough. I gave them the license number. There aren't many Jags in Prague. They just checked the parking garages used by the best hotels. Our couple is staying at a first-class hotel."

"Good for them," said Tobin, putting down the photo of Michael Ormsley.

"Chief..."

Jane Mahoney could not overlook the fatigue and anguish that distorted his face. Russ Tobin had impressed his staff in Berlin station as a man of the old Cold War, not ruthless but capable of ruthlessness and absolutely remorseless. She could not help wondering what had been the personal relationship between the NIO and Mriya Aronovna Meyerhold. In three days this man's wife had been shot and a woman who apparently meant something to him, something more than just another KGB agent, had been murdered. Jane guessed he had not slept in forty-eight hours.

Berlin station had received bits and pieces of the story all day. Mriya Meyerhold had been seized on the street, somewhere between the Aeroflot office and Tobin's apartment. Maybe she'd been snatched from a bus, maybe from a cab. In any case, she had been immobilized by a heavy injection of a morphine-based drug from a needle shoved into her hip, through her clothes. When the wire was drawn around her throat in Tobin's apartment, she died from loss of blood. She'd had no idea of where she was or what was happening to her.

"How did they get into your apartment?"

"That was easy enough. Since when did a lock stop anyone?"

Agents of the BND questioned every neighbor. No one had noticed anyone carrying a drugged woman through the front door. She had been brought in after dark. The medical examiner estimated the time of her death as between eight-thirty and eight-forty-five. The puncture wound from the hypodermic needle was on her right buttock. It was easily found. It was immediately below a small bloodstain on her white nylon panties.

Jane Mahoney knew that Tobin himself had placed the call to Kedrov after a day-long effort to find a number for him. He had given Kedrov the news. He said he believed he had heard shock and grief.

She heard it, too, and saw it, in the voice and on the face of the NIO.

"Keep on it, Jane," he said. "It's very possible the death of Mriya Meyerhold and Debora Benson's trip to Prague are some way related."

"I asked Prague station to keep an eye on her."

"Good . . . good. Now I—maybe I can get an hour's nap before I go to face Nikolai Pavlovich Kedrov."

While she waited in the room for Michael, Debora sat at the little desk and wrote postcards to her father and mother and to her sister, telling them she was in one of the world's most beautiful cities and that she was *happy!*

She was happy. Oh, how few times in her whole life had she known the delicious sensation of happiness! She had quickly suppressed a troubling intuition that there was something unreal about this happiness. Even if there was, she would savor it while it lasted. If it was illusory, she would postpone regret and enjoy what she felt while she could.

He was half an hour late, but he arrived in an exuberant mood, carrying half a dozen boxes gift-wrapped in foil and ribbon. Mock sternly, he demanded that she strip naked; and when she was naked, he began to hand her the boxes one by one, in order. She untied the ribbon and tore the wrapping off each box; and, laughing with mixed delight and embarrassment, she dressed in his gifts.

Dressed. Half-dressed. No bra. Sheer white panties that were almost no panties: nothing but a smidgen of lace and nylon stretched over a little of her backside and nothing much more. A white lace garter belt that held up sheer white stockings. A white silk mini-dress that covered her only from her armpits to halfway between her hips and knees—and clung to her like plastic wrap. Finally, to protect her shoulders against the cool of evening, a white silk stole.

They went for a walk before dinner, through narrow streets in the Old City—streets he knew and that she would never have found as a tourist. It was surely one of the world's most romantic places. The center of the city was medieval, and it was beautiful.

Hand-in-hand with Michael, she walked through narrow cobblestone streets, marveling at old houses that had seen more history than she knew.

People stared at her. If she had been with anyone but Michael, dressed this way for any reason but that he had chosen these clothes for her, she would have been miserable. Shamed.

But not with Michael. He was pleased with her, proud of her. So she could endure it. She might learn to be proud of herself. Why not? Why couldn't his image of her be more valid than her self-image? Why couldn't she change?

He announced they had reached the restaurant where they would have dinner. A cellar. Old brick. Real ivy somehow kept alive. Candles. The smell of tobacco smoke, somehow not oppressive here, mingled with the odors from the kitchen. People jabbering cheerfully in languages of which she could not understand even one word. Here again, people stared; and when Michael took her stole and draped it over the back of her chair, conversation at tables around them stopped for a moment.

The food and wine were called by names she could not even pronounce, even when Michael recited them to her.

He ordered clean-tasting white wine to be drunk with their appetizer and, with their entrée, a red that was almost black. They began their dinner with a freshwater fish that Michael said were caught in streams in the mountains nearby.

For some reason, he began to talk about her hair. "You know," he said, "I think if you cut it very, very short. I mean, you know, that's stylish right now. Some famous stars cut their hair very short. It might give you a certain . . . how shall I put it?"

"Cachet?"

"Yes. A certain elegance. Obviously, it will grow out in time— and then can be styled otherwise."

They had no Beefeater gin here. She loved the dark red wine. They shared two bottles of it. Oddly, the wine went to her head more than the gin did.

"This is a good city for style," he said.

"Michael . . . can you take some time to play tourist with me tomorrow?"

"As a matter of fact," he said, "I had a very successful afternoon. P'raps tomorrow afternoon can be freed up. P'raps we can find a first-class hair stylist for you in the morning, and in the afternoon we'll—"

"Visit the castle?"

"Of course," he said. "Whatever you like. I'll make a point of finishing my meetings on time."

Russ Tobin, Erich Voss, and Nikolai Kedrov met for dinner in the quiet, formal dining room of a club called *Der Herrschaftlichverein*. It was a room frequented more for lunch than for dinner, and only four other tables were in use. Only men sat at them. Conversation was muffled. Each group seemed to demand its privacy. The table reserved by Voss was near a baronial fireplace now cold and filled with potted plants.

Colonel Kedrov was sad and angry. His heavy lower lip protruded more than usual. His blue eyes were narrower, harder. The wrinkles around his eyes and mouth had deepened since Tobin saw him last. Kedrov listened to the others order drinks, then told the waiter to bring a bottle of vodka to the table.

"Nikolai Pavlovich," said Tobin bleakly in Russian, "I deeply regret the death of Mriya Aronovna. As you sent me your assurance that you had nothing to do with the injury to my former wife, and regretted it, let me give you my same assurance and sympathy."

Voss did not speak Russian but understood enough to know what Tobin had just said, and he added his own expression of sympathy in German.

After that, they spoke German, the one language all three shared.

"What are you thinking, Nikolai Pavlovich? Yuryev?"

Kedrov nodded curtly. "Very possible," he said.

"Why?"

"Any one of many reasons," said Kedrov. He glanced across the room, impatient for the bottle of vodka. "Major Yuryev is nothing but a drudge for Chairman Vyshevskii. The chairman long resented Mriya Aronovna. He had his reasons."

"Anti-Semitism," said Tobin.

"He wouldn't kill her for that," said Kedrov. "He was capable of imposing . . . disadvantages because of that, but he wouldn't kill her. No. If the orders for her death originated in Moscow, they were based on a different reason."

"Which is?"

"The matter of Otto Reuss. That episode sat very ill with Chairman Vyshevskii and Vice-Chairman Andronikov. With me, too, for that matter. Except that I held her in . . . very high personal regard, I— In any case, the fact that she was killed in your flat strongly suggests she was executed for betraying the Soviet Union in the Reuss affair."

"But why now? Why now, after all this time?"

Kedrov looked up and saw the waiter coming with their drinks. He waited until everything was on the table, the waiter was gone, and he had poured himself a glass of vodka. "She told me," he said, "that she suspected she was being followed. Part of the time, anyway. As you know, she *was* followed the night she came to your apartment to bring you my assurance that I'd had nothing to do with the injury to your former wife. Whoever followed her could not have known *I* had sent her to you. In any event, she had been there before and stayed all night, had she not? That she was spending nights in your flat may well have suggested to someone that she was again betraying the Soviet Union. The word probably went back to Moscow that Mriya Aronovna Meyerhold was again holding clandestine, late-night meetings with Russell Tobin. The word may have gone back that she was on the verge of defecting. And maybe she was, Russell Georgievich."

"She wanted to go fishing for sharks—but only with you, Nikolai Pavlovich. Not without you."

Kedrov lifted his chin high, and for a moment he stared down into his glass of vodka. The corners of his mouth turned down. Then something in his eyes suggested he had reached some kind of conclusion and drawn himself inward.

"You knew the relationship . . . " he said quietly to Tobin.

"Yes."

"Eleven years . . . "

Years bring a solemn gravity to a man, whether he wants it or not. It had happened to Tobin. He had been acutely conscious of it. It had happened to Kedrov, and it was something more they shared. The Russian remained erect. He retained a strict dignity. But this latest blow had further eroded the spirit that had been Kedrov's. The once-ready smile would have to be forced now, for a long time.

"She warned me against Yuryev," said Tobin. "She was clearly afraid of him. She said he may have ordered the death of Kristin Kuniczak."

"That is very possible," said Kedrov solemnly.

"What would be his reason for doing that?"

"I am not certain," said Kedrov. "My guess is that Kristin Kuniczak, who was once an agent—recruited by me, in fact, from UB—had become a... what is the English expression? A loose cannon. An independent. Pursuing her own agenda, as you Americans say."

Tobin glanced at Voss. He could not say to Kedrov that he knew Kuniczak had been retrained at Zagorsk, couldn't say it without acknowledging that he had a source there. Both men understood. Kedrov was lying.

Then the Russian said, "That was all the more unacceptable because she was one of the few non-Soviet agents selected for special retraining in the new work our agency is now going to do."

"What work is that, Nikolai Pavlovich?"

Kedrov downed the vodka remaining in his glass and reached for the bottle. "The question implies that one of us is a fool, Russell Georgievich. Since you certainly don't think *you* are, you imply that I am."

Tobin grinned. "Well said. My apology."

"Accepted. A not-very-serious gambit."

"You remain a worthy opponent, Nikolai Pavlovich. I regret that we remained adversaries until Mriya Aronovna lost her life."

"A word of advice for you, then," said Kedrov. "If you care about your former wife, get her out of Berlin. Maybe out of Europe. Put her under strong protection. The people who knew Mriya Aronovna was meeting with you also know that André Guyard is in town and that you are meeting with him. You are involved in a dangerous game, Russell Georgievich."

"I thank you for your word of advice," said Tobin. He picked up the menu the waiter had left. He shot a hard, cautioning

glance at Erich Voss. They had decided to ask Kedrov about
Kurt Horst Steiner, but it was obvious now that would not be
a good idea. "What do you recommend here, Erich?"

Debora was a little troubled by the way Michael was turning
her into his fantasy: the woman he'd never had but wanted to
have and now *could* have in this pliant American who would
submit to his every whim. She knew that when he returned to
the hotel again today, he would be carrying boxes, more gifts,
more clothes. This morning he had walked with her to the hairdresser's shop five blocks from the hotel. He had conferred with
the hairdresser in a language she could not understand and had
left, assuring her he would see her in their room at, say, one
in the afternoon.

She'd been unable to talk with the hairdresser. He had done
what Michael had ordered. She'd been tearful as she walked out
onto the bustling street in mid-morning. Except for her certain
knowledge that what the hairdresser had done was in the best
of taste and style, she would have wept.

Almost nothing was left of her hair. The hairdresser had
darkened it first with a rinse, then cut it. On the sides and back,
he had run clippers as high as the tops of her ears, leaving only
a meager dark bristle. On top he had snipped away maniacally
with scissors, leaving a bristle that stood no more than two
finger-widths high—except in front where he left just enough
hair to be brushed a bit, toward the rear and left.

In a calf-length raincoat she walked through the streets, ex-
cruciatingly self-conscious, sure that everyone must be staring
at the nearly bald woman. But . . . but they didn't. They had
stared at her mini-dress last evening, but they did not stare
now. She saw three or four other young women with this same
cut. It was the style, the current fashion for anyone bold enough
to accept it. In fact, she saw, or imagined she saw, some envious
glances from girls hurrying along the streets, probably to their
office jobs.

Before she returned to the hotel, before Michael came, she
gained a self-confidence she'd never had before. When he arrived

a little after one as he had promised, she was ready for him: undressed but for last night's lingerie, with a little more makeup on her face than she usually wore, and wearing a smile that was not artificially brave but real and happy.

He had brought only a bag with a pair of faded and skin-tight jeans plus a bulky, loose knit, multicolored wool sweater. They went out for lunch and for their tour of the castle and cathedral.

Back at the office, Jane Mahoney was gathering information about the Jaguar registered to Michael Ormsley—and about Michael Ormsley. MI5 had checked the address in Belgravia. It was a bed-and-breakfast hotel. Michael Ormsley had rented his room about a month ago. He had been seen there during a few days, then had disappeared and had not been seen since. His rent had been paid a month in advance, and a check had come from Berlin, paying for another month. He had bought the Jaguar at an agency in Mayfair about the same time he rented the room. His British driving license was in order, and he had paid by check drawn on the Bank of Scotland. The Bank of Scotland confirmed that it had an account with him. His current balance was £2,301.50. He had established the account only a few days before he wrote the big check to purchase the automobile, but he had made several deposits since and had written several more checks. His checks had been written to two German banks, one in Berlin.

Except that the address, car, and bank account were all of such recent origin, everything about Michael Ormsley looked ordinary. His passport dated from 1984. His address in 1984 had been Manchester.

Mahoney had returned a question to MI5. What were the sources of the deposits Ormsley made in the Bank of Scotland? And from what address in Berlin did those deposits come?

Tobin was in Marienfelde, meeting again with Ulrich Vogel.

"This guy," he said. He handed Vogel the rear quarter-profile photo that Mahoney had managed to take of the man who'd picked up Debora Benson and driven her to Prague. "Look like anybody you know?"

Vogel shrugged. "You want to know if that's Kurt Horst Steiner? The answer is, it could be. Who can tell, picture like that? But it could be. That's the kind of guy he is. I mean, the guy in the picture is the type."

"This is not your problem," Vogel said to Tobin, tapping the photograph with his finger. "Your problem is Major Yuryev. He didn't kill Meyerhold in your living room as a friendly greeting."

"You're sure it *was* Yuryev?"

"What's sure in this business? Heckler kept up his contacts with The Committee. I haven't heard the name Yuryev, but he laughed about the man he was meeting, called him a little weasel. Does that describe Major Yuryev?"

"I don't know. Does it?"

"You had better find out."

"Who killed Mriya Meyerhold?"

"I'm going to guess. Someone from Moscow. If it was any of our crowd, it would be one of the new-trained ones they put so much trust in, somebody like Steiner. Nobody knows anything about it."

"Nobody *admits* to knowing anything about it."

"Have it your way. If I were you, I'd be careful. Whether it was Yuryev or not, somebody handed you a black spot. It was a warning."

Debora and Michael made love and took a nap before they went out to dinner. Tonight she wore the same white mini-dress she had worn last night, and he hired a cab to take them across the river and up the hill beyond the castle and the cathedral, to a restaurant more elegant than the one where they had eaten last night. Sitting in a room glittering with the light from crystal chandeliers, Debora saw that no woman there was more chic than she was.

Chic—

Cynical realism had reasserted itself as she dressed for this dinner. Chic was superficial. It was also at least faintly ludicrous. This new image Michael had given her was a deception. She was not the woman it suggested. She didn't want to be the woman it suggested. It was fun now, but she wondered how the people back at the LSI labs would react to her when she walked in Monday morning with her hair all cut off. More than that, she wondered what her father would say. He and her mother would be coming to Berlin in the summer. Maybe it would grow out by then.

Michael was oddly quiet and thoughtful tonight. He described the dishes he ordered for them, and the wines, and he talked about the wines and liquors of some of the countries he visited; but the impetus to be buoyantly amusing was absent. She had learned that he disliked strolling musicians in restaurants. They interfered with conversation, he said. They interfered with people's enjoyment of each other. Tonight, whenever the violinist was anywhere near, Michael lapsed into silence and did not try to talk to her above the music, as he usually did. During these silences, he stared at her, glancing at her eyes from time to time, but mostly with his eyes fixed on her shoulders.

"Have you finished your business in Prague?" she asked him.

"We could drive back to Berlin tomorrow," he said. "But I was thinking we would go Sunday."

"Michael, this must be costing you a lot of money. Please let me pay for—"

"The company pays for everything," he said.

"Not for the gifts you've bought me."

"For the hotel, the meals . . . don't think about it, Debora."

"I don't want to make trouble for you with your company."

"Believe me, I'll have no trouble from my company."

As they passed through the lobby of their hotel, he stopped at the concierge's desk and asked that a bottle of champagne be sent up to their room.

In the room, because a waiter would be coming, she did not undress. She pulled back the curtains and looked at the moonlight on the roofs of the city. He stepped close behind her and put his arms around her, cupping her breasts in his hands.

"It's only the first of many beautiful cities we'll see together," he whispered in her ear.

The waiter came. Michael poured champagne. He suggested by gentle gesture that she take off the white dress. She did and faced him in the white panties, stockings, and garter belt. She was stricken once more by returning realism, a troubling appreciation that what she was showing him was not who she was.

"I ordered champagne to make this an even more special night," he said.

"It *is* special."

He raised his glass. She raised hers. They drank.

"I love you, Debora," he said. "You've said you love me. Will you marry me?"

"*Michael . . .*"

God, why hadn't she expected this? They had said they loved each other, said it repeatedly; but for some reason she had not expected a proposal. She was stunned and confused. What had she expected? *He wanted to marry her!*

"Debora . . . ?"

"Of course, Michael! Of course, I'll marry you! I love you!"

And why did she say yes so easily? She was agreeing to change her entire life! Nothing—*nothing* would ever be the same.

She couldn't think about it, could not temper her bewilderment, because he drew her into his arms and began to kiss her. He kissed her for a full two minutes, passionately and yet with the studied gentleness of a lover.

"But Michael. Michael— I'm not what you see. I'm not the woman you're looking at."

He turned away from her, picked up the bottle, and poured more champagne into their glasses.

"I'm not what you think *I* am, either," he said.

She accepted her glass from his hand. "I suspected that."

"Indeed? What did you suspect?"

"Only that behind the facade of the suave English sportswear salesman, you are something very different."

"But suspecting that—"

"Suspecting that, I love you anyway. Maybe more, in fact.

I'm not sure I could be in love with a sportswear salesman."

"What do you suspect I am?"

"Oh, I don't know. A fugitive from justice. A cat burglar. A jewel thief. An embezzler. A deserter from some country's army. A spy. *Not* a serial murderer. *Not* a rapist. *Not* an accountant, *not* a lawyer, and *not* a sportswear salesman."

He put down his glass and reached for her hands. She put her own glass down. They joined hands, at arm's length.

"I'm not English," he said. "I'm Russian."

"A KGB spy," she said dispassionately, with dull fear that she was speaking the truth.

"An intelligence agent."

"Ah . . . yes, of course," she whispered. "All the difference in the world. I— I'd thought of it, actually. And what is your real name . . . Michael?"

He smiled. "Fortunately, it is Michael. Mikhail, in Russian. I am Mikhail Alexeivich Orlov. And you are right. I am no sportswear salesman, no accountant, no lawyer." His smile broadened into a grin. "I am not even much of a Russian anymore, since I have spent most of the past seven years in England and Germany."

"And you have been acting under orders to seduce the mousy American mathematician who knows something about massively parallel processing."

He drew a deep, stiffening breath. "I was under no orders to fall in love with you, none to ask you to marry me, none to *want* you to marry me."

She glanced down over her nearly naked body. "I feel I should cover myself," she said quietly.

"As you wish. But I will be happy if you don't."

Debora freed her hands from his and walked toward the bed, where her mini-dress lay. She stood with her back to him, flexing her shoulders. All her life things like this had happened to her. People had delivered shocks to her, and she'd had no commensurate shocks to hand them to get even. What she would have given to be able to say, "Oh, it's all right, Michael. I'm a Mossad agent myself and had to kill the last four KGB men I encountered."

She had no surprise for him—except maybe one. She resisted the impulse to snatch up the dress and pull it over her head, even to grab a sheet from the bed and wrap herself in it. Instead, she turned and faced him with her firm little breasts defiantly bare, dressed—or undressed—as he wanted her, as he probably thought fixed her role in submissiveness. "So, Michael . . . are you authorized to pay me for what I can tell you about massively parallel processing? If so, how much? Enough to pay for the travel we've talked about?"

"I am not authorized to pay you," he said. "We don't work that way anymore. My assignment is to try to persuade you to help my country overcome one of its paralyzing technological insufficiencies."

"'Persuade.' How were you to do that? By seducing me?"

"Yes."

"Well, you can report back to Moscow that you failed. Because I won't help you steal from my company. Even if we marry, I won't do it. Not even for my husband."

He nodded. "All right. I understand. But—'Even if we marry,' you say. Do you mean you would still consider marrying me?"

"If you defect," she said.

16

THEY SAT AT A small round table on the sidewalk, their backs to a tiny bakery from which delicious smells of hot bread and cakes wafted onto the cobblestone street. Debora had agreed there was no point in driving back to Berlin today. Tomorrow would be soon enough.

"Let me suggest something," he said after their coffee had been set before them. "Prague—I had meant to stay here another day. I was glad you agreed to. But it has got some odd associations now, hasn't it? In two hours we could be in Karlsbad. Beautiful town. Some fascinating sights to see. The mineral baths. Or we could go to Dresden. Both are on the way back to Berlin, or only a little out of the way."

"Karlsbad," she said. "All right. Your recommendations have been good so far."

"I promised you beautiful cities. We can still have them."

"Not impossible, I guess," she said.

"I wasn't supposed to fall in love with you."

"I don't like that cliché, Michael. I've heard it in too many bad movies. Perhaps we can salvage something. I'm not sure what. Don't strain for it."

"Strain . . . reach. Grasp. I probably will."

She shrugged. "I won't play coy. For one thing, I'll still sleep with you if you want. I've enjoyed that."

"So have I. And more."

"I only regret that I let you arrange to have my hair cut like this," she said. "I look like a fool."

"You do not look like a fool."

"I can't be what you wanted to make of me."

"Why talk about it?"

Last night he had been gone from the room most of an hour, between eight and nine, and she had wondered if he had not gone somewhere to make contact with a superior, to get his orders. She was almost surprised when he came back. She had wondered for a little while if he might not just disappear.

They had slept together. He had been gentle and had not tried to enter her—though she remembered he was still caressing her lightly when she went to sleep.

In the jeans and the bulky sweater he had bought for her she felt comfortable, and she focused her thoughts on the hours yesterday afternoon when they had walked hand-in-hand through Hradčany Castle and the St. Vitus Cathedral. She had let herself think there was nothing wrong, when her instincts had warned her there was. They'd warned her the day when he dented her fender and telephoned. They had warned her less and less urgently after that. Still, she hadn't been a fool. Michael *had* made her happy for a while. Why spoil that only because it was imperfect and had never had a chance?

"I first came here when the Russians were the lords and masters of this part of the world," he said.

"You are too young to have come to kill the Prague Spring," she said.

"I was still a child in 1968, as were you."

"I remember 1968. I was an unhappy little girl."

"Odd. I was a happy little boy. I thought of myself as happy. I wanted to be an athlete and didn't see any reason why I couldn't be a good one, a champion, an Olympic medalist. Of course, I had more energy and enthusiasm than skill."

"You must have had something good about you to work for the KGB. I understand a man or woman has to be somebody special to become a—"

"I work in the First Directorate, let me emphasize that," he interrupted.

"What difference does that make?"

"I have always served in foreign intelligence. I am not a policeman."

"Have you ever killed anyone?"

"Yes, as a matter of fact, I have: a defector, a traitor. I found him in Egypt and executed him."

"I must have shocked you when I suggested you defect."

"No. My country has a bad reputation. Americans and others suppose we kill people all over the place, all the time. The Committee—you understand that KGB means Committee for State Security. First Directorate, anyway, is just like the CIA, MI6, BND, DGSE . . . "

"How much like the Gestapo?"

He shook his head. "Once, maybe, it was something like that. That is, some of the other Directorates were. Not First Directorate. That is why I emphasize that I am with First Directorate. I am not a thug, Debora."

She glanced around. "I'm sorry, but I have in mind an image of Russian tanks rolling through these streets."

"We couldn't send tanks here now. Oh, we *have* tanks. And bombs. And missiles. What we don't have is enough to eat. If I lived at home—well, I work for The Committee, so I enjoy extraordinary privileges. My father is a scientist, my mother a dentist. My whole family has privileges. And I am doubly privileged, because I live in Germany. But—" He shook his head. "Nearly three hundred million people . . . live in squalor. I mean squalor compared to what the former fascists in Germany enjoy. Utter squalor compared to what you Americans enjoy."

"And so you try to steal other people's technology," said Debora.

He hesitated, then said, "Yes. If that is what we have to do. It is a question of our survival—survival with any kind of dignity."

"And that is how Mahmud Nedim died. Someone trying to steal technology."

Michael-Mikhail glanced up and down the street, nodding. "Debora . . . in some ways you are an innocent. Technology is a commodity, an extremely valuable commodity. Priceless, some of it. It is bought and sold, ethically and unethically. Think of it as being like cocaine. The stuff sells for so high a price that people kill to obtain it or to control even a tiny segment of the market. The same with technology."

"Then I could be—"

"Kidnapped," he said. "Drugged. Your mind and memory drained. And afterward, they might dump you alive."

"And might not."

"And might not. But let me tell you something. If my superior officer, or his superior officer, had the least suspicion I meant to kill someone in order to carry out an assignment, they would— I would not serve out the day. I would be dismissed instantly. The Committee has renounced that way of operating. Entirely."

"But you'll steal," she said pointedly.

He sighed. "It is the policy of your government, according to its repeated official pronouncements, to *help* the Soviet Union build a competitive economy, not to discourage it or frustrate it. If we are not going to fight, we should compete in fair and open markets. How many presidents have said so? But how can the Soviet Union compete if it is constantly denied access to the basic technologies it needs to build a competitive economy? Are the Soviet peoples condemned to live through the next century as the world's *peasants?* If so... why should we not use our weapons? Who wouldn't?"

"Who denies you these basic technologies?"

"Corporations. Governments say, help the Soviet Union. Companies say, *buy* help if you can; we'll not give it to you. We don't have the money to buy it, so—"

"So you don't get it."

"And we fall further and further behind. Your father said it was good that the Soviet Union should have the hydrogen bomb. And it *was* good. Because both of us had it, neither of us dared use it. Why would it not be equally good for the Soviet Union to have sophisticated computers so that we can build a productive economy capable of meeting our people's needs? Your government says that would be good, but your businessmen continue to shuffle and deal the cards so we cannot win the game. *Win* the game? So we cannot *play* the game. Is it in the national self-interest of the United States for our hundreds of millions to be driven to desperation? Your government doesn't think so, if its statements are to be believed."

Debora stared at him all the time he was speaking, then turned her eyes away and stared at the street. "You give me a lot to think about, Michael. Michael? What do I call you now?"

"Of course, Michael. That is my name in the language we speak to each other."

"I promise you one thing," she said. "I will not report you to that arrogant bastard from the CIA."

"I am grateful, Debora—though he probably knows who I am, anyway."

Major Ivan Stepanovich Yuryev shook the hand of Boris Navrozov. He nodded and gesticulated, grinning and speaking animated Russian. Navrozov, who clutched an Aeroflot ticket in his left hand, stood two hands taller than Yuryev, which still left him a shorter-than-average man. He had a newspaper tucked under his arm. A small travel case sat on the floor beside him.

Navrozov glanced up at the flight board, then pointed at the case sitting on the floor. Yuryev nodded. Navrozov walked off briskly as Yuryev swept his gaze around the departure area and cleared something from his teeth with a fingernail and his tongue.

Navrozov pushed his Aeroflot ticket down in his inside jacket pocket as he approached the men's room. After it was safely in place, he patted it nervously and even put his hand inside and felt it, to be sure the precious ticket was really there and in no danger of falling out.

He was in a hurry, really, to reach the line of urinals. Only one other man stood at one of them. Saturday morning was not the time of many flight departures. In fact, not many flights left Schönefeld Airport at all anymore. The Western lines used Tempelhof, and the airlines of the former fraternal republics had switched there, too. Otherwise the flights on the board had all gone or were scheduled to go after noon.

Navrozov stepped up to a urinal. The other man glanced at him but turned his eyes back to his business after an instant. The other man zipped up his pants and walked out of the room without stopping to wash his hands.

Another man came in as Navrozov let his stream strike the white porcelain and felt the small euphoria of relief. He was conscious that the man was behind him, apparently on his way to one of the urinals a little farther down the line. He was amused. What was superior there to those closer to the door?

That was Navrozov's last thought. He didn't hear the dull pop of the sound-suppressed 9mm automatic. He saw a gout of his own blood, with some chunks of his flesh, strike the porcelain of his urinal. He was confused as to why the electricity should have failed at what had to be some kind of extraordinary moment. If that was his blood in the urinal, he had to be able to see it to understand it. But suddenly it was dark.

When Ivan Stepanovich Yuryev saw the excitement around the door to the men's room, he did not linger to find out what had happened in there. He grabbed his colleague's travel case and strode toward the exit.

His car was in the parking garage across the way. He hurried out of the terminal building into bright spring sunshine, conscious that he was panicking and that his colleague was being forced to fly to Moscow without his clothes and papers. No matter. Standard procedure. You didn't stand around when something nonstandard was happening.

Where had he left the damned car? Third level? Yes, third level. Elevator. Self-service elevator. *No!* Not inside one of those closed boxes, with whomever came in. He took the concrete-and-steel stairs smelling faintly of urine because a few men chose to—

Oh, my god.

"Major Ivan Stepanovich Yuryev."

The man waiting for him on the stairs was not much taller than he was: a swarthy man with a thick black mustache. Yuryev had never seen him before, but he knew who he was.

He was death.

The man shook his head. "So predictable," he said in a German accented almost beyond Yuryev's understanding. "If you worked for me, I would have fired you long ago. You are too transparent for your trade. I'm sorry it is only you. I'd rather have had Vyshevskii. But this will be a message to him. He will understand it. He will understand why I didn't even keep you alive long enough for interrogation."

Yuryev stared in petrified horror. The man with the mustache pointed a huge pistol at him—huge because a big suppressor had been screwed onto its barrel.

"I'm not—"

"Mriya Aronovna. The one in there killed her on your orders. So, *smert*, Yuryev. *Smert!*"

One shot. In the moment of consciousness left to him, Yuryev knew that one shot—producing amazingly little pain—had damaged him far beyond the remotest chance of survival. It was too late for fear. He felt regret.

"How many goddamn things can go to fuck on the same goddamn morning?"

Voss was with Tobin in the CIA station office. Mahoney was with them.

Jane Mahoney had just come in to report: "Gone. They checked out in Prague about thirty minutes ago. Had a leisurely breakfast at a sidewalk café, then made tracks. Oh, incidentally—she's had all her hair cut off. She's stylish as all hell now."

Tobin blew an angry sigh. "Tell Herr Voss what you told me earlier."

"The Jaguar that Mr. X and Debora Benson drove to Prague is registered in London in the name of one Michael Ormsley. Michael Ormsley carries a British passport, dating from 1984. The passport was obtained by showing a birth certificate, indicating that Michael Ormsley was born of Mrs. Duncan Ormsley in Manchester on October 21, 1961. Somerset House—the British repository of vital statistics—confirms that. It has on record a birth certificate showing that Michael Ormsley was born in Manchester, at Dragon's Lying-in Hospital on that date. The difficulty is that Dragon's Lying-in Hospital has no record of a Mrs. Duncan Ormsley giving birth there on that date or any other. In short, the birth certificate is a forgery—forged and slipped into the records sent down from Manchester to London in 1961."

"And left alone there for twenty-three years," said Tobin, "until someone, for some reason, needed a false passport."

"Nothing terribly unusual," said Mahoney. "For decades the KGB—and for that matter Hitler's *Abwehr* and *Sicherheits-dienst*—created false records of births, marriages, and deaths. They seeded the archives with them, for when they might need them."

Voss smiled. "Do none of us do the like?" he asked.

"Whatever the hell," said Tobin, unable to conceal his ire, "a young woman is somewhere in Czechoslovakia or Germany with a man we cannot identify, on her way to who knows where. *And* she knows enough about massively parallel processing to—"

"What she knows is worth billions of dollars," said Mahoney. "Whether she's in the hands of the KGB or—"

"Or the goddam Mafia," said Tobin grimly.

"A problem, surely," said Voss. "But I thought this other problem might dominate our discussion."

"Tell Jane. She doesn't know."

"We've lost our principal villain," said Voss. "I mean, it has been convenient for everyone to blame everything on Major Yuryev. But that's not going to work anymore. Yuryev is dead. And so is another Russian, an identified KGB agent. Both of them were shot with the same 9mm pistol. At Schönefeld Airport. And no one admits to having heard a shot."

"Guyard," said Tobin.

"Working on his own agenda," said Tobin. "Dare we hope he's finished it and will go back to Paris?"

"And our final problem for today," said Voss to Mahoney, "is that Aisuke Hirata has withdrawn his forty-two thousand

Deutschmarks. He hasn't absconded. Just withdrew his money."

"Actually, there is one thing more," she said. "Colonel Kedrov took the morning Aeroflot flight to Moscow. He is accompanying the body of Mriya Meyerhold."

"You are Colonel Nikolai Pavlovich Kedrov?"

"Yes."

The young man in the gray uniform of a police militiaman was deferential. He had boarded the airplane, and a stewardess had led him back to Kedrov's seat. As the other passengers stared, the young man saluted.

"The Chairman sent me to meet you. He wants to see you immediately to convey his sympathy. I will take you past formalities and directly to a car. I am at your service to make everything easier and quicker."

Kedrov doubted that. The young man might be deferential, but his orders involved something more than simply helping the bereaved man to bypass formalities. What was more, Chairman Vyshevskii had something in mind besides conveying his sympathy.

"The coffin—"

"It will be moved directly to the Synagogue on Bolshoi Spasoglinishchevskaya."

"Synagogue . . . ?"

"At her family's request."

An hour later, Kedrov sat in the office of Leonid Ivanovich Vyshevskii. The man with the snakelike head smoked one of his green cigarettes and regarded the colonel with a gaze that did not manifest sympathy.

"I regret the unfortunate death of Mriya Aronovna Meyerhold," the Chairman said woodenly.

"She was a faithful servant of the Soviet Union," said Kedrov, a little defiantly.

Vyshevskii raised his eyes. "Perhaps."

"I assure you."

"Very well. You flew to Moscow from Schönefeld Airport this morning, did you not? Did you see Boris Navrozov on the flight?"

"I am not certain I know Navrozov well enough to recognize him," said Kedrov. "Anyway, I'm not aware of seeing him."

"How long before the flight did you board the airplane at Schönefeld this morning?"

"At the very last possible moment," said Kedrov. "There was some difficulty about getting the coffin aboard."

"Very last moment . . . so you were in the airport terminal for a considerable period before—"

"I was in the freight terminal, fighting paper pushers. I had to order a baggage handler to drive me across the ramp on his cart."

"Do you mean to say you were not inside the terminal?"

"Only briefly."

"Are you unaware of what happened in the terminal and in the parking garage half an hour before the flight took off?"

"I am not aware of anything . . . unusual."

"You are not aware that Boris Navrozov and Ivan Stepanovich Yuryev were shot and killed at Schönefeld Airport this morning less than half an hour before you boarded your flight?"

"I was not aware of that, Comrade Chairman."

"Then of course you have no idea who killed them or why."

"I have no idea who killed them. I can think of several reasons why," said Kedrov.

"I suppose also you have no idea what has become of Vasily Grebenshchikov, who has simply disappeared."

Kedrov shook his head. "No idea. I hope, Comrade Chairman, you are not suggesting I have murdered my colleagues."

The Chairman frowned, then slowly shook his head. "I suppose not," he said. "The Frenchman is in Berlin."

Chairman Vyshevskii took a final puff on his green cigarette and crushed it in the big glass ashtray that, besides his pen-and-pencil set, was the only object on his desktop. He lapsed into a characteristic habit: bobbing his head slowly up and down as he pondered. His upper body swayed in a strange slow rhythm, and the similarity between this and the movement of a swaying snake once more impressed itself on Kedrov.

"I wish to change the subject," he said after about half a minute. "Just where is Kurt Horst Steiner?"

"In Prague."

"He is not in Prague."

"He is in Prague. I spoke with him on the telephone this morning."

"He is not in Prague. He and the young woman left there late in the morning. They have not been seen since."

"Driving back to Berlin," said Kedrov.

"No. They would be there by now. And they are not."

Colonel Kedrov shook a cigarette from a pack and lit it with a lighter of American manufacture.

"What progress is Steiner making with the young woman?" asked Vyshevskii.

"Last night he told her he is a Russian. 'Ah,' said she. 'A KGB spy.' He admitted he works for us. She did not go into hysterics. She slept with him."

Vyshevskii's eyes narrowed, and he lifted his chin and fixed a distrustful stare on Kedrov. "He took that risk? He told her he works for us? What if—"

"Comrade Chairman," Kedrov interrupted. "I am no fool. If she had become hysterical, or threatened to call the CIA, Steiner had only to knock on his hotel room door, and our people would have entered and helped him to subdue her quietly. If we don't know where Steiner and the woman are at the moment, that is only because the people who are following them report to me. If I were in Berlin—or if Mriya Aronovna were alive— we would know exactly where Steiner is."

"The time has come," said Vyshevskii, "to settle this matter. I mean, the matter of the woman. I want her brought to Moscow immediately."

"Comrade Chairman. Let me remind you of our reasons for adopting the original plan. If the woman is kidnapped, the repercussions will be most unfortunate. Among other things, Western technology companies will tighten their control over their employees, thus making our next project doubly difficult. If she comes to us voluntarily, it would only be assumed she is a foolish young woman in love."

"*When* will she come to us voluntarily?"

"Soon."

"That is not an acceptable answer. Let me remind you of how vitally important this operation is. You *know* what's at stake. You're supposed to know, anyway. That's why you were sent to the Conference on the Applications of Higher Technology, so you would learn how much is at stake in this operation and all others like it. Now you tell me, really quite casually, that the Benson woman will come here 'soon.' When is soon, Nikolai Pavlovich?"

"Kristin Kuniczak pressed too hard, too fast—which you and I emphatically characterized as a mistake," said Kedrov. "Now Steiner is being more subtle, as both you and I demanded."

"Nikolai Pavlovich, if you bungle this mission—"

"Allow me to suggest, Comrade Chairman," said Kedrov coldly, "that if this operation is botched, it will not be by me. It will have been by the late Ivan Stepanovich Yuryev, who I assume is the man who attempted to kill Russell Georgievich Tobin—and succeeded only in crippling his ex-wife."

"*I* authorized Major Yuryev's attempt to kill Tobin," said Vyshevskii. He lit another green cigarette, his hand trembling slightly. "I judged that Tobin was within days, perhaps hours, of turning Mriya Aronovna."

"Mriya Aronovna was *not* about to be turned," said Kedrov, suppressing his anger with difficulty—the anger that seized him as strong suspicion changed to a certainty.

"I remind you of the Otto Reuss affair, Nikolai Pavlovich," said the Chairman.

"Which was never proved," said Kedrov. "A suspicion does not make an affair. And I remind you that Mriya Aronovna did very effective work for us for many years."

"Under your sponsorship."

"She would never have come to my attention, I would never even have met her, if she had not already established herself as a highly effective agent, in spite of her . . . handicap. She was *loyal*, Comrade Chairman."

"Then, Nikolai Pavlovich, explain to me why Mriya Aronovna spent two nights in Russell Georgievich Tobin's flat. She met him other times as well."

Kedrov shook his head. "*Two* nights? I know she spent one night there. She telephoned me and—"

"How did she explain the fact that while you were here in Moscow she was arrested and held overnight by the German police? Or the fact that Tobin came to the prison and took her away from there in his car, to a restaurant where they sat and talked for an hour and a half, leaning close together and speaking Russian? What were they talking about, Nikolai Pavlovich? Did she tell you?"

Kedrov shook his head. He wished he could believe Vyshevskii was lying—or repeating lies told him by Yuryev. He controlled himself. Rage and anguish would only blur his focus, which now had to fasten rigidly on his own survival. "I insist," he said dully, "that Mriya Aronovna Meyerhold was no traitor, no defector, no double agent."

"I know how firmly you believe that, Nikolai Pavlovich. I authorized the attempt to eliminate Tobin as an effort to save Mriya Aronovna. When that failed—"

Kedrov stood. He found within himself the courage to end the interview, taking the Chairman's prerogative. "I am glad to know the truth," he said. "It will be difficult to live with. It would have been more difficult to live without it."

Audrey sat in a reclining chair in her hospital room. Her arm hung in a sling. She wore a pink robe Russ had brought her over a white cotton nightgown.

"You can leave here tomorrow," he said.

"I know."

"We won't be going to the flat. I've given it up. I'm moving out of it."

"It isn't safe, hmm?" she said.

"No, I suppose it isn't. Besides, the neighbors don't want me there anymore. They're afraid. Anyway . . . Erich Voss has given us the use of a house in Charlottenburg for as long as we want it. It's a safe house guarded by the BND."

"Where we can live like Don Vito Corleone," she said scornfully. "Inside the walls of a compound, with gunmen at the gate. I think I should go back to Chevy Chase."

"In a week, two weeks at the most, this thing is over."

"And then what?"

"Either I'll retire, as you want me to do; or I'll tell you I never will. That will be soon enough to go home to Chevy Chase."

"My mother will be here tomorrow."

"I'll meet her at Tempelhof."

Michael had returned to the car frowning, to report that the Grand Hotel in Karlsbad could not accommodate them that night. He had something scornful to say about a businessmen's convention that had filled the hotel with *bourgeois*, then had whipped the Jaguar impatiently out onto the road again, speeding south. So they were not at Karlsbad, where they had expected to be, but at Marienbad, which Michael assured her was an equally good, if not better, spa. Anyway, they were comfortably accommodated in the Esplanade Hotel and had time before dinner to sample the waters long-reputed to restore health to those suffering from nearly any ailment.

You drank the water. You bathed in it. You could even sit by one of the steaming pools and just breathe the stinking vapors.

"My grandfather," Debora told Michael, "believed no medicine could possibly be efficacious if it did not have an absolutely nauseating taste. If water is loaded with sulfur and smells rotten, it must be good for you."

The clientele of the spa was clearly divided into two groups: the elderly ill who came in fragile hope of relief and the kind of younger people who also sat under frame pyramids and wore crystal necklaces or copper bracelets. Conversation overheard around the pool was full of astrological terminology.

Debora and Michael had not brought bathing suits. They bought paper suits at the pool desk and ventured into the hot sulfur water in the hope it would not dissolve the paper.

"Goethe took these waters," said Michael. "And Wagner, Chopin, Strauss... the emperors went to Karlsbad. The artists came to Marienbad."

In the dining room two hours later, her mini-dress brought not just stares but gasps and hostile frowns. Debora congratulated herself. Two weeks ago she would have cared.

Over dinner, Michael returned to the subject of technology. "It was our own mistake," he said. "Or... actually it wasn't. Actually the mistakes were made by a little coterie of old and ignorant men who had no mandate from the people. Should the people suffer for that?"

"Ideologues," she said. "Faith. Obsession with believing what is conspicuously not true. Your Marxist ideologues, our Christian faithful, and—worst of all, maybe—the Islamic believers. The most destructive people the world has ever known."

"I understand you, Debora," he said. "But I am different. I was taught to believe. I grew up where the least deviation from orthodoxy condemned a person to lifelong subservience and deprivation."

"We have orthodoxy," she said. "Many orthodoxies, in fact. And Americans have to be very careful to identify which orthodoxy prevails wherever they happen to be. It's more complicated with us, but Americans can be and are punished for deviations from the received truth, religious or secular."

"So we have much in common."

She smiled at him. "Much in common. Which doesn't mean I am going to give you technological secrets from the company that pays me."

"I am pleased that you don't resent the idea."

"I don't resent it," she said quietly. "Your argument is valid. The world might be a better place if we shared our technology."

"We do share medical technology," he said. "At least we do

except when an American pharmaceuticals company develops a new medicine and will allow it to be used to treat only those who can pay for it."

"You have rehearsed your arguments, Michael."

He nodded. "I hoped to convince you," he said simply.

Wrapped in his overcoat, Nikolai Pavlovich Kedrov stood on Bolshoi Spasoglinishchevskaya, staring at the Jewish synagogue. It was, he thought, oddly deserted. This was Saturday, after all—their sabbath. The synagogue was a handsome building, with tall, thin columns in front. He could see dim light from inside.

The night was cold. A sharp wind carried crystals of ice that cut his face. He walked to the door. The big doors were not locked. He pulled one back and stepped inside.

The place was not much different from a church. It *was* a church in a sense, he supposed. He was in a foyer. Another pair of doors led into a sanctuary. A light burned there: a lamp. He knew nothing of their customs or traditions, but he guessed that lamp was kept burning always—or as always as Jews could manage in this country, where these places had regularly been invaded and desecrated.

He had never been quite certain how much being a Jew meant to Mriya. They had rarely talked about it. She had said her Jewishness was something she couldn't change. You couldn't renounce it, at any event. Wishing she were not a Jew was like wishing she had blue eyes, she said.

Well . . . you couldn't escape your Russianness either. There was a story about a man—he couldn't recall the name. Anyway, the man was a writer, and he had spent years in a labor camp in Siberia, for writing something critical of the government. Later he was allowed to emigrate to Paris. After he had been in Paris some years, another Russian, come to Paris for a visit, asked him which had been more difficult, his first six months in the labor camp or his first six months in Paris. The first six months in Paris, the man had replied. After all, when he was in the labor camp he was still in Russia.

Maybe because she was a Jew, Mriya had not been a Russian in that way. She could talk about leaving forever, to go fishing for sharks in the Caribbean.

A man walked toward him: a small young man with a dark black beard and small round eyeglasses. He wore the little black skullcap the Jews liked to wear.

"Welcome," he said. "May I help you?"

"I was a very good friend of Mriya Aronovna Meyerhold. I was told her body was brought here."

"You are Colonel Kedrov?"

"Yes. I was long detained on business this afternoon."

"I am Rabbi Oblako. I regret we could not delay the burial any longer. Mriya Aronovna had remained too long unburied under our law. We waited for you as long as we could. Her mother was with her, and her brother. They asked me to convey their regard to you but to ask you not to contact them."

"I will conform to their wishes, Rabbi," said Kedrov. "Give them my respect and my sympathy."

Kedrov glanced around the synagogue one more time before turning away from the young rabbi. Warmth. That was his impression: a great warm chamber, with little light except for the lamp hanging at the front. He wondered if the warmth were Russian or Jewish. Like an Orthodox church, the sanctuary was intimate in spite of its size. It was inviting—indrawing, if there was such a word. People found comfort in it, no doubt.

Dismissing such old-fashioned sentimentality, he nodded at the rabbi and walked out into the cold and dark and wind.

He drove north, toward Gorki Street and the building where Mriya had lived with him most of eleven years. He was not certain he wanted to spend the night there.

So. Chairman Vyshevskii himself had ordered the death of Mriya. No surprise. Yuryev would not have carried enough authority to do it on his own. But why?

Why? In the end, for all his deficiencies, Vyshevskii was no fool. What was more, he was uncompromisingly rational. He was an anti-Semite and didn't like Mriya, but he would not have ordered her death for that reason. He didn't just suspect her role in the Otto Reuss affair, he knew; but he would not have chosen just now, after so many years, to punish her for that—unless he had another compelling reason.

Tobin. The Chairman believed Mriya had been once again compromising herself with Tobin.

And maybe she had been. Yes. Maybe she had.

Which endangered the mission. Which was important. It was worth the life of Mriya Aronovna Meyerhold.

It was worth the life of Nikolai Pavlovich Kedrov.

He wondered who would be in the shadows behind him, now that Major Yuryev was dead. Someone. Without doubt. He understood now that he was only the front man of this mission. The mission belonged to the Chairman himself.

His apartment on Gorki Street was not far from Red Square, and tonight he drove along the Moscow River and into Red Square, beneath the walls of the Kremlin. Snow had begun to fall. It sparkled in the lights. Wind drove it across the great square. How many nights had he paused here just to look at this: snow falling past the red stars that had glowed from the tops of the Kremlin towers, and through the lights and onto the pavement of the square? As a schoolboy carrying books, he'd sometimes stopped here while his companions ran on, mocking him for stopping to stare at something they could see any time, when it wasn't cold and windy.

He stopped the car. He got out and stood and raised his face into the snow. Suddenly Nikolai Pavlovich Kedrov knew something. He wanted to live. He would perform this service for his country, and survive, and be honored for it. It was his patriotic duty. And when the time came, they'd give him his *dacha*.

17

"WHY SHOULD THERE be talk about defecting?" Michael asked. "I mean, isn't that something from the old time? If an American decides to go to England to live, no one says he's defecting. If a German goes to live in France, that's not defecting. The word implies hostility. More than that. It implies war, almost. And that's not the way it is between our countries anymore—or so everyone says."

They had left Marienbad not long after nine. They would not return to Berlin the way they had come, he had said. He would show her some different country. Instead of driving north, he had turned west and crossed the border into Bavaria. Driving through magnificent mountain scenery, they had crossed the divide and come upon the headwaters of the Main River. This brought them shortly to an entrance to the Nürnberg-Leipzig-Berlin Autobahn, on which they sped north.

Michael, she had already seen, knew a great deal more about history than she did. When they passed not far east of Jena, he pointed to an exit sign and said, "Jena. There is a famous and beautiful university there. Hegel taught there. But I supposed it's best known for the battle Napoleon fought there in 1806. A famous victory."

And later: "Torgau. About fifty kilometers east of here—say thirty miles. That's where the American Sixty-ninth Division met the First Ukrainian Army on April 25, 1945. That cut Germany in two, and the war was all but over."

But he talked more about nations and the loyalty people owed them.

"My father and mother would love to visit America. Would this be called defecting? If you and I marry, who defects?"

"I think you are missing the point, Michael," she said. "We are not talking about treason. Your government has asked you to engage in—I guess the term is industrial espionage. You want technological and business information from Laser Solutions, Incorporated. Whoever killed Mahmud Nedim wanted the same and killed him to get it."

"Maybe for a million dollars," said Michael. "Maybe paid by a competitor who was willing to pay any amount, even to kill, to steal the profit your company expects from a technology it has developed."

"Maybe. That's possible, I suppose."

"Suppose," he went on, "your government said to LSI, 'We will pay you a generous price for this technology so we can give it to the whole world, so everyone can benefit. We will pay enough to cover your costs and give you an ample profit.' Suppose that. Would the company sell?"

"That would depend on the price," she said.

"That this would be good for your nation and the world would not influence your company's decision?"

"I don't know," she admitted quietly.

He seemed to drop the subject. He switched on the radio and tuned it to a symphony broadcast from Berlin.

Debora closed her eyes. Northeast of Leipzig the scenery visible from the autobahn was not spectacular. Michael caressed her leg. She welcomed his touch, though she felt it only through the denim of her jeans. She was comfortable. She had even decided she liked what the man in Prague had done to her hair. A couple of swipes of the brush was all she had needed to do to it each morning; and, whether anyone liked the style or not, it was the current style—among people with the nerve to wear it.

Comfortable... sure. She was in love with an agent of the KGB. He was pressing her to give away what she knew about massively parallel processing. Comfortable—

"Will I meet your parents when they come to Berlin?" Michael asked.

"Uh—" She was so surprised by the question she did not know how to respond. "Uh . . . I suppose so."

"If I meet them, will you tell them who I am?"

"Yes. I won't lie to them about it."

"I don't know about your mother," he said. "But you spoke about your father, and I don't think he will be disturbed to find out you have a Russian friend."

"I have a feeling you're right about that. That my Russian friend is an agent of the KGB raises another question."

"What I know of your father suggests he is a broad-minded man with an intelligent perspective on the world."

"My mother is equally intelligent and broad-minded."

"And they have a lot of courage," said Michael.

"Yes. Yes, they do."

Michael flipped on his left-turn signal and pulled into the left lane to race past a Mercedes tractor pulling two trailers. European-style, he left the signal blinking all the time he was in the left lane, then flipped on the right signal to say he was returning to the right lane.

"I have thought about your parents meeting mine," he said. "Such a wealth of contrasting experience!"

"My parents don't speak Russian."

"Mine speak English," he said. "Not very well, perhaps, but they can converse. And German."

"My father and mother can make themselves understood in German."

He smiled. "They would be able to talk. And you . . . you and my parents can talk happily together."

Debora nodded and looked away through the windshield at some town or other that they were passing: at red tile roofs, at stucco houses, at the orderly German countryside.

"What would we have to say to each other, Michael?"

"Many things. All kinds of things. They are hungry for information about America."

"I think— I think they would be surprised by America."

"I think you will be surprised by Russia."

She turned appraising eyes on him. He'd said nothing since Friday about her going to the Soviet Union. He'd said nothing about it since he confessed he was Russian.

"We grew up on a diet of lies about each other's countries," he said. "So did our parents. Our governments worked constantly at making us hate each other. I was taught that American workers were cruelly oppressed." He smiled. "You know an American cartoon strip with a man called Dagwood? Our teachers showed us episodes of that cartoon, showing Dagwood's employer striking him, knocking him down, and so on. That, we were told, was how the capitalist boss treated the American worker."

"Seriously?"

"Absolutely. Americans thought that kind of thing was funny, we were told. That is, the capitalist bosses thought it was funny. The cartoon was one of their favorites, our teachers said."

"I guess we were taught some pretty stupid things about the Soviet Union," said Debora.

"So . . . my father and mother would love to hear you talk about America. They would ask you endless questions. And they would love to show you Moscow and the Russian countryside. It is still covered by snow now. Snow covers a lot of ugliness, you know. Mother Russia is at her best right now, at the end of winter, when bright sun shines on the snow."

"Are you asking me to go to Moscow?" she asked.

"Would you?"

"My company—"

"Debora, you are not a prisoner of LSI! You are not Dagwood Bumstead, either. Your boss cannot treat you—"

"Michael. When?"

"Will you go? You are not afraid to go?"

"I'm not afraid. But I want a promise from you. No talk about technology."

He nodded. "Absolutely. No talk about computers."

Russ took Audrey to the house in Charlottenburg in the morning. Then he drove to Tempelhof, met the flight, and drove

Audrey's mother to the house. He could not stay with them for lunch. He had to meet André Guyard.

He and the Frenchman sat over lunch in the dining room at the Potsdamer Hof, a bottle of white wine in a bucket by their table, a fish appetizer on their plates.

"Why?"

"I had excellent reasons, Roos-ell," said André Guyard. "Excellent reasons. Compelling reasons."

"Personal reasons," said Tobin grimly.

"As you wish," said Guyard. "Reasons shared by us, just the same."

"If you mean revenge," said Tobin, "I do share that motive. I think Yuryev hired the man who injured Audrey. I'd have liked to kill him myself. But—"

"The other man, Navrozov, was the one who killed Mriya Aronovna Meyerhold," said Guyard.

"I'm glad they're dead, André. But having revenge on Yuryev is not my job right now."

"Do you know why they have killed Mriya Meyerhold?"

"I can think of several reasons."

"I don't mean speculations, Roos-ell. I *know* why."

"How can you be sure?"

Guyard took a sip of wine. "I have interrogated someone."

Tobin drew a deep breath. "Did he survive?"

Guyard shrugged. "They have killed Mriya Meyerhold because they thought she was a threat to Colonel Kedrov's special mission in Berlin, which is of course to steal the technology. They suspected she was betraying the mission to you. They killed her in your flat as a warning to you. That has been Major Yuryev's personal touch, not ordered from Moscow."

"Who did you interrogate, André?"

"A man you will remember. Vasily Grebenshchikov."

"That old-line thug! What was *he* doing in Berlin?"

"Working for Yuryev."

"You say Kedrov's mission is to steal technology. Did you find out anything about where and how?"

"Grebenshchikov did not know."

"What good did it do to kill Yuryev and Navrozov?"

"That," said Guyard, "has been a message from me to Chairman Vyshevskii. Mriya Aronovna Meyerhold has been a friend of mine."

"Your personal agenda doesn't match my official one."

"Oh, no? Well, more may be at stake than just your assignment to protect LSI technology. Major Yuryev's assignment in Berlin has been to back up Colonel Kedrov, to see that he does not fail. If he does, that may be the fall of Leonid Ivanovich Vyshevskii."

"Another personal vendetta of yours, André."

"Is it important to change the nature of the KGB? Under Vyshevskii, the agency is not very different from what it has been, at least in the foreign-intelligence field. They talk about a new KGB, one that wouldn't go about the world killing people. There will be nothing new about it so long as Vyshevskii is Chairman."

"They will still be desperate for Western technology and will still fight to steal it," said Tobin. "No matter who is Chairman."

Guyard shrugged. "Chairman Vyshevskii will have to send in a new team, anyway. Maybe we can defeat Kedrov before his new backers are in place."

The villa where the BDN housed Tobin, Audrey, and her mother was in what had once been a quiet residential neighborhood of Charlottenburg, only a few blocks southwest of the great Charlottenburg Chateau. It had been quiet before the autobahn was built. Now the noise of traffic penetrated the house, and no matter how comfortable it was otherwise, it was a noisy house.

Besides, Mrs. Tickhill complained, "The tay-ee in the kitchen is all China tay-ee, no Ceylon tay-ee. I suppose it's all roight, but it's nowt nearly so good as Ceylon tay-ee. It's sort of... orangish in color, nowt gray-eenish black loik the best tay-ee."

"We won't be here long," said Audrey.

"Well, Oi want to see Berlin before we go 'ome."

Coming from the hospital in a car, settling into this house, and receiving her mother had tired Audrey. She sat apart, her eyes dull as she looked out through leaded windows at a garden and a high brick wall. She had noticed the armed guards that patroled the premises, and she had remarked again that they would be living like a Mafia don in his compound.

At odd hours over the past few days, Russ had tried to give some kind of name to his feeling for Audrey. He had decided the name really was love. He had decided it was not just sympathy and not the sense of guilt that she had been so badly hurt because of him.

She had brushed out her red hair this morning and had put on a little makeup, to be ready to leave the hospital with him. She had dressed, too, in a checked gray skirt and jacket, plus a black sweater. A nurse had helped her pull the sweater and jacket over her injured shoulder. Russ could only guess what pain she had endured to manipulate her arm that way. The arm hung in a sling, of course. She had sweated a little in the car— from pain, he understood.

"Berlin . . . " mused Mrs. Tickhill. "Oi never thought Oi'd see the die when Oi'd come to Berlin. Cahn't see much bomb damage no more, cahn you?"

One of the BND agents came in. He approached Russ and leaned down to speak quietly—"Ulrich Vogel says he wants to talk to you. He called the downtown office to ask where to find you. We can put the call through without telling him where you are."

Russ nodded, got up, and left the room with the agent. The switch was completed, and Vogel came on the line.

"I can tell you something about Steiner," he said. "Moscow has put out a kill order on everybody who works for Kedrov. Steiner has left Berlin."

"I don't think that's why he's left town," said Tobin.

"Well, there's a real bloodbath among the Committee people in Berlin. Besides Mriya Meyerhold, there've been four other deaths. Kristin Kuniczak, Vasily Grebenshchikov, Boris Navrozov, and Major Ivan Stepanovich Yuryev himself. What's more, Kedrov is gone. Dead or alive, I don't know."

"I know all this, Ulrich."

"Ah. Well, I can tell you something more about Steiner, if you're still interested in him."

"I'm still interested."

"He's got a suite in a residential hotel at 788 Emserstrasse. Bachelor quarters, you might say. Posh. Drives an expensive English car."

"Good information, my friend. You say 788 Emserstrasse?"

"Yes. But he's not there. He wasn't there Thursday night, Friday night, last night—"

"You've been watching?"

"Since I got the address. The windows have been dark the last three nights."

"Keep watching. Call me the same way."

"Is this worth money?"

"This is worth money, Ulrich. Don't worry about that. You've earned a piece of money."

Debora asked Michael to stop by her apartment, so she could leave soiled clothes and pick up clean ones. There was no point in pretending that she wanted to sleep alone. She didn't. Others from LSI lived in her building, and she did not want them to see she had a man with her overnight. Besides, his bachelor suite was compact and cozy.

She would make different living arrangements soon. Whether she married Michael or not, they would live together. Or if they didn't, at least she would have a place where tongues wouldn't wag if he spent the night with her.

She smiled to herself as he drove her to Emserstrasse. She ran her right hand over her all-but-absent hair. Then she grinned.

"He is home," said Vogel. "With a young woman. She went in with him."

"Describe her."

"Very stylish. Tall. Nicely dressed."

"Blonde? Brunette?"

"Who could tell? Almost no hair at all."

Tobin put down the telephone and went back to the table where Audrey and Mrs. Tickhill were having dinner.

"I put the question to you very plainly, Debora," said Steiner (a name she had never heard). "Will you fly to Moscow with me to meet my parents, to see my home? And will you marry me?"

Debora was naked, as was he. She had in her hand a glass of Beefeater on ice. "The answer to both questions is yes," she said. "And you know my conditions for going to Moscow."

He grinned. "That we not set up a meeting for you with computer scientists from the Academy of Sciences."

"And for the marriage, a condition. I don't want you to defect. I don't want you to betray your country. I just want you to get a job as . . . as a sportswear salesman."

"Agreed. When can we fly to Moscow?"

She shrugged. "Tomorrow. Tonight! Actually . . . when you've called your parents to say we are coming. When I've told LSI I'm taking two weeks' vacation. When I've bought a Polaroid camera to take pictures of your parents and your home—for my parents. Tuesday! Wednesday! Quick, before I turn cautious!"

18

"SHE'S A RATHER different young woman from the person you last saw," said Max Wenzel with an amused smile.

The tall, gaunt director of the Dahlem laboratories of LSI sat behind his uncluttered glass desk. Tobin had heard that the director's penchant for tidiness was the subject of much amusement and not a little annoyance among his staff. *"Ordentlisch Pult, ordentlisch kopf,"* he had been heard to say—Tidy desk, tidy mind.

He was committed to punctuality and promptness, too, and was now a little annoyed that Debora Benson had not yet arrived in response to his call to her office.

"While we wait, there's something else we can talk about," said Tobin. "Aisuke Hirata."

The director frowned. "I would rather not talk about him, if you don't mind."

"I'm afraid we have to talk about him, sooner or later. You know about the big cash deposit he made to his bank account. Well, now he has withdrawn it."

Wenzel raised his brows and turned down the corners of his mouth. "Aisuke Hirata is an odd fellow," he said.

"I asked you last week to give me a list of your people who are working on phase shifting. Is Aisuke Hirata on that list?"

"Well... I said we weren't doing much in that field. But Aisuke would be on such a list."

"I want to talk to him."

"I'll send word."

Debora knew Director Wenzel was waiting for her, and she knew of his impatience. She had heard the CIA man was in the building, and she suspected he was with Wenzel. She would have gone to the director's office immediately, except that when the call came she had been sitting in her office talking to Aisuke Hirata. Aisuke did not want to leave.

And for the moment she would not ask him to leave, even if Wenzel and the CIA man were waiting, because Aisuke had just said something very strange—

"The man you were with in Prague and Marienbad obviously made a strong personal impression on you."

She'd had her hands on the arms of her chair, about to rise and leave her office, when he said that.

"If you will forgive the observation."

"Marienbad! Aisuke, how do you know I was at Marienbad? We only went there after we couldn't get a room at Karlsbad."

The grim Japanese allowed himself a faint smile. "Is that man trying to buy secrets from you?" he asked bluntly.

"No! And why do you ask?"

"What you know about massively parallel processing is worth a large sum of money. A *very* large sum of money. If the man is trying to buy knowledge from you, I hope you understand what it is worth."

"How do you know I was at Marienbad?"

He focused an intent gaze on her for a moment, then said, "I represent some people who are interested in you."

"Interested in—*So damned interested they had me followed?* What the hell is this, Aisuke?"

"The man . . . your new friend. He may not be who and what you think he is."

"I know who and what he is—and I'm not sure it's any of your damned business."

Aisuke stood. "Very well, Debora. If he makes you some kind

of offer, please let me know. I might want to make a higher bid."

Debora Benson walked into Wenzel's office looking angry and confused. Tobin wondered why.

Wenzel was certainly right in saying she was a different woman. The conspicuous difference was her hair, of course, she'd had it cut extremely short. That was superficial. His distinct impression of her had been that she lacked the self-possession to carry off such style; but right now she was carrying it off with élan.

It *was* attractive. Bold and attractive.

"If you don't mind a personal word, Debora, I'd like to say I very much like the way you've had your hair styled. It's most becoming."

"Thank you."

Blonde or brunette, who could tell? Vogel had said. The woman who went into Steiner's hotel with him last night had almost no hair at all.

Steiner. Michael Ormsley. Tobin wondered which she thought the guy was.

"I'd like to ask for your help," he said.

"In a CIA investigation?"

"Yes. I need only a minute of your time. I would like to ask you to identify a photograph."

She shrugged. "All right."

The labs had done an excellent job on the old photograph of Steiner. They had done art work to age the man in the Egyptian photograph. The picture was exactly what Tobin had asked Mahoney to arrange.

Steiner stared into the camera. The youthful smile had been altered and turned into a defiant sneer. Still, the image was of Steiner, unmistakably of Steiner. A board in front of him was lettered, white on black:

STEINER, KURT HORST
ACCUSÉ MEURTRE AVEC PRÉMÉDITATION

07/11/87
POLICE, BRUXELLES

"I'm sorry I've no better or more recent photograph," said Tobin. "The man dislikes having his picture taken. I just wonder if you've ever seen this man."

Debora stared at the photograph. Tobin saw her lips stiffen, her jaw harden and twitch. Then she looked up and said, "No. I don't think I've ever seen this man."

"He is a dangerous man," said Tobin. "A killer."

She looked at the picture again. She shook her head. "Accused of premeditated murder in Brussels in 1987," she said. "Was he acquitted? Did he escape?"

Tobin and Mahoney had rehearsed an answer for a question like this. "The process was abandoned for lack of clear evidence," he said. "There was some diplomatic pressure."

"Why?"

"Because he was an important agent of the *Ministerium für Staats-Sicherheit. Stasi.*"

"Where do you think he is now?"

"We know where he is. Berlin. And we know what he's doing. He was retrained at a special KGB facility at Zagorsk, a few miles from Moscow—trained to be a new kind of intelligence agent. Kristin Kuniczak was trained there, too. Kristin Kuniczak, you know . . . Anne-Lise Hein. Their new intelligence mission is to steal technology."

"Steal technology. Why?"

"Because they are ten or twenty years behind the West. Because they can't compete. Because they can't feed, clothe, or house their people. To catch up, they are willing to steal. They are willing to kill."

She handed the photograph back to him. "If I see this man, I'll let you know," she said.

When she left, Tobin was quiet for a long time, first staring after her as she walked briskly through Wenzel's outer office, then turning and looking at Wenzel.

"She's lying."

"Obviously."

Tobin scratched the corner of his eye. "I want to talk to Aisuke Hirata."

Wenzel picked up his telephone and punched in some numbers. In a moment he turned to Tobin and said, "He's left the office, leaving no word as to where he was going. I feel sure he will be back within the hour."

Colonel Nikolai Pavlovich Kedrov broke off a chunk of sweet pastry, shoved it into his mouth, and moistened it for chewing with a sip of strong black coffee. Kurt Horst Steiner watched, not entirely approving of the way the Russian ate.

It had occurred to Steiner before today that he and Kedrov might have been mistaken for father and son. They were much alike: blond, muscular, handsome. They were also much different. The Russian—*all* Russians, in Steiner's judgment—had the coarseness of a peasant. No matter how much polish he put on himself, he was a Slav. The word meant slave, and, damn them, that was what they were fit for: slaves. Uncouth.

It did not occur to Steiner that Kedrov might have similar thoughts about him: that he represented an inferior people, too long inbred, too . . . pretty. They made fine servants. They had the polish for it. They had a studied capacity for taking orders, which was what they had been doing for the past forty-seven years: taking orders from Russians. They had become reasonably good at it.

"She will come?"

Steiner nodded. "Voluntarily. I've convinced her she should travel with me to Moscow, to meet my 'parents'—though I wish we had established an interrogation center in Germany. We should have such a facility available, in the unlikely event she changes her mind."

"Well, we don't have," said Kedrov. "We are constantly reminded of the importance of this mission, but—well, never mind. We have no choice but to deliver Debora Benson to Moscow.

Two agents will play the roles of your father and mother. That's been arranged. Have you mentioned a sister? Your sister will be Olga Alexandrovna Chernov. She is a computer expert and will know what questions to ask."

"I am satisfied she will come with me voluntarily. But if I need help—"

"We are alone, Steiner," said Kedrov. "For a day or so. Mriya Aronovna is dead. Kristin Kuniczak is dead. Only the four of us knew the dimensions of the mission. Oh, I've got some errand-runners here and there, but we are all that is left of the command group. What is more, Chairman Vyshevskii's snakes are all dead. Yuryev, Grebenshchikov, Navrozov. And the enemy is closing in on us. Tobin, Voss, Guyard. Killers, every one of them. We have run out of time."

"She is willing to go . . . say, Wednesday."

Kedrov shook his head. "I'm not sure we have until Wednesday. I was handed a report as I left Moscow early this morning. British intelligence has been making inquiries about Michael Ormsley. About Michael Ormsley and his Jaguar automobile."

"Thank god for the leaks in MI5."

"As a matter of fact, the information came from the old man at Dragon's Lying-in Hospital. He has worried for more than thirty years about having filed a false report of birth; and sure enough, the inquiry came at last. He came crying for help. Of course, no one identified the false report with him, so— anyway, they know now that no Michael Ormsley was born at Dragon's in 1961. From which they have deduced the rest of it."

"So Michael is dead."

"The car must disappear, too."

"I've prepared for that," said Steiner. "Into the lake. Into the Grosser Müggel See. I know a place where I can drive to the water and shove it in. It will be found, of course, but not for a few days—with any luck."

"The small problem," said Kedrov. "But returning to Debora Benson. What is your plan?"

"Well, it *was* Aeroflot to Moscow."

"No. Not now. The airports may already be under close surveillance. You will have to drive her. I will get you a car, a different car. You will have to give her some explanation as to why you are not driving the Jaguar."

"We are still talking about small problems, Comrade Colonel. The real problem, the difficult problem, is to find an explanation as to why we must leave today or tomorrow, and not Wednesday. I am not sure how I am going to explain that."

"You must solve that problem, Steiner. Solve it one way or another. From this point forward, I will be nearby. If we have to use force—"

"*I* will use it, Comrade Colonel," said Steiner firmly. "I have come this far with this difficult young woman. I will do whatever is necessary."

"*Mittagessen*," said Debora Benson to her secretary about a quarter after twelve. Lunch. "*Nicht später als halb zwei.*" Back no later than one-thirty.

She drove out of the parking lot in her MG. Suspecting she might be followed, she drove east to Berliner Strasse, then northeast into the complex Schöneberg interchange, confident she could lose anyone in that tangle of thoroughfares. Five minutes out of the interchange she pulled to the curb on one of the streets leading into Bayerischer Platz. There she went to a telephone kiosk.

Anticipating something like this, she had allowed Michael to give her a special telephone number. ("My telephone may be tapped. Yours may be. Let's have a way or reaching each other privately.")

"*Hallo. Mit wem wollen Sie sprechen?*"

"*Mit Michael, bitte.*"

"*Ihre nummer, bitte. Ich rufe Sie wieder an.*"

She gave the number of the telephone in the kiosk—and waited.

After three minutes, it rang.

"Michael?"

"Debora?"

"I need to see you. Right now! We have trouble!"

"What kind of trouble?"

"The CIA."

"Debora . . . the dining room of the Bristol-Kempinski. They'll never think of looking for us there. Half an hour."

"Half an hour, Michael."

Aisuke Hirata did not accept failure without anger and resentment. He had seen Debora Benson's MG speed out of the parking lot and had taken after it in his BMW. But the maneuverable little car, in the hands of a driver who conspicuously knew how to handle it, had raced through the turns of the Schöneberg Interchange and off into a street—exactly as if she had meant to lose someone following her.

When he was sure he'd lost her, Aisuke pulled the BMW to the curb and sat for a full minute, sweat pouring, muscles tensed, angry. He would encounter Debora Benson again—and then she would not rid herself of him so easily.

Jane Mahoney sat in a car across the street from Debora Benson's flat. Glancing around, she could see that BND agents watched from doorways and from other cars.

She picked up her microphone and called the station.

"MH here. I've got a lot of company. Is this local?"

"Will advise, MH."

"He's blown," said Tobin.

That was not altogether certain. How could you tell if a man had abandoned quarters so little marked with his personality? The place was like a hotel room a man had recently checked out of. He'd taken his clothes and toiletries, anyway.

He'd left one thing in a bureau drawer. A white silk chemise.

Odd. Why would a man who had taken everything else from a room when he left it—clothes, toiletries, and so on—leave a white silk chemise?

You could spend an hour looking around this residential hotel suite—and agents of the BND would spend an hour, and more—without finding any clue about the personality of the man who had occupied this room. Why had he been so careless about an obviously expensive chemise?

Michael met Debora in the lobby of the hotel and led her into the dining room. They sat near a window where they could see the traffic on the Ku-damm.

"He showed me a picture of you—or what purported to be a picture of you. A police picture. What Americans call a mug shot. Do you know what I mean?"

"Now that you've told me, I do."

"It was taken in Brussels."

"I swear to you I've never been in Brussels."

"I believe you. Anyway, the name on the picture was Kurt Horst Steiner."

Michael smiled. "*Steiner*. I've been called by several names, but *Steiner*? Stone? No."

"Also—have you ever heard of a Japanese by the name of Aisuke Hirata?"

Michael shook his head.

"He is a scientist working for the company. He confronted me in my office this morning and spoke about Marienbad. How could he have known we were at Marienbad? He said he represented some people who are interested in me. He warned me about you. He said you aren't who you say you are."

"I wasn't, of course."

"He said you and Kristin Kuniczak were trained at the same school."

"Every man or woman who works for the KGB is trained at the KGB training school."

"At Zagorsk."

"Zagorsk? There is a famous monastery at Zagorsk."

"I have an uncomfortable sense that something bad is happening."

"Are you sure no one followed you here?"

"I'm sure. I drove to Tempelhof and parked my car, then

came here in a taxi. If they find my car there, that will give them something to worry about, won't it?"

He grinned. "One would think you were trained for conspiracy."

She looked up at the waiter who put a glass of Beefeater in front of her. When the man was gone, she looked again at Michael and said, "Tobin, the CIA man, said you're trying to steal technology. He said that's the new mission of the KGB."

Michael nodded. "In a desperate struggle to catch up. I haven't denied it."

"Let me tell you what he said to me. Of your country, he said, 'They can't compete. They can't feed, clothe, or house their people.' Michael, he said that as if it were something to be proud of! As if he were *glad* the Russian people suffer!"

"The old Cold War mentality."

She took a sip of gin. "What do you know about massively parallel processing?"

"Nothing. Really, nothing."

"It could be extremely valuable to a country that has fallen behind in computer technology and wants a way to catch up quickly. It won't solve all problems, not by any means; but with massively parallel processing a group of older, less sophisticated computers can do some of the work the new, big super-supers can do. Not everything. But much of it. Enough to—"

"Enough to give my country a boost into the twenty-first century?" he asked.

"Something like that. A boost, yes. A quick boost."

"Yes . . . But companies like yours monopolize this technology."

Debora glanced around the room. "I'm half-convinced I should help you," she said.

"Maybe my father and mother could put all this in a better perspective for you."

"When are we leaving?"

"You said tomorrow or Wednesday. I have reserved seats on an Aeroflot flight to Moscow on Wednesday morning."

She scowled. "I'm not sure someone won't try to prevent my going. First I find out we were followed by Aisuke, or by someone working with him. Then Tobin tries to confuse me with a faked photograph. And it *was* faked, Michael. Something about that picture was unnatural. It was you, and yet it wasn't you. It might have fooled someone who didn't know you as well as I do, but to me there was something wrong with it, as if it had been crudely retouched. What are they trying to do, for God's sake?"

"Debora . . . can we leave this afternoon?"

"Can you get tickets?"

"We'll drive."

"A thousand miles?"

"To Kaliningrad. Three hundred miles. Fly from there."

"Take me to my apartment and—"

"Debora. If you think someone is really following you—and me—we can't go to your apartment. They will be waiting for you there. We can't fly. They'll be watching for us."

"Dammit! We're not doing anything illegal. I'm entitled to go where I want, when I want. You said it yourself, that I'm not a prisoner of LSI."

"When did the CIA begin to trouble itself with legality or illegality?" he asked. "And this man Aisuke Hirata . . . remember what I told you about people willing to kidnap a scientist? He may be no one of the kind, but—"

"Are we fugitives?"

Michael softened and smiled. "No . . . no. In a week or two, we'll come back. You'll say 'I took some time off to visit the family of the man I love.' And what can they do about that? As you said, you are entitled to go where you want, when you want. In the meantime—" His face hardened again. "It is an unfortunate fact that someone might try to prevent your going with me to visit Moscow. Why, you might even decide to help the Soviet people to feed and clothe and house themselves!"

"I might," she muttered. "I just might."

"Don't decide, Debora. Not now. Don't decide until you've met some of our people. Don't decide until you've seen Moscow, and some of the towns around it, and some of the country—

until you've met some Russians, see how they live, learn what kind of people they are. Then decide."

A little smile appeared on her face. "An adventure," she said. "The revolt of Debora Benson! The mouse that mutinied!"

Russ was at the house in Charlottenburg, where he had arrived a little after one for a quick lunch with Audrey and Mrs. Tickhill. He was interrupted by a telephone call.

Erich Voss was on the line.

"Debora Benson left the Dahlem labs about noon, saying she was going to lunch. She hasn't come back. Wenzel is in a panic. He thinks she's been kidnapped."

"I wouldn't jump to that conclusion. The young woman I saw this morning is unlikely to have been kidnapped," said Tobin. "More likely, she's with Steiner voluntarily."

"She didn't go home," said Voss. "She didn't go to any of the places where she ordinarily has lunch. Steiner has not appeared anywhere. Kedrov had lunch in the dining room at the Bristol-Kempinski. We have a tail on him and haven't lost him. We're watching the airports and rail stations for Benson and Steiner, but we haven't spotted them."

"Suppose she *has* been kidnapped. Or suppose she's gone somewhere voluntarily. Where would Steiner be taking her?"

"To a place where they can isolate her and apply whatever means they choose to drain her of every idea and scrap of information they want. That could be in Berlin. It could be in the Soviet Union."

"She was last seen, what? Two hours ago? What chance do we have to find her now?"

"We have compelling reasons to try," said Voss. "What do you think they will do to her after they have extracted from her everything she knows?"

"Where's the Jaguar?"

"It developed a cracked valve. I had to rent this car."

Debora stared skeptically at a luxurious, leather-upholstered Mercedes. It was painted dark green, and it was fully equipped, even to the little wipers on the headlights.

"I'd got to thinking of the Jag as *our* car," she said.

"We'll recover it when we come back," he said.

"When we come back... I wonder, Michael, if we ever will."

"Why shouldn't we?"

"We'll be a pair of renegades. I will be, anyway."

"Debora. We will be back in no more than two weeks. And the only thing that will have changed will be that you will be Mrs. Orlov instead of Miss Benson."

He leaned over and kissed her, then started the powerful engine of the big car.

At noon, Jane Mahoney was at Tempelhof. She found Debora Benson's MG.

About the same time, a man who worked for André Guyard had recognized one of Erich Voss's agents hurrying purposefully along Tauentzienstrasse. The man's anxious purposefulness had aroused the Frenchman's curiosity. He had followed along for a block, only casually interested in what the German was doing—yet interested enough to stride after him in the hope he might learn something useful. He did. The BND man was following Colonel Nikolai Pavlovich Kedrov. The French agent decided to join the tail. At his first opportunity, he telephoned Guyard at the Potsdamer Hof.

Ulrich Vogel sat at a small desk in a small room in the CIA station. Personnel found reasons to walk past and glance in through the window in the door at the fat old man who had once been a dangerous agent of *Stasi*. Apparently the Chief thought he was important. He had ordered a car sent for him. Vogel was working a telephone, calling god-knew-who, one call after another.

The Chief called every few minutes, but he did not come in. He had gone from Charlottenburg to the Berlin headquarters of BND. He and Voss were coordinating the search for Debora Benson from the larger and far more fully equipped BND center.

Max Wenzel allowed little to interrupt the pleasant daily schedule he had fixed for himself when he became director of the Dahlem labs. An important element of that schedule was his round of lunches, in good restaurants and in his club in the Mercedes-Benz building. Today he saw no reason not to enjoy his usual Monday lunch at his club.

The only difference was in his choice of guests. This was only the second time he had invited Aisuke Hirata to join him there. Wenzel liked a fine whiskey before lunch and was sipping Glenfiddich. Aisuke had never acquired a taste for whiskey and was content with a glass of Perrier water.

They spoke English. Aisuke's German was weak.

"It was not a casual departure," said Aisuke. "When she entered that interchange, she accelerated that little car and whipped it through the turns like a racing driver. My car is faster, but I couldn't keep up with her. She didn't do that for fun."

"I have no idea what we can do about it," said Wenzel. "Furthermore, you understand we could not have held her, could not have prevented her from leaving."

"We won't see her alive again."

Wenzel frowned. "Let's not be dramatic."

"No, let's not be. Let's be rational. She knows as much about massively parallel processing as any computer scientist in the world. She—"

"Well, she might," Wenzel interrupted. "She developed some of the basic ideas."

Aisuke glanced around the club dining room. As Wenzel had noted before when he brought him here, this Japanese held the quiet, comfortable little world of successful businessmen in utter contempt.

Abruptly Aisuke changed the subject. "What did the American want?"

"He is highly suspicious of you. The BND checked your bank

account and found the cash deposit. Also, they know you've withdrawn it."

"We shouldn't have deposited that money," said Aisuke. "We should have hidden it."

"An unacceptable risk," said Wenzel. "If the German government discovers you're hiding forty-two thousand marks in cash, it will assume you're dealing in narcotics or supplying explosives to terrorists. No, it was better to deposit it, though I thank god the BND didn't check *my* account."

"Are you sure they didn't?"

"I think there would have been repercussions by now. But anyway, what have you done with the money?"

"I was going to offer it to Debora Benson."

"For god's sake, why?"

"I thought maybe I could outbid the Russians. I might have asked for your forty-two thousand, too. In fact, I may yet get a chance to bid—if we can find her."

Wenzel shook his head. "I'm afraid we don't make very good conspirators, Aisuke."

"To the contrary," said Aisuke. "We sold Rikuchu Corporation something quite worthless and put them in a position where they can't complain or demand their money back. I regard that as highly successful."

Wenzel shrugged. "At least they can't blame us for the disappearance of Debora Benson."

"Being blamed or not blamed is the least of our worries about Debora Benson," said Aisuke.

19

COLONEL NIKOLAI PAVLOVICH KEDROV knew he was being followed. The tail might have picked him up as he left the Bristol-Kempinski Hotel after lunch. Or maybe—actually far more likely—the tail had picked him up earlier, followed him to the hotel dining room, waited while he had lunch, and fallen in behind him when he left.

If the latter was the case, the Debora Benson operation had come appallingly close to disaster. He had eaten lunch in the Bristol-Kempinski because Steiner had phoned to say he was meeting Benson there. It would be well, Steiner had said, for the colonel to have a good look at her. He had never seen her, after all, and it was essential that he know who she was.

He had sat three tables away from Steiner and Benson and had a very good look, indeed—so good a look that he was sickened by what he saw. The young woman was conspicuously in love with Steiner. She doted on him. That was obvious. Obvious, too—except to her—was that the arrogant young man only tolerated her. He had deceived her, seduced her not only physically but mentally and emotionally, didn't give a damn about her, was prepared to injure or kill her without hesitation.

Kurt Horst Steiner was an effective agent. Kedrov acknowledged that. He was also a something less than human. He didn't have a single decent instinct.

Before he left that dining room, Kedrov had formed a resolution. Sooner or later he was going to destroy that son of a bitch. For self-protection if for no better reason.

Yes, he'd had a good look at Debora Benson. And so should his BND tail have had, if they had come into the dining room. Here was a lesson in how trained professionals mucked up assignments. In their dutiful concentration on Kedrov, could they have overlooked the young couple dining three tables away? Or had they not been shown pictures of Debora Benson and Kurt Horst Steiner, not been told to look for that pair, too? Or had they conscientiously kept their expense accounts low by just covering the exits and never entering the dining room?

Anyway, it had been close. For an hour and a half, the BND had had Benson and Steiner within their grasp.

Half a minute after he walked out after lunch, onto the busy Kurfürstendamm, Kedrov had become certain he was being tailed. If they had been following him before he went into the Bristol-Kempinski, they had been subtle. They were not subtle now. Maybe their patience had worn thin.

So—he had stopped and taken a full minute to light a cigarette, watching for Steiner and Benson to come out on the street. When they did, Kedrov had waited until they walked past him; and then, when they were half a block ahead of him, he had walked after them. He had wanted to see if there was a separate tail on them.

After walking a block or so, he had concluded that no one was tailing the young couple. He'd had many years' experience tailing subjects, setting tails on subjects, throwing off tails.

He had known of course where they were going: to the garage where the green Mercedes he had rented waited for Steiner. As the couple had neared the garage, he had fallen farther back and crossed to the wrong side of the street. When he had his last glimpse of Steiner and Benson, they were entering the garage. He was certain the BND tails had not identified them.

Which left him with a problem: how to rid himself of these sticky nuisances. He could do it, of course. No problem. The point was to do it without making them aware that he had outsmarted them and intentionally lost them. The point was to make them think they had *inadvertently* lost him.

He had ordered Steiner to wait for him at the safe flat in Köpenick. Kedrov was not sending this vitally important couple off on a drive across Poland alone. He was coming, too, in a separate car. He would carry the heavy arms they might need if the green Mercedes got stopped on the way.

"One piece of good news," Jane Mahoney said to Tobin as he arrived at the CIA station. "I picked up your Porsche good as new. It's in the garage. It took them a week, but you'd never know what happened."

He did not ask her what came to his mind. Did they get all the bloodstains out? Replacing shattered glass was one thing. Cleaning blood off upholstery was another.

"Draw two Uzis," he said to Mahoney. "The little ones. Put them in the car."

"We going duck shooting?"

"It might turn out that way."

He went in to see Ulrich Vogel. The heavy old man had filled the little room with pipe smoke, so much that Tobin's eyes teared when he came in; but he was still on the telephone, mumbling, asking questions, nodding as he listened to the answers.

"*Die Arbeit ist nicht leicht,*" he said to Tobin. The work is not easy.

"But have you found out anything?" Tobin asked, in German.

Vogel shrugged. "The girl with no hair. There aren't many like that."

"It's a style."

"I suppose so. I've been asking some of the fellows if they've seen a girl with no hair. Two of them have."

"Where and when?"

"One of the men works as a guard at the Pergamon Museum. A girl with no hair is in the museum now—or was there ten minutes ago. He described her. I don't think she's tall enough. I don't think she's the one. Another old friend of mine sells newspapers and cigars in the lobby of the Bristol-Kempinski.

Sooner or later, everybody who is anybody in Berlin walks past his counter. He saw a bald girl twice. She went in the dining room. She came out. An hour ago. When she came out, she was with a man who *could*—notice I only say could—have been Steiner."

"Keep working the phone," Tobin said. "You'll be paid for this."

In his own office, Tobin called Wenzel. It was possible—and wouldn't *that* be a hoot!—that Debora Benson had a long, leisurely lunch with Steiner and was back at the labs.

"No," said Wenzel. "She has not come back."

"How about Aisuke Hirata?"

"He's here."

"I'm thinking of having the BND pick him up for interrogation. He's been ducking me."

"Let me bring him to your office," said Wenzel, an odd note of urgency in his voice.

"He'll come?"

"I promise you."

"I can't promise I'll be here."

"I'll bring him anyway."

When he put down the telephone, Mahoney rapped on the frame of his door. She had been standing there waiting.

"André Guyard on line four," she said.

Tobin grabbed the phone and punched the button. "*Ici* Tobin."

"My friend. You want Colonel Kedrov? I have him."

"You have him where? How?"

Guyard chuckled. "Voss has a tail on him."

"Voss's men lost him."

"Mine haven't."

"Where is he, André?"

"He's at the zoo."

"The *zoo?* What the hell—"

"Strolling around, looking at the animals."

"Promise me you won't touch him. I want him alive, André."

"You have my word."

Jane Mahoney remained standing in the doorway. Tobin

looked up. "You got those Uzis? Soon as I talk to Voss, we're going hunting."

Debora sat slumped and glum in the grim living room of the flat in Köpenick. The adventure, the revolt of Debora Benson, had come to an abrupt end. Instead of racing across Poland in their luxurious Mercedes, she and Michael sat here and waited.

Waited. He hadn't made it clear why.

"I might as well go back to the lab," she said.

"Please, Debora, don't even think of it. We won't be here long."

Discovering he had a bottle of Beefeater in this shabby house, she wondered if he hadn't all along meant to bring her here—if in fact maybe she was in the clutches of the KGB and this was as far as they were going. He encouraged her to drink. She had—a little too much.

"I have to know why we are here. Tell me the truth!"

"We are waiting for a friend."

"A friend..."

"My superior officer, Debora. The man who *pays* for things. The car, for example."

"My clothes."

"No."

"Our hotel rooms."

"Things like the cars, Debora. Things that are beyond the means of a man of my age and rank."

"Provided by your superior officer, to impress me."

"Debora...I love you. I want to marry you. I want us to have a happy life together. Maybe have children. Have you thought of that? A home. Well...I am an intelligence agent. That is my occupation. It is how I earn a living. So I have superiors, and I take orders."

"Orders..."

"A CIA agent takes orders. So does an FBI agent. British agents with MI5 and MI6. BND agents. Are we all bad fellows, just because we have superior officers and have to take orders?"

"But why are we sitting here? What does your superior officer want?"

"Debora. My superior officer is going across Poland with us. Not in our car. In a separate car. He is a man of high rank. He is doing us a very great favor. He is going to expedite everything for us. He will take care of formalities, like a visa for you. He will see to it that we have first priority for the best class of transportation to Moscow. We may in fact go by train, a luxury train. Because he respects our privacy, he is driving his own car—when he could just as well be riding with us. He is a fine man. I know you will like him."

"What is his name?"

"His name is Colonel Nikolai Pavlovich Kedrov. And just to give you an idea of what sort of fellow he is, I can tell you he is a warm friend of the CIA man, Russell Tobin. They have lunch together occasionally. What better proof could you have that he is not one of the old-fashioned menacing KGB men? He is a professional intelligence officer, and has been all his life, just like Tobin."

"When will he be here?"

"I had expected him before now. He is late."

Colonel Kedrov sat on a bench within the grounds of the *zoologischer Garten*, staring at a pair of hippopotami rubbing against each other. He wore a gray suit and a gray hat, plus a raincoat, and he held a folded newspaper. He hoped he looked casual.

The tail still stuck to him. The personnel had changed, but that was standard procedure, and he was sure the two men were his tail. Shaking them and making it took like a mischance was not going to be possible.

He had not walked into the grounds of the zoo without purpose. An experienced intelligence officer always had several identified escape hatches, in every city where he spent any time. An experienced tail knew that. It was a game, with the quarry trying to approach his exit port with deceptive casualness, the hunter trying to guess when and where the quarry would make his attempt.

The hippopotami shoved each other, their huge, ungainly bodies stirring the muddy water in which they stood.

Mriya had liked this place. He had a score to settle for her. Maybe he'd never find the opportunity, but he would never forget, never stop looking for the opening.

The essential of the game he was playing with the tail was to affect nonchalance. He stood. He walked closer to the fence where one hippopotamus now opened its cavernous mouth and showed its great yellow teeth.

Kedrov glanced around, as if not quite sure where he would go next. Then he walked decisively toward the building that housed the toilets.

He did not glance around to see if the tail was following. There was only one entrance and exit to the low, brick building. To remain inconspicuous, they would probably wait outside. In the antechamber he stopped at a vending machine and bought a pack of cigarettes. That gave him a moment to watch the door. The tail did not enter.

He went into the men's room and used a urinal.

In the short corridor between the men's and women's facilities, there was a locked steel service door—as Colonel Kedrov well knew.

The folded newspaper he was carrying was not just a newspaper. It was a small kit containing several things he might need on a day like this.

He reached into it and pulled out a paperboard tube about the size of his thumb, though longer. It looked much like the tube a woman used to insert a tampon, except that the paperboard was brown. He tore off a cap taped to the tip; and, holding the paperboard tube in his left fist, he pressed the uncapped tip hard against the keyhole of the lock on the steel door. Pushing his right index finger into the other end of the tube, he forced a wooden piston through. A yellow, waxy substance oozed into the keyhole. Because of its color and consistency, it was called by the Russian word *maslo*—butter.

Kedrov had practiced with *maslo* many times, and he needed only a few seconds to empty the tube into the keyhole. He needed only two or three more seconds to shove a thin copper tube into the *maslo*-filled lock. The tube was his detonator. Two thin filaments sticking out of it were not wires but fuses: two of them for certainty. He lit the fuses with a cigarette lighter and stepped a few paces back.

In the days when Czechoslovakia was a fraternal republic, Czech scientists had developed *maslo* for just this purpose: quickly breaking small locks. The explosion was a sharp crack, like the report of a 9mm pistol. Kedrov stepped up and turned the knob. The shattered pieces inside the lock crunched. The knob resisted but turned, and he shoved the door open.

Glancing once at the startled people in the corridor, he walked outside and closed the door after him. He strode along a service road, then turned into a small grove and climbed to a road a little above. Four minutes later he was out of the zoo and walking along Budapesterstrasse.

He had lost his tail.

"Son of a *bitch!*"

As soon as he saw the police cars at the zoo, Tobin knew the French had lost Kedrov. He could only hope the KGB colonel had not killed one or more of Guyard's men.

Then he saw Guyard.

"*Le beurre!*" Guyard spat. "*Merde!*" Butter! Shit!

Tobin recognized one of the French agents who had lost Kedrov. He had seen him somewhere. The man spoke to him in English.

"He blew the lock with *maslo* and escaped through a service door."

"Do you have any idea where he was going?"

"Somewhere not far from the Kaiser Wilhelm Church, somewhere on the Kurfürstendamm, I imagine. He kept circling around and going back. I thought he was reluctant to go very far away from something that seemed to draw him."

Tobin nodded. "Very good. Very observant. The question is, what was drawing him?"

"I've got an idea," said Mahoney, who had overheard. "We've

got the airports covered. And the train stations. If they're taking Debora Benson away from Berlin, they're driving. Maybe he needs to get back to his car, which he has parked somewhere. We know he had lunch at the Bristol-Kempinski. He's trying to return to his parking garage."

"Why would he insist on recovering one particular automobile?" asked Guyard. "What would he risk to return to that one car?"

"God knows what he has in it," said Mahoney. "Maybe Debora Benson, unconscious in the trunk."

"So the problem becomes easy," said Tobin impatiently. "There couldn't be more than twenty parking garages within a kilometer of the Kempinksi."

"And he's still thirty minutes or more ahead of us," she said.

Voss arrived, accompanied by six BND agents. A minute later he radioed commands to the *kriminalpolizei* as well as to his own headquarters.

Erich Voss stood on the grass, staring at two hippopotami, wondering whether their rubbing and snorting signified affection or hostility, wondering what it meant when the grotesque beasts spread open their extraordinary jaws.

Voss, Mahoney saw, was near the end of his career. His hands trembled. His cigarette trembled. She wondered if he had not put in too many years in a profession so demanding that it aged a man before his time. She formed a sudden resolution that she would not stay with the CIA until it destroyed her. She looked at Russ Tobin and was stricken by an impulse to rush to him and beg him to leave this thing before it did to him what it had done to Voss.

She suppressed the impulse. She hoped Audrey could do it for him. She knew she couldn't.

"So where the hell are we now?" Russ asked.

Mahoney took that unhappy question for resignation. *She* had several ideas.

Jane Mahoney had been absolutely right. Nikolai Pavlovich Kedrov would have given up the Saab parked in the garage on

Joachimstaler Strasse if he had to, but it was important enough to make an effort to return to it.

He had guns in it. And documents.

He drove out of the garage and turned southeast, toward Köpenick.

Tobin, Mahoney, and Guyard rushed with Voss to the Berlin headquarters of the *Bundesnachtrichtendienst*, the best-equipped communications center in the city. Within a minute, Voss established an open telephone connection between his office and the CIA station. Tobin could speak to his office just by picking up the phone, without dialing.

Max Wenzel was at the CIA station with Aisuke Hirata. Tobin told them to come to BND headquarters.

Voss settled into the chair behind his zebrawood desk and lit a cigarette. Tobin, Mahoney, and Guyard sat in the cube chairs facing him.

"I'm going to make a guess," said Tobin, speaking German. "Steiner and Benson are still in Berlin, but they're leaving soon. Kedrov is going with them."

"You deduce that from what?" asked Mahoney.

"Kedrov," he said. "Why would he be so anxious to break away from his tail if he weren't about to do something significant? He had someplace to go, something to do. He led his tail to a place where he knew a way of evading them."

"And he evaded them," said Guyard.

"What's become of the Jaguar?" asked Mahoney.

Voss turned and tapped the keys on one of his computer consoles. "*Verdammt!*" he muttered. "The Jaguar registered to Michael Ormsley is in a police garage in Köpenick. It was dragged out of the Grosser Müggel See this morning."

Tobin grinned. "Steiner... His notorious penchant for the dramatic. He couldn't just abandon the Jaguar in a parking garage or on the street. He had to sink it in the lake."

"But this means he has to have a new car," said Mahoney. She shook her head. "So all we have to do is check every automobile sales and rental agency in Berlin."

"Not impossible if we had a day or two," said Voss.

"Kedrov had lunch at the Bristol-Kempinski," said Tobin. "Debora Benson was seen in the hotel, too, which means Steiner was probably there. At least we can check the car-rental agency in the hotel and the ones in the immediate area. Have agents with descriptions of Kedrov and Steiner—"

"Done," said Voss. He picked up a telephone.

Tobin met Max Wenzel and Aisuke Hirata in a small office down the hall.

"All right," he said curtly. "What's the story? You tell me, or you're out of the loop."

"Who are you, Mr. Tobin, to make demands on us?" asked Aisuke.

The Japanese was grimly defiant. Wenzel was nervous and uncomfortable.

"I'll tell you who I am," said Tobin. "I'm the guy who's going to have your jobs—both of you—for withholding cooperation from an investigation into a conspiracy to steal technological information from your company. How am I going to do that? I'm going to file a report that will get into the hands of the top management of Laser Solutions, Incorporated; and top management is going to realize that if my agency and others find LSI leaky, it will be cut out of government contracts. Okay? Understood?"

"Just what is it you wish to know, Mr. Tobin?" Aisuke asked icily.

"I want to know about the 42,455 marks."

"The correct figure is 84,910 marks," said Aisuke. "It is an odd number because the transaction was in yen. It was in cash because that was the only way Rikuchu Corporation would deliver the money."

Wenzel sighed loudly, then spoke. "Russ. Maybe I should have told you earlier that Aisuke Hirata is a security officer of LSI."

"There is more than one way of defending a company's secrets, Mr. Tobin," said Aisuke. "What we sold Rikuchu was worthless.

We accepted their bribe and gave them worthless information."

"Does your company know you deposited the money in your own personal account—and then withdrew it?"

"LSI has a full report of it," said Wenzel. "But only orally. I can tell you who heard the report, if you need to know."

"We put the money in our own accounts so an audit of LSI would not find it," said Wenzel. "Rikuchu probably still believes that Aisuke and I outsmarted it for our personal advantage. I doubt its management has guessed they were deceived by LSI itself. Anyway, the money belongs to the company."

Tobin turned and for a moment stared out the window. He shook his head. Then he looked at Aisuke and said, "If you're the company's own internal security agent, what do you know that I don't about the death of Mahmud Nedim and the disappearance today of Debora Benson?"

"I know nothing you don't know," said Aisuke. "Except that I suspected when she left the office today that she was not planning to return. I followed her, but she shook me."

"We found her car at Tempelhof, but she didn't take a flight from there," said Tobin.

"She has been staying overnight with a man who lives in a residential hotel on Emserstrasse," said Aisuke. "She went to Prague with him, then to Marienbad."

"Kurt Horst Steiner," said Tobin. "Formerly an HVA agent, now KGB. She thinks his name is Michael Ormsley."

"No longer. I warned her this morning that the man was not who and what she thought he was, and she told me she knew who and what he is—and that it was none of my business."

"Do you have any thoughts as to where she might be?"

Aisuke shook his head. "I should be honored to be allowed to join your team that is searching for her."

Tobin returned to Voss's office, where Voss still sat tapping keys on his console, drawing up information from computerized data banks. Mahoney and Guyard watched him. Tobin brought Wenzel and Aisuke into the office. There were not enough chairs. The Japanese murmured that he preferred to stand.

"Nothing from the car-rental agencies," Mahoney said to Tobin. "Not yet."

Tobin did not want a chair either. He stood at the window and looked out over Berlin. It was like looking at New York or London or Chicago or Los Angeles. A view of the city told you dramatically how impossible it was to find one or two people in all that space.

"Suppose they are driving to the nearest crossing point on the Soviet border," said Aisuke. "I have thought about this. They would go, would they not? on the Autobahn E 74, to Stettin. Then across Poland to Danzig and then to Kaliningrad."

"They could go on E 8 to Frankfurt-am-Oder, to Warsaw, then to Brest," said Voss.

"Two autobahns to watch," said Mahoney. "Easy. But for what car?"

Tobin hardly heard them. He stared down at the teeming streets. Damn, but he loved this city! And—

A puzzle. The uninitiated assumed that every puzzle had a solution. He had learned in his first year in this work that most puzzles did not. In fact... It wasn't true just of intelligence work. In all of life, more puzzles had to be abandoned short of a solution than were ever solved with a flash of brilliance. More were solved by dull, plodding work than were solved with flashes of brilliance; but most were not solved at all.

Something—his mind was struggling to bring up something. It was like a word or name that people described in that ludicrous cliché, "It's on the tip of my tongue." Nothing was ever on the tip of your tongue; it was behind a gate somewhere in your mind. Computer types talked about "gates" in their computers. Well, the brain had gates, too.

"While we wonder, they go," said Guyard.

Traffic was heavy late in the afternoon. The last thing Kedrov wanted was to be stopped by some diligent Berlin policeman. He settled into the flow of traffic and drove along the Spree

River toward Köpenick. He was impatient, but he had lost his tail and overcome the last obstruction to moving his quarry to Moscow.

He thought about her. It was difficult to believe the young woman was important enough to justify all he had invested in her; but Olga Alexandrovna Chernov had reassured him only yesterday.

Yesterday. Could it have been only yesterday? Yesterday morning in Moscow, before he went to the airport and flew back to Berlin. He had telephoned Olga Alexandrovna. Obviously he had wakened her. But she had invited him to come to her flat for breakfast. They had tea and some smoked fish, black bread, and cheese. Her husband had not appeared, and she had not said where he was.

They had talked about Debora Benson. "She is important, Nikolai Pavlovich. Don't entertain any doubts about it. I've read two of her monographs. If we could recruit her, or—"

"I understand."

He had wished he did not have to fly back so early.

Russ Tobin turned abruptly away from the window, where he had stood for five minutes staring down at the streets, all but ignoring the talk behind him in Voss's office.

"Erich," he said quietly. "I'd like to speak with you outside."

The others watched, some of them resentfully, as Voss left his desk and walked out into the hall with Tobin.

"Erich... One day last week—I think it was the day when I came in to tell you about Aisuke Hirata's cash deposit—you said to me you had traced Kedrov to a house in... where?"

Voss frowned. "Uh... Köpenick. We followed him to a house in Köpenick. On Salzstrasse. We once followed Mriya Meyerhold there, too."

"Salzstrasse. We've got nothing better to do than have a look."

Voss glanced toward the door to his office, where Mahoney, Guyard, Wenzel, and Aisuke waited. "Which of them goes with us?" he asked.

"I want Mahoney. Nobody else. I want to speak with Vogel for a moment before we leave."

"We'll patch the telephone connection into our radio system," said Voss. "You can talk to him while we're on our way."

The KGB colonel was a handsome man of imposing presence and even some charm. Debora Benson was surprised. She had thought she might meet a pockmarked, beetle-browed apparatchik with tacky clothes and hairy hands. Instead, he was an amiable, genteel man in a handsomely tailored suit. He invited her to call him Nikolai and asked if he might call her Debora.

"If there is anything to eat in the house, I suggest we have a quick snack before we leave," he said. "I'm going to suggest we don't stop for dinner until we reach Stettin, which we should reach in about two hours. I know a good place there."

"Will we drive on across Poland tonight?" she asked.

"Yes. It is about four hundred kilometers from Stettin to Kaliningrad. We'll be there before dawn. We can fly on to Moscow immediately or check into a good hotel for some sleep, as we wish. Or maybe . . . maybe, if there's a good cruise ship in port at Kaliningrad, we'll take a restful cruise up to St. Petersburg and go down to Moscow by train. We shall see. Let us make it a pleasant journey, as it should be."

Though the house was well stocked with liquor, there was little food there. Colonel Kedrov—Nikolai—drank a glass of vodka and ate a piece of cheese. Debora took one more drink of Beefeater. Michael did not drink. He made some comment about not being stopped for erratic driving—which made Nikolai laugh.

"Well, then," he said. "You go ahead, and I will follow. If I want to stop for any reason, I'll blink my lights. Otherwise, we'll see each other as we sit down to a fine dinner at Stettin."

The helicopter hovered above Salzstrasse at five hundred meters. Tobin sat in the right seat, the pilot in the left. Voss and

Mahoney sat behind. All three of them scanned the street with binoculars.

"*Diese Richtung*," Tobin said to the pilot, pointing to his right, to the east.

The chopper was a Messerschmitt light utility helicopter, of a design that had proved useful for so many purposes that it had become all but ubiquitous in Germany. So many of them flew, for so many reasons, that they were inconspicuous and therefore ideal for police and security use.

The pilot eased the helicopter to the east a hundred meters or so to give the observers a better look at the front of the house on Salzstrasse.

Two cars sat on the street in front: a big green Mercedes and a blue Saab. The Mercedes was out of place on that street; no other car was in its price range. It kindled Tobin's interest.

He glanced at the altimeter, then said, "*Tausend meter, bitte.*"

He wanted to climb to a higher altitude, where the helicopter would be less likely to attract attention.

As the chopper climbed, two people came out of the house. The observers peered through their binoculars.

"Damn!" said Mahoney. "You can't tell if it's a man and a woman or two men."

"Men rarely open doors for other men," said Tobin. "I'd call that a man and a woman."

Now another man came out and walked to the Saab.

"Gray suit, gray hat," said Tobin. "Guyard's men said Colonel Kedrov was wearing a gray suit and hat at the zoo."

The two cars pulled away from the curb. The pilot didn't have to be told to follow them. He came down again to five hundred meters and skillfully kept above and behind the cars as they worked their way through traffic to the northeast, toward an entrance to the Stettin autobahn.

Voss clutched a microphone to his mouth, muttering orders.

Shortly, they were joined by a second Messerschmitt helicopter, which flew five hundred meters to their west and slightly higher.

"I'm ordering a roadblock set up on the autobahn," said Voss.

"It will take a while. We'll have to let them get fifty or sixty kilometers out of Berlin. That's better, anyway. Traffic lighter. The roadblock will be set up between exits, so they'll be trapped on the autobahn."

Tobin glanced around behind them. "We should take them before sunset," he said.

"It will be just before sunset," said Voss.

They flew above the two cars for another twenty minutes, until the Mercedes and the Saab entered the autobahn and sped northeast. A third helicopter took up station above the moving cars, flying at a thousand meters.

"We'll look like proper fools if we're following the wrong cars," muttered Mahoney. She shrugged. "On the other hand . . . Salzstrasse to the Stettin autobahn—looks right."

Voss ordered the pilot to fly at maximum airspeed and to race ahead of the two cars. He wanted to be at the roadblock when the cars reached it.

"Out of Berlin traffic, we'll be in Stettin in an hour and a half," said Michael. "Can you see Colonel Kedrov back there?"

She turned and looked back. She could see the Saab following a hundred meters or so behind. "I see him."

"One of the most effective intelligence officers who ever worked the game. There aren't many tricks he doesn't know."

"He has to be of the old days. I suppose he . . . "

"Has killed people? I don't know. I suppose so. They all did in the old days. Don't harbor any doubt that Tobin did."

She shook her head. "I don't know if I dare hope we've moved on to a better world."

"We have. I promise you."

The helicopter landed to the west of the autobahn. Tobin scrambled out, followed by Voss and Mahoney.

"Teutonic efficiency," Tobin muttered to Jane Mahoney as they walked across the grass toward the pavement.

The roadblock consisted of heavy steel booms on wheels that

could be pushed across the pavement of both lanes at the appropriate time. Each would extend five meters or so onto the grass at both ends. Trucks were parked in the median strip, blocking that. Police cars were parked behind the booms, making sure that no one was going to speed around the booms.

"We do not want to cause a monumental traffic jam, even to stop these people," said Voss.

"I don't see how you're going to avoid it," said Mahoney, pointing at the stream of cars and trucks moving northeast on the autobahn.

"The helicopters are keeping us advised by radio. The Mercedes and the Saab have just passed the Joachimsthal interchange. When they pass the Greiffenberg interchange, the autobahn will be immediately closed. Traffic will be sent onto a detour. A few cars may get by before the closure is effective, but they will be stopped by officers stationed along the way. When the Mercedes and the Saab reach the roadblock, there will be no traffic behind them."

"What about the cars ahead of them?"

"We will not run the booms across the pavement until the target cars are, say, three hundred meters from here. The few cars ahead of them will be flagged down and directed to pull off to the sides. In the meantime, five hundred meters back, another set of booms will be run across the road. Our friends cannot turn around and race back toward Berlin. By then, too, the helicopters will be hovering directly over them. They will be surrounded. They will surrender."

"I wouldn't count too much on that," said Tobin grimly.

"Scheiss!"

Debora was almost as startled by that as she was by what they had just spotted ahead. Michael had sworn in German, not in English, not in Russian.

What was the name Tobin had mentioned? Steiner. Kurt Steiner. *Jesus Christ*, that's who he was! Steiner! A German! Not a Russian! Everything was a lie. Everything—

The autobahn was blocked. A heavy steel boom, painted black

and white, crossed the highway. Strobe lights flashed blue. Uniformed policemen with helmets, carrying ugly automatic rifles, stood at the boom and along both sides of the pavement.

Steiner hit the brakes. He had no choice. The boom was too heavy to hit head-on, and vehicles to both sides blocked escape by turning right or left. They were deep in a trap. Looking back to see where the Saab was, she saw an identical boom being dragged across, a quarter of a mile back.

My God, was she this important? Had she made this big a fool of herself?

She felt as if the Beefeater she had drunk back in Köpenick had suddenly all reached her head at the same time.

Steiner had pulled a pistol. He threw open the door. He grabbed her by the arm and dragged her across the car, under the steering wheel, and out onto the pavement. With his left arm clutching her tight to him, he shoved the pistol to her temple.

"Let us pass!" he yelled. "You want her to live? Let us pass!"

Russ Tobin held his Walther PPK in his hand. The Mercedes was bathed in eerie green light. It was blindingly bright, and Steiner was squinting. Tobin started toward the circle of light.

"With you, Chief," said Mahoney. She had her own PPK, drawn from her purse. "Two hands are better than one."

"No," he said. "No way. It's going to come down one of two ways, and either way you can't help."

"Russ . . ."

He focused his eyes on hers for an instant. "Stay back, Jane," he said quietly.

He walked toward Steiner.

Debora Benson was limp in the man's grip. Tobin wasn't even sure she was conscious.

He glanced around. Kedrov had stepped out of the Saab and stood beside it. No one was paying him much attention.

"Steiner. Let her go. You don't have a chance. There's absolutely no chance. Even if we wanted to let *you* go, we're not letting *her* go. It's all over. The game is over."

"Not over," muttered Steiner.

"Oh, yes. Over. You hurt her, I swear I'll shoot you in the balls. Think about that one for a minute. It isn't going to be easy and clean, Steiner. You hurt her, we're all going to stand around and watch you writhe."

"You talk big. Suppose I put a bullet through her spine?"

"Then we'll turn you over to Guyard."

As they talked, Tobin kept walking slowly forward.

Kurt Horst Steiner... what made that kind of man? Tobin stared into his eyes, and what he saw was the end of Western civilization. Steiner was the kind of man Hitler had made. Was it only the Germans who could do it? Was it only the Germans who could be turned into what this man was?

"Steiner," he said firmly. "You are a rational man. You can see it's all over. Drop the pistol. Let Debora go. Whatever you thought you were going to accomplish, you didn't. It's over."

Steiner jerked his pistol away from Debora's head, took quick aim on Tobin, and fired. Tobin fell to his knees, then sprawled forward, shot through the chest. He coughed, and blood sprayed through his mouth. He rolled on his back and lay gasping.

"Who writhes now?" Steiner asked. "Does anyone else want to test me? Now, I say, move back. Open the barrier."

"Steiner . . ."

Fifty heads jerked around. Not half those who turned to stare at him knew the man who walked toward Steiner was Nikolai Pavlovich Kedrov, Colonel, KGB. He was a tall, erect man in a gray suit and hat; and he carried himself with an air of confident authority as he strode across the pavement toward the big green Mercedes and the man shielded by the trembling woman.

"Steiner. Let her go," he said in English. Then he switched to German and said, "*Alles ist vorbei.*"

Steiner stared at him dumbly, blinking, licking his lips. He had returned the muzzle of the pistol to Debora's temple.

"*Alles ist vorbei, Kurt. Machst du Debora los!*"

Steiner began to nod. He loosened his grip on Debora. He lowered the muzzle of the pistol. His eyes never shifted from the commanding figure of Kedrov.

"*Machst Sie los!*"

Steiner dropped his arms to his side, and Debora staggered away from him.

Kedrov drew a Tokarev automatic from inside his jacket. Steiner stood gaping at him as the colonel aimed and fired one shot. Steiner stumbled back against the Mercedes, then slumped and fell.

Kedrov threw the automatic on the pavement and stepped quickly to Tobin. He knelt beside him.

Tobin whispered weakly, his voice fluttering with blood blowing out on his breath. "Now we'll go fishing for sharks, Nikolai Pavlovich."

"We will, Russell Georgievich," said Kedrov. He nodded toward the body of Steiner. "Basic defect in the German character," he said. "Why they always lose. They always obey orders."

━━━ EPILOGUE ━━━

TWO YEARS LATER—actually, two years, two months, and two weeks, Debora said—a thirty-six-foot fiberglass sports cruiser named *Audrey* churned through the rush of an incoming tide in the Hillsboro Inlet and headed for the Gulf Stream. Although some of the people on board had seen each other from time to time, this was what Russ called a reunion. He had sent written invitations.

Three people had sent regrets. Jane Mahoney remained in Berlin and wrote that she was expecting the birth of her first child and felt she could not travel. Erich Voss sent his best wishes from his retirement home in Bavaria and said he would be thinking of the others on the day of the reunion. André Guyard wrote cryptically that he was deeply committed to a critical investigation but was arranging for a case of fine champagne to be delivered in his stead—which he had done.

Russ was at the wheel on the flying bridge. He was trim and tanned, wearing a dark blue golf shirt and a pair of khaki shorts, and a long-billed cap and sunglasses. Sometimes when he took a very deep breath, he felt a twinge of pain, and he had a shiny white scar along his side. Otherwise, he was fully recovered.

The bullet had shattered a rib and punctured his right lung. For a few hours he had been in danger from shock and loss of blood; but by the time Audrey arrived at the hospital in Angermünde, Erich Voss had been able to tell her that Russ was going to make it.

After a week, he had been moved to a hospital in Berlin, where he was visited by the DCI himself, who had flown over for the purpose. During that visit, Russ retired.

He was a consultant on corporate security. He traveled a good deal still, often to Europe. He and Audrey kept a pied-à-terre in Berlin, not far from the Tiergarten, in fact so close to the zoo that at night they could hear the lions roar.

He and Audrey had remarried. After her mother's death, Audrey had decided to give up the house in Chevy Chase. She and Russ lived in Fort Lauderdale. The sign on her office door, in a one-story, palm-shaded medical building, still read—

Audrey S. Tobin, M.D.
Certified, American Board of Psychiatry
Adult and Adolescent Psychiatry—Psychopharmacology

During the two months she stayed in Berlin, while Russ could not yet be moved from the hospital, she had renewed her association with Professor Heinrich Draeger, the psychiatrist whose conference she had come to Berlin to attend. From time to time, particularly when Russ was going to Berlin, she went there and lived in the pied-à-terre while she took part in seminars, taught, and worked with the professor on the treatment of difficult cases.

Standing on the bridge beside Russ, Audrey wore a tiny white bikini, but because she tended to burn rather than tan, she also wore a loose white shirt to cover her shoulders. The shirt covered the complex and varicolored scars on her left shoulder. Her left arm was thinner than her right. Because she could do nothing strenuous with it, the muscles were smaller and softer.

Only when the boat was out of the tidal rush did she take the wheel. Handling the boat in a strong and shifting current was a little too much for anyone to do with one arm, and she did not have enough strength in the left to whip the wheel around.

Debora sat in the stern with the man she had come to call Nick Kedrov. He was dressed like Russ, she in a red bikini a little more fully-cut than Audrey's.

Kedrov had been held in the Siemensstadt prison—the same

one where Mriya had spent one night—for five months. The Soviet government claimed he was a diplomat—he carried a diplomatic passport—and demanded his immediate release. He asked for political asylum. The German government found it diplomatically difficult to grant it and instead held him in prison until something else could be worked out. Something else was. His release was not announced until he was already in Virginia.

For the past eight months he had taught Russian at the United States Naval Academy at Annapolis.

He remained wary. He believed the KGB would still try to kill him. The abrupt retirement of Chairman Vyshevskii had encouraged him a little, but he was ever alert. At first he had rarely ventured off the campus of the Academy. This was, though, the third time he had flown to Fort Lauderdale, the third time he had gone fishing for sharks. Though they had put down deep lines baited for sharks, he had not caught one yet. He had caught bonito and a barracuda and a huge mackerel, but he was dissatisfied that his shark had so far eluded him.

Debora Benson taught mathematics at Columbia. She was also a consultant to Laser Solutions, Incorporated, in the field of massively parallel processing. She had twice visited Nick Kedrov at Annapolis, and once she had driven him to New York in her MG. They were not lovers.

Debora had been Audrey's patient for a while. Audrey had told her that she, too, had been wounded; and she, too, had to convalesce and recover. Debora worked at it. Last night, alone with Audrey on the deck by the Tobins' swimming pool, Debora had happily told Audrey that she was involved with an associate professor of astronomy. He had asked her to marry him.

"Ask Russ how you get an FBI check on a man," she had said.